PRAISE FOR MOISÉS NAÍM'S *THE END OF POWER*

"A remarkable new book by the remarkable Moisés Naím."

—Richard Cohen, *Washington Post*

"Naím is a courageous writer who seeks to dissect big subjects in new ways."

—*Wall Street Journal*

"[A] highly original, interdisciplinary meditation on the degeneration of international power . . . *The End of Power* makes a truly important contribution."

—*Washington Post*

"This fascinating book . . . should provoke a debate about how to govern the world when more and more people are in charge."

—*Foreign Affairs*

"After you read *The End of Power*, you will see the world through different eyes. Moisés Naím provides a compelling and original perspective."

—Arianna Huffington

"[Naím] makes his case with eloquence."

—*Financial Times*

"A timely and timeless

—*Booklist*

"Having served as editor in chief of *Foreign Policy* and executive director of the World Bank, Naím knows better than most what power on a global scale looks like . . . [A] timely, insightful, and eloquent message."

—*Publishers Weekly* (starred review)

"*The End of Power* will change the way you read the news, the way you think about politics, and the way you look at the world."

—William Jefferson Clinton

"In my own experience as president of Brazil, I observed firsthand many of the trends that Naím identifies in this book, but he describes them in a way that is as original as it is delightful to read. All those who have power—or want it—should read this book."

—Fernando Henrique Cardoso

TWO SPIES
IN CARACAS

OTHER TITLES BY MOISÉS NAÍM

The End of Power

Illicit

TWO SPIES
IN CARACAS

A NOVEL

MOISÉS NAÍM

TRANSLATED BY DANIEL HAHN

AMAZON CROSSING

Text copyright © 2019 by Moisés Naím
Text copyright © 2019 by Penguin Random House Grupo Editorial, S. A. U.
Travessera de Gràcia, 47-49, 08021 Barcelona
Translation copyright © 2021 by Daniel Hahn
All rights reserved.

Previously published as *Dos espías en Caracas* by Ediciones B in Spain in 2019. Translated from Spanish by Daniel Hahn. First published in English by Amazon Crossing in 2021.

Published by Amazon Crossing, Seattle

www.apub.com

ISBN-13: 9781542016698
ISBN-10: 154201669X

Cover design by Rex Bonomelli

Printed in the United States of America

For Emma, Lily, Sami, and Ari

AUTHOR'S NOTE

One February morning in 1992, at dawn, an unknown lieutenant colonel in the Venezuelan army named Hugo Chávez led a military revolt against the Venezuelan government. While the coup failed, it made Chávez a household name in his country and, in the ensuing years, in the world. Six years after the coup, freed from jail thanks to a presidential pardon, the lieutenant colonel ran for president, won the democratic election, and then proceeded to stay in power until his death from cancer in 2013. During that time, Venezuela was transformed from one of the wealthiest countries in the world to one of the poorest. But this book isn't about that. It's about people and their passions, living and loving during an extraordinary period of time, in a beautiful, tragic country on the edge of the Caribbean Sea.

Except for historical figures like Hugo Chávez and Fidel Castro, I invented all the characters that appear in this story. Some are completely imaginary, and others are composites of multiple real-life characters.

Not only did I take liberties creating the protagonists of this story but I also played with time. I converted a historical time span into a fictional time frame, compressing events that occurred in the two decades of Chávez's influence into a much shorter time period.

Finally, many of the hard-to-believe historic events that serve as the backdrop of this novel are true and easy to verify. They are part of the public record.

Chapter 1

Two Calls in the Night

February 1992

There is no sound more annoying to a couple making love than the ring of a telephone.

The woman gripped the man tighter and gasped, "Don't even think about answering!"

Ignoring her, he pulled away from her lips and wrenched free of the tangle of hands, legs, and sensations in which she'd had him trapped. He sat up and brought a finger to his lips to indicate silence, then answered the old-fashioned black phone. He managed to speak without giving away the fact that he'd been close to orgasm just moments before.

"Hello?"

"Iván. What the fuck is going on in Venezuela?"

He recognized the voice immediately: Gálvez, his boss.

The woman didn't give up, touching him in every way and in every place she knew he found irresistible. She deployed lips, tongue, nipples, and hands in the service of reconquest. She wanted to restore the moment the telephone had destroyed.

To Chloe, her lover's behavior was incomprehensible. What could be more important than making love to someone for whom you felt such passion? The young Dutch activist had come to Cuba to "study" how a revolution is made and how it might be exported to the rest of the world. Her idealism was exceeded only by her passion—and her naïveté. And that political passion manifested in bed with this man, a man she thought could be the love of her life.

But Iván Rincón had obligations she knew nothing about, obligations that were much more important than sex. Impatiently, he stepped away from the bed.

Finally, she gave up. She went out to the balcony, naked, to try to calm her anger. She breathed in the sea breeze deeply. Havana, silent in the small hours of the morning, was lit only by the moon, which silhouetted the city and sparkled on the Caribbean Sea.

"I don't know . . . I told you, nothing ever happens there," said Iván, cautiously, surprised.

"You couldn't be more wrong . . . It's fucking chaos in Venezuela," replied Gálvez.

"What? What do you mean?"

"What I mean is that at this very moment, while you're fast asleep, there's a coup underway—tanks attacking the presidential palace and mortars shelling the president's residence. We don't know who the soldiers are, or who's giving them orders. But I'm sure the Americans are behind it."

"What?"

"I'm disappointed that you're surprised . . . I thought you had Venezuela in hand. Look, get your ass over here immediately!" Gálvez hung up.

Iván slammed down the phone angrily and dressed in a hurry. Chloe, back from the balcony, lay provocatively on the bed.

"I'll see you later," Iván said. He gave her a quick, chaste kiss and an apologetic glance and then turned to the door.

Iván drove his rickety old car as fast as he could. It was times like these he regretted not paying more attention to the engine. The thing was falling apart. Wherever it went, the streets filled with smoke, and it shattered the silence of the now-deserted city. He'd taken this route a thousand times, from his home to G2, Cuba's Intelligence Directorate.

No, Gálvez is wrong, Iván thought. *He just sees Americans everywhere. How would a military coup possibly help Washington? How much more influence over the Venezuelan government do they need? They're allies! But if not them, who the hell is behind this coup? Could Gálvez be right? If so . . . they've caught me with my pants down this time. How could I not have seen this coming . . . ?*

Iván pressed the gas pedal harder, but nothing happened. The engine was already at its limit.

He finally arrived at the G2 building and bypassed the slow elevator, running up the stairs instead. Reaching the office, he saw Gálvez and others, soldiers among them, in the meeting room. Several were on the phone. Iván knew them all. And he knew they weren't all his friends. He walked in and greeted Gálvez timidly, avoiding eye contact. His boss was furious.

"You finally made it . . . Welcome to doing your job! Well, better late than never, huh?" Gálvez said.

He turned to address the group and said, voice dripping with irony: "Let me introduce you all to superagent Iván Rincón. You know him . . . our legendary colleague, responsible for the success of so many of our most dangerous operations. Who's never let anything get away . . . and an agent whose pride is deeper than the sea. Unfortunately, he neglected to tell us that he retired and is now devoting all his energy to playing romantic lead, to bedding every pretty young thing who happens into his life. Shame he's been too busy to keep an eye on Venezuela for us . . ."

Iván felt like he was hearing Gálvez through his stomach, not his ears. His insides were in knots, and a volcano was erupting in his chest. With each word, the flames rose higher. Iván was used to being praised by his bosses. They'd never humiliated him before, least of all in front of colleagues. The fire in his chest was raging. At last, he managed to swallow and speak.

"You're right, boss. We messed up. None of my agents in Venezuela indicated that something like this could happen. I was just there for nearly a month. I went everywhere, but I didn't see anything suspicious. Just the usual things: a lot of politics, a lot of talking shit, a lot of money, a lot of theft, and a lot of poverty, but nothing new. We were convinced that, so long as there's oil, nothing would ever happen in Venezuela."

Gálvez interrupted him.

"Congratulations, Rincón. Great analysis. Really brilliant. Too bad it's completely wrong. While you were busy developing these carefully considered opinions, the Americans were plotting behind your back. You screwed up, Romeo."

Iván's humiliation was multiplied by his colleagues' smiles.

"You're going to Caracas, right now," Gálvez continued, "and you're going to prepare a detailed explanation about what's going on. You know that Venezuela's always been a key target for us. You hear me? Get a grip on this situation and turn it to our advantage."

At almost the exact same time the phone call in Havana deprived Iván of his orgasm, a call 1,800 miles north in Washington, DC, interrupted Cristina Garza's meditation.

That device was nothing like the ancient black telephone. It was cordless, and it not only rang but vibrated too. It was impossible to ignore, especially when it was a call from one of the preprogrammed emergency numbers, like this one. Cristina opened her eyes, annoyed, and looked out through the enormous living room window of her small, elegant apartment at the last flakes of the snow that had ground

Washington, DC, to a halt for days. She had found it hard to get used to winter. The truth was, she knew she never would. For her, cold and happiness were incompatible.

She'd just spent half an hour trying to defeat another night of insomnia. Her psychiatrist said meditation might help her sleep. But she found meditation difficult too. The same images appeared night after night, covering her with cold sweat and forcing tears out from somewhere that should have been dry by now. Who could sleep like that? Bombs exploding. A woman screaming, heartbroken, hugging a helpless little body. Men and women, bloodied and dazed, walking aimlessly and alone. Bodies strewn about the streets. And she's standing in the midst of it all, in her bloody uniform, an M1 slung over her shoulder.

Cristina had tried everything to escape those memories: pills, psychotherapy, hypnosis, Reiki, pranayama exercises, qigong, and much more. But the images kept coming back, like ghosts determined to ruin her life.

"It's post-traumatic stress," her psychiatrist told her. "It'll pass, in time . . ."

"But time is the only thing that *has* passed, and the nightmare is still there, always."

More real than a nightmare, what haunted Cristina were images from her time as a Marine lieutenant in Just Cause, the Pentagon's code name for the invasion of Panama. Their mission was to remove General Manuel Noriega from power, after the dictator had transformed his country into a narco-state and entered into a lucrative alliance with Pablo Escobar, head of the Medellín cartel. And though what happened that day left her with indelible scars—the grenade shrapnel in her leg and the images in her mind—Cristina regretted nothing. Joining the Marines had allowed her to find her place in the world, to take on new challenges, and to vanquish old fears.

At that hour, Cristina would have liked to continue her attempt at meditation, but the phone's insistence forced her back to reality. The ringtone told her that it was her boss, Oliver Watson, calling.

He didn't even give her a chance to say hello. "Cris . . . ? What's going on in Venezuela?"

Cristina opened her eyes wide and asked: "What?"

"The soldiers are staging a coup," Watson said.

"Which soldiers?" Cristina asked, to her boss's annoyance.

"That's what I wanted to ask you. Which soldiers, Cristina? Your job is to know what's going on in Venezuela before it happens. And you don't know? Not even when it's already happened! It's worse than I thought. Do you think it could be the Cubans?"

Cristina answered that her network of agents in Venezuela was keeping a close eye on the Cubans, and on the Venezuelan soldiers, but they'd reported nothing suspicious.

Watson went silent for several interminable seconds.

"Get over here at once," he said sharply and hung up.

Cristina froze. This was an attack on one of the two pillars of her life: her job. She had no long-term partner, no children, no hobbies, and no religion. Her family, her other pillar, lived in Arizona. She'd gradually transformed into her family's caretaker, and she supported and protected them from a distance. Her family and her job. Those were her anchors, her identity, the only certainties she had in life.

She dressed with military speed, choosing a conservative cream button-down shirt and a pair of black dress pants that didn't manage to hide her yoga-toned figure. She grabbed her tailored black Italian overcoat and shoved her feet into a pair of winter boots. To hide the bags under her eyes, evidence of yet another sleepless night, she had picked a pair of thick-framed glasses, but in the elevator mirror she could see the glasses weren't enough. Insomnia and nightmares were there on her face for all to see. As the elevator descended to the garage, she put on a little makeup, a faint-pink gloss on her lips and, just to make herself feel better, a touch of her usual perfume, Ma Liberté by Jean Patou.

Even in the most stressful moments, Cristina was a perfectionist, a trait that was only accentuated when she joined the Marines. Before, her life in the United States as an undocumented immigrant had been so uncertain and so risky that it left no room for error. With her parents, Cristina endured the constant, dizzying fear of being captured in a raid and returned to Mexico by force, just one more family on the long list of deportees. Everything needed to be done perfectly to keep from falling into the hands of *la migra* and getting deported. As a child, she'd perfected her ability to go unnoticed, to not draw attention to herself, a tactic essential for her future career. As a little girl, she'd acquired the skill of making herself invisible.

It was then, when she was still a little girl, that she'd gone through the traumatic experience of crossing the border on foot with her little sister and their brother, who was still a baby. Together they'd suffered the desert heat that dries your entrails, the thirst that turns saliva to sand, and the constant fear of snakes, of border guards, and, worst of all, of coyotes, those predators her father had paid to help them cross the imaginary line separating despair from hope. *Never again, never again,* little Cristina kept repeating to herself. She learned that for this "never again" to become reality, she had to make herself invisible. To be present without other people noticing her presence. That was one of the earliest and most lasting lessons life had taught her. And it made her the person she was today. A person who sees everything, but is seen by no one.

When she finished high school, Cristina Garza discovered a possible relief for the panic that was always with her: a new law opened a path for undocumented immigrants to the US to legalize their situations and those of their families. The condition was a commitment to serve in the US armed forces for five years.

Cristina wasn't troubled by the distress of her mother, who thought the risks of the military were as bad as those of being undocumented. To Cristina's mother, both were minefields. If anything, joining the Marines was, perhaps, moving closer to death. But Cristina didn't see it like that. Despite her shy demeanor, she ended up surprising her superiors and her colleagues. In the first months of difficult academic tests and strenuous physical training, she demonstrated her great intelligence and a tireless capacity to endure the hardest of struggles.

The journalists and photographers who accompanied the Marines in their 1989 invasion of Panama recorded the moment Cristina risked her life to save a fellow Marine. Under fire from militias loyal to Noriega, a young Marine lay bleeding in a small square. Without hesitation, Cristina zigzagged over to him and, dodging bullets, dragged him behind a tree.

In that moment everything freezes. The gunfire stops, and after long moments of silence, Cristina hears a woman's screams from the other side of the square. She sees her, on the ground, with a little boy in her lap crying ceaselessly. Without thinking, Cristina runs over to her. The gunfire begins again. The militiamen shoot in Cristina's direction, but they quickly disappear from view again when the rest of her unit lays down cover fire. Reaching the woman, Cristina sees that the boy is no longer crying. Or breathing. The child is riddled with bullets. From that moment on, her memories are both very vivid and very confused.

She remembers that as she tried to move the mother, wounded but alive, she heard a loud noise and was thrown several yards back. She felt something tear through her right leg. She learned later that a grenade had exploded nearby, and she'd been hit by the shrapnel. Despite the wound, she managed to drag herself back to where the dying woman lay, still hugging her little boy, the same boy who would live in her own soul and keep her from sleeping. The child became a daily protagonist in her unbearable, permanent guilt. "I almost saved him," she repeated over and over.

Later, when her CO left the force to take a senior job at the CIA, he'd asked Cristina to go with him. Oliver Watson trusted her implicitly. "Cristina can do anything, and she does everything well," he'd tell his colleagues. And so it turned out to be. Cristina accepted Watson's invitation, and, once installed in the CIA, her perfect Spanish, her highly decorated military service, and above all her total devotion to work and excellence ensured a dazzling career marked by regular promotions. She'd quickly reached her current position, one that was seemingly made for her, as the woman in charge of an important Latin American country: Venezuela, the nation with the greatest oil reserves on the planet, situated just a three-and-a-half-hour flight from the coast of the US, its traditional ally.

But none of that mattered now. As she fired up her shiny new red Jeep, she felt as though she were about to lose it all. Forcing herself to face up to the situation, and to the snowstorm, she pulled out of the building at an irresponsible speed. She left the US capital's monuments behind her, crossing over the Potomac, and in under half an hour arrived at the CIA's headquarters in Langley, Virginia. She went straight to the situation room and found there was already a meeting underway, chaired by Watson. She sat at the table, and all eyes turned toward her. No one said a word.

Nor did she.

Cristina hadn't been completely blindsided, even if it felt like it. She reviewed the latest intel from her network in Venezuela. President Carlos Andrés Pérez had left a week ago for Davos, Switzerland, for the annual economic forum. The defense minister and his head of military intelligence had requested an urgent meeting with the president just as he was about to leave for the airport. Cristina had listened to their conversation herself—one of her agents had placed a listening device in the president's office. She listened as the distressed generals told the president that a number of officers had been recruiting soldiers at every rank and were preparing for a coup. The conspirators thought that the poor economy and the president's corresponding fall in polls would elicit popular support for the uprising. The president was dismissive.

"Nothing but rumors. This alleged cabal is just a group of officers who read all kinds of garbage that passes for analysis, track opinion polls, and like to talk politics. Show me an army in the world where that doesn't happen! Don't worry so much. Nothing's going to happen here."

President Pérez didn't think the rebel soldiers had enough power to do any real damage, much less force him out of office, and Cristina's informants were of the same opinion.

"Forty years of democracy can't be destroyed overnight by some confused military kids and a handful of people too gullible to know better," he said to his generals. "I know this country. Venezuelans love their freedom, and even if there's discontent, they still prefer democracy." President Pérez laughed. "Your soldiers have too much time on their hands, General! Keep them busy! That's all."

Chagrined, Cristina remembered sending this analysis and endorsing its conclusions to her CIA bosses in Washington. The mistake was going to cost her dearly.

◆ ◆ ◆

After going over the details of the plan for the thousandth time, two officers lingered, talking, drinking rum from small opaque plastic tumblers, worried and excited.

"We've been working on this for ten years, man," Colonel Hugo Chávez said to Colonel Manuel Sánchez. "And here we are, at last, the moment we've been waiting for, for so long! The day this democratic sham comes to an end and those lying, thieving politicians leave the stage forever."

"Here's hoping," Sánchez answered, pensively.

His companion's doubt irritated Hugo.

"No pessimism. We're going to win. And the people, our people, will finally have a chance to benefit from this country's wealth," he said with passion. "The people and the army. Together. Without middlemen."

The men had another drink. And another. Their blood warmed and their hearts raced with alcohol, nerves, and, most of all, anticipation. But fear too.

"But if we fail . . . we'll have some hard times ahead, some real hard times!" Hugo said, quieter and more reflective after a few drinks. "Death is a real possibility. If I die before seeing our dreams fulfilled, I want you, my dear friend, to carry the torch and continue our fight. And take care of my kids."

Chávez was trying to play on Sánchez's emotions, but they'd been friends since they were teenagers, since they were at the military academy together. Sánchez knew that Hugo had said exactly the same thing to several other comrades, Ángel Montes for one. So Sánchez ignored him. Besides, he didn't want to think about death, neither his friend's nor his own.

"Forget it, Sánchez, it doesn't matter," Hugo said, his tone changed. "It was just a turn of phrase—no one here is going to die. It'll all work out. You and I are going to lead this country. And we're going to give the people what they need."

In barracks all over, soldiers were already gathering in squads, and those in turn were coming together in brigades. Together they swore on God and Simón Bolívar, the *patria* and honor. Very few knew what they were preparing for, but they could tell something unusual was happening, or about to happen.

And two men devoted to a single cause poured themselves another drink, and Hugo made an optimistic, emotional toast.

"Bolívar said it himself: 'Anything's possible with a bit of guile.'"

The next afternoon a harmless rain hung over the capital's streets. Offices and stores were starting to close and people were heading home. Cars and buses crawled through traffic. It was a regular Monday, a day just like any other in the country's history, until a group of 150 baseball players arrived at the Military Museum in Caracas. They looked like ordinary players, but as soon as they got off the buses they disarmed and detained the surprised museum guards. As shotguns, crates of munitions, balaclavas, and armbands were unloaded from the buses, the baseball uniforms transformed into military uniforms and the large open space in front of the museum into a light artillery post. From there they had a clear view of Miraflores Palace, barely a mile away, historic and imposing. The heart of power.

From a camouflaged ops car serving as a control post outside the museum, Manuel Sánchez, the colonel commanding the group closest to the palace, addressed his troops:

"Comrades! Today will be a very long day. A day of both waiting and action. Two hundred officers and more than two thousand soldiers, acting simultaneously across the country, are counting on us. From now on, we are one. And united we will all share the same fate. The *patria* is counting on you!"

He shouted the sacred slogan: "Bolívar . . . !"

"Forever!" the soldiers responded.

Many of them only learned the purpose of their trip to Caracas at that moment. For the great majority, poor people from rural areas, it was the first time they had visited their nation's capital.

Across the city, soldiers supplied small groups of civilian sympathizers with arms: rifles, submachine guns, a few hand grenades. Not a lot.

As the other commanders reported that they were in position, Hugo took refuge in the museum. Alone and nervous, he talked to himself in the bathroom mirror, giving himself strength. He arranged and rearranged his paratrooper's scarf and, straightening his red beret, smiled in a victorious pose. He felt deeply that Bolívar's spirit was bonding with his own liberating soul.

From a hill twelve miles away near the international airport, Colonel Ángel Montes watched the runway with night-vision binoculars, listening to the conversations between the control tower and the planes on his radio and reporting to his comrades. As soon as he'd detected the approach of President Pérez's flight back from Switzerland, he'd given his troops the order to advance on the airport, arrest Pérez, and take him immediately to the secret location prepared for his detention. The order was to eliminate anybody who got in the way. But as Montes watched, ten assault vehicles moved onto the runway. Forces loyal to the government were taking position.

"Damn it!" he shouted, furious.

On the runway, hundreds of loyal soldiers formed a secure perimeter around the plane after it landed. The president disembarked and immediately got into an unmarked black car, which peeled out, followed by vans full of soldiers.

"Comrades, the target escaped," Montes reported curtly. "I'll leave my position here and bring reinforcements. Where should I bring my soldiers?" No reply. "Comrades? Comrades!"

Angry at God and at the world, Hugo finally gave the order: "We'll take him at the presidential palace. Surround the residence!"

Inside La Casona, the president's official residence, the first lady, the president's daughters, grandchildren, and staff cowered as mortar rounds rained over the elegant residence. Some ran to the underground wine cellar while others desperately hid under beds or the long cedar banquet table in the dining room. Everyone was terrified. If he'd gone to La Casona, as a minister had suggested, the president would have probably been killed. Instead he ordered his motorcade to go to Miraflores, the presidential palace, where he arrived safely and his entourage made their way briskly through its courtyards and corridors to the president's office.

Colonel Manuel Sánchez, whose soldiers were in the streets beside the presidential palace, saw their arrival and radioed him for reinforcements. "Hugo! Attack now! I repeat, attack now! We're ready but we need your forces. Once you advance we can take them by surprise from behind. Follow the plan! Follow the plan for God's sake, Hugo!"

But Hugo wasn't at the radio. While his comrades were preparing, Hugo had decided to honor Simón Bolívar. Armed, he slipped into a hall of the Military Museum that was filled with immense paintings of great battles from the War of Independence against the Spanish Empire. Hugo trembled with emotion. He was immersed in the din of two-century-old battles. He and Bolívar were the protagonists. The two of them were one, in so many ways.

Suddenly, a babel of gunfire, blasts, shouts, the clamor of fighting, orders, and screams, exploded in the distance. A few blocks away, Colonel Sánchez decided he couldn't wait any longer and gave the order to attack. In an instant, everything he had feared became apparent: his soldiers weren't numerous or experienced enough, and they were facing all the troops of the presidential guard. They were supposed to have been the second flank when Hugo's troops entered the palace. But Hugo and his troops never showed up, and Sánchez's assault was being repelled. Desperate, he ordered a retreat from the palace, but a government tank appeared on their flank, cornering them.

"Where the hell's Hugo? We need his soldiers and anti-tank weapons here, now!"

Meanwhile, Hugo was still in divine communion with the portrait of Simón Bolívar. He saluted him, a military salute:

"I swear to you. I swear on the God of my ancestors . . ."

Bolívar's eyes were expressionless, insensible to the words of his idolater.

Hugo's trance was interrupted at last by an armed group approaching him.

"With all due respect, Comandante Chávez, now's not the moment . . . ," one officer began.

"Our comrades are surrounded—they need us!" another shouted.

Hugo finally reacted. "Sur— . . . surrounded?"

An explosion shattered a wall. The loyalist troops were surrounding the museum. The colonel, imagining himself as Bolívar in the Battle of Carabobo, took cover.

"Kneel and fire at will, my great patriots!" shouted Hugo, anachronistically. Without stopping their fire, the rebels exchanged looks of astonishment.

"Bolívar is watching us! Bolívar is lighting our way and guiding us!" Hugo cried. He started to stand, exposing himself to gunfire, and a soldier made him take cover.

"It's the song of war!" said Hugo, rapturous.

Just minutes later, the president addressed the nation from a local radio station, denouncing the military coup, declaring its defeat, and exhorting any rebels still fighting to give themselves up. At the Military Museum the gunfire of the loyalist troops had begun to prevail. The rebels were almost totally wiped out, and yet they kept fighting all the same.

Flooded by his very private reliving of the battles of Bolívar, Chávez walked out, disoriented, calling for cease-fire. He walked toward the enemy, seemingly possessed, mad, with a distant gaze in his eyes. He surrendered. The only remaining sounds were the long, piercing wails of the wounded, like the cries of hungry cats. Operation Zamora had failed.

Chapter 2

The Three Powers

An orange light gave way to daybreak in Caracas. The TV stations assembled pictures of the hellish night before: military and civilian corpses, the wounded waiting to be evacuated, ruined houses, overturned cars, and finally soldiers surrendering, lying facedown in the street.

Head lowered, hands clasped between his knees, Hugo listened distantly to the general in charge of military intelligence. A few hours earlier the president announced that the government had successfully defeated the cowardly military attack on the legitimate government. There were just a few cells of resistance left, who refused to surrender.

"Look, Chávez," the general said, "you were the commanding officer of this fool's errand. It's your responsibility to prevent further bloodshed. Here—read this!" He handed him a sheet of paper. "You'll be live on every radio and TV station. You'll read this statement accepting defeat and asking those still fighting to lay down their weapons and surrender. You understand the order?"

"Yes, General," Hugo said, quietly.

"I can't hear you!" the general shouted, close to his face.

"Yes, General!" the defeated man shouted back.

"And listen up." The general dropped all formality, and his tone became threatening. "You'll do exactly as I've ordered . . . just as I've ordered you to. You'll read it exactly as it's written on that piece of paper. You won't screw this up for me, because if you do, the bullet that was meant for you this morning is sure as hell gonna find you now. You hear what I'm saying?"

"Yes, General, I understand."

A dejected Hugo was led to a hallway full of journalists, microphones, and cameras. He was surrounded by officers loyal to the government, exhausted from the long night of fighting.

"And in this live broadcast we have a statement from the ringleader of this thwarted coup attempt: Colonel . . . ," a minister spoke from the podium.

Hugo appeared in the background, still in his military uniform and wearing a red beret. He was the picture of a defeated insurgent. But as soon as Hugo spoke, the generals and officers there realized he was much more than that—he was a charismatic officer who knew how to speak to his men, and to the country.

"Good morning, my dear compatriots. I am the man responsible for this action to restore decency and honesty to our nation, the action officers and soldiers from our armed forces carried out last night."

His captors exchanged glances of alarm. He wasn't reading the text prepared for him, but nobody dared interrupt.

"I apologize to my comrades-in-arms for having failed in the mission that was assigned to me," he said and paused. "And to those heroes still fighting, I ask them to lay down their weapons. There is no need for any more blood to be shed by our patriots.

"You haven't failed. I have, and I am ready to face the consequences." He took a deep breath. "If the death of this humble son helps Venezuela's long-suffering people demand their rights from a corrupt, inept system, then our sacrifice won't have been in vain. There will be no future if it is not on the side of the people!

"You will live forever in our history even if I die, because I come from you . . . I am you. We were defeated today, but we have not been truly defeated, because the struggle is not over. Regrettably, the goals we laid out haven't been achieved . . . for now."

Millions of expectant Venezuelans—the president and his wife, his daughters, his ministers, the *golpista* soldiers in all the barracks—all heard this definitive "for now."

Clara, Hugo's grandmother in her modest house in Barinas, heard it, too, and began to cry, unsure whether from fear for what awaited her little Huguito or from pride at having such a grandson. His parents and siblings watched, too, somewhere between alarmed and moved. And the many women he'd kissed. His ex-wife, Flora. His three small children. His schoolteachers. His comrades from the military academy. His baseball friends from back home. The whole country listened, absorbed and surprised, to the message from Comandante Chávez.

But the most remarkable thing about it was the sight of a leader publicly taking responsibility for his failure. The politicians who filled the airwaves daily with routine phrases, like characters from soap operas, never did such a thing.

"This guy's telling it like it is!" said one young man to the people gathered around a TV at an appliance store.

"And he's so brave! That's my kind of man!" an old woman said, to general laughter.

But nobody watched with greater interest than the leaders of three powerful organizations that hoped to shape the future of both the rebel soldier and his nation. From their offices in Havana, Iván Rincón and Raimundo Gálvez listened with excited recognition to this young officer demanding greater social justice.

"This guy's the best news we've had from Venezuela in decades," Gálvez said. "He thinks like we do. He's one of us."

"He really is, boss," Iván agreed.

Cristina Garza and Oliver Watson, along with their team of analysts, spies, soldiers, and diplomats, were puzzled as they followed events from their situation room at CIA headquarters. To Watson, the speech seemed to be a confirmation that the Cubans were behind the military coup. But there was no real evidence.

"This isn't something we're going to be able to decipher from here in Langley, or with surveillance. We need a lot more HUMINT." CIA slang for "human intelligence," HUMINT is information obtained not through surveillance but directly by people. Spies. "Without reliable HUMINT we're never going to know what's really happening," Watson said.

And in a luxury prison cell in *La Cueva*—the Cave—the man known to everybody as Prán was the first to predict that the defeated soldier would become Venezuela's next president. Prán oversaw a vast criminal empire from within his cell, and his instincts had gotten him a long way. These instincts told him that the man on the TV was not only going to be the next president but was also the missing piece that would allow his own organization to achieve the ambitious destiny he'd dreamed about.

"Man, I'd like to get that rebel in here for a bit, let him have the full treatment," he said out loud, with a faint smile.

During the past few weeks an uncomfortable feeling of defeat had taken root in Iván's soul. He knew just where it had come from: after years of leading the Cuban Revolution's most successful espionage operations on several continents, he was now confined to his small office in G2's headquarters. Something strange was going on.

On the night of the coup, Gálvez told him he wanted to see him operating from Venezuela as soon as possible. But then he started to delay. Whenever Iván asked about it, Gálvez responded with vague answers and ambiguous promises. He'd obviously changed his mind, but Iván didn't understand why. On top of that, Gálvez was holding meetings about Venezuela without him. It was maddening. Nobody knew more than he did about that country, its government, its politicians, and the people in power there.

But Iván was a professional, and he decided to get his work done as best he could regardless of the circumstances. *Things will be sorted out soon enough,* he told himself. And when things were sorted out, he knew he'd be leading the intelligence offensive his government was preparing to deploy in Venezuela. So he spent his time widening his network of spies and informants there and studying the events that led to the coup. Who was this Hugo Chávez, anyway? He analyzed maps and main players, speculated about those involved and about possible allies within the country and outside it. But doing all this from Havana had its limitations. He needed to operate from Caracas.

As he always did in difficult times, Iván sought advice from his father, the General, a legendary member of Cuba's military elite. When Iván was a boy, his mother had run away with a Spanish merchant. Left behind on the island, he and his father had a bond based on respect, admiration, and deep affection. And a mistrust of women. Iván, tall, with a swimmer's shoulders, deep, brown soulful eyes, a strong jaw, and prominent cheekbones, was easily seductive. But he never let himself fall in love with any of the beautiful women he met. He took great pleasure in the wooing, but he always made himself look for someone else soon after. Love wasn't his thing.

The General had focused his life on a single objective: preparing Iván to be heir to the family business, the defense of the revolution.

The General never hid his hope that Iván would be among the small group of leaders that governed the island. He managed his son's studies, and later his professional career, as if training a champion athlete. And Iván never disappointed him. His success gave the General a pride that lessened the discomforts of his sickly, lonely old age.

Many years ago, as a young, idealistic lieutenant, the General had been with guerrillas in the Venezuelan mountains, fighting forty-two different kinds of venomous snakes, the Venezuelan National Army, and Cuban bureaucracy. Munitions, medicines, and the reinforcements they so desperately needed never arrived. Their mission had been to unseat the Venezuelan government and refound the nation along the principles established in Cuba. The General had coordinated the operation on Machurucuto Beach in 1967, during which about a dozen Cuban soldiers arrived on the Venezuelan coast and were immediately ambushed and captured by troops loyal to the government. After years of trying to foment a popular uprising and guerrilla war, the leaders in Havana had to acknowledge their failure. "The conditions in Venezuela are as yet not ready for the socialist flame to burn there," the internal report concluded primly. But the experience helped Iván's father understand the significance Venezuela could have for the future of his island: oil.

"Nothing's ever going to happen there, Papá." Iván was getting ready to head home after visiting his father one evening, days before the military coup. As usual, they'd been discussing his career and his growing frustration with his assignment. "Venezuela isn't a real espionage operation like what I'm trained for. And it's not an international mission like the ones you did in Africa either. Venezuela's an office job. I'm being kept on ice for God knows how long."

"You can't be all risk and adrenaline the whole time," his father said. "You serve the revolution where the revolution tells you to go."

"Well, I don't think there's any future in Venezuela. I don't think it's ever going to become socialist," said Iván.

"They've got you there for something important, son," his father insisted. "For God's sake, think about it! Venezuelan oil is the fuel for Latin America's revolution. You don't think that's a big deal?"

"It's never going to happen, Papá. Trust me," Iván said despondently, shutting the door behind him with a sigh.

The coup changed everything. In the country where nothing ever happened, suddenly everything was happening. But Iván was being kept out of the loop. And he didn't know if he was being excluded because of his mistakes or his father's. Was someone exacting revenge on the General, making him pay for something by derailing his son's career?

Iván knew his own tendency to take serious risks on missions and his decadent personal life had earned him criticism. The helicopter crash in Chiapas, the funds he'd hidden in the Rome account, and that messy public fight with the mother of a discarded lover—all that counted against him.

One afternoon the General appeared in Iván's office. He said, in a hoarse, emotional whisper: "Start packing, son. I've just done what I'd refused to do before, what they demanded from me. I informed against one of my best friends. Don't ask questions. What matters is that you succeed in bringing Venezuelan oil to us. Please, look after yourself."

Without another word, the General turned and walked away, slowly, his age suddenly apparent. Iván stood to follow, but the General, without turning, waved him off.

"Not now, son. Leave it. I know my way out. You get back to work."

A few hours later, Iván received the order.

"If Chávez doesn't get killed," Gálvez said, "and if he doesn't turn out to be a Yankee agent, it's your job to get into his circle and make absolutely sure he becomes our ally. And you've got to neutralize the CIA agent running the American operations in Venezuela."

Iván was thrilled. He'd just been given the greatest challenge of his career: move to Caracas, find the top CIA agent in Venezuela, and eliminate them. At the same time, he would expand his network and infiltrate all aspects of the country's society, politics, and economy. The military especially.

"I can do it," he replied, decisively.

On the flight to Caracas from the Dominican Republic, where he'd gone to polish up his story, Iván looked out the window. Descending, he saw the airport runway along the coast, in front of the imposing mountain range.

"Get ready, Venezuela," he said to himself, excited. "Here comes Cuba . . ."

◆ ◆ ◆

In Langley, Cristina was busy preparing a report of who's who in the failed uprising, starting with Colonel Hugo Chávez.

Until now, being responsible for Venezuela hadn't particularly excited her. It wasn't as challenging or career advancing as other positions she'd held. She was, however, grateful to work closely with Colonel Oliver Watson, her boss and mentor. He'd trained her, taught her the most valuable skills for war and espionage, and brought her into his elite unit in the Marines, and then into the CIA, watching over her as if she were his own daughter.

Nonetheless, the work Watson had been assigning her recently was somewhat routine. The feeling of treading water was new to Cristina, and she'd been stewing for months now. She knew that she was easily bored and that her talent for passing unnoticed coexisted with a powerful ambition. Both had protected her from the dangers she'd lived with since she was a girl. The threats that used to scare her no longer existed, but the anxiety that motivated her continued to be very real. Success was her antidote to these fears.

None of this was evident to her colleagues and friends. People saw her as a strong, intelligent, courageous woman. Nothing could hold her back. And her problem wasn't the CIA, an organization she found fascinating, but Venezuela, a country that bored her. She'd been doing everything she could to get herself assigned somewhere else, somewhere more challenging. She didn't want to go back to open warfare, to being in the middle of a battlefield like in Panama. But there had to be something better, more interesting, more useful to her career, than sitting at a desk monitoring a country where nothing ever happens. Besides, agents who aspired to higher positions in the CIA knew they needed to specialize in the Middle East or Asia, not Latin America. "They should put me on Jordan, Pakistan, or China, not Venezuela," she'd said to Watson more than once, to no effect. Heading up a mission that seemed insignificant began to depress her. This depression was fueled by the ups and downs of her secret relationship with Senator Brendan Hatch, whom she thought she loved and who said he loved her, though he still hadn't left his wife.

Outside the agency, only the senator knew she worked for the CIA. Cristina's mother thought that her daughter worked at the Department of Agriculture and that her depression was because of winter and loneliness. "Have faith, child. Things will change for the better. Talk to your boss again and insist you need to turn your career around," her mother said again, on the phone.

A few days before the coup, while having lunch with Watson in the cafeteria, Cristina took her mother's advice and put her discontent back onto the table.

"So . . . when are you getting me out of Venezuela? I told you I'm not interested in that country."

Watson looked at her warmly, understanding her frustration. But he didn't want to pull her out of Venezuela; there was nobody better than her for the job. He was impressed by her mastery of the subject— the information, the history—and her ability to use all this knowledge to support her theories.

"You said recently the political situation there is getting complicated. What do you think could happen?" he asked. Cristina answered without hesitating.

"Venezuelans are taught from childhood what a rich country they live in, with all that oil. And since the oil is state-owned, it belongs to everybody. But in reality, the great majority of people are poor. There's a lot of corruption and bad economic policies. Nobody wants to hear about that. What people want is to be given their share of the wealth. And this is the contradiction: 'The country's rich, so I should be rich. Yet I'm poor. Somebody is stealing what's mine.' That's a toxic political bomb," she concluded.

It was true that Venezuela had one of the oldest democracies in Latin America, and that it hadn't had military dictatorships like Argentina, Brazil, and Chile. But Cristina wasn't sure this was enough to protect the country from sudden institutional destabilization. She brought up the low price of oil, the subsequent need for the government to make more cuts, and how unpopular these measures were.

"Things aren't going well for *el pueblo*—the people. That's why there's so much discontent. And it could get worse with the new economic changes. Who knows what might happen?"

"And what about the military?" asked Watson. "There hasn't been a military coup there in forty years."

"Right," said Cristina. "Democracy seems very well embedded. There's popular discontent, but everyone agrees their democracy is solid, and Venezuelans don't want soldiers in power. They like democracy and aren't going to give it up. The consensus among our experts is that nothing's ever going to happen there. I don't want to wait to see if something does. I want to work on a country that's a priority for the White House."

Watson looked at her carefully for a few moments.

"I'm late for a meeting," he said, standing up. "We'll see each other later."

Cristina left lunch the same way she'd arrived, feeling that her capabilities as a spy were being underutilized.

She had been wrong. It hurt, but Watson's anger was justified. Predicting the military coup before it happened was her job, and she hadn't done it. She'd failed. In response, trying to remedy it, she contacted her agents in Venezuela, who sent her incomplete, brief, and somewhat unreliable information. She was struggling with a half-assembled jigsaw puzzle, trying to gather reliable information about the *golpistas*, their motives, and the effects of all this on the country and beyond. But that was all she could do. She read the first of several briefs on Colonel Hugo Chávez.

> Chávez was the second of six sons born to school-teachers in Barinas, in Venezuela's Los Llanos region. The 1950s were difficult for the Chávez-Frías family, with many children and little money. Hugo's mother sent Hugo to live with her mother-in-law, though she, too, lived in poverty. He lived with her for his whole childhood.

The Chávez-Frías family's slow economic improvement was part of the social transformation that Venezuela experienced in the 1960s. After the Marcos Pérez Jiménez dictatorship ended in 1958, democracy legitimized the political parties that would govern the country. The first beneficiaries of the social development policies established in the following years were party members. The Chávez-Fríases became affiliated with the Social Christian Party and received better-paid positions in the Ministry of Education.

Prosperity never reached Chávez's grandmother Clara; she and her grandson struggled to survive. Clara cooked *arañitas,* traditional sweets, and Hugo sold them on the streets of Sabaneta, where he came to be called *El Arañero.* Hugo and his grandmother are still close.

Scattered bits of information kept arriving from Venezuela. Chávez's passions were baseball, women, and politics. He'd been an altar boy at the Sabaneta church and had an intense, if undisciplined, religious fervor. People who'd known him since childhood mentioned Hugo's immense mood swings, from acts of great kindness to episodes of uncontrollable rage and extreme cruelty. Cristina wondered if this was why his mother decided to send him to his grandmother. As a young man, he'd enrolled in the military academy, where he'd had a distinguished career. He'd married a childhood sweetheart, had three children, and then divorced.

She shared this information with her team, hoping someone might see something interesting that eluded her. But no one did, and Watson only wanted to know one thing: Was he a puppet of the Cubans?

"There's a lot we can't confirm from here. You should go to Caracas." Cristina's eyes gleamed as Watson described her mission. "I'll give you a few hours to think about it."

Cristina accepted immediately. Her mission's status was high priority, and she would do everything possible to secure the US government as much influence as possible in Venezuela, the country with the greatest oil reserves on the planet. Her most urgent task was to find the Cubans' main agent.

"When you're sure of their identity, you know what to do," Watson said.

On the plane, Cristina reviewed the latest intel from her agents within the government who had carefully hidden listening devices and cameras in the presidential offices at Miraflores. Every so often, they were discovered and destroyed, and just as regularly her operatives would replace them in new spots. The agency had the benefit of access to the very latest and most expensive technology, and the counterintelligence agency within the Venezuelan government couldn't keep up. Since the coup, her agents had sent daily summaries, along with relevant video or audio clips for further analysis. From everything she could see, surviving the attack did not make President Pérez the victor. On the contrary, the unexpected figure of Colonel Chávez had awoken the spirits of a nation tired of fraud, austerity, and corruption scandals. Restoring true order wasn't going to be easy for Pérez. After all, he had something in common with the soldier who tried to topple him: they had both failed, one as a leader of a coup, the other as a president.

Chapter 3

In *La Cueva*

Things weren't easy for Hugo. "If we fail, we'll have some hard times ahead," he recalled saying to Sánchez, who had died in the fighting. It was hard being in prison, knowing that his brothers would never again sing revolutionary songs with him. It was hard being held in a lightless cell, without news of his comrades. *How many had died? How many were wounded? How many arrested? Where were they being held? What about my children? And my lawyer? When will the trial begin?*

For a moment, hope appeared. Visitors started arriving, like pilgrims to a holy shrine. He received letters from his lover, cards from hundreds of new militants, priests, relatives, reporters, and even politicians offering him support and inviting him to join their party. A crowd of sympathizers marched in front of the barracks day and night.

One morning, the wardens got an order to transfer Hugo to *La Cueva*, the biggest, most terrifying prison in the country. Hands cuffed, he was led through a maze of courtyards and cells crammed with prisoners. Before he could take in the true scale of the inhumanity, he was dumped like trash into a yard filled with inmates, puddles of urine and excrement, flies, rats, shadows of humans sniffing drugs, and guards who turned a blind eye to it all. He had no time to give a revolutionary salute to these poor unprotected prisoners before he was stripped of his shoes, clothes, military authority, his friendly nature, and his faith. In moments, this leader of armed men was transformed into a prisoner with no name, no history, nowhere to hide. And nobody to defend him against the men driven mad by imprisonment who beat him and pelted him with vomit, shit, rotting food, and dying rats.

"Not even Prán's gonna save you, faggot!" one shouted at him.

"Long live Prán!" chanted the others.

"Oh, heavenly Prán, bring your saving power to this poor, damned soul who has gone astray," came the pagan sermon intoned by a popular inmate who played the role of shepherd of souls in this soulless place.

For interminable weeks, Hugo was a pupil in a Dantean classroom, where he witnessed rapes, torture, and murders. He forgot all Bolívar's moralizing words. His faith in the revolution disintegrated. He buried his passion for baseball and for women. He stopped thinking entirely. Just one word, like a drumbeat in his head: "Prán . . . Prán . . . Prán . . ." And Prán, like the god he was, saw and knew everything.

Can one avoid the horrors and hardships that, for the vast majority of humanity, make up the everyday? Some people, very few, manage to. For them, loneliness, poverty, hunger, scarcity, and discomfort are alien. They are the richest and most powerful people in the world. They have everything they want. They live in paradises built according to their wishes.

Yusnabi Valentín was one of those people. And not because he was blessed by the gods or born into a rich family from whom he inherited a fortune. Nothing of the sort. Poor boy, they used to say about him. He never met his father, and the last time he saw his mother she was lying in a puddle of blood in a Caracas alley: a bullet had carried her off, with all her wretchedness. He was eleven and had nobody else in the world.

Master of his own destiny, Yusnabi grew up with other orphans in the city's poorest slums. The street boys learned to sniff glue, use knives, mug old ladies, sell drugs, kidnap girls, and rob banks. Although he was the weakest and smallest, his courage was as great as his desire to possess it all. It wasn't long before the police officers knew all about him: those who refused to accept cash from him received a gift made of lead.

In time, even he himself had lost count of his dead. A trivial piece of information, because he'd already stopped being a man and instead had become a legend: a being with the bones of a contortionist and the brains of a genius.

He was short, thin, and haggard. His bald head, always gleaming, made his green eyes stand out. He spoke loudly, lips close together, hiding his teeth. His penetrating stare intimidated men far larger than him. His brain was prodigious and horrifying. He was a born leader, a genius with numbers, attentive to detail, and capable of making tough decisions. "Fear is a cricket to be squashed with your shoe," he liked to say.

By thirty, at the height of his criminal career, Yusnabi Valentín retired from killing. He left that to the contingent of hit men willing to do anything he asked of them.

Yusnabi remained in prison by choice. Having been captured, he decided that the safest thing would be to run his empire from a cell. Or rather, a suite of cells. He chose *La Cueva*, the most terrifying of all—to other people, of course—because for him it was just another of his businesses. From prison he bought politicians, lawyers, police officers, workers, and security guards. He sentenced himself to at least forty years, and there he built his office-mansion complete with guest rooms. From there he committed himself to directing one of the most diversified and lucrative enterprises in Venezuela. It specialized in the trafficking of drugs and women, kidnappings, bank robberies, smuggling, and, of course, a chain of luxury gentlemen's clubs, regularly frequented by the country's most powerful men. He controlled a significant portion of the country's black market. His crime was very well organized indeed.

Yusnabi Valentín knew that a good manager is surrounded by other good managers. So over time he'd gathered an effective team of lieutenants, managers, and staff until he'd assembled an army of over five hundred men charged with maintaining order. On the outside, that number was tenfold. He supplied his mercenaries with rifles, shotguns, pistols, machine guns, grenades, and anything that could be used to scare people to death.

La Cueva, then, was his fortress, his center of operations, his central bank, and his personal club. Nobody came into or out of the prison without permission from his organization, including the authorities whom he personally selected. Or disposed of.

He paid exorbitant amounts to his civil servants and his squires, while charging prisoners a weekly sum as a kind of income tax. He modernized techniques for torture and selective disappearance. From *La Cueva* he had two or three bodies removed daily to purge the plague.

But he wasn't all bad: he gave the inmates a private security service, alcohol or drug delivery, room rental, telephones, weapons, and prostitutes. And he was religious too, a devoted follower of Juan Cash, a magnetic Texan televangelist who combined Christianity with New Age self-help and African rituals. Prán revered him like a saint. He'd built him an altar in his office and made large monthly donations as a down payment toward the sanctification of his soul. He was convinced Cash's words were divine philosophy: "God wants you to be rich! In this life!"

Flaunting your wealth wasn't a sin. When he turned forty he hosted an unforgettable party in his mansion. He hired a merengue group from the Dominican Republic. He doled out money, whisky, caviar, and cocaine. He was thrilled to watch so many politicians gathered to drink champagne with beauty queens, high-ranking military officers toasting with investment bankers, journalists with pimps. It was his way of celebrating the miracle of still being alive, the gift of being a remarkable executive. Because that was very clear. The fact that his businesses tended toward the illegal was of secondary importance. The truth was, he had a genius for organization, for complex logistics, for opaque financial structures, and for manipulation of all kinds.

Like any successful businessman, Prán found it easy to connect with other powerful men, especially politicians. He was good at reading them. Very early in his career, he understood that any large firm needs access to and influence in the government—regardless of who's in charge. "Those who govern are temporary; we businessmen are permanent," he would say, with a smile that showed he understood the irony better than anybody.

He had government employees on call—politicians, ministers, judges, and generals. But that wasn't enough. He wanted more. A president.

Prán was an ambitious businessman; he knew how to take advantage of opportunities as they presented themselves. And Hugo looked like a very interesting opportunity. This defeated colonel might be the vehicle for his business consortium to one day include a president of the republic.

So he ordered Hugo to be brought to *La Cueva*. It was he who'd decided Hugo should be dumped like trash in the most depressing and violent wing, that he be mistreated and humiliated until he felt utterly consumed by his defeat. It was he who ensured that his own name be repeated endlessly. It was important that this *golpista* soldier knew that here, deep in the underworld, there lived a giant and powerful mollusk, whose tentacles were his only hope for salvation.

Prán, nothing if not cautious, waited until his prisoner reached rock bottom. Then Hugo was escorted by three hefty guards in plain clothes in a fast-paced transfer to the Garden of Delights. He couldn't tell if they were wardens or inmates. They led him through secret doors, down shortcuts, and through warrens until they reached Prán's "private club." There he found two beautiful women waiting. They took him to a shower, then a sauna, and finally a tub where they bathed and massaged him head to toe. For the first time in weeks he got a plate of decent food, clean water, and a menu of wines, spirits, and cocktails. They brought him to a clean room with all the amenities: music, TV, DVD, the lot. They showed him his new double bed, towels, toiletries, and a dozen books to read. In this way Hugo was revived from his agony, becoming again the charismatic leader with a seductive voice.

A couple of days later, the mollusk surfaced. He sent a note, impeccably handwritten:

Welcome to La Cueva, Colonel Chávez. I'm eager to meet you. We have much to discuss. Allow me the pleasure of having you dine with me tonight at eight. I'll be waiting.

Yours, in admiration,

Yusnabi Valentín (Prán)

Prán's suite was on the top floor, four stories above the filthy yard Hugo had originally been brought to. Prán's space was isolated from the rest of the prison and very well protected. Impregnable.

"Did someone cook capybara?" Hugo asked as the hulking bodyguard closed the door behind him, without even saying hello.

"Your grandmother," Prán said, laughing. "She cooked it at her house yesterday. It's one of a few little surprises I have for you."

Hugo laughed, more hungry than pleased. He hadn't seen a dish of capybara for six years. But he restrained himself. He remembered what his grandmother always said, especially in those frequent days when there was nothing on the table: "If you let them see how hungry you are, you won't get to eat."

He sat at the table where his host was waiting for him, hand extended. Prán's enormous green eyes met the colonel's, and the silence of mutual recognition gave way to a superficial conversation about the menu, the dessert, and the drinks.

They had a lot in common. There weren't many years' difference between them. They had both lived through a childhood without parents. They were both brave, rash, intelligent, and unscrupulous. Both crazy about women, but without truly loving them. They were both trained to be leaders in battle, to show their claws and teeth, never show their weaknesses, and *always* show the power they had, even if, at times, it was only illusory. The similarities of the arcs of their respective histories—the true ones as well as the ones they invented—ran deeper and deeper as they talked.

Finally, the topic turned to the military coup. Suddenly, Chávez was on an imaginary stage, addressing not the most dangerous of all criminals, but *the people*.

"We cannot tolerate such betrayal of the *patria*, such dishonor, such injustice, such wickedness, steering the destinies of the people. I'm not talking about myself alone. We're a revolutionary movement made up of thousands of soldiers united, our hearts all galloping toward the same dream of liberty."

"And most of them in prison, or exiled!" Prán laughed, sarcastically, but Hugo continued.

"In this country we're all victims of a dictatorship, of a small group that is depleting our national treasures. But prison is not defeat. We have an existential obligation. We have seen with deep pain how our Venezuela has broken apart, how there's no path, no map, no compass to guide us. The current challenge is to gather these fragments and remake the map, define the path toward blue horizons of hope."

Hugo took a breath and another swig of rum. Prán took advantage of the pause.

"And here, just between us, Colonel, tell me . . . what do you prefer: fucking women, or fucking over a president?"

Both men laughed, recalling their conquests.

"I haven't found my other half," Prán continued, "but I can still get plenty of action. We have amazing parties in here! I'll invite all the women, so you can stop giving speeches and have a good time, for once."

The new friends toasted.

At what seemed to be the high point of the night, Prán cut the conversation off with an order disguised as a question.

"Shall I call you a cab?"

Mónica Parker was the presenter of the most-watched TV news program in the country. With dark curls and a petite frame, she exuded a glamour exceeded only by her bravery. She wasn't just a pretty face reading the news on TV. Her millions of admirers looked forward to her legendary segment, "Mónica Parker on Special Assignment." In these special investigative broadcasts, Mónica would venture into a dangerous border town to confront a crooked chief of police, or barge into a fancy restaurant to confront a wealthy financier who'd been hiding from the evidence she had of his bank's money laundering, or visit an orphanage where hungry, dirty, and desperate kids were chained to their beds.

Like the rest of the country, Mónica was fascinated by Hugo Chávez and his story. The journalist devoted all her resources, contacts, and intuition to understanding who this man was. Ever since she heard his fateful "for now," she'd been trying to collect enough pieces to complete the puzzle that was this young officer. She sensed Hugo might become the driver of historic change for Venezuela. Mónica, a brilliant reporter, was determined to be the journalist who knew him best, understood him best, and best shared her discoveries with the world.

Mónica managed to construct a reliable profile of Hugo that began with his childhood in the small town on the plains, his life with his grandmother, his studies at the military academy, and his trajectory through the armed forces, and ended with a detailed chronology of his actions on the day of the coup. In fact, it was her well-researched profile that had provided most of the information in Cristina's brief. Mónica found it striking that this gregarious, womanizing, charismatic officer had previously only been known as the organizer of the armed forces' fiestas. How had he come to be the ringleader of this ambitious plan to forcibly take power? So much investigation, compiling, and questioning over the past few weeks had worn her down.

Mariana, a journalist on her team, knocked on the door to her office, pulling her back out of her thoughts.

"Hi, Mónica. How's the story coming? You look like you haven't slept in days."

Mónica laughed weakly. "Well, to be honest, I haven't. There's just so much to consider . . . It feels like I'm missing something important, but I just can't put my finger on it. It's like he came out of nowhere. It doesn't make any sense yet." Mónica got that distant, dreamy look she always got when trying to untangle a complicated story.

"You need a break," Mariana said, interrupting her reverie again. "That's actually why I stopped by. I wanted to show you this." She pulled out the latest issue of *Diva*, a women's-interest magazine focused on Caracas. It was folded open to an interview running beside a full-page picture of a beautiful young woman in a flowing white pair of pants and a turquoise button-down shirt standing in front of a newly restored old mansion.

LUNA: New Holistic Beauty Center Opens in Caracas

> "Not just a spa or a gym, LUNA is a place for connecting body, mind, and spirit. A holistic beauty center," said Mexican Eva López, the owner, in an interview. "Here at LUNA we'll help you find balance, peace of mind, awareness of your body, and spiritual well-being through a range of holistic disciplines and practices."

The owner, a thirty-five-year-old yoga instructor, had moved to Venezuela from Mexico City a few months ago with a dream. She talked about finding the perfect house, the renovation and restoration of the building and gardens, and her love for Caracas. Mónica examined her warm, open face with its big golden-brown eyes and inviting, confident smile, framed by long, dark strands of straight hair that had escaped her elegantly messy bun. She sounded intelligent, interesting, and, most importantly, grounded. In the bottom left-hand corner of the page ran a list of their services, every one of them appealing to Mónica: yoga, Pilates, spa, meditation, aromatherapy, reflexology, holistic Japanese healing practices, traditional Chinese medicine, Ayurvedic therapy, astral charts, family astrology.

"I went last weekend, as soon as I saw the article, and it's amazing," Mariana continued. "It's the most relaxed I've felt in years. You should give it a try. Eva teaches an incredible yoga class that even you would find a challenge." Mariana laughed, knowing Mónica's regular yoga practice made her a near expert. "Anyway, you could at least use a massage." Mariana left the magazine with Mónica and turned to go.

Mónica picked up the phone and made an appointment for that Saturday.

LUNA had been open only a few weeks and was already a hit among the women of the capital's elite. Mónica, like everyone else who went there, was immediately enchanted by the atmosphere, the stylishness, the elegance. Eva López knew how to make a great first impression. She met every new client personally and showed them around the beautifully maintained late-nineteenth-century house she'd transformed into a holistic palace.

"I read the piece in the magazine. Very nice," Mónica said by way of greeting, with a professional handshake. "I'd been thinking I need something like this, a new yoga class, a massage, meditation. I don't know . . . something."

"We all do, but we rarely make the time," Eva said. "Let me show you around, and we'll see what appeals."

From the reception area in the foyer they went into a spacious hall on the right with a parquet floor. It used to be the mansion's ballroom, and Eva had left the original French wallpaper and paneling, adding mirrors where paintings would have once hung and wiring ornate brass electric candelabras where candlelight would have flickered. If you cleared away the yoga mats and piles of foam bolsters, you could imagine the room filled with the Caracas elite in their finest dress, waltzing across the floor. Eva paused, allowing Mónica to take it all in.

"We have yoga classes all week, at all different levels. I teach a hatha yoga class—maybe you'll join it sometime?"

Walking back across the foyer, they came to a large room filled with trapezes, ropes, mats, and weights, with human anatomy illustrations on the walls. It had clearly been the formal dining room, with open rosewood pocket doors connecting it to the parlor.

"And this is our Pilates studio . . . If you haven't tried Pilates before, you absolutely must. It's quite different from yoga." Eva closed the doors and guided a captivated Mónica up the central grand staircase.

"On the second floor we have our holistic services. Three rooms for massage and physical therapy, one for guided meditation, and another for astral chart readings." Eva led her down a softly lit, plushly carpeted hallway, gesturing to the rooms to the right and left. The doors were closed, indicating they were all in use. At the end of the hallway, they came to a spacious room with a balcony. It was furnished with reading chairs and a library of books on everything from astrology to Zen meditation.

"There's no talking in this room. Here we encourage our clients to learn as much as they want to about our practices, or just to sit in silence and reflect," Eva said, as they stood on the wrought-iron balcony looking over the Japanese garden below.

They went back downstairs and finished the tour by going back through the kitchen-turned-café, out onto the terrace furnished with elegant French-inspired marble tables and upholstered chairs facing the garden beyond. Just to the right, French-paned glass doors with sheer curtains looked onto the terrace.

"And that's my office," Eva concluded, gesturing to the doors, as they took a seat with a pot of jasmine tea.

"How lovely!" Mónica said, a little surprised. "It's a miracle finding a place like this in Caracas. And that's coming from someone who knows this city really well."

"Thank you. It was a lot of work, but I think it's worth it." Eva smiled proudly. Mónica was suddenly struck by Eva's Mexican accent, and her journalist instincts kicked in.

"Why did you come to Caracas, if you don't mind my asking?"

"Not at all!" Eva replied. "I had a Venezuelan boyfriend. We'd visited together a couple of times. We'd been talking about moving here, but then . . . he died. Cancer. It was hard to recover, and I felt like I really needed a healing place, and I got this crazy idea, y'know? I'd always wanted to start a place like this. And . . . well, I guess I needed an adventure. Living in another country, and . . . well . . . I do love Venezuela and Venezuelans."

Mónica and Eva had a natural connection. Mónica was intrigued by this confident, beautiful woman with an intelligence to match her own. That was rare, in her experience, and she felt immediately that they could become good friends. And Eva was surprised to sense that Mónica could be not only a rich source of information—which was why she'd told Mariana to suggest that she come to the spa—but also someone she genuinely liked. They talked for an hour over tea, sharing dating horror stories and commiserating over the challenges of being a professional woman in a man's world. Before leaving, Mónica scheduled yoga classes twice a week and a series of massages and facial treatments.

After her employees had gone home, Eva closed the door to her airy office, lit a white candle, and breathed deeply for several long minutes. Then she turned on her computer, drank a glass of water, and sent an encrypted report to her boss, Oliver Watson.

LUNA OK.

◆　◆　◆

Iván Rincón had visited Venezuela often, and traveled through its most remote regions as well as the cities. Sometimes he felt he knew the country better than some Venezuelans. This time he arrived at Maiquetía International Airport near Caracas from Santo Domingo with a Dominican passport in the name of Mauricio Bosco.

Adalberto Santamaría, his "cousin," met him at the airport and took him and his luggage to his new home. Mauricio was ostensibly there to expand Elite, a chain of stores selling high-fashion clothing, handbags, shoes, and accessories at bargain prices. This would allow him to make his way into the wealthy circles of the Caracas business world.

Adalberto was already very well connected. He was one of the Venezuelan agents working undercover for the Cuban Revolution. Mauricio's second-in-command, he'd already used the facade of his company to travel the country and recruit new spies, informants, and friends.

In Mauricio's first few months he visited all Venezuela's main cities, especially those where the largest military bases were located. The number of Elite locations had been growing quickly, attracting all kinds of customers, especially the wives and daughters of senior military officers. In each branch there was a manager and a pleasant saleswoman who befriended the customers and knew precisely what to ask about their husbands' or fathers' activities. "We welcome everyone here," they repeated happily. And that's indeed how it was; the wives of politicians and businessmen found themselves running into their husbands' secretaries in the stores. "It's a gift," some of them would lie when they happened to meet someone they knew in line for the cashier.

Of course, the Elite stores were operating at a loss. It's impossible not to if what you're selling costs more than you're charging. And the losses were being absorbed by G2, as a cost of doing business in Venezuela. They sold cheap clothes in order to one day obtain the oil the island needed from the Venezuelan government at prices every bit as discounted. Or maybe even for free . . .

As the chain of stores grew, Mauricio played the role of international businessman in Caracas with aplomb. He attended galas and high-society dinners, and eventually secured invitations to join a secret, members-only organization where the rich and powerful men of the city gathered to drink and smoke and discuss their affairs. There were always beautiful women there, serving the most expensive scotches and whiskies, and a maître d' who could obtain anything the members might desire. Though Mauricio was only playing a role, he felt at moments as though this was the life he was supposed to be living: wearing the finest Italian suits, with a private chauffeur to drive him from his luxury top-floor condo with sweeping views of the city to the velvet-covered chairs of the club, where he rubbed elbows with the country's most influential men. He quickly befriended several politicians, senior military officers, businessmen, and leaders of the widest possible range of backgrounds and occupations.

Mauricio already had a substantial network of information and influence, even agents who had infiltrated Prán's circle in *La Cueva* and gotten close to Hugo. He needed to bring this to the next level and help transform Hugo's Bolivarian ideology into a practical proposal for true socialist governing. He knew just the person: Professor Torres had the right academic profile and a thirst for prestige. Mauricio called him through the university switchboard, always safer than speaking on their cell phones.

"Good afternoon, Professor. It's been a while, but I've got an intriguing idea for you."

"Well, Mauricio, you always have something exciting going on. Maybe you can spice up my academic days."

"I've always admired your grasp of the theory and practice of Marxism. I wonder if you would be willing to offer a private tutorial to an influential person. You would have the opportunity to be part of Venezuelan history."

"Now you have my full attention. Who would this private student be?"

"I can't tell you over the phone. Could you meet me at Café Solar at noon tomorrow? I could take you to meet him."

As Mauricio suspected, Professor Torres was delighted at the prospect, and eagerly stepped into the highly charged world of Hugo Chávez.

Eva had quickly consolidated her effective network of informants and undercover agents, spread through the heart of the country's economic, political, and military elite. She had paid spies in the barrios, the universities, the trade unions, the media, and the public sector. She had recruited a number of women ready to do anything needed, some of whom had managed to get themselves invited to Prán's parties, where, in addition to seducing Hugo, they had obtained information about his plans and accomplices. But perhaps her most valuable sources of information were the influential people she'd befriended thanks to her spa. Like Mónica Parker.

"I don't know, Eva. Gangs in the barrios keep killing each other, and the country's problems keep getting worse. There isn't enough money or political power to confront them. President Pérez can't seem to do anything. No one supports him anymore, and Chávez is on the rise. But I don't know about him . . . ," Mónica said to Eva over a glass of wine one afternoon. She'd taken to staying and chatting on Eva's private terrace overlooking the Japanese garden after her massage treatments. They were becoming fast friends.

Eva knew that Mónica had been after Hugo for an interview for weeks. Finally, she had been allowed to come to *La Cueva* with her cameras.

"It was like I wasn't even there. He completely ignored my first question and just started rhapsodizing. It was like he was giving a speech. He went on about 'the commitment and the values of a people who would never let themselves be crushed by the leaders of the day and their campaigns of deception and alienation.'" Mónica imitated the ponderous self-importance of Hugo's speaking voice, eliciting a smile from Eva. "He's not entirely wrong though. He said his revolutionary movement was responding to the suffering of the *patria*, the hunger, and the decay into which the country has fallen. But then he started talking about the revolutionary fire that had been lit in the souls and consciousnesses of Venezuelans, which nobody could ever put out. He kept saying: 'Our goal is to get the ship out of the storm and on course for a blue horizon of hope.'" Eva cocked one perfectly groomed eyebrow and sipped her wine. She'd learned that Mónica could home in on just the right observations and pieces of information, even without prompting.

"Of course I *tried* interrupting him. I'd been preparing for days, and had some good questions. But he barely even acknowledged them with banalities before resuming that monologue he'd clearly been rehearsing." Mónica sighed, pausing.

"Did he answer any of your questions?" Eva asked, skeptically.

"No! So finally at the end I said to him: 'Well, Comandante, I hope you'll grant me another interview soon, not to give a speech but to answer my questions, which are the questions all Venezuelans are asking.'" Mónica threw up her hands. "He thinks he's so charming, so slick. He might have the public fooled, but I know a bullshitter when I see one."

"What did he say to that?" Eva prodded.

"It was unbelievable. He *smiled* at me, like he was flirting with me." Mónica rolled her eyes. "He leaned forward, and put his hand on my knee, and said: 'Well, Mónica, you're tough as well as beautiful and smart. But that makes you even more attractive. And I'm sure that's what our viewers are all thinking too. Isn't that right, Venezuela?'"

Mónica blushed angrily at the memory, the same furious flush of her cheeks Eva noted when rewatching the interview later. Despite her personal reservations, Mónica's interview with Hugo seemed to have an immense impact. Hugo's popularity soared, as did Prán's ambitions.

Faced with the vertiginous speed with which things were progressing, Mauricio needed to send a status report to Havana. He wrote that he knew his rivals' espionage network was led by somebody merciless and effective. Although his own network was expanding quickly and getting close, he still hadn't been able to identify who was leading CIA operations in Caracas. He requested patience and tried to convey confidence that he would have this key intelligence shortly. Of course he knew that his boss would scoff. He had to get moving.

He reported particularly on developing a contact within Prán's organization: Carlos "Willy" García. Willy was a member of the Venezuelan bourgeoisie, a graduate of Harvard Business School, who managed the "legal" firms in Prán's consortium. He was also a regular member of the club Mauricio frequented, and had delighted in taking the newcomer businessman into his confidence, giving him advice on managing his affairs and introducing him to other important people. Mauricio's charm was just as effective a tool for cultivating sources as was his ruthlessness, and he knew how to wield them equally well. Through Willy, who within weeks considered him a close confidant, he learned about Prán's hopes for Chávez and his plans for achieving them.

Willy, on his third glass of scotch, leaned back into the plush armchair at the club, satisfied with himself. Mauricio watched, patiently. He knew that, given time, Willy would open up. After a few minutes of silence, Willy pulled a cigarette case out of his breast pocket, offered one to Mauricio, and lit it with a gold lighter in his perfectly manicured right hand. He smiled, conspiratorially, and looked around to make sure no one was listening in.

"We had a meeting last week. In the 'presidential suite.'" Willy winked. He'd told Mauricio that's what his boss, Prán, called the apartment from which he ran his organization within *La Cueva*. "The boss gave me an assignment. He wants broad social and political support for *the candidate*." That's what they had taken to calling Colonel Chávez, whom Prán was determined to make the next president of Venezuela, an objective that suited Mauricio and his bosses perfectly.

"We'll start with some marches and demonstrations demanding the candidate's release," Willy said.

"An interesting challenge," Mauricio replied, feigning mild disinterest. "I'm sure you're the perfect man for the job." Mauricio knew that Willy was, in fact, the perfect tool for this project; with his money and influence he could set in motion a vast and well-funded movement. And Mauricio was perfectly positioned to support it.

Soon, every Monday and Thursday—visiting days—dozens of supporters and admirers were waiting in long lines to see Hugo Chávez in prison. Mauricio had met a renowned criminal defense lawyer with socialist leanings, who after several leading conversations offered to defend Chávez and the other *golpista* soldiers who were also political prisoners. This lawyer, and newly minted revolutionary, with Mauricio's guidance, created a Bolivarian human rights group consisting of lawyers, academics, university faculty, and artists in support of the imprisoned soldiers. Within weeks, popular demonstrations supporting Chávez stretched out across the whole country—some of them spontaneous, many others funded by Prán, supplemented by Mauricio's organizational network.

Mauricio had also succeeded in setting up the distinguished sociology professor Dr. Torres to tutor Chávez privately in Marxism. Their long sessions would help transform his Bolivarian ideology into practical ideas that could be used for governing. It was essential that Chávez's sense of being Bolívar's heir was encouraged to develop along socialist lines. Mauricio felt confident that the language of the socialist revolution would appeal to Chávez. He also knew that what Prán was doing in the neighborhoods and through the media was a perfect complement to promoting a new socialist order.

While all this was happening, Prán moved ahead with the next phase: directing his efforts at the release of the popular icon in order to launch him into political stardom. To this end, he made use of sophisticated media campaigns, secret bribes, and threats. He controlled all the news relating to him, making sure to frame him as the new champion of the poor. The world believed him, unquestioningly. And once again, Hugo played his part perfectly because he, too, genuinely believed it.

Hugo's persuasive eloquence, his friendliness, his Creole appearance, and his natural cunning led the poor to love him. They saw themselves in him. He talked about the fight against poverty, inequality, corruption, exclusion, and social injustice. And his message reached the many Venezuelans for whom the country's oil wealth had been as insubstantial as the scent of coffee.

Much of the middle class and even the wealthy elite were also drawn to his speeches about restoring honesty: citizens who'd been victims of embezzling banks or unexpected bankruptcies in which they'd lost their life savings. His charisma, boosted by sustained and orchestrated media exposure, resulted in a broad—and well-funded—popular movement in support of him being freed.

His ex-wife was ancient history; they'd been separated for several years, and all they had in common were their three children. His lover of eight years decided to end their relationship, and it didn't take long for popular magazines to dub him Venezuela's "Bachelor of the Year."

The current president was approaching the end of his term and facing a trial for embezzlement of public funds. His political destiny was written. And if that weren't enough, another group of soldiers had rebelled and attempted to unseat him in a second failed coup.

All the candidates promised to free all the *golpistas*. But the people didn't just want their idolized colonel freed. They wanted him for president. Prán showed him a few polls in which he was the electorate's top choice. And so Prán nudged Hugo onto the electoral path toward power.

"Votes are weapons too," Prán told him. But his protégé was inscrutable.

Not Prán, nor Mónica Parker, nor Mauricio Bosco, nor Eva López, nor anyone else had any idea what Hugo would do when he regained his freedom.

Chapter 4

REDDER THAN RED . . . LIKE THE COCK OF THE ROCK

When Hugo Chávez was released from prison two years later, a media circus was waiting for him. Two people had dissolved separately into the throng: Eva and Mauricio. They each scrutinized every detail, weighing up the event, Hugo, the crowd, and the relationship between Hugo and the people who clearly adored him. Using their networks, and following the famous ex-soldier closely, Eva López and Mauricio Bosco had gathered similar information and come to similar conclusions. Both were surprised at his political savvy.

"This guy's no average soldier, he's a politician!" Mauricio said to himself again, while reading an agent's report.

The report detailed the whirlwind of activity Hugo had thrown himself into: public speeches and marches, daily radio and TV interviews, and private meetings with the most varied groups. He accepted almost every invitation he received, and there were many, using each one to reinforce his message about who he was, where he came from, and where his main interest lay. The candidate revealed a remarkable talent for reading his audience and tailoring his speech to fit their hopes and fears. His personality, even with the rich, whom he openly scorned, was magnetic.

Mauricio had seen it himself. He had been a guest at an elegant dinner at the mansion of a businessman, a friend from the club. Hugo arrived in his full military uniform, as always, and insisted, as always, on using the service entrance, stopping in the kitchen to greet each of the waiters and cooks. He deliberately devoted more time than necessary to chatting with the staff, posing for photos with them, asking about their families, and charming them, as his hosts exchanged nervous looks. But as soon as he was seated among the rich guests, he was as charming and charismatic as could be.

Hugo seemed to know, though, that only *el pueblo*, the people, showed him sincere, warm enthusiasm, and he never passed up a chance to stress that this popular support was "the reaction of a people who've been exploited and are tired of suffering. Who know to count on me because I come from the people and I will never abandon them." All the polls indicated that this message had resonated widely, and that Hugo's popularity rose with every passing day.

The ex-colonel's attitude pleased the Cubans. Mauricio had devoted himself body and soul to getting "his people" close to Hugo, securing key posts in his electoral campaign. His determination over the past two years had already paid off. The professors who visited Hugo in prison were Mauricio's unwitting agents. In these "prison seminars," Hugo received—without realizing it—a Cuban education in economic theory and political philosophy, while developing close friendships with these generous teachers. This intellectual network around the prisoner had become very useful to Mauricio, now that Hugo was moving closer toward power.

As Mauricio prepared the ground, he watched for the best moment to use his most powerful secret weapon: Fidel. His plan, since arriving in Caracas, had been to arrange for Hugo to have a personal meeting with Castro. These meetings never failed: the visitor always succumbed to the bearded comandante's charms and returned to their country converted to the cause. The moment would come; it was only a matter of time. What mattered most was that when it happened it should feel absolutely natural, so Chávez never suspected any ulterior motives. And disguising his ulterior motives was Mauricio's specialty, after all.

◆ ◆ ◆

It was obvious that this crusade for the presidency was short of neither money nor popularity. To Hugo's delight, the campaign also generated a continuous flow of alluring women who wanted to "get to know him better." But his advisers warned that womanizing was putting his victory at risk. Playing Casanova, caught in magazines flirting with one woman or another, kissing this one or hugging that one, was unpopular among women in the opinion polls. It was a matter of necessity—and urgency!—to secure him a wife. Marriage was a tactic for polishing up his image—an irreversible political decision.

In a visit to the country's interior, the journalist Eloísa Márquez requested an interview with him for her radio program. The cock-of-the-rock candidate showed off his best poses and deployed his most effective tactics of seduction. She was a vision! A former beauty queen—lovely, blonde, blue-eyed. The cock of the rock sang to her, danced with her. He wanted to electrify this lady, having been electrified by her already himself. She acted as though she were interviewing him, but she'd already given him her heart. She stared at him, lovingly, admiringly. At the end of the interview, the cock of the rock winked, brushed her hand, and asked for her phone number, then made her wait several days. He prepared a sublime courtship before calling.

When he called, he recited passages from love letters between Manuelita Sáenz, Bolívar's lover, and *El Libertador* himself. Without missing a beat, she said goodbye with the words Manuelita herself used: "your friend and patriot." She felt like a character in a novel, accepting that she'd succumbed to a strategist of love, a poet, an otherworldly romantic. Within days, they began appearing together in public, in magazines, and on TV programs—including on Mónica's program.

"So, tell me, Eloísa, what's it like being with the most sought-after man in Venezuela?" Mónica asked.

Eloísa looked at him sweetly, mischievously, squeezed his hand, and answered grandly: "I'm the luckiest woman in the world, but I have a huge responsibility too. Being at the side of this wonderful man means that I, too, am committed to building a new country."

Hugo looked at her tenderly, pleased, then smiled at the cameras and fixed his eyes on Mónica.

Eva had seen all this on Mónica's program. The next day, Mónica came in for her usual yoga class, and they retreated to Eva's private terrace with a pot of jasmine tea to catch up. These weekly chats had become a ritual for them over the past two years, and despite Eva's hidden agenda, the friendship they felt for one another was genuine.

"You'll never believe it," Mónica started, right away. "As soon as the interview ended, Hugo came right over and, while pretending to hug me, whispered in my ear: 'Don't think that because I'm with her I'm not thinking about you. I think about you constantly. You drive me crazy. Call me anytime, I'll drop everything for you.'" She shuddered, flushed with indignation. Mónica's mocking impression of Chávez's pompous voice made Eva laugh curtly.

"Well, of course, I didn't know how to react. I'm sure I blushed and looked nervous, which Hugo probably interpreted as a sign of interest, because he *smiled*, looking way too pleased with himself. I should have slapped him. Made a scene. But I guess I was trying to keep a professional demeanor. So I stepped back and glared, and said: 'You ought to be ashamed. Eloísa's right there—pay attention to her. I'm a professional trying to do my job. Have some respect!'" Mónica's eyes gleamed with the memory of Hugo's surprised face.

"You know, I don't think anyone's ever spoken to him like that before. He clearly didn't expect to be rejected." Mónica laughed, delighted, and Eva with her.

Their conversation turned to how his "serious relationship" had raised the candidate's standing by several points. "Beauty and the Beast," read the headlines from the entertainment critics, at which Mónica rolled her eyes.

"He's not so much the Beast as the *Rupicola peruviana*," she said. Eva looked confused. Sometimes Mónica forgot that Eva wasn't actually Venezuelan, she had become so much a part of her landscape in Caracas. "You know, the official bird of Barinas, his home state. The Andean cock of the rock: ostentatious, with bright-red plumage on its head, like a beret, flirtatious, and seductive. And always unfaithful."

In the following weeks, the relationship developed at great speed. News leaked that Eloísa was pregnant, and a few weeks later the press reported that the couple of the year had married in a discreet but very romantic ceremony. Displaying her incipient belly, the new bride launched herself into the whirlwind of politics and began campaigning. Her voice rose tenderly when she spoke her candidate's name, and she brought the campaign a glittering touch of romanticism and courage.

"As a woman and a mother, I am afraid. Of a lack of safety, of schools and hospitals dismantled, of speculation, of unemployment. Do not allow all this fear to rob you of your hope." She gave her advice with a lovely smile: "Vote for Hugo Chávez, the solution to your problems."

While the country's political future was still hanging in the balance, in the middle of the electoral cycle, a daughter was born to the colonel candidate and his new wife. The voters now saw Hugo as an admirable father and loving husband, devoted to his beautiful new family. They seemed happy. Eloísa especially. She didn't yet know that cocks of the rock aren't completely trustworthy. They bewitch and enchant, but they also abandon their nests. It's in their biology. An uncontrollable impulse written into their genetic code.

◆　◆　◆

It was time. Mauricio arranged for the University of Havana to invite Hugo to give a lecture. On the future of Latin America, no less. When Hugo received the invitation, Mauricio's agent in his inner circle reported, the candidate's eyes flashed with sparks and he clasped his hands with delight. Cuba! But—ever the negotiator—he quickly hid his excitement and said he'd discuss it with his team first. He called Ángel Montes and told him about the invitation. Eva listened to the call, through a tap on Ángel's home phone.

"Imagine, Ángel, Fidel might even receive me—the actual Fidel Castro himself!" Hugo was excited, and was of course going to accept.

"Things are going well for us, Hugo. Why stir up this wasps' nest? Leave it be." Ángel worried it could be counterproductive for the campaign. The soldiers didn't like Castro. The Americans even less. "It would be worse if Fidel did receive you and a photo came out of you two hugging. Just imagine! We've got everything to lose and nothing to gain, Hugo. Don't do it."

But Ángel knew his friend well and knew he was fighting a losing battle. Hugo was going to Havana. Ángel had no choice but to prepare responses to the questions this visit would prompt, and to try to limit the damage. That was his role, and he accepted it. Ever since they were in the military academy, he'd been both Hugo's conscience and the person cleaning up the messes he left along his path.

Already an expert on the relationship between Cuba and Venezuela, Eva focused on learning everything she could about the trip. She devoted her best agents to monitoring Hugo and his associates' contacts with the regime in Havana. But the unknown Cuban agent was too careful, too skillful to leave traces: there were hardly any direct contacts, and none that led to anyone in power in Cuba. Eva was convinced the Cuban agent was behind this trip, but she couldn't find a single person out of place, a single piece of information to point to someone orchestrating the invitation. It appeared to come directly from the university, through one of the professors who had been Hugo's tutors in prison. She sighed. Leafing through the archive she'd been assembling, she found and reread a report written months earlier by an analyst in Caracas:

> Around the time Hugo turned five, the revolution-
> ary movement in Cuba was victorious. A few young
> bearded guerrillas had managed to unseat the dicta-
> tor general, Fulgencio Batista. Castro, the revolution's
> leader, became a living legend. The best-known Latin
> American in the world.
>
> Fidel's rise coincided with great political change
> in Venezuela. In 1958, the year before Fidel assumed
> power in Havana, the dictator Marcos Pérez Jiménez
> was toppled in Caracas. Though this revolution
> wasn't due to leftist guerrillas, the country was hope-
> ful about the new democracy and demanded signifi-
> cant change. Political parties, who came out of hiding
> after the dictator was taken down to participate in
> democratic politics, eventually came to power. Getting
> votes, gaining supporters, and transforming them into
> militants became the priority for Venezuelan politi-
> cians and their organizations.

Hugo's parents, both schoolteachers, realized that joining one of the parties would secure them a public position, and along with that, more food, a better house, and more money for the family. All they had to do was choose one, attend meetings, applaud at party gatherings, and bring people to vote on election day. When they did, things began to improve.

The triumphant Fidel Castro's visit to Caracas in 1959 thrilled the country. His purpose was to ask for financial and political support for the young regime in Havana, and the Cuban leader's popularity was immediately clear, inspiring the anemic Venezuelan left. The visit was a political failure, however, as the new Venezuelan democracy was unwilling to support a dictatorship. "Come back when you've had free elections in Cuba," they told him.

Fidel Castro would not return to Caracas until 1989, for the inauguration of President Carlos Andrés Pérez for a second term.

If the Cubans were behind Hugo's admiration of Fidel, and interest in socialism, she had yet to find any real evidence of their interference. One of the men who came for weekly manicures, always booking the beautiful Patricia—one of Eva's employees and a trained agent—was Willy García. She learned early on about his importance in the vast criminal organization run by a man called Prán from within *La Cueva*. In his attempts to impress Patricia, García often let slip valuable information about the goings-on in the "presidential suite," as he called Prán's luxury apartments within the prison. Willy was anything but a socialist revolutionary—a man addicted to luxury and power, fussy to the point of obsession about his appearance, and easily manipulated with a little flattery and admiration.

"Do you really know Colonel Chávez?" Patricia asked, while massaging his cuticles in a bowl of warm, rose-scented water. Eva, as always, watched from the camera hidden in the light fixture.

"Of course I do," García said dismissively, with a small, predatory smile.

"What's he like?" Patricia asked, with just the right amount of awe in her voice. Eva had taught her well, that men like this need to feel like they're in charge of the conversation.

"Well, he's a great dreamer, of course. A man with big ideas. With the right support"—García gestured toward himself, before turning his hand back over to Patricia's ministrations—"he's going to change Venezuela."

"Everyone knows that," Patricia said, playing her hand deftly. "I mean, what's he *really* like? In private."

"I'll tell you something only a few people know." Willy leaned toward her, conspiratorially, as if about to share a great secret. "I knew him while he was in prison, and it was there, thanks to my guidance, that he formed the basis of his political ideals. He was just a militant revolutionary until he went to *La Cueva*. I made sure he had tutoring from the best professors and a library full of political and economic texts. He went to *La Cueva* as unformed clay, and left a political savant." Willy leaned back, self-satisfied.

"What were his favorite books?" Patricia asked, wide-eyed in feigned adoration.

"He kept a copy of Fidel's 1959 speech in Caracas in his room, which he read over and over." Willy smiled. "He learned a lot about how to talk to the people from that."

Eva knew the speech. For hours beneath the afternoon sun, Castro had moved thousands of students with his heroic words:

> Let us hope the destiny of our two peoples will be
> one single destiny. How long will we remain in this

slumber, how long will we be divided, the victims of powerful interests? If the union of our two peoples has been fruitful, why would the union of nations not be even more so—that is Bolivarian thinking. Venezuela should be the country to lead the peoples of America.

A few weeks later, Hugo packed his suitcases, buttoned up his *liqui-liqui*, placed his red beret on his head, and alongside his loyal comrade Ángel, boarded a commercial flight. Also on board was an agent of Eva's. The Venezuelan group was small, just Hugo and Ángel, so Eva had to rely on secondhand intelligence, which frustrated her. According to her agent, as soon as the plane landed in Havana, two imposing military officers boarded and demanded to speak to Colonel Hugo Chávez. Standing, he gave a formal salute and he and Ángel were escorted off.

It wasn't until after they had returned to Venezuela that Eva learned what happened next. Ángel, unaware of the tap on his phone, discussed the meeting with a confidant.

"Hugo seemed dazzled by Castro. He told me afterward that the meeting didn't just give him new perspective on his own country and the possibilities of an alliance with revolutionary Cuba, it also altered his perception of himself. Fidel told him to think big, just as he himself had done. That it wasn't enough to change a country—they had to change a continent. And, if possible, the world. This was no megalomaniac madness, but an essential mission. Colonel Chávez had to act beyond Venezuela, for all the oppressed people of the Americas, with the support and guidance of Fidel Castro. It worries me, to be honest." The worry was evident in Ángel's voice, though his words were always extraordinarily carefully chosen. "The whole trip, he kept repeating to himself one of the last things Castro said to him: 'Take care of yourself: you might go far, but before you do, people will try to kill you.'"

Upon their return, without Ángel Montes or anyone else able to stop him, Chávez's speeches became radical and aggressive, against the corruption of the traditional parties and "the oligarchy," a new term he'd incorporated permanently into his vocabulary. He also insisted upon the need for a decisive attack on poverty, inequality, and "imperialism," another new addition to his lexicon.

◆ ◆ ◆

Once upon a time, not that long ago, villains were good people. They were called *villains* because they lived in a *villa*—they were, in other words, farmhands. But like other words that change with the arbitrariness of time, the humble nature of the villains was converted into a synonym for obscenity, coarseness, and malice. It seems not even the villains themselves understand why history made them into the bad guys.

Once upon another time, even less long ago, Carlos "Willy" García was a good guy too. He'd been born and raised in a bourgeois family, part of Venezuela's business elite, in a country that was prosperous and democratic. He became a lawyer and earned a master's degree in business administration from Harvard. As his destiny dictated, he married a society lady and had three daughters with her. It was a perfect marriage, so it seemed. With no need for miracles, Willy had been directing successful firms that allowed him to live his own version of heaven for years. One day, however, a banking crisis devoured all his passions and projects.

In Venezuela, every ten to twelve years, something like this happened: a rumor would start that some large bank was facing problems because its owners stole the public's deposits or loaned them to themselves, their other firms, their families, or front men. Somehow, the money had vanished. These immense, unrecoverable debts jeopardized people's savings, so as the rumor grew, panic spread, resulting in a run on the banks. In order to cover the money withdrawn, the banks, both the bankrupt ones and the solvent ones, immediately demanded payment of their loans. The result was always catastrophic.

One day, Willy's turn came. In a matter of days, the bankers, some of whom had been his lifelong friends, demanded that he settle his debts immediately, which he of course couldn't do. He insisted that they give him a bit of time to make the payments, but they all refused. Within a few weeks, Willy was on the verge of losing his house in the Country Club, his mansion on the beach in Miami, his yacht, and his plane. He and his family were about to be turned out onto the street.

Just when he'd lost hope, his ever-loyal head of security approached him: "Sorry for the presumption, sir," he said. "But I think I know someone who can help you. He's a good friend of mine and he helped me when I needed it. You might even know him."

"And what's your friend's name?"

"Everyone calls him Prán."

At first, Willy scorned the idea of asking for help, especially from a stranger. But eventually, with the boldness of a person with nothing left to lose, he agreed to meet him. Things could hardly get worse. And when he met this potential savior, they clicked at once. The tentacles of *La Cueva* wrapped themselves around him, and after some drinks and long conversations, Willy realized he had received a miracle: this strange man was going to save him from bankruptcy. He was going to instruct a leading Swiss bank to extend him sufficient credit to pay off the Venezuelan banks and give him time to salvage his companies. Willy, moved, struggled to hide his tears. Salvation for himself and his family! Regaining control, he prepared himself for the worst. *He's going to ask me for something impossible,* he thought.

"In exchange for what?" he asked quietly.

Seconds of silent torment. And Prán, with his expression both sharp and friendly, surprised him again.

"For nothing. The only thing I'd propose, and this isn't a condition, is that we might work together as partners. I'm building a business empire, all legal, respected, and well run . . . and I'd like you to manage it. You'd report to me, of course, but I'd be totally invisible. You understand? Let me put it in your terms: I'm proposing that you be the chief executive and shareholder of a *diversified consortium of high-growth firms*, which I control. Does that appeal?"

Willy jumped to his feet with excitement, his right hand thrust out enthusiastically. Prán smiled triumphantly. Instead of taking his hand, he embraced him, like the best friend he already was. And so Willy became, in theory, the head of a bank and several firms in the construction, transport, and telecom sectors. While in practice, and in absolute secret, their true owner was a businessman no one had ever heard of: Yusnabi Valentín.

◆ ◆ ◆

After two years in Caracas, Eva López had earned a reputation as an intelligent, pleasant professional, always eager to help her customers. Many of these women had become friends and had allowed her into their lives and their social circles.

She spent several hours each day working from a secure hidden office she had secretly built deep within LUNA. From there she watched Hugo's political movement grow and expand, and she was the first to realize that the colonel was unstoppable. He would become Venezuela's president.

She created a universe of invisible networks spun by expert agents, anonymous helpers, and others who, whether they realized it or not, fed into her suspicions and certainties. She (always indirectly) bought alliances and created friendships with unsuspecting informants who fed her news of politicians, soldiers, bankers, and journalists. She won a small victory when one of her agents managed to gain the trust of one of the people's candidate's many lovers. She was also pleased that her true identity and work remained indisputably secret. She operated through two CIA superagents in Venezuela, and it was they who managed the rest of the agents and carried out missions. Even they had never seen her in person; they received their instructions and passed on information via encrypted messages. They usually received their orders in the middle of the night.

Eva never slept well. She hardly slept at all, in fact. During her unsettled nights, she defeated the usual nightmares by simply remaining awake. And so, in the small hours of the morning, when she had no more orders to send out, questions to ask, reports to read or produce, Eva battled against sleep by reading novels. Not spy novels, nothing violent. She only read love stories.

These novels didn't just protect her from sleep and the nightmares; they forced her to think about her own love story. Sometimes she didn't know whether her relationship with the very married, very Republican, very attractive senator Brendan Hatch was a great love story or just a cheesy Mexican telenovela, the kind her mom watched.

The relationship with Hatch allowed for both possibilities. Whenever together, they made love as if for the first time. Afterward, they had long conversations about their shared interests: espionage, intelligence, international politics, the maneuverings of the politicians in DC, the elections, who was up and who was down, who was going to reach the summits of power, and who would crash along the way. And, of course, who was sleeping with whom.

Hatch was the chair of the Senate Intelligence Committee, which gave him not only power but also access to the most classified information. And Eva, who went back to being Cristina with him, had access to all the information handled by the CIA. The combination of what they both knew with their analytical powers gave them a perspective they both realized was unique and privileged. The relationship went well beyond their passionate sexual encounters. Or was that just the delusion of a woman in love? That was the question Cristina asked herself often. And the answer was what she was trying to find in the love stories she was constantly reading.

Hatch was mentioned regularly as a potential presidential candidate with a good chance of winning. This brought Eva great satisfaction as well as profound sadness. If, as he had occasionally promised her, Hatch were to get a divorce and marry her, his journey to the White House would be over. Republican voters wouldn't forgive him for abandoning his wife and kids to marry a CIA agent who was a Mexican immigrant. She knew that between the presidency and a life with her, Hatch would always choose the presidency. A part of her understood this, and even admired it. But another part hated the political ambition that stopped him from being her man. She wanted him always, every day and every night. She was no longer satisfied with the intense but occasional encounters they were able—with considerable precautions—to have on a discreet Caribbean island not far from Venezuela.

Each time she came back to Venezuela after one of these meetings, she fell apart. She was filled with a sadness more intense than anybody could understand. The only way she had of facing this sadness was through work.

She was not short of work.

The Venezuelan elections were coming, and the country seemed to be going through something between a hurricane and a political carnival. This meant she had a lot to do, many obligations and urgent tasks. She continued to be surprised at the natural gift for politics that Hugo demonstrated.

She had been following his campaign closely, analyzing everything, down to his silences. Besides studying all his speeches, statements, and interviews, she also received reports on every step he took, and sometimes her agents were able to gain access to his telephone communications, including some of his most private conversations. But Eva wanted more. She wanted to see him again, even if only from a distance, and she knew that Hugo would be in central Caracas at one of the final popular rallies. She decided to attend and observe the people's fervor for their magnanimous leader with her own eyes. LUNA had a small but efficient security team, well trained and totally devoted to the owner of the firm, who treated them well and paid even better, and they would accompany her to the rally.

When she reached the square, she ordered her minders not to attract any attention and to keep a reasonable distance from her. She saw the candidate from afar, standing on a dais, surrounded by a ring of bodyguards. Beside him, his blonde wife smiled and raised her left fist devoutly. Hugo presided over a lively red fiesta, where people could buy berets, T-shirts, and tricolor sashes with his name on them. There were drums, flags, and posters. Women and kisses rained down. Eva decided to plunge into the crowd and expected her minders to retain visual contact while keeping their distance. The bodyguards followed her, but not quickly enough, and they lost sight of her.

The candidate told the people what they had come to hear: dignity, equality, justice. Savoring every syllable, he said: "You must all remember the words of *El Libertador*, Simón Bolívar: unite, or anarchy will devour us!"

To the people's alarm, he then claimed that there was a plan to sabotage the electoral process, and, furthermore, there were mercenaries with orders to kill him. He held the current president responsible in the event anything were to happen to him. Eva followed his speech, filled with its incendiary, anti-imperialist phrases, with interest. They were the same words he used in every setting. And they always worked. The crowd, angry at what the candidate was telling them, got fired up. The festive atmosphere turned dangerous. The crowd was starting to crush and overwhelm her. But just when she thought it was time to go back home, a magnetic visual contact froze her to the spot.

Only a few steps away, a man was looking at her, making no effort to hide his interest. He looked rapt. Eva, taking refuge behind a large pair of sunglasses, acted indifferent.

He tried to move closer, but there was an unbreachable wall of bodies between them, a chorus of voices shouting in response to each fiery phrase from Hugo, a million hands applauding like a runaway train.

Suddenly an explosion of violence interrupted the silent flirtation. A group of well-built men armed with sticks burst into the crowd, striking everyone in their path. It was not clear, but Eva suspected they were hired by one of Hugo's rivals. The violence escalated as the throng responded with stones and pipes. The riot police intervened; the bodyguards got the candidate down off the dais. His followers dispersed, running in all directions. Petards exploded, there were gunshots, and a thick cloud of tear gas blinded everyone. It was impossible to see, and Eva didn't know the labyrinth of streets and alleys around the square where she was. She looked for one of her security team, but saw no one. She began to run, trying to escape the tear gas, and finally reached a square she knew. There she got a taxi and asked the driver to take her to LUNA.

In the taxi, she was surprised at herself: instead of thinking about the candidate and what had just happened, her mind kept returning to the man who'd been looking at her.

"This year has been sealed by the hand of history," said Hugo in one of his last rallies. It was the first week of December, the final week in the presidential campaign. The candidate was already certain of his political future. "Nobody and nothing can prevent the people from triumphing next Sunday!" he shouted.

And so it was. His call to fight for dignity and courage and his repeated claim that his was the only path to peace produced the majority of votes necessary to get him to Miraflores Palace.

Barely a month earlier, the results of the state governors and Congressional elections similarly reflected the rapid ascent of the recently created revolutionary political movement he was leading.

Almost every senator, deputy, and governor who had Hugo's support won. Everything, then, pointed toward his being able to govern unconstrained. So what would he do next, with all that power?

In his first press conference as president-elect, Hugo repeated the words of Jesus of Nazareth, moving his devoted followers to tears: "It is done."

The skeptics were the minority. At family meals, in classrooms, in bank boardrooms, and at trade unions, everyone passionately discussed the changes his mandate would bring: a new constitution for a new Venezuela. The prevailing emotion was optimism; the country was expecting everything from him, even if the economy looked rocky: the price of oil, the country's main export, had tanked well before the elections. There was a shortage of money, and unpopular cuts to public expenditures would be needed.

In a rare moment alone with Ángel, the new president said: "Sometimes I don't think it can be true, Ángel. I still can't believe it. We did it. And now we're gonna turn this country upside-fuckin'-down!"

Ángel looked at him thoughtfully, then cautioned: "Be careful, Hugo. We've got to be realistic. The way things are, it's going to be hard to keep all our promises to the people. You've got to lower expectations among your voters. If you don't, they're going to feel duped, and it's going to come back to bite you. We might find ourselves all on our own if our people become disheartened with you and with our project."

Hugo didn't like the warning.

"It's not like that! You're always such a pessimist, Ángel! It's going to go great for us. Anyway, I've never forgotten the pronouncement of the warrior Sun Tzu, the ancient Chinese strategist. It was the first thing they taught us in the military academy—you do remember, don't you? He said: 'You, soldier, when you return from the battle, after your victory, sheathe your sword. Look up to the Lord, give thanks to God, and withdraw to celebrate your triumph with humility, silently, because more battles will be coming tomorrow.'"

Ángel just looked at him silently.

In the shadows of the celebrations, bets were laid on who would have the greatest influence over Chávez's government: Cuba or the USA? Prán, too, savored his victory and prepared to wield more power than ever.

Mauricio Bosco and Eva López were exhausted. The challenges they faced tripled with the ex-soldier's accession to the presidency. In Havana there was elation, and in Washington, concern. In the situation rooms of the two spy agencies, they watched the theatrical arrival of hundreds of senators, governors, reporters, and special guests from all over the world on TV. One particular special guest came from Havana. They watched the armed forces paying tribute. They watched the new president beaming, accompanied by his wife. They watched him place his hand on his heart: "I swear before God / I swear before the *patria* / I swear before my people that / upon this dying old constitution / I shall carry out, impel / the necessary democratic transformations / for the new republic to have / an adequate constitution / for these new times / I swear it."

The oath delighted the mollusk in *La Cueva*, though he did frown when he saw Fidel sitting among the most important guests, smiling and applauding. The outgoing president, Rafael Caldera, another champion of democracy who had become its gravedigger, tremblingly placed the presidential sash on the people's savior. In the most solemn moment of the ceremony, when the country burst into applause, the first lady, visibly moved, gave a long kiss to her husband, the president. Prán and Willy raised their glasses and toasted: this president was theirs too.

Chapter 5

THE COLONEL ON HONEYMOON

Mónica arrived at La Casona, the presidential mansion with spacious gardens and courtyards, a chapel, halls and more halls, fountains and more fountains, all of them marble. She was there for the official reception, but in the flurry of activity managed to slip away and wandered through the offices, halls, and bedrooms, looking at the luxurious pieces of furniture and the oil paintings. She had, of course, been to Miraflores Palace before, the official seat of government, but this was her first time inside the presidential residence.

It was bustling with a considerable retinue of servants, cooks, aides-de-camp, bodyguards, and security personnel. Though nightfall had marked the start of the official reception, and the guests were already arriving and the first lady was ready and waiting for Hugo, he was nowhere to be found. Mónica took advantage of the newness of the staff, and her own confidence, which gave her the appearance of always being exactly where she was supposed to be, to explore the upper floor of the mansion. A door that had been left ajar caught her attention, and carefully she peeked through the crack. She couldn't believe it: Castro and Chávez, sharing a glass of Chivas whisky—the Cuban president's favorite, and now the Venezuelan's too. After the long day of his swearing-in as president, master and disciple had met to talk in private. Mónica held her breath, pressed up against the wall, keeping an eye out for bodyguards or staff as she listened.

"These are the moments when it's worth recalling the greats," Fidel said, thoughtfully. "To me, Lenin was one of the greats. And he said something that perfectly captures what's happening here: 'There are decades when nothing happens and there are weeks when decades happen.'"

"What a great line!" Hugo exclaimed. "That's exactly how it feels, Fidel."

"Make the most of it, Hugo . . ."

"I'll try. But I'll need your help, Fidel."

"You'll have it," said the master, eyes fixed on his pupil. "You'll have it." He raised his glass in a toast.

Mónica exhaled and turned back to return to the reception, uneasy.

The palace was filled with the most distinguished figures: heads of state and the cream of the worlds of diplomacy, politics, the military, the arts, sports, media, and business. Mónica took it all in, ever observant. There was His Royal Highness from Spain, the Prince of Asturias, Felipe de Borbón. And there was the energy secretary from the US and the secretary-general of the OAS. There was a leftist Colombian senator, wearing a red turban, hugging by way of greeting an indigenous activist in ritual Amazonian ceremonial garb. And there, joining a Dominican baseball player, was the unmistakable Fidel.

With Mónica in the corner of the room, watching the spectacle equally discreetly, were a couple already very close to the household: Willy García and his wife. She looked dazzled, wide-eyed, as they chatted politely. The guests waited ninety minutes for Hugo to appear. In the palace halls, people started to get uncomfortable. They felt themselves being watched by a vast portrait of Simón Bolívar occupying one wall and harassed by a three-meter-high clock marking the endless seconds of their host's non-arrival.

When the presidential couple arrived at last, Hugo puffed up his victorious chest and exclaimed, radiantly: "Six years ago, I tried to get into this house with tanks, bombs, and bullets . . . and I couldn't do it!" Everybody couldn't help but laugh, and even Mónica smiled. "Today I'm managing it at last, thanks to the vote of the majority. Welcome to the house of a servant of the people!"

The guests applauded so hard the oil Bolívar trembled in his frame. Music immediately began to play, marking the beginning of the celebration and litanies of congratulations. The president and first lady smiled easily.

At one point, taking advantage of his wife's being at the other end of the enormous hall, Hugo approached Mónica, pulling her away from the group she was talking to. Once again, the experienced, calm, and always prepared journalist was visibly nervous. And—once again—Hugo assumed that it was his charm.

"Mónica, on a night like tonight, you are the queen of this palace. I won't rest until we can be together, and you allow me to make you happy in a way no other man has ever before made you happy, or ever will."

Mónica said nothing and turned back to the safety of the group she'd been talking to before Venezuela's new leader had approached her. Nobody noticed, and the party went on.

The president and first lady debuted their new roles as monarchs of a country without a monarchy. Eloísa didn't know that, in time, she would change from loving wife to fierce critic. And he didn't know that, in time, he would find himself compelled to choose between the two Hugos he had in his soul. As Gabriel García Márquez wrote after first meeting the leader at a gathering organized by Fidel Castro: "I was shaken by the sudden realization that I had traveled to speak with two opposite men. One, whom cruel fortune has given an opportunity to save his country. And the other, an illusionist who could go down in history as just another tyrant."

◆　◆　◆

The real celebration, the post-party party, began in the small hours, when the most excellent first lady, the most beloved relatives, and the most honored guests had all left. Some departed without saying good-bye, not wanting to interrupt the host's warm and lengthy conversations. The president made everybody—even those he'd just met—feel like their conversation was unique, private, and intimate, a chat between good friends. Everyone was fascinated by the young leader whose promises inspired such hope and admiration.

The staff had withdrawn, too, and only a few waiters remained. The Venezuelans, safely back in their homes, were waiting to see the dawn of a new country.

Fidel had been patient. During the party he hadn't wanted to show how moved he was by his friend's triumph. Nor how close he was. Of all the invited leaders, he was the one who'd spent the least amount of time with the new president. More than thirty years had passed since he'd asked for help and was denied. But it seemed as though life was about to reward him for his long wait.

So when no other sounds could be heard in the house but the second hand of the clock, the patriarch suggested to Hugo that they withdraw to his study to discuss the tasks that he would have to carry out.

In the president's study, Hugo switched on an incredibly old and incredibly beautiful lamp. In carved mahogany armchairs, the two lions—both men astrological Leos—began to roar. From one wall, a third, atop a horse, watched them silently. Hugo saluted the equestrian portrait of *El Libertador* respectfully, then said to his friend: "Look what I've got, Fidel." He took out a bottle of Chivas and two beautiful Baccarat crystal glasses.

They poured, and clinked.

"Good luck to you, comrade," Fidel said.

Hugo was still reveling in the thrill of victory. "Total popularity! The whole country is at my feet!"

Fidel stroked his leonine beard and frowned in warning. "Be careful. Don't buy it. You should be suspicious of any power that doesn't come from weapons. You have too many enemies, and if you really want to help the poor, you'll have to make profound changes that will make you even more. Very dangerous enemies. People you won't be able to handle within a democracy. You need to neutralize them entirely and in any way you can."

Total hegemony. The president made a note of this.

"Mao says power grows out of the barrel of a gun, and he's right! Democracy is a bourgeois farce," said Fidel, threateningly. "Power is exercised entirely, or lost completely. A true leader does not consult, he *commands*."

A lot of information at the end of a perfect day. Hugo listened respectfully and nodded, but deep down he didn't think he'd have to go to such extremes. He said nothing, however. On the contrary, he paid careful attention to the deluge of advice and warnings. Fidel insisted that his personal security was the most important thing, not to ever stop watching out because, without a doubt, when the honeymoon with the country ended, his opponents would start to move their pieces.

"Here's hoping what happened to Allende doesn't happen to you," he said, referring to the Chilean socialist president who came to power by winning an election in 1970 and three years later was unseated by a military coup. "Look, I know that story. I moved to Santiago for a month to help Allende and I saw it all. I saw the traps they laid for him with these very eyes. Not to mention the ones they've been laying for me all these years. But with me they never managed it. And I want to give you all the help and the knowledge we have on the subject so it doesn't happen to you. Because if they kill you or topple you, the revolution's over. And you can't let that happen."

Hugo engraved Fidel's words in his memory. They would return to his mind on many occasions to come. Meanwhile, with his atheist friend's permission, Hugo offered an enthusiastic recitation of the Sayings of Agur from the Book of Proverbs he'd just revisited:

> *There are three things majestic in their gait*
> *And a fourth of elegant bearing:*
> *The lion, most powerful of the beasts,*
> *That nothing can make to retreat;*
> *The rooster, that stands proudly up;*
> *And the he-goat too;*
> *And the king, when his army is with him.*

Biblical tongue twisters meant nothing to Fidel Castro; he wasn't interested in the fact that Jesus Christ was also a lion, the Lion of Judah. So he resumed his advice giving:

"Not all your enemies are going to play fair." He again gave himself as an example, talking about the economic blockade of the island, and the fact that he'd already been the target of more than six hundred assassination attempts. But his precocious disciple responded with another Biblical proverb, a simple one: "Fidel, my brother, 'The dread of the wicked will come upon him, but the desire of the righteous will be granted.'"

As the sky lightened again, the lions fused into a goodbye hug.

"You know you can always count on me," the bearded man said, and took advantage of the moment to put one of his most trusted men in the mix. "If you don't mind, I'm going to send you my best guy. You must have an intelligence expert by your side, and I've got one for you: his name's Mauricio Bosco."

Hugo thanked him, and Fidel got up to leave after another long, heartfelt hug.

The president was at last left alone to think. In spite of the respect he had for Castro, he dismissed most of his warnings: *Fidel is right about a lot of things,* Hugo thought, *but he doesn't know Venezuela the way I do, and he doesn't know how much the people love me. There's no reason for me to go to the extremes he's suggesting. His story is different from mine. And his was a different time too.*

Meanwhile, Eloísa was remembering. She went back to nights not so long ago when Hugo was courting her. She remembered how her heart leaped when he recited poems over the phone inspired by her smile. Dazzled by love, she answered him with some piece of the correspondence between Manuelita Sáenz, Simón Bolívar's lover, and *El Libertador* himself. "You know well that no other woman you have met could delight you with the fervor and the passion that binds me to you. You should get to know a real woman, a loyal one, with no reservations." Eloísa read Manuelita's declaration as if it was a message she alone could have written.

If only it were all love letters . . . Was Hugo listening when she read "no other woman"? Perhaps confusing her patriotic dreams with *El Libertador's Libertadora,* and confused in real life by the frenzy of events, the provincial journalist had been elevated to the role of first lady, a profession they didn't prepare one for at any university. God had put her here for some reason, she thought. With little time for prayer or contemplation, it felt as though the woman who was suddenly the most important in the country had to learn to combine her roles of mother, political leader's wife, friend of the people, and servant of the revolution. "I will never tire of thanking God and the Venezuelan people for having answered this call we have all made for peace, for social change," she said to the press on one of her first days. "I thank you all for the huge support you have given us."

However, the honeymoon of her reign was already dissipating. Within a few days, she would come to understand the scale of her alliance with the man who had seduced the country and was the center of attention at all times and in all places. Torrents of dark water would soon flow into the sea of love.

◆　◆　◆

In the morning, the presidential motorcade moved slowly through rush-hour traffic despite the motorbikes and the security unit that were deployed. Traffic got snarled up whenever the president moved around the city. Wherever he went, delirious popular demonstrations of support followed. Everybody wanted to see him, to touch him, to shout that they loved him. They had to pass through a densely populated shantytown, and from the window of his armored car, Hugo looked at the hillsides covered in the thousands of precarious jumbles of cardboard and tiles that passed for houses, pressed up against one another. His eyes followed the long, narrow flights of stairs that snaked through the middle of the destitution, tracing a labyrinth of earth, cement, and people. At one bend, a little space opened up, a court where sometimes the young men played basketball. And sometimes they played not with a ball but with automatic weapons. Just a few moments ago a young passerby had been hit by gunfire.

The commotion caught the president's attention as eight people rushed down the hillside, carrying the wounded young man. His mother followed, devastated and panicking. Traffic was slow and dense. The few available taxi drivers refused to help. Someone suggested putting him on a motorbike.

"Stop!" Hugo shouted. To his guards' alarm, he jumped out of the car and approached the group, taking charge of the situation. He ordered that the wounded man and his mother be taken to the hospital in one of his escort cars. The motorcycle security detail traveled ahead, clearing the path for the improvised ambulance.

Everything happened so fast that passengers on buses, peddlers, tramps, street kids, and schoolchildren barely had time to recognize this benefactor. Like ants attracted to sugar, people rushed in from all over to greet him.

"It's him, it's him!" they shouted. What could his entourage possibly do to control such excitement? He didn't turn away from the crowds. On the contrary—he gestured for his bodyguards to step back. The people looked at him adoringly. They couldn't believe it—"It's him, it's Hugo!"—and they surrounded him until he was unable to move. They didn't want to waste a second. As if he were a family friend, they made every petition they could think of:

"Hugo, gimme some help to fix our shack!"

"Hugo, I'm homeless!"

"Hugo, I need an operation for my old lady, it's urgent, and I got no job!"

"Hugo, gimme a grant to study!"

"Hugo, those punks bully us day and night!"

"Hugo, give us water and electricity!"

And Hugo heard the entreaties from his people, he talked with them, he asked their names and about their lives. The bodyguards didn't know what to do with the hundreds of requests written on little slips of paper people were trying to get into the president's hands. Eventually, they fought to get him out of the throng that had surrounded them.

Luz Amelia Lobo was there, a young woman, just twenty, fighting to hand him a piece of paper. She finally managed to grab him by the sleeve and shout: "Hugo, help me!" He got a look at her, and noticed her pregnant belly. He took a piece of paper from her, folded in four.

In the hospital, doctors were trying to save the young man's life, and on the streets the bodyguards finally regained control of the situation.

Hugo got back into the car, the hopeful multitude dissolved, and Luz Amelia was lost in the dangerous labyrinth of streets and hillsides.

Mauricio had to put all this street activity in context for his bosses in Havana. He explained that President Chávez had called a massive popular rally to celebrate his victory and thank the voters. A vast crowd of citizens answered his call. They were commemorating the start of a new era of justice and dignity. Chávez passionately told them that governing wouldn't be easy, that they'd need to work together to defeat many monsters. And that this was his rationale for signing his first decree, an order to hold a referendum on reforming the constitution to have a "true participatory democracy." The plan was that in two months, voters would return to the ballot boxes to decide whether or not to convene a Constituent National Assembly. If they voted "yes," Congress would be dissolved and the constitution replaced with a more modern one better suited to the twenty-first century. Chávez's proposal was met with applause and he seemed to feel their unquestioning love.

Mauricio went on to report on the ins and outs of Chávez's meetings and consultations. In the first week, his schedule of events and meetings seemed to consume almost his entire day. According to his sources, the president spent long days in meetings with advisers, drafting the new constitution, while also analyzing alarming reports on the country's dire social conditions with Ángel Montes. Poverty was as widespread as criminal violence. Homicide rates had skyrocketed and were now among the world's highest. Caracas at night was more dangerous than a war zone. The price of oil had plummeted, and the state's revenues made it impossible to increase public spending, or to do all the things the president had promised to do. Mauricio stressed insistently to his bosses that the social situation was horrible and unsustainable. Hugo needed to do something soon to avoid a social explosion and a massive wave of protests that could bring an end to his presidency.

Between their yoga classes, long conversations, and meals out, Eva López and Mónica Parker had become good friends. Eva genuinely liked Mónica and admired her professionally, which is why the spy often felt a little guilty about the sensitive information Mónica shared without the slightest suspicion that she had become a CIA informant.

The conversations often turned toward their personal lives. Mónica spoke about the trouble she had finding a man who lived up to her expectations. Among other things, they were united by solitude, a catalog of failed relationships, and the hope of love.

Mónica also talked to Eva about her family. Her father came from an old Boston family, and an American bank had sent him to Caracas when the country was enjoying an oil boom. The young businessman settled in Venezuela and married her mother, a Caracas society lady, with whom he had Mónica and her sister. Her mother had died ten years ago, her sister now lived in Boston, and her sixty-seven-year-old father was now retired and living alone in the big family house in Caracas.

What Mónica didn't tell Eva was that a few years ago, Charles "Chuck" Parker had been caught falsifying financial statements to hide massive embezzlement. This tropical Madoff was the author of a protracted fraud that made victims of anybody who deposited their savings with his bank. The bank handled the situation with discretion; they fired Parker, but gave him a way out of criminal charges: replace the funds immediately, or go to jail.

Mónica Parker didn't tell Eva that her father was shut away in that house, permanently drunk and grief stricken. She didn't tell her that she loved him so much she'd do anything to protect him. She didn't mention any of this to her friend because, as one of the most respected figures in the country, she needed to tread very carefully. Her morning news bulletin dominated the ratings. On it, she interviewed politicians, bankers, and powerful people with whom she was relentless but respectful. Her program often generated headlines and articles in the print media. What Mónica showed each day defined what the country was going to be talking about.

Eva López, meanwhile, knew all the things Mónica thought she didn't, and more. Though she would've liked to help her friend, she didn't know how. And though she would've liked to stop using her as an informant, she couldn't do that either. The information she got through Mónica was invaluable.

Besides, Eva herself was under enormous pressure. In her most recent contact with Oliver Watson, she received urgent orders to *neutralize* her Cuban counterpart, of whom Eva confessed to have not found a single clue. But she reiterated her commitment to work toward that end.

Over the past few months, her networks had been investigating the deep-rooted links between Prán and Willy García, who, according to the best informants, had gotten close to the new president. She sat at her desk, with photographs spread in front of her. The photos, taken at a considerable distance, showed Prán and Willy having lunch with somebody only seen from behind who might have been Hugo. They were taken during the current president's imprisonment. The group looked to be enjoying themselves. They were drinking champagne and laughing. Eva pressed PLAY on her remote and watched yet again the moment when Willy García gave a smug smile when paying his respects to the president and first lady in a video of the inauguration party in the presidential palace.

Eva pulled out recent pictures from *Granma*, Cuba's official newspaper, showing Castro and Chávez together during one of the latter's frequent visits to Cuba, and put them on top of the surveillance photos. There had to be some kind of connection between them all.

Who are you, Mr. President? she murmured to herself.

Eva looked at the time and realized she was due to teach her weekly hatha yoga class in ten minutes.

Light cascaded in through the windows of the yoga studio, and Eva stood on one leg in front of her class of students. She gently eased her lithe body into downward-facing dog pose, and the class dutifully followed her lead. Mónica copied the rest of the class, but her heart wasn't in the stretches that afternoon. Her mind kept wandering to that new dark-haired man in the front of the class. He stood a head taller than everyone else in the room, and when he was setting up his mat, he had cast a quick glance her way. Their eyes met for only a second, but that glance had pierced her deeply. Eva, too, was distracted by him. She recognized him, but it took her most of the class to figure out from where. He was none other than the man from the rally.

After class, Mónica lingered, waiting for Eva and their standing tea date, helping Eva roll up the yoga mats. Mauricio hung back, too, as the rest of the class thanked Eva and took their leave, hoping to catch a moment with the woman whose gaze had captured his attention, twice. As he waited, Mónica appeared beside him.

"You don't strike me as the yoga type," Mónica said confidently.

"No? I like to think I'm quite graceful. I guess you should never judge a book by its cover." He recognized the famous journalist but wasn't intimidated by her. In fact, in person he found her quite alluring. He stepped closer, a subtle way of asserting dominance and flirting at the same time. She stood her ground, and he could feel the heat between them. Smiling down, he said, "Hi, I'm Mauricio."

It was 9:00 p.m. when Prán said hello into the receiver of the most private and secure of his telephones. On the other end, Hugo said he wanted to repay him for everything he'd done for him while he was in prison. He was holding the decree for his pardon. Prán smiled and, with solemn respect, turned down the offer. He had so many enemies *outside*, so many debts unpaid to his rivals in organized crime, that as soon as he was out on the street he'd be a dead man.

"I thank you for your noble gesture with all my heart, Mr. President, but I'm safer here, you understand?"

Hugo insisted on returning his support in some tangible way, and Prán thought this could be the right moment to call in some favors.

"Very well . . . if you insist . . . The truth is, I don't want anything for myself. But I'd like it if you would consider some recommendations for your team. There are people I trust absolutely, talented people who admire you and who could be very useful to have working alongside you."

A worrying silence. Prán and Willy exchanged glances. Then the mollusk went on happily: "Of course, I can give you names! Carlos García, for example, or . . . Willy, as you know him. He's a brilliant economist, very well respected. He knows the country's problems well. Put him in charge of the economy, and there's nobody better to inspire confidence among private-sector investors, inside and outside the country. He's a Harvard guy, you know? Bilingual, incredibly gifted!"

Prán gave his partner a wink, said goodbye to "my dear Mr. President," and raised a glass of rum.

"I told you, Willy. I'm not the master of the world, but I'm the master's son! God loves me!" he said, laughing at his brilliant idea.

A few days later, Prán watched a crowded press conference broadcast from the presidential palace. Hugo was introducing the country to his first ministerial cabinet. Mónica Parker reported live:

> The president has taken some time in announcing his ministers. Usually they're named on the same day the president is sworn in, but our new president often

disregards established norms, and has kept the ministries vacant until he was ready. Some critics claim that the real reason for his delay was to prevent anything overshadowing his presidential swearing-in. He wants to be the only character in the story, as if he weren't already. The good news is that today, at last, he's ready to make these crucial nominations.

Mónica didn't report that among the ministers there was dismay and mutual distrust, but she told Eva over drinks that week.

"Every social group with influence is represented: academics, economists, leftist politicians, social activists, and, most of all, various ex-soldiers. Every sector that's been courting the president since the night of the coup. It's obvious the president is creating a vast bureaucracy," Mónica said and sipped a glass of red wine.

"What's your take, really?" Eva asked.

Mónica worried the public sector would be an expensive, inefficient monster, which is what the critics predicted. But Hugo didn't seem to care. He believed in the state, so in his government, the state would be as big as it needed to be and there would be as many ministers as he required. He repeated this at every opportunity.

"Well, everybody hoped that the first appointments would give some sense of where the government was headed. But it doesn't make any sense. It's like he's trying to collapse government under its own weight." Mónica paused. "And Willy García, a minister! Absurd!"

"How so?" Eva looked at her quizzically, playing the uninformed foreigner. She was careful not to reveal that after months of intel and research she already knew everything there was to know about Willy García.

"He's a snake. I mean, they all are, but him more than the others. It's a little embarrassing, really . . ." Mónica took a large gulp of her drink. "I don't really understand how I fell for his bullshit. Willy and

I were lovers, a few years ago. He kept promising he would leave his wife, that we would start a new life together in Europe. He'd devote his time to business, and I'd make documentaries. We would travel the world and live happily ever after." Her voice grew increasingly sarcastic. "Miraculously the affair never made it into the press. Thank goodness."

"How did it end?" Eva asked, genuinely curious about her friend's newly revealed romance.

"You'll love this. I was making a documentary about some neighborhood, and the camera crew decided to move us closer to this beautiful, deserted beach in a little hidden bay. And there he was, walking along hand in hand with a top model." Mónica smiled at the memory. "Of course, Willy didn't know what to say, but I did. I broke it off then and there, in front of the model and the camera crew and everyone. I realized I'd rather be single. Maybe it's lonely, sometimes, but at least it's honest."

Mónica couldn't know how closely the story resonated with Eva's own. Eva turned her thoughts to work, as she always did when her heart started to ache. Mónica's confession only confirmed what Eva already knew about Willy: that he was vain, egoistic, petty, and untrustworthy.

But how had he managed to get so close to Chávez? How had a man like him ended up becoming a minister? How was Prán involved in this? And the Cubans? She couldn't see how it all fit together, though she knew all too well things like this didn't happen by chance.

The nomination triggered celebration in the mollusk's cave, of course. With the new president "number one" on his speed dial, and several ministers on his personal payroll, Prán was starting to reap the benefits of his master plan. He felt certain he'd be able to expand his businesses, the legal and illegal ones, more than he'd ever dreamed possible. He would open up new markets, he'd buy up new industries. Of course, it wouldn't be all smooth sailing. He knew that powerful enemies would appear, including from within the regime of his friend the president. But fear is a cricket to be flattened under your shoe. And Prán knew just how to do that.

◆ ◆ ◆

Hugo was determined to create a radio show. Every Sunday he would speak about new government programs, talk to his ministers, and receive calls from compatriots, friends, and counterparts from around Latin America. He decided to call the program *Hello, Mr. President*.

While the government's radio station had limited reach, the private media owners offered him a vast radio network that covered almost the entire country. The opposition was surprised at such an audacious tactic of media activism on the president's part. "He'll burn out. It's not sustainable. You'll see, he'll give it up," his critics and some communications experts all predicted wrongly. During the first few broadcasts, the program had no prepared script apart from an announcement of the day's events and of a trip to some province. There were two announcers with him in the studio and it was their job to flatter him, between one subject and the next. The president took the opportunity to show off his gifts as a singer of popular and protest songs. To cheer up his listeners' days, he extensively discussed his childhood, his military career, his aspirations as a baseball player, and even his days as a young lad when he was a hit with the girls. But at the center of it all, at first, were the protracted conversations with listeners who called in to the program with complaints and requests. Many insisted on speaking to him personally, inviting him into their lives to tell him about their problems in detail. The president always asked for their phone numbers and told his staff to contact them after the broadcast.

"How are you, Mr. President?" Pedro Marrero, one of the listeners, asked.

"Very well, kid. I'm here with our patriot friends," replied the president.

"Look, Mr. President, I live just back here, at the end of the block, and I wanted to ask you a favor, but I wanted you to see it *with your own eyes*. Let me invite you to come for a nice little Criollo coffee with me and my family."

"Wait for me when I'm coming out," the president said, "and we'll see if I can, because you know that at the door of the radio station there are always hundreds of people, and I almost always stay behind for at least an hour talking to them, hearing their complaints, taking notes."

"I know, I live right next door," Marrero said.

"You live next door, Pedro, you're our neighbor. I'm going to try to grab a coffee with you. Here's hoping the public will let us! But either way, I'm so grateful to you and your family, though you know I'm devoted to the collective. Here's hoping I can do it, if our people, who're just there outside, will let us . . ."

For the first several weeks on the air, in his famous, pleasantly plainspoken, folksy manner, Hugo urged his people to understand him without making any actual commitments. On average he took twenty calls each show and always seemed determined to resolve each person's troubles. However, as the weeks passed, the format became unsustainable, since, to his great irritation, some of these followers criticized the new government's policies live on the air. So *Hello, Mr. President* was transformed into a marathon monologue, totally controlled but with a pretense of being spontaneous and improvised. This new version could last up to nine hours, and though it still included calls from the people, they were prescreened and only praised the president, thanked him for some favor or gift, and criticized the "enemies of the revolution."

Hello, Mr. President was broadcast on TV too. It was a kind of political variety show, with special guests, music, phone-ins, and all kinds of surprises that gave it a large audience. Hugo periodically chose different places in the country to broadcast from, managing to convey the impression that the president was everywhere. An omnipresent leader. The turmoil outside each local radio station, far from worrying the president, strengthened his belief that Venezuela was a poor, wayward flock in search of a good shepherd. "Venezuela was lost, nobody loved her . . . and then I found her," he said once.

Chávez governed from the screen. His program was his medium of choice for announcing his next acts or intentions, whether political, social, economic, military, electoral, national, or international. One afternoon, for example, before boarding a plane for Brazil, Hugo explained to the Venezuelan people why the trip was so important:

"I'm going to the first summit of heads of state from Latin America and the Caribbean, and the European Union. Last night, in the small hours, I was reading an old book of mine . . . I've been thinking a lot about Simón Bolívar's idea of forming a confederation of formerly Spanish states in Ibero-America. That will be my main message at this summit. Latin America can and should be a global power. We should unite Venezuela, Brazil, Colombia, Ecuador, Peru, Bolivia, Argentina, Chile, all of Central America, Panama, Cuba, the Dominican Republic, Jamaica, Haiti, this whole Bolivarian world. It's the only path open to us."

Broadcast by broadcast, the people felt as though they were a living part of the government. The program's media impact was unstoppable.

For the first time in the history of the annual gala of the Association of Women for Venezuelan Childhood, the attendees would include the president of the republic himself. The event, to raise funds for a well-known home for abandoned children, was a social occasion that the country's elite already considered unmissable, since it gathered the cream of the Criollo jet set in one single space. The organizers, most of them wives and daughters of bankers, businessmen, and politicians, were proud to devote their time and energy to this worthy cause.

President Chávez accepted the invitation to the gala as part of his publicity strategy. It would keep him center stage and promote his image as a good man and a positive example, since he himself was living proof of the possibility of overcoming the social barriers created by poverty.

Because this was the twentieth such gala, and because some of the organizers were among her closest friends, Mónica Parker agreed to be the evening's MC. She arrived late and full of anxiety at having left her father alone, drowning in his third bottle. Paradoxically she gave herself strength by drinking two glasses of rum before assuming her ceremonial role.

Following a script agonized over by the organizers, Mónica started off by thanking the president of the republic and first lady for the honor of their presence and the more than six hundred attendees, who, thanks to their donations, "are writing a chapter of hope in the lives of millions of needy children." Then she awarded a plaque of recognition and gratitude to the most generous donor that year: the Elite chain of stores. The guests, many of them wearing items of luxury clothing purchased at one of the Caracas stores, burst into applause when the company's senior executive, Mauricio Bosco, rose from the table he shared with the president. As he approached the platform to receive the plaque and a hug from Mónica, she was surprised to recognize him as the same Mauricio from Eva's yoga class. She blushed as they embraced politely.

Once the formalities were over, Mónica was led to the table of distinguished guests, where she was seated directly between the president and Mauricio Bosco, who rose simultaneously to greet her. Under the watchful eye of his wife, Hugo winked at Mónica, conveying what he'd said to her so many times before. Mauricio took her hand and introduced himself again, with sober formality. She smiled as he pushed her chair in and sat back down to her left.

Mónica half regretted having accepted the invitation. It was impossible to break away from the president's tireless monologue, enlivened as he always was by the attention of the crowd and the occasional questions from Mauricio, whom he addressed as if he were a close friend. And dozens of guests came over to shake Hugo's hand, hug him, and make themselves available in case he needed anything. Mónica could see Eloísa's blood boil each time Hugo lingered a bit too long in a hug with one woman or another. Though Eloísa maintained a courteous smile for most of the evening, Mónica noticed that several times she whispered to him that they should leave, requests that disappeared as fast as the glasses of whisky.

But on the other hand, Mónica was delighted to have the chance to talk more to Mauricio. He clearly knew how to respect the president's desire for the limelight, but he spoke with self-assured authority when Hugo addressed him directly. And when Hugo's attention was otherwise occupied, he made casual small talk with Mónica, asking her about her professional life with a combination of genuine interest and confidence that was rare. Men were usually overbearingly aggressive and egoistic, or a little starstruck by her. Mauricio was neither.

After many drinks, hugs, and kisses, the president seemed satisfied and began buttoning up his jacket, signaling he was getting ready to leave. The party halted for a few minutes while Hugo and his wife left, and then Mauricio turned to Mónica.

"At last. I thought he'd never stop talking," Mauricio whispered to Mónica with a laugh, close enough that only she could hear him. The warmth of his breath on her ear made her shiver a tiny bit.

"Always the same Hugo," she said, knowingly.

Mauricio didn't waste a moment. He put his warm hand gently on hers, looked into her eyes for a breathless moment, and made an invitation she didn't want to refuse: "Care to dance?"

Chapter 6

BILL CLINTON, QUEEN ELIZABETH II, SADDAM HUSSEIN, AND MOTHER NATURE

Mauricio had heard about the globe in President Chávez's study, covered with little red circles. Sitting in front of it like it was a magic crystal ball, the president had marked—one by one—the hundreds of places he wanted to go on what he called his "geopolitical missions."

He'd made it clear in his TV program, in interviews, and in public speeches, that he didn't travel for fun: he traveled to bring the revolutionary message to every corner of the globe. He didn't say it out loud, but deep in his heart he dreamed of changing the world. Fidel had urged him to think big, and that's what he was doing.

Mauricio was always up to speed with Hugo's comings and goings, his meetings, and his work schedule, thanks to the close friendship he'd cultivated with now-minister Willy García and the agents he'd placed as bodyguards and staff within the presidential home. And he at least partly believed the president's repeated statement that these weren't pleasure trips but work for the Venezuelan people and for a revolution that would restore their dignity.

As he put the finishing touches on rewriting the national constitution, he put red circles over Bonn, Hamburg, Hannover, Berlin, and

Rome, for his first European tour. A few days later, he and a group of eight ministers boarded the presidential plane. First stop: Berlin.

In one of his many speeches he used recent German history to make himself understood: "Just as the Berlin Wall was raised here fifty years ago to divide Germany in two, forty years ago in Venezuela invisible walls also divided us: the walls of hunger, of wretchedness, of inequality. Just like you, we are today beginning to knock down those walls to reunify our country."

Such euphoria with each burst of applause!

Weeks later Hugo traveled to the most sublime stop of his tour, the private study of Pope John Paul II in the Vatican. He brought gifts, and, as a devoted Catholic, a follower of the teachings of Jesus, he asked His Holiness to bless his revolutionary cause. The pope, according to Hugo, looked at him "with an expression that was youthful, lively, and mischievous" and gave him the supreme blessing that he shared with his people via *Hello, Mr. President*.

Shortly after the benefit evening, Mónica and Eva met for dinner at a restaurant, a date they'd kept postponing because of the many demands on their time. They sat on the terrace, with a full view of the vastness of the mountains surrounding Caracas. They ordered their food and a bottle of wine.

"At last!" Mónica began. "I've been dying to tell you something."

Eva guessed her friend had some explosive news about her love life to share, and she asked playfully: "Well, who is he? What does he do? How did you meet?"

Impressed at Eva's intuitiveness, Mónica laughed, and then summarized that recent night at the benefit. Eva followed the story, expectantly.

"Mauricio, Mauricio Bosco. From class? He's Dominican, he runs Elite—you know, the clothing store? I don't really know much more than that, except he acts like a real TV soap star."

"Acts?" asked Eva, concerned.

"Oh no," Mónica said, correcting herself. "It's just he seems like a TV star, like he's from another world. I was seated next to him at that charity ball. At first I was bored out of my mind, Mauricio barely said a word, and as usual Chávez monopolized the conversation. But the moment Hugo and Eloísa left, he asked me to dance. And we danced, Eva, like I've never danced with anyone before. The guy is a pro. It's true, Dominicans are the best dancers. We didn't need to exchange a single word. I thought I'd been properly inoculated against seductive men. My anti-ladies'-man radar is usually in a state of red alert. I won't let myself be caught again. But this guy's different. I don't know why . . . but he's different."

Mónica kept talking, fast and excited. Eva had never seen her like that before.

"After six songs in a row, I excused myself to go to the bathroom. I was exhausted but thought a little rest would be enough to dance another six. But when I got back to the table he'd gone, and next to my glass he'd left a note on a napkin: 'We'll do this again, yes?' and his initials: MB."

Eva followed the story, containing her emotion. She was a romantic at heart, even if her line of work seemed to have toughened her.

She asked if they'd seen each other again, if the night of dancing had indeed been repeated.

"Not yet," said Mónica. "He hasn't been back to LUNA, at least not to any of the classes I've been to. And of course I looked into him. All I could find out was that he's Dominican and he is constantly traveling all over the Caribbean, where he's opening more stores. But he sent flowers twice, delivered to the production company. And this note came with the last delivery."

Eva and her friend read it simultaneously:

"There isn't a woman in the Caribbean who salsas better than you. Can't wait to see you soon. MB."

Mónica admitted that she couldn't think about anything else, that she came to the office every morning wanting nothing more than for this strange guy to show up, for something to happen, anything.

The friends finished their bottle of wine, but Mónica wasn't ready to leave just yet.

"And what about you?" she asked Eva. "Any 'romantic' news?"

Eva laughed, and lied with the usual ease: "No news, but I'm fine the way I am."

Deep down, however, Eva would have loved to be able to tell her friend about her relationship with Brendan Hatch. She'd have liked to know what Mónica made of the fact that she had met a US senator for a secret love tryst in Puerto Rico just two weeks earlier, and that she did so whenever she felt an urgent need to be her real self.

"The people who voted so passionately in the presidential elections are not excited about the matter of a new constitution," Mónica said into the cameras. "Polls show that disinterest and apathy reign among voters."

Mauricio watched as Mónica reported astutely on the president's call for new elections to determine a new constitution.

"People aren't looking to President Chávez for a new legal document, but for more jobs, higher salaries, better education, housing, pensions, and a better life." She concluded with her usual professional sign-off: "I'm Mónica Parker. Good night."

Mauricio smiled. Mónica was right, of course. But a new constitution could be just what they needed to ensure that Venezuela stayed on the path to revolution. Mauricio knew that the president would take advantage of his official visits up and down the country to set out, with all his power of persuasion, the need for a new constitution for a new Venezuela. And Mauricio would do everything in his power to help. He picked up the phone and called one of many publicity and campaign experts he had in his network. After arranging a meeting between the PR expert and the president's team, Mauricio looked at the clock. Not too late. Without even putting the receiver down, he dialed again.

"Hello?"

"Hi, Mónica. It's Mauricio. Are you free for dinner?"

Mónica had planned to have a quiet night at home with her father, but the butterflies in her stomach made it impossible to say no to Mauricio. She went home to change, picking a classic black dress that highlighted her long neck and muscular calves. Not too sexy, not too serious. She added low heels, a simple gold chain necklace, and swept her hair up into a casual bun. She arrived at the restaurant and found Mauricio was already there, waiting for her. She couldn't help but smile when he rose to greet her, pulling her chair out for her as he had at the gala dinner.

"I'm so glad you could make it," he said softly. "I've been wanting to see you. But I've had to travel for work so much . . . I just got back today. You were my first call." He lied with ease.

The part about wanting to see her wasn't a lie. He had been thinking about her more and more often. More than if she had been just another informant he was manipulating. He was surprised to realize that he was genuinely drawn to this brilliant, courageous woman.

"I'm glad you called," she said with a little smile, though there was reserve in her voice. She was glad he'd invited her to dinner, but she wasn't fully ready to surrender to his charms. Caution and skepticism were the trademarks of her career, and she'd learned the hard way that they were just as important when it came to relationships. "Where were you traveling?"

"Oh, my work is boring. Just opening clothing stores, meeting with suppliers. Nothing compared to yours," he deflected, laughing. "I saw your report on the elections today. Very interesting. Do you have any new stories in the works?"

"I'm working on something I've wanted to do for a while, a human-interest piece about people in the barrios who are affected by gang violence. I want to show what it's like for them to live every day with the fear, the uncertainty, without any options." Mónica paused.

"It's so important people understand the conditions of the poor," Mauricio said admiringly. "Most of us can't imagine what it's like to live like that. Are you focusing on one or two people, or will it be a broader overview?"

Mónica smiled, this time with no reserve. She loved her work and was excited to talk more about it with this insightful man. She was used to men who only talked about themselves, trying to impress her. Or who asked routine questions without actually wanting an answer. Mauricio was different. He listened attentively, asked smart questions, and seemed to actually care. They talked intently about poverty, about the conditions in the barrios, and then as they finished their first bottle of wine, about lighter subjects. Travel, where they had been, where they wanted to go. Before they knew it, they were the last people in the restaurant, the tired waitstaff waiting politely for them to leave so they could go home. It was well into the small hours of the morning. Finally, Mónica put on her coat. Mauricio walked her to the door, where their cars were waiting, and took her by the shoulders, looking long into her eyes.

"Thank you for a lovely evening," he said softly.

Mónica held his gaze. "It was my pleasure."

They stood in the doorway for a long moment, looking into one another's eyes, trying to decide on their next move. They both wanted the night to go on, but they knew that dreams are made more potent by waking.

Mauricio leaned in to delicately brush her cheek with his soft lips, shooting electricity through her body.

"Good night," he said, holding the door to her car open for her. Still tingling from the feeling of his lips on her skin, she got in with an almost inaudible sigh.

A few weeks later, the vote demonstrated that Mónica was right, at least in part: less than half the electorate went to the ballot box. But there were enough votes to trigger the process of drafting a new constitution, made to Hugo's specifications.

"The president is back on the campaign trail, traveling the country, not in order to fulfill his executive responsibilities, but to drum up support for *another* vote, this time ratifying the people he has handpicked to be members of the Assembly that will draft our new constitution. Democracy is suffering at the hand of these electoral tricks," Mónica said, concluding her report with passion.

"What's happening here can't be allowed," Mónica said to Eva one day, several months later. "These *most sovereign* people think they own the will of the nation. It's not enough for them to draft a new constitution, they want to destroy the whole thing."

The Assembly, upon being convened, had immediately eliminated government institutions, passed a national budget, reduced the functions of Congress, taking over its facilities, and dismissed hundreds of civil servants and judges who were "not revolutionary."

Eva had watched from her secret office in LUNA as the representatives wrote a draft constitution that did indeed change everything, from the name of the country to the way power was distributed. Eva understood better than anyone how profound the changes were, how they concentrated more power in the office of the president. They transformed him into an autocrat disguised as a democrat. She also realized that neither the outside world nor Venezuelans themselves really understood what these changes would mean for the country. She was at a loss as to how to stop it, though. In her reports to Watson, she repeatedly suggested the need for aggressive intervention to prevent Venezuela from becoming a dictatorship, but so far she had been left on her own.

Eva was aware that despite his constant traveling, Hugo was following the drafting of the document in detail. If he disagreed with something, he called the drafters directly and persuaded them to change it. He even drafted the text of some articles himself, in the small hours of the morning, before sending it to his representatives, who ensured it was this version, no other, that would appear untouched in the final document. Nobody resisted.

And finally, the president called his beloved Venezuela to the polls for the fourth time in under a year. It wasn't enough that the constitution had been drafted and approved by the representatives elected for just this purpose. "The sovereign people must now give it a massive vote of approval," he insisted.

"Why do you think he does it, Mónica?" asked Eva after their yoga class, as they drank tea in LUNA's Japanese garden.

"I think," Mónica said, "he's trying to teach his opponents a lesson, show them how much popular support he has. He knows that people in power need to look democratic even if they aren't really. But keeping up the appearance of democracy is something Hugo's interested in . . . and he's very good at it."

Eva nodded. Mónica was more right than she knew.

"They want democracy?" Hugo had said to Fidel in one of their frequent midnight conversations. "Well, I'm going to give them more democracy than they've ever seen. Though this doesn't mean a handful of people are going to tell me what I should do. I have the support of the majority, and in this case you do what the majority wants."

This private conversation reached Eva's ears directly, having been intercepted via her wiretaps. Mauricio learned of it, too, though via a less modern method, albeit a much more efficient one: Fidel told Raimundo Gálvez, who told Mauricio.

"Hmm," Eva said noncommittally. She had kept up her appearance as a mostly disinterested foreigner, letting Mónica believe she was only following politics on the most cursory level. "Let's talk about something better. How are things going with Mauricio?" Eva grinned, knowingly.

Mónica and Mauricio had been seeing each other regularly since that first dinner, and Eva had gotten all the gossip. He had been back to LUNA a few times, but Eva hadn't really gotten to know him, except through Mónica. She was the one friend Mónica trusted with her most intimate details, and Mónica had told her all about how the romance had unfolded.

Like she did with everyone who came to LUNA, she'd run a check on him. Dominican, working for Elite, some family still in the Dominican Republic, and some here in Caracas. She'd found nothing unusual and nothing she saw as a potential source of information. Unexpectedly relieved, she allowed herself to enjoy hearing about her friend's developing relationship without all the skepticism and scheming the rest of her life called for. And if Eva was honest with herself, she was a tiny bit envious of Mónica. Not because she wanted Mauricio, of course, but because Mónica seemed so happy with him, so at ease. She wanted that kind of freedom for romance for herself, though she knew that the career she'd chosen made it all but impossible.

◆ ◆ ◆

On the eve of the vote, the gale-force storms that had persisted over the past three days were still not letting up, threatening to destroy everything.

"Good morning, Venezuela," Mónica greeted the viewers of her morning bulletin, Luz Amelia among them. "Unprecedented tropical storms have the entire population in a state of growing alarm. As the rains continue down the coast, there is an imminent risk of mudslides and water surges pushing massive rocks down the hillsides. This is bound to affect voter turnout for the constitutional referendum."

The news team had managed to secure an interview with the president, who was in the studio, sitting across the table from Mónica.

"Will you delay the vote, Mr. President?" she asked.

"If nature sets herself against us, we will fight her and make her obey us," he said, to the surprise of Mónica and many of the TV viewers, quoting Simón Bolívar from 1812, when the city of Caracas was destroyed by a terrible earthquake. "Citizens, defy the elements, and go out to the ballot boxes!" he exhorted.

At a certain point, it stopped raining water and started raining mud. Vast torrents fell from the summits of the mountain range, along with rocks as huge as the terror of those in their path. It was as if the earth had become enraged and was flattening entire towns, burying them in mud or hurling them into the sea, along with thousands of inhabitants carried by the fatal tide. It was a meteorological apocalypse.

While Mónica reported on the disaster live, Luz Amelia fought to save her mother and baby from the brown avalanche. The entire neighborhood seemed to be running, everyone trying to dodge the landslide in their own way. The young mother prayed fervently, asking her president to send help to save her beloved village.

But that didn't happen. Neither God nor Chávez nor anybody sent by either came to Luz Amelia's village. Nor to any of the hundreds of other villages along the coast that had disappeared, buried or washed away into a Caribbean Sea that was no longer blue. Conquering a paralyzing panic, spurred on by her determination to save her little boy and dear mother, Luz Amelia finally pulled them out of their shack, into the torrents of mud. They moved as fast as they could, careful to keep their footing, down the winding, flooded streets of the barrio. Finally, they reached the sturdy four-story town hall and climbed up to the roof, where they watched what used to be a street become a wide river of mud dragging away animals, cars, furniture, motorbikes, cribs, mattresses, and people. A lot of people.

"Officials report more than thirty thousand dead as of tonight in this unprecedented natural disaster." Mónica was still on the air that evening, reporting tirelessly on the events as they unfolded. Luz Amelia could no longer watch, stranded with her family on the rooftop in the rain, but millions of viewers across Latin America tuned in to learn as much as they could about what was happening. Some were hoping for news of friends or family; some merely watched in horror as the relentless storm continued. "There's no word from the government yet about evacuations or relief efforts. We'll continue reporting as information becomes available." In an address to the country that afternoon, the president had mentioned the tragedy only briefly, using most of his airtime to urge people to go out and vote.

When the rain finally stopped, the entire coastline of Vargas, the state next to Caracas, was changed. Mother Nature had redistributed the physical arrangement of a whole region. Families who had lived there for generations no longer knew where they were. The street they'd lived on forever, along with their houses, relatives, neighbors, and pets had disappeared, gone in a cascade of mud and stones.

But it wasn't all bad news. The president was informed that, once again, the people had shown him their boundless love with their vote. In a few short weeks, the country would have a new name, the Bolivarian Republic of Venezuela, and a new constitution.

◆ ◆ ◆

Clearly anxious, Ángel Montes kept Hugo abreast of the scale of the tragedy. But Chávez couldn't bear to hear about the worst climate catastrophe his country had suffered in modern memory, instead taking refuge alone in his study in Miraflores Palace. For the whole day, he stayed away from radio and TV microphones, unconcerned that his silence puzzled everybody and even struck fear into some of his supporters. What could have happened to him? Why was he taking so long to respond, and why wasn't he at the front lines of the crisis? There was a rumor that he'd fallen into a state of paralyzing depression.

But just before his critics mobilized to denounce his silence about the catastrophe and the government's lack of preparedness, he unleashed his leadership and charisma all at once. He took a helicopter over the disaster zone, where everything was chaos and improvisation, and showed up at the aid centers himself. He ordered paratrooper units to carry out rescue operations for those isolated by the water. He went by SUV to remote areas, where he was received with delight by the survivors. He offered the presidential residence to accommodate a large group of victims and then, finally, he addressed the country on TV. Without downplaying the gravity of the situation, he shared information about the emergency, along with plans of action, and brought a sense of comfort and order to the traumatized national spirit. Once again, the poor recognized Hugo as patron of the defenseless. If Hugo was in charge, it would all be okay.

Following this crisis, the US government offered immediate and substantive humanitarian aid. During the days of the rain, Eva López had been secretly mobilizing all her contacts in Washington, especially through Senator Brendan Hatch, to launch a humanitarian mission with the US Navy. At the same time, using her network of agents within the government machine, she'd managed to arrange for the Venezuelan Ministry of Defense to immediately accept the help Bill Clinton's government had offered.

Ángel Montes was the messenger for the request: "You know very well, Hugo, our government hasn't got the resources or the equipment, let alone the experience, to deal with this tragedy," he said, holding out a document for Hugo's signature. "We can't refuse help."

Hugo signed grudgingly, and two days later several ships from the US Navy set sail from their base in Norfolk, Virginia, headed for Venezuela. Meanwhile, tens of thousands of people were totally isolated in the disaster zone, and there were fears of an outbreak of disease. Hunger reigned.

As fast as the emergency warranted, the US government, which had experience with similar events in Central America, the Caribbean, and elsewhere, offered to reconstruct the coastal highway, which the rain had wiped off the map. Officers were bringing ships loaded with the heavy machinery needed for establishing access routes to the areas that had been isolated. They also made experts available from the army engineering corps, along with rescue personnel and hundreds of doctors, paramedics, and nurses, and they supplied helicopters, field hospitals, and tents for the families who had lost their homes.

The Venezuelan Ministry of Defense, with the support of the president's ever-present adviser, Ángel Montes, coordinated activities, while media in both countries broadcast images of the US ships approaching on the high seas.

During the worst phase of the emergency, Hugo received a call from an extremely alarmed Fidel Castro. With little by way of preamble, the Cuban leader made him see how bad it would be to allow the Yanks to build goodwill with this gesture of humanity and solidarity.

"You must understand, they aren't engineers or doctors," Fidel said. "They're an occupying army! Fucking Marines! They're invading, and you didn't even notice!"

Hugo recalled something that had happened a few weeks earlier, when nobody had suspected the tragedy was looming. As a part of the doctrinal alliance between the two governments, the Venezuelan president had gathered a group of officers close to him in a hall in the palace to watch a film suggested by Fidel himself. It was a movie produced in Cuba that brought together two speeches by the late Chilean president, Salvador Allende, the first socialist to come to power via the ballot box in Latin America, in 1970.

In the first clip, Allende was addressing the heads of state gathered at the UN: "People have put their trust in us. What increases our faith in the great human values is the certainty that these values must prevail—they cannot be destroyed."

In his youth, Hugo had followed Allende's ideals very closely. Seeing him again moved him deeply. In the second part of the film, the group of officers, including the president, watched with anger a series of pictures of war: planes from the Chilean Air Force bombing La Moneda, Chile's presidential palace. Allende wore his military helmet and was holding the machine gun Fidel Castro had given him not long before. The painful final scene announced the death of the Chilean president.

It did not need repeating, and Hugo already had an image engraved in his mind of the violent death of Allende, a leftist leader who, like himself, had won elections and tried to govern democratically. He imagined Allende cornered by greater military forces, compelled to surrender and resign. He imagined him reaching the crossroads in a hall in the presidential palace, where he died from self-inflicted gunshot wounds, later ruled a suicide.

From Havana, in the middle of Venezuela's catastrophe, Fidel was determined to convince Hugo to reject the "humanitarian aid" from the US, reminding him what happened in Chile.

"That's what the gringos did. You've gotten further than Allende; you can't become another martyr. I promise you'll meet the same fate if you don't stop them."

The Cuban leader's call had its desired effect. Hugo called Ángel Montes to his study to give him the counterorder to reject the US's help. "We won't allow their warships into our country."

Ángel couldn't hide his surprise, or his unease. Up till now, Hugo had been willing to accept the Americans' help. Ángel tried to dissuade him. He spoke about the urgent need for their equipment and their engineers to open up roads to get to people dying from a lack of aid, medicine, water, and food. The cargo on board the US boats would save lives. And it would give temporary homes to the tens of thousands of people who had lost theirs. And medical attention too.

Ángel expressed his genuine solidarity with those who were suffering. But this just enraged the president.

"Nobody loves the people more than I do!" he exclaimed. The look in his eyes was icy, filled with restrained rage, as he shouted at his friend: "If you can't carry out this order, Ángel, just say so. There are plenty of other compañeros ready to obey without objection. Your refusal to comply is insubordination!"

All this happened in the presence of expectant senior officers, who made a mental note of the rabid anti-US attitude. They were also surprised Hugo was so aggressive with his closest friend and brother-in-arms. An obedient Ángel lowered his eyes, and with clear distress and humiliation, said: "Your order will be carried out, Mr. President. If you'll excuse me . . ."

Within a few hours the US ships found themselves obliged to change course and return to their base. The president celebrated his decision. Fidel gave a satisfied smile as he watched the boats returning on CNN. Meanwhile thousands of victims isolated in the mire continued to wait for help, food, and medicine.

The president addressed the nation and announced that he had rejected the US's help, to the anger of Mónica, Eva, Hatch, and thousands of incredulous Venezuelans. He gave a vague statement that his government had sufficient resources to manage the crisis by itself and he would not allow foreign powers to "come and tell us how we should be saving our people."

Hugo's effusive message reached a group of victims via a transistor radio. As usual, the leader's decisions divided his people.

A woman surrounded by sick children burst into tears. "Without the Americans' medicine, my kids are going to die!"

But the man beside her scolded her: "Don't be a fool, woman! Hugo knows what he's doing. He'll get us out of this. I bet he'll even give us a better house than that little wooden one that fell down. You'll see!"

The first day of the twenty-first century dawned full of rants of love for Venezuela and cries of suffering. On the one hand, Hugo celebrated the fact that his beloved people had voted for the new constitution and so set in motion what he called the planned refounding of the new Bolivarian Republic of Venezuela.

At the same time, Hugo knew that part of his beloved country had been destroyed by the most serious natural disaster in its history. Tens of thousands of his compatriots, in particular some of the poorest, who he felt were his own people, had died. Death and the *patria* were intertwined in Hugo's soul. But there was no time to mourn. Hugo couldn't save the victims, but he could save the country.

A few weeks later, in Santo Domingo, Mauricio met with his boss, Raimundo Gálvez.

"Chávez is an extraordinary communicator who knows how to make an emotional connection with the people, but he doesn't really have a political apparatus." Mauricio reported his analysis of the man on whom so much of the Cuban future depended. "He doesn't really control the military, or the oil industry either, which is everything in Venezuela. He lacks expertise, so it's likely he'll make mistakes. It's obvious the administration of the state bores him, and sometimes it's like he isn't governing so much as conducting a permanent campaign. He's impetuous and rash, and he's gotten lax in his personal security, which puts him at risk of being assassinated. You've seen it for yourself: he's always adding to his list of enemies—real and imaginary. I worry there might be a military coup in his future."

"And what about your second mission?" Gálvez asked with a steely look in his eyes.

"No change from a few weeks ago," Mauricio replied. "We had some successes . . . but still no clues to the chain of command in Venezuela. There's no doubt Langley's spies are acting effectively. They've also managed to infiltrate the government and the armed forces."

Gálvez wasn't satisfied with Mauricio's report. "The CIA man clearly knows what he's doing and is highly strategic. He's probably already tracked you down, and he'll kill you if you don't wake up and get him first."

Mauricio returned to Caracas, annoyed and frustrated. He needed to move his pieces some other way. Years of experience had taught him that to find a way around conundrums it's useful to put them aside for a time. So he called his new lover and invited her to dinner.

Mónica looked at Mauricio through the candlelight. "I have to admit I was impressed with your dancing at the gala." She blushed at her own honesty.

"My aunt was a salsa instructor in Santo Domingo." He smiled at the memory. "It was heaven on earth the way she moved. She taught me how to dance when I was a little boy. She would glide with me across her hardwood dance studio, and my heart would sing. That's how I learned to love to dance."

This was a rare moment of truth. The only falsehood was that his aunt had been a salsa instructor in Havana rather than Santo Domingo. He knew that mixing in sprinkles of the truth made him a better liar. But he also realized, to his own surprise, that he wanted Mónica to know something real about him. He wanted to share something meaningful to him with this amazing woman.

The waiter poured Mónica a taste from the bottle of tempranillo she'd ordered, and she took a slow sip, then nodded in approval. The waiter poured both their glasses.

"Are you ready to order?" Mauricio asked Mónica. She nodded.

"I'll have the pork chops." She smiled at the waiter. Mauricio raised an eyebrow, quizzically.

"And I'll have the steak." The waiter scurried away with their orders.

"Pork chops?" he asked, almost laughing.

"Oh, yes," she laughed. "They're my favorite! Every time I visited my family in Boston, my uncle made everyone pork chops after Sunday Mass. It was always the best part of the trip for me."

"The best pork chops I ever had came from a tiny hole-in-the-wall restaurant in Venice. I was attending the opening of a new textile shop, and they had plenty of wine and no food. When I left, I just went into the first place open and asked what their specialty was. The waiter brought me a huge plate of pork chops! I ate so much that I almost lost them again in the gondola later that night." He laughed a little to himself at the memory. "So, how did you get into journalism?" Mauricio wanted to steer the conversation around to Mónica again. She leaned back in her chair and thought a moment.

"I love to get to the bottom of things. To dig deep and find the truth in humanity." After a short pause she said, "I also see it as my way of serving my country." With those words she remembered all the times

Chávez had hit on her, and a chill went down her spine. Mónica took a long drink from her glass of wine.

"And what about you? Fashion?" she countered. The conversation flowed naturally, each sharing details about their lives, laughing easily, and opening up more and more as they relaxed into the bottle of wine. At some point the waiter wordlessly placed their food in front of them, knowing not to interrupt new couples in the throes of budding love. They barely stopped talking long enough to eat their meal.

◆ ◆ ◆

"Our economy and our lives depend on those oil prices," President Chávez said on TV, announcing his upcoming travel schedule. Eva watched with concern. She had sent an encrypted report to Watson just the day before: the president was preparing to call an international gathering of oil-producing countries, and he would shortly be beginning a tour of the Middle East, to persuade the leaders to coordinate their actions to raise the price of crude oil. Eva had managed to learn some of the details of the trip ahead of their announcement, thanks to Willy García's developing "friendship" with Patricia, the skilled manicurist at LUNA. García, now a prominent minister in Chávez's government, would be joining the president in his travels.

"I don't know what I'm going to do without you for so long," Willy had said to Patricia on the tape Eva reviewed, as she always did, after his weekly appointment. She'd never seen a man so fastidious about his nails.

"What do you mean?" Patricia asked coyly. "You're not leaving me, are you?"

Willy smiled. "The president has invited me to accompany him on his tour of the Middle East," he said self-importantly, in a low voice. "We'll be going to Iraq, to meet with Saddam Hussein himself and stopping in the United Arab Emirates to meet with Sheikh Zayed bin Sultan Al Nahayan."

"Wow," Patricia said, feigning admiration. "Such important men. What will you do there?"

"It's quite complicated, my dear," Willy said patronizingly. "Venezuela is a great oil-holding country, and we need to have strong relationships with them to make sure we're getting everything we deserve in exchange for sharing our resources with the world."

Eva informed her bosses about these plans immediately, along with her analysis that Chávez was aligning himself with these dictators in an attempt to control global oil prices, but other than that there was nothing she could do.

As the UN had put a travel embargo on Iraq after the invasion of Kuwait, Chávez's arrival was as complicated as it would have been in the time of Marco Polo. After long days of traveling, after several cars and helicopters, they finally arrived. Saddam himself drove them along streets decked out in honor of the visitor, across the city toward one of his many palaces. They talked about cooperation agreements and the Organization of Petroleum Exporting Countries. And about their common resentment toward the United States.

The public reaction from Washington fired Hugo up, and he took advantage of the opportunity to rant and rave against "the Northern Empire."

"If those people in the US say my visit is unworthy, I tell them we are worthy. Venezuela stands for self-determination and freedom for all."

Back in Caracas, his wife awaited him unhappily. Eloísa, like most of the prominent ladies in Caracas society, had become a regular at LUNA and had come to confide in her regular masseuse, who had been treating her for years now with her healing hands, aromatherapy, and a comforting ear, always willing to listen to her problems.

"I can't believe we matter so little to him," Eloísa said, still upset, in the middle of her weekly massage at LUNA. "He didn't even come to see us when he got back—he just went straight to his office in Miraflores. I called five times before he even answered the phone! He pretended he wanted nothing more than to be with us, but he had to attend to the country's needs. 'Eloísa, our Bolivarian Revolution shouldn't just span the hemisphere, but the whole world. You should be pleased we're right at the center of this,' he said."

"Oh, querida, that's terrible," Patricia said sympathetically.

"Of course, I hung up on him," Eloísa finished, with a sigh, wiping away a tear that had spilled out despite her best efforts to suppress her heartbreak.

◆ ◆ ◆

Boosted by his growing international visibility, Hugo was determined to fulfill his new aim: becoming an anti-US leader of global renown.

"It shouldn't be hard," he said to Ángel one morning in the early hours in his study. "The whole world hates the Yanks, and nobody likes that hick George W. Bush. I'm going to mess with him and you'll see how much people like it when I do that. Here and everywhere."

Ángel, like Eloísa, found it harder and harder to talk to his old friend.

"The eyes of the world are on me now, and on what we're doing in Venezuela," he said to Ángel, excited. "I've persuaded the oil-producing countries to raise the price of crude oil. And people are no longer prepared to tolerate injustice and inequality. Here in Venezuela we're making more progress than anybody, and people know this, and that's why they admire us; they admire us."

What won him the most goodwill were the televised accounts of his meetings with emperors, kings, and presidents where he broke with protocol. Hugo made his country laugh with his stories: how he tried to give a big, friendly Caribbean hug to the emperor of Japan, a sacred being whom nobody touches, or when he informed the protocol services of the British royal family that he intended to greet the queen of England with a little kiss.

"We always greet ladies here with a kiss on the cheek, and we say 'sweetheart' to them all, don't we? Well, then! You can't imagine the reaction from those Englishmen at Buckingham Palace! They're pink already, and they turned even pinker. They started whispering and couldn't work out how to tell me I wasn't allowed to do that. Finally, the head of protocol, the tallest, skinniest guy I've ever seen in my life, came up to me and, very formally, told me that they were going to cancel the meeting. I was laughing so hard! I promised I'd behave myself and it didn't make any difference if they believed me or not because they couldn't stop me now; I was already there, and the place was full of journalists. They made me wait a bit longer, and then I was invited to a huge room where the queen of England was waiting for me. We had a nice chat, and in the middle of our conversation I told her, 'Your Majesty, I wanted to greet you with a kiss on the cheek the way we do it back home, but they wouldn't let me.' I thought she'd find this funny, but the old lady's expression didn't change even a bit. She acted like she hadn't understood what I'd said. And she left me still wanting to give her that kiss."

The president's disdain for royal protocol and Queen Elizabeth II set laughter running through a whole society. He had learned how to transform laughter into power too.

Chapter 7

A Change of Skin

By the end of their first turbulent year of marriage, Eloísa had learned that she was required to share her married life with an interloper to whom she would always lose: Hugo's schedule. Her husband stopped being the impassioned, coquettish cock of the rock who sang to her while she cooked, read her revolutionary poetry, made love to her wildly. He was a different person now. A man who'd totally surrendered to a clamoring population whose problems seemed to grow, multiply, and become more complicated with each passing minute.

The young woman recognized that her husband was ever more distant and that, even when they were together, he was really elsewhere. Maybe, she agonized, he was with another woman.

At times the first lady managed to resign herself to it. God put her here for a reason, she told herself over and over. And so she tried to adjust to the circumstances and embrace her role in this performance that had already begun. In interviews she spoke about rescuing homeless children. About improving education. About updating policies on adoption. About being a friend and ally to Venezuela's women.

Despite criticism, she decided to take part in the Assembly for drafting the new constitution, and she had joined her husband in a few rallies where he demanded the people vote for the constitution, which would "sweep away poverty and inequality." The first lady also set herself up in a small office in the presidential palace, where she made plans to head up social projects. And to get her husband to pay more attention to her.

When Eloísa complained to Hugo that they didn't spend enough time together, he invited her to move her residence into the palace, where an excess of work kept him for long days and nights. But she preferred to return to the La Casona residence to sleep. She complained that in Miraflores there were too many dark energies—it felt steeped in tediousness, jealousies, and power plays—that were harmful to her.

Hugo, meanwhile, didn't like La Casona. He was repelled by everything that place symbolized: a home that wasn't really a home. A home should be permanent, and that place was transitory. Each president was forced to hand the residence over to his successor. He knew that's what makes a democracy—there were no permanent leaders. But though he never said this to anyone, the idea troubled him. That's why he became irritated at the portrait gallery of past presidents of Venezuela, his predecessors. These pictures reminded him all too clearly that power was ephemeral. Too ephemeral, sometimes.

And Hugo wanted to be there forever.

Besides, Hugo preferred the high-security barracks of Fort Tiuna, the capital's military base. That Eloísa couldn't stand the place was also appealing. The fact that she never showed up there allowed for possibilities of which he took the fullest advantage.

Meanwhile, the first lady was discovering power of her own, and the possibilities that it allowed. Unable to compete with her husband's charisma or get in his schedule, Eloísa's haughtiness, beauty, and ambition thrust her into the spotlight. There were some events, like certain official dinners or her daughter Margarita's baptism, that made her feel good—so much so that at times she fell into the temptation of thinking that she was almost as important to Hugo as Manuelita had been to

Bolívar. She was delighted when she'd hear people say: "Behind every great man there's a great woman." Or "This is the woman who rules the president's heart." Only her! One in a million, one in a billion! Because of course all women melted with love for the president, and how many dreamed of occupying her position as the first and only! Even Hugo's security chief was impressed. Every day and at every public event, he saw Hugo fielding the love and seduction thrust upon him. Sometimes it appeared to him that every woman in Venezuela desperately wanted him for her own.

And he, the adventurous cock of the rock, a seemingly faithful married man, of course couldn't let so many opportunities pass him by. Strategically minded and discreet, he shielded himself with Óscar Rojas, his security head and a close friend since their military academy days. During the first months of Hugo's administration, Rojas's generous salary covered duties that included acting as mediator between the president's libido and his fervent groupies. Rojas and his agents served as a containment barrier for the "female avalanche," and tactfully and inoffensively held back those women clamoring to meet the president. Only a few carefully chosen ones would discover what it was like to make love to this seducer who had mutated into a leader of global renown.

From the raised dais in his public appearances, a hungry, insatiable Hugo would scan the room, and his eyes would indicate the women he fancied. During the rally, a female captain in an impeccable Venezuelan Navy uniform would come down from the rostrum and approach the chosen women. "Miss," she would say to each one, "the president would like to speak to you later. What's your name? Here's my phone number. Call me, and I'll send someone to fetch you." Eight out of ten responded, and in the houses of his most discreet friends, in little nooks around the palace, in Fort Tiuna military base, and even in his limo, Hugo seduced, courted, took, and abandoned these conquests.

But the first lady was not blind. Despite what the media might suggest, her married life was far from blessed. As the months passed, she'd begun to understand the extent of her husband's infidelities and the handling of his sexual encounters by Rojas and his team of complicit guards.

Imagining him with other women drove her crazy. She chastised her husband, without success. She wept with the inconsolable sorrow of knowing she'd been deceived. She screamed at the captain, accusing her of being a pimp and demanding that she be transferred somewhere far from her husband. The jealousy threw her soul into chaos. All the women who approached Hugo awoke her suspicion and often a rage she couldn't contain. Scandalous scenes unfolded in the daily gossip at the court of the cock of the rock.

Rather than Manuelita Sáenz, Bolívar's lover, breathing promises of everlasting love, the first lady's words were now closer to Doña Inés's entreaties to Don Juan in the Zorrilla play, imploring her lover to either love her or just tear out her heart.

The first lady wasn't the only woman to want more attention from the president.

Just over a year ago, thanks to a heavenly miracle, the very young, very poor Luz Amelia had caught Hugo's eye. It had changed the young woman's life. The encounter was now just another anecdote for the president, but to Luz Amelia it was perhaps the most transcendental thing that had ever happened to her.

Hugo had made the presidential motorcade stop to help a young man who'd been shot in a confrontation between two gangs. Luz Amelia, in the middle of the whirlwind of locals surrounding Hugo, had managed to reach out, grab his sleeve, and hand him a piece of paper. She had been twenty, and she was expecting a baby in just a few weeks. The child's father was a dangerous delinquent with a criminal record that included murder, part of a gang of dealers in one of Caracas's poor, dangerous barrios.

Hoping to offer the child a better future, no sooner had Luz Amelia become pregnant than she'd dumped her boyfriend and gone to live in her mother's precarious *ranchito*, with rickety brick walls, furnished with cardboard and wooden crates, finding work selling vegetables at a stall in the town market. From the very beginning, she and her neighbors had felt drawn to Hugo, who was like them. Luz Amelia had attended several electoral rallies and soon joined one of the "collectives," the popular networks of Chávez supporters that proliferated in the country's most densely populated barrios—part of a popular movement designed and coordinated by the hundreds of Cuban agents in Mauricio Bosco's network.

In the quest for a special connection to their leader, or at least in the hope of getting his attention, the president's followers started to find ways to get *papelitos* to Hugo—little slips of paper with requests for help: to pay for treatment for costly illnesses, to get a home, a grant, a job, a position in the government. So overwhelming were the number of requests that the president dedicated an office in Miraflores Palace just to reading and processing the petitions. The guards christened it the "Room of Hopes." That was where the little piece of paper that Luz Amelia had given Hugo the first time she got close to him had been filed.

Luz Amelia's efforts to keep her baby safe were not without challenges. Although she believed her boyfriend couldn't care less what happened to the baby, he had shown up a couple of times, high and armed, attempting to force her to hand him over. The incidents were only resolved because the boy's grandmother managed, wisely and heroically, to intervene and make the man leave with a promise that the baby would be given to him later. But before he could come back, Luz Amelia, her mother, and her newborn son escaped to the coastal village of Carmen de Uria. They took refuge in an aunt's tumbledown house, waiting for a miracle. Luz Amelia kept faith, idolizing the hero of the poor. She was waiting for him to give her a house for her family, which was what she had petitioned for on her little slip of paper, since "decent homes for everyone" was one of the president's electoral promises and she believed in him fervently.

However, just as she started to recover her strength safely away from her baby's father, an even more powerful force overwhelmed her. On the day people were preparing to vote for the new constitution, the sky and mountains fell on Carmen de Uria.

A few days later, at the end of her resources, faint with hunger and thirst, Luz Amelia and others were finally rescued by an army helicopter that took them to the international airport, now converted into a refugee camp. Despair, which had hitherto been on her like a birthmark, gave way to a spark of hope when the president promised his government would provide homes for the survivors of the landslide.

A new, clean house. What more could Luz Amelia want? Only *her* Hugo could do miracles like that.

Eva reread her report one final time:

> President Chávez's oratory—sometimes solemn and messianic, sometimes warm and witty, and always showy—is being transformed into the official language of the regime. He's not short on material: he receives petitions from preselected members of the public and gives away houses and cars, awards grants, and authorizes surgical interventions. Once he even ordered repairs to the pipes of a small town. He goes over his political ideas, notifies people of his plans and the measures he intends to take, chastises

his ministers, insults his opponents, and defends his government's work. Or he simply shares whatever's going through his head, what he had for lunch that day or what he talked about with someone very important, or with one of the people. He makes sudden announcements of important economic measures or nominations to critical roles, forcing both his supporters and his opponents, equally interested in the government's activities, to watch the show from beginning to end.

At one point in his monologue, for example, he explained what it meant that the Assembly had granted him special powers to rule by decree for a year. He reported that hundreds of Bolivarian schools had been opened in the barracks for the purpose of studying the work of *El Libertador*, along with revolutionary leaders such as Ho Chi Minh, Fidel, Che Guevara, and others. He also decided that thousands of soldiers would no longer be trained solely in military matters and would also serve the community. He proposed the removal of the current labor leaders and new elections to fill these roles. He proclaimed that in a not-too-distant future, Venezuela and Cuba would end up a single nation and that today they are already sailing side by side toward the seas of happiness.

To the delight of the poor and unease of the rich, Chávez asserts repeatedly that he plans to wipe the old oligarchic powers off the map. He said he'd soon begin the process of property expropriation. "In Venezuela, large estate ownership will come to an end or my name's not Hugo Chávez . . . and I'm not going anywhere, and my name *is* Hugo Chávez."

Hugo swears his voice makes not just oligarchs tremble, but the whole world. His program is an extension of his throne, and he takes it very seriously. He wants to take full advantage of his unusual and appealing combination of popular leader, statesman, and—the part he likes most—presenter of the longest and most-watched TV program in the nation. While his ministers wait days or weeks for him to make decisions critical to the functioning of the government, Hugo devotes a significant amount of his time to planning and producing his weekly show. It's clear that he's more interested in public communication than public administration, and that if he is to consolidate his power it must be on camera with millions of viewers rather than in a cabinet meeting with just a handful of ministers.

There's one connection that I still don't fully understand how to operationalize. We know Chávez is connected to Prán, but Prán seems to be devoted to an evangelical preacher in Texas, Juan Cash. We need more intel on Cash's operations.

Eva felt if she could just solve this puzzle, a lot would become clear, and it might even open up channels of influence over Hugo that she didn't currently have.

Mónica had produced a program about the country's prison problem, which included an interview with Prán, who had received her in a tiny, filthy room. Prán had two books with him by the Texan pastor. Mónica was struck by that, and dedicated a large part of the interview to Prán's devotion to this man. The inmate explained to her how these books and the pastor's preaching gave him the serenity to survive in prison.

Watching Mónica's program as she always did, Eva became even more interested in what was behind his devotion to that Texan televangelist. She put together a short but thorough biography of the eccentric pastor. At some point early in his career, Cash discovered he had a huge number of Hispanic followers in the US and decided to learn Spanish. Eva watched a few broadcasts and found a thin, elegant man with very white skin and long black hair. Besides being handsome, he was an engaging speaker with a magnetic personality and a persuasive and emotive rhetorical style, expressed in his own highly distinctive Spanish.

Thanks to his skillful preaching, Cash's church had grown enormously across Latin America, so he traveled constantly to visit his faithful flock and spread his message. Cash preached a kind of prosperity gospel theology based on economic progress and faith in God in the service of what he called "personal missions." Each person had to, through their faith, discover what their own personal mission was. "God wants you to be rich, in this life, now, here on Earth," he said. This required first identifying your personal mission and then complying with what this mission demanded.

His preaching extolled material gain; being rich was no sin. His devotees were struck by how the televangelist made no attempt to hide the luxury in which he lived, his mansions, his private jet, his yacht.

In her interview, Mónica established that, although Prán had never met his guru in person, the jailbird watched him every week on TV, in programs broadcast live from his megachurch in southern Texas, which easily held twelve thousand people. Eva learned that Prán was perhaps the most consistent follower of this unusual doctrine and one of its teacher's most generous donors.

"Thanks to my pastor, I understand why I am still alive," Prán said to Mónica. "And why I am happy, despite having come from the most total wretchedness."

Eva followed her hunch and dove more deeply into Cash's activities, and Prán's relationship to him. She sensed it might be useful to her, since Prán's devotion verged on fanaticism. Every week, Prán received doctrinal correspondence and spiritual counsel from the church. And while they had never met in person, they communicated regularly via email and video call. Audiences with Pastor Cash, incredibly hard to secure for the majority of his followers, were regular for Prán. Cash made himself available to his wealthy Venezuelan acolyte. And Prán made his substantial resources available to the Church of Cash.

Eva requested that her colleagues in the FBI, the DEA, and the NSA investigate Juan Cash. A clearer picture of the preacher quickly took shape. Behind the dazzling facade of his megachurch was a money-laundering operation, willing, for a generous commission, to process large quantities of illegal money that needed to be made usable and lawful. The immense sums of money, in cash, that the church deposited every Monday to dozens of banks were not entirely, as claimed, donations from the faithful. They were the proceeds from drug sales. The Cash religious organization was a gigantic money-laundering scheme for drug traffickers.

That information could be vital to her Venezuelan mission. She decided, for the time being, to focus all her attention on Juan Cash, and, through him, she might get to Prán. If she got to Prán, she'd have privileged access to Hugo and the kind of influence over his decision making that the Cubans could only dream about. Or at least, that was what she hoped.

Eva traveled to the US and approached Cash under the pretext of being a scholar who wanted to interview him for her book. Right from the start, her beauty and intelligence dazzled the "millionaire bishop," as many called him. In their conversation in his luxurious office, she allowed their first meeting to fill with flirtations, compliments, insinuations, and spellbound looks. The religious leader, seductive and seduced, invited her to his house for dinner that night, so they could continue the interview.

"I'd rather talk to you in private; it might loosen my tongue and I'll tell you things I've never told anybody before. If things go well, you'll have a world exclusive for your book. A guaranteed hit . . . ," Cash said with a knowing smile.

She accepted, and not long into their predinner conversation, the evangelist moved in to kiss her and she pushed him away.

"Before you kiss me, there's something you should know," Eva said. "Look at this, Juan. You'll find it of interest. It's the story of your life, in a version the world doesn't know. I'm giving you the exclusive . . ." She handed him a summary of the long criminal record of Juan Cash—activities from his past as well as current ones.

He leafed through the documents and looked at her, indignant, surprised, furious. He couldn't believe it. He threw the folder to the floor, stood, and got a revolver from a nearby drawer.

Without getting up, Eva looked at him calmly and said: "Relax, Juan. I work for the government, and this house is surrounded by federal agents. There are sharpshooters with rifles pointed at your heart right now. Drop the gun, and don't make any sudden moves if you want to stay alive. You'd better calm down and have a seat in this chair with your hands up, because I'm going to give you some good news. You might get out of this better than you think. All you have to do is cooperate with us. I can't promise to keep you out of prison, but I can make sure you don't spend the rest of your life behind bars. It's up to you."

Juan Cash was trembling, his blue silk shirt soaked with sweat. He sat down. "What do you want?"

"We want to know everything about Yusnabi Valentín, your Venezuelan devotee: Prán."

◆ ◆ ◆

That Sunday the president had accepted an invitation from a large private agro-industrial group that was launching a modern dairy plant using cutting-edge technology.

In order to encourage good relations with the government, the firm's managers considered it of critical importance to extend a very special invitation to the president. They wanted him to see the country's advances in this area in person.

Since he was accustomed to traveling with his production team, the star of *Hello, Mr. President* decided his program would be broadcast from the plant. He also wanted to show his followers that he wasn't against private property. On the contrary, he was a friend to businessmen and respected the important part they played in the national economy.

The first minutes were filled with the conventional politeness of pure propaganda. Hugo was as lively and chatty as ever and praised the modernity of the facilities, how new it all smelled. To make the most of the setting and the guests, at one point the script suggested that the president chat with the firm's workers and managers.

That was when the friendly atmosphere warped. The group's major shareholder respectfully explained that prices had been frozen for a long time but that production costs kept rising, leaving only the tiniest profit margin. The businessman asked the president to authorize a price increase.

"If we go on like this, we'll go bankrupt and the country will be left without any farming production; there will be hunger here, Mr. President, if you don't act."

The mood turned aggressive. Although Hugo hadn't studied the circumstances of this firm in any great detail, and he hadn't been the one to buy his own milk or cheese, his reaction was an impassioned defense of the rights of the people. This business about *profit margins* made him so angry that he shouted: "You get rich on the people's food, and you want more, always more!"

The managers were unnerved. They didn't understand how a request that seemed justified to them had managed to awake the president's ire. The conversation with the businessmen came to an abrupt end. Continuing on as if they no longer existed, Hugo turned to the TV cameras.

On the subject of food, he spoke about promoting the development of rice production, a project that would start soon, as arranged with the Chinese government, one of the *almost*-signed agreements from his Asian tour.

"You all know China has 1.3 billion inhabitants and they produce all the food they need for that enormous number of people. Meanwhile here in Venezuela we've only got twenty-four million people and we've got to import sugar, oil, rice, and meat? How crazy is that? We've got so much land, so much water; in the medium term we should be producing all the food—or the great majority—we need for subsistence. We can't go on importing everything! We should be more than capable of feeding our own people. Hunger can't be allowed to exist in a country as rich as this. I promise you, in just a few years, nobody in this country will go hungry. Nobody!"

◆ ◆ ◆

Mauricio arrived at his secret office after a night with Mónica. The office was full of notes, speeches, photographs, and videos. But alongside all these pieces of the jigsaw puzzle he'd been tasked with assembling, Mauricio was also facing an unexpected challenge: Mónica. It had become hard to come back down to earth and focus on his job after sharing a few hours with this woman who made him feel like no other woman had before. He couldn't believe how obsessed he'd become with her these past months.

He remembered their first night together. It had been after dinner the night he had returned from "Aruba." He'd brought her a larimar pendant, set in waves of warm yellow gold, like the waves of the sea. Larimar, he'd told her, was only found in the Dominican Republic, and it was said to help you find your soul mate. The blue reminded him of Mónica's eyes. They were sitting in his car, talking. He was about to drive her back to her house after dinner, but neither wanted the evening to be over. He'd handed her the small velvet box, and when she opened it, he took her right hand and kissed it. He knew he had to hide his truth from this captivating woman, but his body could tell her what his words could not. He kissed each individual finger, punctuating his story about the stone, and when he finished he pulled her into an embrace. She seemed to melt into his arms. He felt his heart starting to open to this woman like a rosebud in the morning sunlight. They kissed, long and hard, all the way to his apartment, barely making it inside the door before they tumbled down and made love on the floor. He awoke the next morning with Mónica in his arms.

When they were together, Mauricio had to make considerable effort to avoid saying anything about Venezuela, its government, its politics, let alone Cuba or Fidel. He continued to act the part of an apolitical businessman interested in nothing but his company.

But he was worried. First, because the feelings the journalist had awakened in him were new to him, and he wasn't quite sure how to handle them. And second, because he felt so comfortable with her that he was afraid that his *true self* might leak out in some little phrase that could allow Mónica to see the lie he was living. Though they talked a lot, their conversation tended to center around books they'd read, movies they watched together, recollections of trips they'd taken before they'd met each other, music, trivialities. Each time she made an effort to discuss the president, or the government, or the ambition of the Cubans, he smiled sweetly and listened to her silently, as if spellbound.

"Fidel is coming to Caracas in one week, and today we got his schedule: visits to the National Pantheon, to the cell where the president was imprisoned, the house where he was born, and a bunch of trips around the country. The whole thing looks very picturesque, but this relationship is a threat to our democracy."

Mauricio felt he had to redouble his precautions and decided to change the subject the best way he could: he wrapped her in his arms and whispered sweet nothings into her ear, until she melted.

Mauricio had to be especially vigilant because, in view of Fidel's visit to Caracas, the diplomatic whirlwind was increasing its intelligence threefold. In his secret office, Mauricio switched on the latest episode of *Hello, Mr. President*, dedicated to the eagerly awaited visit.

"On Monday, we will sign the total cooperation agreement between Cuba and Venezuela. We will be selling them oil at solidarity prices, while they, in turn, will pay us by sending over hundreds or even thousands of doctors, an abundance of medicine and medical equipment, as well as education, culture, sport, tourism, farm products—in short, they'll give us everything."

The spy remembered the days leading up to the military coup, when he'd complained that being assigned to Venezuela meant that his career had stalled, since, as he had said to his father, the General, "Nothing ever happens in that country, and nothing's going to change." And his father had told him, "You're wrong. Sooner or later Venezuelan oil will be the fuel that will keep the Cuban Revolution going."

Hugo's speech continued: "This is just one of the agreements we're going to sign with our great friends and their remarkable leader, Fidel Castro. To hell with those who are too mean to acknowledge the size and scale of this leader not just for Cuba, but for the whole world. A man of universal scale, whatever others may say."

The spy gave an involuntary laugh at the TV. He looked for his notebook and made a to-do list. But he couldn't concentrate. Fidel and Mónica. Mónica and Fidel. If only he had a week to go to some solitary beach with her . . . And if Fidel's visit could coincide with him solving the mystery of who the lead CIA agent was in Venezuela. And getting rid of him. How nice that would be . . .

Chapter 8

Everyone against Hugo

Hugo brandished the day's papers furiously. He was angry at the headlines, at what he'd seen on the TV news, and at what he'd heard on the radio talk shows. In the midst of preparations for Fidel Castro's visit, the troubled mainstream press was laying out the consequences of his latest *Hello, Mr. President* broadcast from the dairy production plant.

Businessmen and investors, domestic and foreign, were alarmed at both the tone and the content of the president's reaction and his rhetoric about the private sector. The currency plummeted, and several firms announced they would postpone their investment plans until there was clarification of the government's intentions. Private-sector leaders held an emergency meeting to consider the president's threats.

Hugo offered statements to soothe investors, but they didn't work. The media kept calling the president's outburst an attack on the principle of private property. The leader of the country, in turn, exploded in front of the ever-faithful Ángel Montes and his closest allies.

"Who do they think they are? That Mónica Parker, those reporters, and the media owners, they're taking advantage of democracy! What we have here isn't press freedom, it's press free-for-all! What they're doing to us isn't criticism, it's a media lynching! They criticize everything! But

I'm going to stop this at all costs. I'm going to do what's got to be done; I won't stand for this."

Ever since the Constituent Assembly, the media, and Mónica Parker's bulletin in particular, had been getting in his way. They'd stopped being shrewd worshippers begging for interviews and had become irritating stones in the revolution's shoes. They'd criticized the dissolution of Congress and establishment of the new unicameral Assembly. On TV, comedians ridiculed him daily. The TV station owners used all kinds of tricks to avoid suspending their regular programming to broadcast *Hello, Mr. President*, or any other public event where the head of state was speaking. Accusations of corruption and reports revealing newfound wealth among public officials close to the president and his family were made daily. And they even dared to criticize his relationship with Fidel Castro!

In his study in the palace, the president watched the latest programs from "that Parker woman" and other news bulletins criticizing him. A surprised Ángel Montes listened as Hugo hurled threats against the media, starting with Mónica. He ordered telephone taps on the station owners and directors, and for taxes to be imposed on them. He swore he would shut down newspapers and TV stations if this "counterrevolutionary campaign" didn't stop.

"I'm not some asshole like Allende! They won't do to me what they did to Allende!" he yelled at the top of his lungs.

Montes asked, apprehensively but directly, if he planned to impose press censorship. At that, Hugo lost his temper and rebuked him bluntly. Montes, ever respectful, insisted that the constitution—"*your* constitution, Mr. President"—enshrined freedom of expression and there were certain things that he simply couldn't do without violating it.

But Hugo was in no mood for legislative lectures.

"The will of the people is my only constitution," he said, annoyed. "If the current constitution isn't working for me, I'll change it."

"You can't simply change it, just like that, Hugo," Montes insisted.

"Oh no? You'll see what I can do!" he shouted and told him to withdraw. Nobody dared say a word.

Not long afterward, a secretary informed the president that he had a phone call from a famous reporter in the US. Still raging, Hugo agreed to speak to her for a few minutes about the counterrevolutionary campaign of disparagement against his government.

"What are you referring to, specifically?" the journalist asked from the other end of the line. The conversation was being recorded for her international news program.

"No less than an organized campaign against me," the president replied, sounding calm. "Some complaints are natural when you start a process like the one we have going here, making such profound changes . . . There have been fears, doubts, some distorted information, and it's our responsibility to communicate to the world and tell them to be patient, to stay calm, that we're rebuilding Venezuela on the basis of democracy and peace."

"Mr. President," the reporter continued, "the media is obliged to report on what's happening in your country. We've rebroadcast your speeches when you asked the Constituent Assembly to dissolve Congress, that the Supreme Court judges be removed; the new positions you now hold on private enterprise. All these things took place . . . Are you saying the media shouldn't report on what's happening there?"

"No, not at all! I'm very happy with social communication," he replied cautiously, stifling the lion that wanted to roar. "I argue for total freedom of the press and of expression. And I'd invite you and all the world's other journalists to visit my country and see the total freedom to think that we have here! Long live intelligence! Long live freedom! But there are sectors that are destroying this society, who oppose our changes and are trying to avoid them at all costs."

"Are you prepared to talk to these sectors?" asked the journalist.

"Of course! I love dialogue and consensus. I've always been a man of dialogue," he emphasized, bringing the interview to a close.

And so begins another battle, he said to himself. *And I'll win this one too.*

◆ ◆ ◆

Living in a sandcastle, a house of cards, or in a ruin amounts to much the same thing.

In the first lady's life, the castle was La Casona and the fairy tale was turning into a terrifying psychological drama. In this tale, the wolf had taken off his sheepskin, and his real, threatening nature had become as visible as his huge white teeth.

There were many things Eloísa couldn't bear. She absolutely could not bear them! But the worst of them all was that her husband had brought the three children from his first marriage to live with them. Hugo wanted his children to be a part of his life, but Eloísa wanted them to be a part of her husband's past, not their present, let alone for them to share her family's future. Finally, after months of fighting, the two girls asked if they could go back to their mother in the town where they belonged. The first lady never imagined how different Hugo's family was from her own.

"They're just rural peasants," she told a friend in a moment of careless sincerity.

But the real problem was the boy.

From the day he'd arrived, this badly behaved, disrespectful child hadn't stopped annoying her. She forbade the servants to wash his clothes or make his bed or prepare his food. She took the TV out of his room. She forbade him to use the swimming pool.

"He needs discipline, order," she'd say to anyone who would listen.

But nothing seemed to have any effect on him.

Finally, one afternoon, Eloísa blew up at some bit of his mischief and ordered that he be thrown out, taken somewhere else where she'd never have to see him again. That night, the president was returning from one of his trips and no sooner had he disembarked than he found his son waiting for him at the airport, crying. The security staff didn't know what to do with him, but they dared not disobey the first lady, so they'd brought him there. Hugo listened to the story with tired disinterest and delegated the problem to Rojas.

The efficient, discreet service that Hugo received from his security chief might have been secret, but Eloísa knew about it, and it was one more wrong she could no longer bear. She couldn't bear the rumors, nor Rojas, her husband's accomplice in his constant infidelity. She wasn't the only woman in the world to have been deceived by her husband. But not all betrayed wives were married to the leader of a country. She knew things and had resources that gave her power.

Eloísa was crushed by the failure of her marriage to this man she so loved. Gone were the days when she would devotedly pack his suitcase for a trip, surprise him with a special breakfast, or recite a revolutionary poem to him. She no longer worried when he caught a cold, complained about gastritis, or had an asthma attack, which all happened frequently. She could barely focus on her own stability. She cried fitfully, bemoaning that she was ignored by her husband, hated by his family and, of course, his entourage. She knew they called her crazy, unhinged, rude, unstable, stupid, and a lot more besides. But they wouldn't be able to stop her; she couldn't remain on her throne, watching as Hugo continued to deceive her and the whole country while the sandcastle collapsed into ruins. How could the whole world see him as a dedicated father and an exemplary husband, when he'd been just the opposite, an extreme example of an absent, toxic, unfaithful one?

She knew she'd been the victim of physical and psychological mistreatment. The press was already murmuring rumors about it, which gave her a certain sense of justice. But deep down, everything was more complicated than that. Her friends suggested she seek professional help. Finally, Eloísa got in touch with a renowned psychiatrist, who treated her depression and prescribed her tranquilizers and sleeping pills. All this brought some relief, but no cure.

After her sessions with the psychiatrist, the first lady decided to leave La Casona with her daughter, return to the city of her birth, and shut herself away from her close friends and the press.

"What's up with Eloísa?" Mónica Parker asked on the air.

"It's been days since we've seen any trace of Eloísa," a couple of the first lady's friends said, chatting at LUNA, where they were spending a day at the spa.

The real-world version of Monopoly that Prán played from *La Cueva* was a modern, sinister adaptation of the board game. As an exceptional player with an implacable ambition to win, he rolled the dice with skill, identified the properties he wanted to buy, ordered his partner to acquire them at any cost, and bit by bit, took ownership of the entire board.

Making up his own rules led to him being the only player who wasn't affected by having to play from prison. With his partner Willy García as finance minister, Prán's hustles and muscles were powerful weapons for buying perfectly legal companies. For now, his main objectives were the bank, telecom companies, an airline, and—why not?—an oil company too. The game was now easily won; all the other players had surrendered before him.

Willy García had an arsenal of resources to help him acquire whatever Prán wanted. Above all, he was closely acquainted with the financial and business worlds both within and outside the country. He was up to speed on their weaknesses and their often-unlawful practices. He knew that having part of the economic sector under his control meant that many bankers and businessmen were going to try to buy his favors, just as they had done in previous governments.

Prán's strategic partner didn't forget, however, that the bankers and businessmen, his *lifelong friends*, had been prepared to leave him on the street, refusing to give him the help he'd needed to save his businesses. Neither did he forget that Prán had been the only person willing to help him in that difficult time.

But there was no point being chained to the past. The future he was building with Prán was exciting, ambitious, and, thanks to the president, possible. In the latest moves, a terrific and unexpected card helped clear the way: the leader's anti-capitalist rhetoric. The uncertainty of an environment as hostile to business as the one Hugo had been creating prompted a lot of fearful businesspeople to be compliant with the minister of finance, well before he ever needed to ask them to be.

Willy had the best of both worlds. As in any corrupt government, he could deal in influence by selling favors, knowingly issuing illegal licenses or charging commissions via front men. But he could also act as an anti-capitalist, taking control of major businesses via fiscal terrorism. When he saw a company he wanted, he accused it of not having paid taxes and imposed enormous fines that gave the owners no choice but to sell it for a song. His gift for using the language of the far left was combined with his capacity for acting like the most ferocious far-right capitalist. A true predator.

The legal facade of Prán's growing empire gained strength, and the number of his properties on the Monopoly board increased daily, protected by the revolutionary leader's favor. However, the core of his business remained his lucrative drug-trafficking network. Prán was aware of the difficulty of imposing himself over the business's multiple owners and dangerous competitors, but he intended to exploit a route to Europe through "transit" countries in Africa.

The mollusk always thought big, but he was increasingly unsettled by the strident speeches of the president, who publicly expressed his rejection of the US treating the FARC—one of the guerrilla groups in Colombia—as a narco-terrorist organization. In fact, he demanded on

Hello, Mr. President that the FARC be recognized as a legitimately warring army in the neighboring country's internal conflict.

Prán was apprehensive as he monitored this group's increasing closeness to his friend the president. He didn't care about the Americans, only that the FARC were a tough competitor for his business, along with the Mexican cartels.

As they considered the board, Prán and Willy decided that their best option was to find some senior military officers opposed to Hugo's pro-Castro slant and put them on the payroll. More than this—get them involved in the drug-trafficking business themselves. These officers would be first flattered and then invited to adopt the "Willy García technique," as Prán called it, which consisted of saluting the president's revolutionary, anti-US, and socialist flags, while at the same time acting in the business world with mobster-like capitalist aggression.

Prán and Willy García considered each possible name and weighed up their business opportunities, considering each one as a potential property for acquisition. Among the many officers and résumés, they separated the wheat from the chaff and made a list of the generals they planned to recruit in the coming days. "We will launch a new cartel, the Generals' Cartel," Prán said with a smile.

After a long and exhausting episode of *Hello, Mr. President*, Hugo sat in brief solitude in his study in the palace, drinking his third coffee, lighting a second cigarette with the butt of the first before stubbing it out in a crystal ashtray. He gazed at the oil paintings of Bolívar and focused on the anti-imperialist thoughts in his mind.

His thoughts about the reconquest of the continent, fed by Fidel's advice, merged with the problem of his own government that concerned him most and kept him up at night: the goose that laid the golden eggs—that is, oil. The source of 90 percent of the government's revenue. Up till now, Hugo had been careful in his relationship with Petroleum of Venezuela, PDVSA, the company that extracted the country's oil and sold it to the world. Though it was a state-owned company, the president didn't control it. He had left the technocratic, specialist elite who governed the industry—whose autonomy had always been respected by politicians and leaders—to work at their own pace. He thought politicizing the company would endanger the flow of capital, and he understood that they were technical experts and he needed them to produce the revenue he planned to use to make his revolution.

In frequent, serious meetings with senior management, the president had applauded their plans for ambitious expansion and approved the multimillion-dollar investment budgets they presented him with. Hugo had led them to believe he was an ally. The most senior oil executives, the subjects of verbal attacks by the president during the first campaign, celebrated his change of tone, courted him, and kept him happy and well informed. They believed they were indispensable and therefore untouchable.

Chávez smiled to himself. Believing themselves indispensable meant not being able to detect that, despite his pleasantness and his apparent support, the president loathed their airs of superiority, resented their elitism, and couldn't stand that they controlled the most important firm in the country.

Sitting in front of his globe, Hugo had one eye on the company's financial reports, while the other traced imaginary lines between Venezuela, Cuba, the US, other parts of Latin America, and the world's oil-exporting countries. He was preparing—after a fashion—for the Summit of the Americas, a meeting to be attended by the continents' presidents, in Canada in a few days' time. He wanted to use the opportunity, indeed any opportunity, to push his dream of uniting neighboring countries. His explicit topic was the integration of the Americas, but he really wanted to derail the US, the dominant power and the greatest consumer of oil in the world. Fidel had made the importance of this plan very clear to him. Since Fidel hadn't been invited, it was up to Hugo to be "the only devil of the summit," as he put it.

A few days later, the Venezuelan president, along with a team of seasoned diplomatic experts from Cuba, joined thirty-four heads of state from across the two continents in Quebec. Chávez missed no opportunity to veto, object, criticize, and manipulate the group's deliberations. He raised his voice in disagreement with the final document, the only person to do so. "I can't approve the point saying we commit to strengthening representative democracy, because in Venezuela representative democracy was really a trap that brought a heroic people to poverty and misery."

He knew this so-called continental integration was a setup by the Yanks to gain power over the Latin American market. And he wasn't afraid to be David standing up to Goliath. He would form his own alliances with South America, Cuba, the Caribbean, China, Russia, and the Middle East. Just let those Washington guys and their puppets leave him in peace.

After refusing to sign the documents, on his way out of the summit, Hugo ran into President Bush and they chatted for a few minutes. They greeted each other via an intermediary, shook hands for the first time, looked each other in the eye, exchanged a few brief phrases, and said goodbye without time for photographs to be taken.

"What did you say to each other?" the press asked.

"Bush wants to be my friend," Hugo said. "And I told him in my bad English: 'I also want to be your friend. Our political differences of opinion are very big, but I think we can get along.' I even invited him to play some baseball!"

The relationship wouldn't make it quite that far. George W. Bush, his vice president, Dick Cheney, and the rest of the government didn't look too kindly on Hugo's closeness to Fidel Castro, Saddam Hussein, Mu'ammar Gaddhafi, or Vladimir Putin, let alone his budding economic relationship with China. But for the moment, it was a convenient petro-friendship: Venezuela had the oil the US needed, and the

US was one of the few customers who bought it at market price and paid on time.

In the months that followed that first meeting between Chávez and Bush, something unexpected changed everything, at least for the United States—the terrorist attacks of September 11, 2001. Hugo, like most people who witnessed these scenes of war on TV, declared his and his country's solidarity with the US and its people.

But in the following months Venezuela's president was fiercely critical of the bombings in Afghanistan, denouncing them as a violation of human rights, calling for an end to the killing of innocents. He quickly decided to set out on a new tour of the Middle East, which in the eyes of Washington was a sign of Hugo's support for countries that tolerated, or even promoted, terrorist activity.

And so the petro-friendship between the US and Venezuela entered a tense stalemate. President Bush was on his guard against foreign governments that set themselves against his military policy; Venezuela and Cuba were on the list of "hostile nations." Hugo, in turn, was on his guard. What did he care about new enemies? He had his goose that laid golden eggs. The flowing rivers of oil were the weapon that would allow him to conquer the world.

◆　◆　◆

"The honeymoon is over. Everyone is annoyed," Mauricio told his colleagues in Havana over their secure phone line. "The priests, the soldiers, the oil producers, the media, the universities, the unions, and the businesses are all against Hugo. It's too much. And I'm sure the CIA is planning something." He sighed, hanging up the phone.

He had a lunch date with Mónica. He had wondered in the past if he was even capable of falling in love, but now he had no doubt that he was feeling the real thing. Mónica was brilliant, ambitious, and stunningly gorgeous. Their chemistry was off the charts. And he was so comfortable with her. Something about being with her felt right, like a puzzle piece fitting into place. There were moments when he forgot that his cover story was just a story, when he felt the possibility of what they could have if he were really just a Dominican businessman, unconcerned and uninvolved with political intrigue. But love wasn't part of his reality, and it could never be, so whenever he felt himself opening his heart he slammed it back shut, reminding himself that Mónica didn't even know the real him.

Mauricio arrived at Mónica's house for lunch. Chuck, her father, opened the door and didn't hide his displeasure. He had taken to calling Mauricio "that Caribbean guy"—within earshot—after a few drinks. Mónica ran up behind her father and threw her arms around Mauricio, bringing her lips to his in an inviting kiss. She took his hand and led him to the patio, where lunch was already served. Mauricio raised his eyebrows slightly at Mónica, seeing three places set for what was supposed to be their romantic afternoon lunch. She shrugged almost imperceptibly.

"Dad was able to join us for lunch after all!" she said cheerily, just a hint of pleading in her voice.

Mauricio smiled widely. "How wonderful!" he said, without a hint of sarcasm.

"I've been working on a special report on the invasion of Cuban civil servants into Chávez's government." Mónica steered the conversation deftly toward a subject she knew they could all agree on.

"Those Cubans are devils," her father said, approvingly.

"They tried taking the Dominican Republic in '73, but we didn't let them," Mauricio added. "They've got to be stopped before it's too late. They're dangerous."

Mónica launched vehemently into a description of what the Venezuelan government was allowing the Havana regime to do in Caracas. "Thousands of them are coming into the country as everything from sports trainers to doctors. But a lot of them are really soldiers, spies, and Cuban government agents," she said. "Besides, this anti-US attitude and the friendship between Chávez and Castro upsets a lot of people who still matter in this country. We're many things here, but we're no communists. And that's something Hugo doesn't seem to understand."

No matter how disinterested he appeared, Mauricio had learned he couldn't avoid politics entirely with Mónica, since it was her favorite topic of conversation. As the months had passed, Mónica had become increasingly critical of the government, and increasingly passionate about discussing it. He kept his comments brief, allowing her to go on at length about her work, her analysis, and her discoveries. Of course, she had no idea that much of what she shared with him ended up in his reports.

"You've seen it on the show, my love. The guests we have on, my reporters, and my own analysis of the concrete cases I present to the public say it all: the government isn't governing, and everything it does goes wrong. Unemployment, criminality, and the danger on the streets have all skyrocketed—and of course corruption too. We've always had it, but now it's like never before. And Hugo does nothing. He doesn't care."

"Yes. I hear customers criticize the government all the time," Mauricio added blandly.

As usual, Mónica's father had too much to drink with lunch, so he withdrew to his wing, leaving them alone on the terrace with their coffee. She pulled out her laptop and showed Mauricio pictures from the massive anti-Chavista marches, with placards that read: ALL WE WANT from Cuba is Guaguancó music, or We don't want communism in our country, we want freedom, we want democracy. Chávez out!

But Mauricio was tired of playing the anti-Castro Dominican.

"Why don't we leave these matters for the news bulletin, and focus on something better?" He placed his warm hand lightly on her knee, letting his fingers trace small lines up under her hemline.

She shivered. "Like what?" Mónica smiled, teasingly. Her skin felt like it was on fire under his touch.

"I can think of something . . ." He leaned over and kissed her, deeply, taking her breath away. Breaking off the kiss suddenly, he stood, the desire in his eyes making her tremble. He took her by the hand and led her down the hall toward the bedroom.

They went in and locked the door.

Eva sat in her office at LUNA, waiting for Mónica to finish her class and join her for tea in the garden, their usual midweek ritual. Though she appeared to be working on the spa's finances, she was actually finishing a report to her bosses on the constant, huge protests, public gatherings, work stoppages, and strikes.

> There are no longer Venezuelans; there are Chavistas and anti-Chavistas. The president has managed to alienate groups that should be his natural allies. The trade unionists and the universities—both faculty and students—oppose him. The president can't bear the fact that these groups are refusing to blindly follow his plans, and he has reacted furiously, lowering their budgets to the barest minimum and enacting decrees that take away their power and autonomy.
>
> Still, the president's attention to the needs of the poor has yielded him many political dividends. He's

built some schools and homes and has fixed a couple of big hospitals and important highways. He's also starting to assign money to finance new food, health, and education programs in the neediest areas. Which is why many still support him.

But it's not just about what he's done. The most important thing is how much he promises and how well he does it. The people believe in him. And he works hard to make the most of any chance he gets to remind them he's one of them, that he is like them and his interests lie in "defending their interests" and not those of the wealthy. He's a virtuoso in what a lot of people disdain as populism and what he, meanwhile, sees as the only way of staying in power. But at the same time a considerable opposition block has started to rebel, asking him to step down. The political situation in Venezuela is explosive, and the president is taking very serious risks.

Eva was trying to identify the leaders of a possible insurrection, but she hadn't managed to yet. She knew something might happen, but she didn't know what, or when, or who would lead it. She clenched her fists in frustration. She had tried to get names from her customers at LUNA, but nobody ever went further than criticizing certain actions by the government.

Some criticized the constant attacks on private enterprise and the freedom of the press. Others declared that their husbands (bankers, heads of companies, senior military officers, oil company employees) were worried about the new set of laws that the Assembly approved for the president in recent months, granting him extraordinary powers. They feared Hugo would use PDVSA's enormous oil revenues to fund social programs instead of paying for the maintenance of the oil operations that provided the exports on which the nation's economy critically depended. Others were concerned about large areas of farmland expropriated by the government, which defined them arbitrarily as "undeveloped land."

Just as Eva was getting lost in her reverie, there was a light tap on the French door leading to the patio. Eva encrypted her work, closed her computer, and called out a cheerful "Come in!" The door opened and there was Mónica, freshly showered and radiant as she always was after an afternoon at the spa.

"I hope you're not working too hard," she said, seeing Eva's furrowed brow.

"Oh, no, not at all! Just looking at the quarterly projections. You know how much I hate quarterly projections!" Eva said, laughing lightly, standing to greet her friend with the customary kiss on her cheek. "I'm more than ready for a break."

They walked out onto the terrace overlooking the garden and found an unoccupied table still catching the last slanting rays of the summer sun. As they sat, a waiter appeared with their usual pot of jasmine tea, two cups, a plate of fresh fruit and cheese, and two glasses of water. This ritual was familiar to everyone on staff by now.

"So, tell me everything," Eva began, as she often did.

Mónica laughed. "Good news or bad news first?" Mónica countered, her usual response.

"I think good today," Eva replied. "I could use a distraction from worrying about numbers."

"Well, Mauricio came over for lunch yesterday . . ." Mónica grinned, unable to hide her delight.

"That's the third time you've seen him in the past week!" Eva said with a gasp.

"And we have plans for Friday night. He's taking me to some business associate's party. I'm sure you've heard about it—the theme is going to be *Alice's Adventures in Wonderland*."

Eva had heard about it, one of the extravagant parties the nouveau riche in Venezuela had taken to throwing. But she shook her head, feigning ignorance.

"Well, I'd normally never go, but Mauricio has to go for work, of course, and . . . well, he sent me this to wear!" Mónica took out her phone and pulled up a picture of a crimson evening gown with a deep V-neck and long sleeves that trailed down to the floor to join a pooling silk skirt. "It's Chanel. Preseason. One of the perks of dating someone in the fashion industry." Mónica couldn't help but be delighted—her ambitious career hadn't left much room for frivolity, and she was reveling in Mauricio's pampering.

"Stunning," Eva gushed appreciatively, though she knew little of fashion herself.

"It's the most beautiful thing I've ever put on," Mónica said, a little quietly. "I don't know, Eva . . . He seems really serious about me. He calls every day, sends gifts. He's even making an effort with my dad." She sighed. "But I still haven't met any of his family. And sometimes I get this feeling, like he's closed off somehow. I can't explain it; he's so attentive, and when we're together it's magical. But it's like there's another side of him that I can sense but haven't ever gotten to see. That must sound crazy."

Eva shook her head. "No, no, not at all. You have to trust your instincts," she said reassuringly. Of course she had looked into Mauricio when he and Mónica had started getting serious a few months ago and had found nothing of particular interest, but he did have a reputation for being a bit of a playboy. While he seemed to be devoted to Mónica, Eva couldn't help but wonder if he was taking advantage of her friend.

"And what about the bad news?" Eva asked with a knowing smile. That was their private code for talking about politics, a perennial favorite subject for them. Mónica loved that Eva seemed as engaged and interested in Venezuelan political happenings as she herself was. They often spent hours talking over pots of tea or bottles of wine, really letting loose about their hatred for the Chávez government, analyzing every aspect of the current administration and prevailing public feelings.

But even Mónica, no matter how much she investigated, was unable to anticipate what might happen. "Well, there are still no obvious leaders among those opposing Hugo," she said to Eva. She sighed heavily. "Nobody stands out. The opposition is still at a loss."

◆ ◆ ◆

Things had begun to build to a climax with a series of special programs by Mónica Parker, starting with the report on Cubans and followed by the president's furious responses. Eva watched her recordings of them again, intently.

"The concessions granted to Castro have upset a large number of senior military officers," Mónica said into the camera. "Many are concerned by President Chávez's closeness to Castro, who formerly attempted an invasion of Venezuela and was defeated by our armed forces. According to one retired general who wished to remain anonymous, President Chávez is straying from the path 'in order to take possession of the country and impose a system that has failed in other countries and brings nothing but misery and poverty.' Another retired general says officers are being promoted who lack the necessary expertise or credentials, just on the basis of their professed loyalty to the government. All our sources within the military have condemned the Venezuelan president's aggression toward the United States.

"One distinguished retired general, who claimed to speak on behalf of a large number of currently serving officers, was willing to appear before our cameras, with his identity disguised."

The camera showed a shadowed figure in profile, speaking to Mónica: "We reject the sustained deterioration in international relationships with our traditional allies in exchange for forging links with nondemocratic governments. For this and many other reasons we demand the president's resignation. He is a fascist, a totalitarian, and a threat to the democracy and sovereignty of Venezuela." In order to preserve democracy, they proposed replacing Chávez with an interim civilian and holding early elections to allow the people to select a legitimate leader. Military officers, they said, should not be elected to take on public political posts.

Eva skipped forward to the next broadcast. It was Mónica again, appearing several days after the initial broadcast of her groundbreaking report. "Following my latest broadcast, the president expelled a number of generals and officers from the armed forces. Certain other generals reported finding vast sums of money deposited in their accounts. I ask you, is this the government we want for Venezuela? One that punishes legitimate criticism to silence dissenting voices?"

And then, as if to rub their faces in it, the president organized a great celebration for Fidel Castro's seventy-fifth birthday. On live television he honored the Cuban leader with an important decoration previously reserved only for great national heroes and announced an extension of the oil accord with the island.

"According to the agreement," Mónica reported, following her coverage of Castro's birthday party, "Cuba will continue to receive Venezuelan crude oil at a steep discount and on credit, payable in-kind over the long term. So in exchange for the oil that keeps Cuba's economy afloat, they are providing grains, vegetables, and Cuban advisers for security, intelligence, culture, education, and health. Additionally, the president has called on people to create Bolivarian Circles in every barrio and in every organization."

And his followers had indeed united, because to the great disappointment of the opposition, the people still loved their leader madly.

Eva skipped to a clip of Chávez shouting into a camera. "Don't be mistaken, oligarchs. Don't go getting your math wrong now, oligarchs.

Don't go believing your own lies. I'm telling you this as a warning. I'm warning you in the name of the people. Maybe, in your irrationality, you don't realize that you're awakening a force out there, that you're helping to increase the strength of the people and their irrevocable decision to defend the revolution *whatever it takes*."

The camera cut back to Mónica, a clip of Chávez mid-shout frozen on the screen to the left of her concerned face. "The people are hungry because there is no food," Mónica explained. "There's no food because there's no transport. There's no transport because there's no gas. There's no gas because of the oil crisis. There's an oil crisis because our government refuses to acknowledge what's going on."

The streets of central Caracas had become a hotbed of emotions. The country was paralyzed and, judging by the shouts in the street, very clearly divided.

"Yesterday, after hours of civilian uprisings," Mónica reported, "President Chávez ordered the military onto the street, dispersing a massive opposition march with unprovoked violence from the riot police and the army. The president had this to say."

Mónica's face was replaced by a jubilant Chávez, a clip taken from *Hello, Mr. President*. "They launched a strike and they crashed. Oligarchs, union leaders, bandits, *escuálidos*: let them keep coming out. They'll see what'll happen to them, one defeat after another." Chávez laughed on the TV screen. "They marched to call for my resignation. I will go, I tell them, but not right now in 2001—in 2021!" he said and burst out laughing again.

Mónica's face returned to Eva's screen. "Tonight we bring you a response to these matters, with special guests from within the government and the opposition." Eva fast-forwarded while these special guests called him a communist, controlling, an enemy to private property, antidemocratic, conceited, retrogressive, and an anachronism. Still, despite the unrest, the opposition was without any clear leadership.

"How can he sleep with this crisis on his conscience?" Mónica wondered to Eva after their yoga class later that day.

"What I don't understand is how the opposition hasn't found a leader yet," Eva responded.

"I know. The president's own friends are abandoning him: his lover, Eloísa, the fellow *golpistas*, and even his former head of security are against him now." Mónica grinned, reveling in her insider information. "I almost feel bad for him, but of course the real victim here is the nation," Mónica said, suddenly angry. "Venezuela is deteriorating at an alarming speed. The public sector has never been so inefficient. Do we deserve this lunatic with delusions of being an immortal caudillo?"

Eva looked at her with resignation.

"Right, no, I don't understand either. But yoga and Pilates are what I know about. I leave politics to you."

The TV played messages directed to the president himself, as Mauricio hurriedly rechecked contingency plans for his operatives, in case things got out of control. Everyone had instructions in case of a coup, to flee to a particular consulate, to create a presence on the streets in strategic places, or to retreat to a particular safe house. Mauricio, of course, had his own individual escape route, but he didn't think he would need it, despite the increasingly direct threats against the president coming from the television:

"You are the only person responsible for the gas shortages, for the food shortages, for the violation of the constitution, for the militarization of the country, for the embezzlement of public funds, for financing terror groups created under the protection of the government, for giving our oil away to Cuba, for the murders in the streets, for the lack of safety, for the unemployment, for the corruption, for the closing down of businesses, for the politicization of oil production, for the lack of respect toward institutions, for the politicization of the armed forces, for the strike, for the division in Venezuela. Resign now! Elections now!"

Mauricio had been working intensively and secretly to try to shape the results of these dramatic events in Cuba's favor. But he was essentially unprepared for the sheer strength of this leaderless opposition movement. He felt blindsided, a feeling he wasn't used to and didn't particularly like. And he hadn't seen Mónica in days—a week? He found himself thinking more about her than he expected, maybe even missing her, another feeling he wasn't used to.

Private TV stations broadcast the president's speech on a split screen while simultaneously showing the live progress of the huge opposition march that was beginning to surround the palace: "Earlier today, opposition groups gathered to march toward the oil production company's main building on Veracruz Avenue. At some point, the demonstrators turned toward Miraflores Palace, calling for the president's resignation. In response, the president's supporters gathered around Miraflores Palace, which was surrounded by soldiers, the National Guard, paramilitary groups, and heavily armed civilians."

Hugo seemed different from the arrogant man who'd dismissed the oil company managers. "Don't forget I am the president of all of you, even of that small minority who do not love me," he said with ironic tenderness.

Suddenly Mauricio heard the sound of automatic gunfire and, turning to the TV, saw several demonstrators fall, brought down by well-aimed shots to the head. The defenders of the revolution started hurling stones, bottles, Molotov cocktails, and tear gas at the opposition. Cameras showed the dead live on TV, and then in a moment a general appeared, speaking on behalf of the armed forces:

"We do not recognize the current government or the authority of Hugo Chávez."

"What?!" Mauricio was astonished. Hugo's friends in the army, betraying him! This was a blow he hadn't foreseen.

Mauricio immediately picked up his encrypted phone and called Havana. He didn't have long to formulate a plan, but everything hinged on keeping Chávez safe. No matter what. They could still recover from this blow, but not without Chávez.

Minutes later, with seemingly divine omnipresence, Fidel called Chávez directly in his office:

"We mustn't talk for long, Hugo," he said, Mauricio listening in. He asked the essential questions Mauricio had insisted on getting the answers to: how many soldiers he had, how many weapons, who was still loyal within the government. Finally, all information gathered, Fidel ended the call: "I'm going to say one more thing: don't sacrifice yourself. This doesn't end today."

By four in the morning, the Chavistas and snipers had dispersed, the families of the dead were grieving their losses, loyal ministers and deputies were in hiding at embassies and friends' houses, and the president had handed himself over to the opposition generals, who took the palace and assumed volatile, contested power.

Washington had sent the orders Eva was expecting: "Try to get into the Cuban embassy before the staff destroys everything of interest to us. Get ahold of the communications codes, the computers, and any information you can." Eva wanted to oversee the attempt herself, so she pulled her hair up and pinned it under a baseball cap, dressed in baggy, dirty jeans and a loose, torn T-shirt. Looking every bit the part of a young man from the barrios, she slipped out onto the streets and made her way to the embassy. Thanks to Mónica's exposé on the Cuban influence within the government, protesters had already come to understand that a number of senior officials would take refuge in the Cuban diplomatic mission, so by the time she got there it was surrounded. The energy was intense, inflammatory, furious. Protesters were destroying cars, cutting off electricity and water, smashing security cameras, throwing Molotov cocktails, and getting ready to take the building by storm.

Eva, along with her usual entourage of bodyguards, blended seamlessly into the crowd, provoking people when necessary to keep the energy high. Though Eva already knew the building had no particular weak points, she hoped the crowd's sheer force could get her and her agents inside.

Within the diplomatic mission, seventeen Cuban diplomats, all veteran G2 agents, destroyed documents and got ready to defend the embassy with their lives. They had practiced what to do in the event of something like this occurring.

As the sun started to rise, new demonstrators arrived, and someone—Eva thought she recognized the voice as belonging to one of her masseuses—began shouting, "Down with communism! Down with Castro! Down with Chávez!" The crowd of protesters surged with new energy, someone threw another useless Molotov cocktail at the impregnable building, and the TV crews arrived.

"Chávez doesn't represent the poor, Chávez represents Fidel Castro!" a man shouted into a megaphone outside the embassy and live on TV.

"Venezuela will never be communist!" another shouted.

"Down with the Cubanization of education!" yelled an angry mother. "They're indoctrinating our young people with ideas from Cuba to make them turn their parents in if they say bad things about the government!" another called.

Finally, Eva thought, *things are about to turn in our favor.*

Chapter 9

THERE'S NO SUCH THING AS A SMALL ENEMY

A warm Caribbean breeze blew through a small white-walled bedroom and enveloped a man curled in bed, almost in the fetal position, crying silently. A prisoner of his enemies on La Orchila, a remote island with nothing but a small navy garrison, Hugo was contemplating the end of his political career, his dreams, and probably his life too.

I'm going back to prison, he said to himself. *And for the same reason: for my loyalty to my people.*

Then he fell silent. He was unnerved, broken. How had it come to this? How had he not seen the treachery in the military high command? *Cowards! Traitors!* Crushed by depression, the man who was still president allowed himself to be carried off by musings in which Bolívar—frowning and patriarchal—appeared to him to bring him courage: "If my death contributes toward the consolidation of the union, I will descend into the grave peacefully."

Fidel Castro, his other hero, also appeared and held him back: "Resist, Hugo—resist!" he said. "You need to finish Bolívar's task!"

Through the windows of the bedroom that had been transformed into a cell, parts of the sky were visible. The darkness of the Caribbean

Sea made the stars shine even brighter. For a moment, he focused on the distant morning star, asking it to enlighten him as he fell into a meditative state. A kind of weightlessness that made his body seem to disappear. Was he floating in space? The question prompted an answer that shattered his momentary serenity. Once again he heard Prán say to him: "Nobody and nothing can imprison you—only your own mind."

The idea shook him, woke him, and suddenly he was filled with optimism and determination, and he felt the weight of defeat evaporate.

The strange silence of the past few hours, a silence that had never been part of him before, suddenly gave way to manic, unstoppable verbosity. He started talking amiably and without interruption to the two sentries posted outside his room, who were under strict orders not to speak to him.

"You men are not my enemies. You are soldiers obeying orders. We are all sons of Bolívar, and his example guides us along the same shining path of freedom. These things are a part of the revolutionary's life."

The two Marines exchanged a baffled look. They didn't know what to say, and the president of the republic didn't stop talking.

Once again, he invoked *El Libertador*, who never gave up, and also Mao and his Long March, and Gandhi: "Listen to me, men—you know who Gandhi was? No? And what about Che Guevara? Not him either? Well, let me tell you . . ."

And bit by bit, with his usual charisma, energy, and eloquence, he won over the silent sympathy of the two young Marines.

"Did you resign, Mr. President?" one of them eventually asked him, almost shyly.

"No, comrade, I haven't resigned, and I am not going to. Most likely, they're going to make me disappear or have me shot."

"To me, you're still president," one sentry said quietly, and then the other, quieter still, said: "To me too."

The president confided in the young recruits that he resolved to refute the claim that he'd resigned his post and created a constitutional vacancy that the *golpista* soldiers had been obliged to fill.

"Look, it's already time for our changing of the guard," one young soldier said. "I have a piece of paper and a pencil. If you want, you can write a message to your family or to the people and leave it in the trash, and I'll collect it. I swear to God—and on Bolívar and the *patria* and my blessed mother—that I'll make sure it gets to wherever it needs to go."

Hugo was moved and looked gratefully at the young man, feeling his lips tremble and his heart beat faster. He wrote down a name and quickly scribbled a message that would change his history. And that of millions of his compatriots.

> *To the Venezuelan people and to whom it may concern.*
>
> *I have not resigned the legitimate power that the people have given me.*

He signed it, threw the paper in the trash, and walked back to the window, looking for the star that had pulled him from the emotional pit into which he'd fallen. But it was no longer there. The early morning light had already made it disappear.

Meanwhile, the messenger kept his promise. He retrieved the message from the trash and made his way to the garrison's small, deserted admin office. He searched nervously and finally found a huge white book that, covered in dust, looked yellowish. It contained the telephone and fax numbers of the Navy offices, the Ministry of Defense, and the main units of Venezuela's armed forces and their respective commanders.

He couldn't turn on the light for fear of attracting attention, but in the darkness he was going to have to find a name in the massive phone book. He moved closer to the window and used the faint glow of dawn to illuminate the pages. Finally, he found the name of the person the prisoner president had given him. He was amazed to see that the man was the general in charge of the Maracay military base.

The biggest, most heavily armed military base in the country.

Everybody knew that somewhere behind the events that led to the fall of a leader who'd so aggressively antagonized the US must be its main government-toppling arm: the CIA.

But the anarchistic, unpredictable, improvised nature of events caught Eva and her organization off guard too. Neither she nor her best-connected informants had anticipated the coup, and they certainly weren't responsible for it. That, of course, was a problem for Eva. She had heard over and over throughout her training: "Good agents surprise, they are not surprised." And this was the second time she'd been surprised.

Back in the safety of her office, Eva watched as Mónica's program opened with what, to the opposition and to her government, might have been the best news in the world. One of the opposition leaders declared, euphorically: "Today our children, our youth, and all of Venezuela have had the right and the hope of a better life restored to them."

The chief of defense followed, his tone victorious: "We regret the disgraceful events that took place last night in the capital city. In light of these occurrences, we have asked the president of the republic for his resignation, which he has agreed to tender."

But Eva knew things weren't going well. Her informants told her that the *golpista* generals couldn't decide what to do with Hugo. Chaos reigned, along with a lack of leadership. The political ineptitude of the offices and the *golpista* civilians alike was quite apparent. It was clear that this was not a carefully planned coup but a protest that had escalated beyond anybody's control. Nobody was in charge.

She concluded her report to Watson:

> Some generals want to comply with the conditions
> stipulated by the president at his surrender to be flown
> to Cuba with his family and his closest allies. Others
> are insisting he be brought to trial in Venezuela, and
> of course some suggest he should have an "accident."
> But the real problem is that there isn't anyone capa-
> ble of forming a government that could be considered
> legitimate by the country or the international commu-
> nity, or of calling for new elections.

She sighed and sent the message. This was a huge opportunity, if only she had time to maneuver . . . She'd already been warned that the US ambassador would never support what was ultimately a coup d'état. There had to be something she could do.

"The decision has been made to form a transitional government," Señor Salvador Estéves announced in a sort of presidential address. "And I have been charged with leading it, following an agreement between parties, including representatives of Venezuelan civil society and the leadership of the armed forces. Here, before the nation, I take on this historic responsibility."

In an unprecedented act, Salvador Estéves declared himself president of the republic, dissolved the National Assembly, dismissed the legitimately elected governors, and rescinded all the laws passed during the previous term. And to conclude his first set of orders, he demanded that the supply of oil to Cuba be halted.

Outside the palace, popular pressure was growing like wildfire. Hugo's followers arrived from every corner of the country to protest the new government, which they considered a dictatorship. Chávez remained their president.

"Chávez won't go!" they shouted in the barrios, in the squares, on the streets.

Mauricio and his agents had quickly organized to support the spontaneous popular movement and increase its impact. Mauricio had clear orders from Havana: "Keep the Chavista population active, keep them protesting in the street—this is your top priority. Do whatever is necessary. Inform us of anything you need. We will support you fully. And another thing: make sure Hugo's family is safe and out of harm's way. If necessary send them here."

◆ ◆ ◆

General Raúl Mujica, a comrade from the failed military coup a decade earlier, received a fax with a note written by his former comrade-in-arms, saying he had not resigned. He recognized the handwriting and signature at once and didn't need to think long before deciding to act.

Mujica commanded a well-armed elite unit stationed in Maracay, a couple of hours from Caracas. He had several army and paratrooper brigades under his command, as well as a unit of helicopter gunships.

Mujica, whom his comrades had nicknamed "the Yogi" for his interest in East Asian spirituality, looked for guidance in the Tao Te Ching, where Lao Tzu said: "There is no greater disaster than underestimating an enemy. If I underestimate my enemy, I risk losing my greatest treasure: love. Which is why when two similar armies face up to each other, the winner is the one that does so with sorrow in his heart."

If he had been uncertain, that decided it. He quickly organized a commando unit of his best men, and he and his officials agreed on a plan of action. The plan was built on the idea that the leaders of the coup against Hugo had neither the organization, the capability, nor the firepower to repel a counterattack to restore the president to his position.

"We're not underestimating them, General?" one of his officers asked, nervously.

"No. We're taking advantage of how much they're underestimating us and my comrade Hugo. And they're underestimating the love the people have for Hugo Chávez."

Before boarding one of the three helicopters that was headed toward the island to rescue the president, General Mujica visited a radio station and announced that President Chávez had not resigned and that troops loyal to him were about to rescue him.

"Our true, legitimate president, the only president elected by the people, will soon be back at Miraflores," he said, giving no further detail. Then he read the note Hugo had sent and passionately entreated the radio listeners to spread the caudillo prisoner's message by word of mouth, to go out into the street and defend their constitutional president. Dozens of stations up and down the country broadcast his words.

The great wave of hope mobilized the people. In the middle of the night, the poor ran from barrio to barrio spreading the good news. They loved Hugo and wanted him back in charge of the country.

At the same time, private TV stations agreed to maintain a news blackout, hoping that the situation would stabilize in favor of those who had taken over the government.

The situation couldn't have been any more uncertain, and that's how Mónica described it to the foreign correspondents who sought her out. She sensed that everything was getting out of hand, that anything could happen. She watched, in shock, as the group that brought down Chávez buried itself in squabbles, spurred on by the different economic groups' desire for influence.

In the dawn, three helicopters were landing at the remote island where the prisoner was being held. The military personnel there, officers as well as the rank and file, didn't even try to repel the rescue mission. On the contrary, without any fuss, they assisted with the landing, indicating their unequivocal support.

Hugo celebrated the miracle from heaven. He said goodbye to his sentries with lively displays of affection and gratitude. They all cheered for him. Everybody hugged.

"Good luck, Mr. President, and don't forget us!" shouted one young soldier.

General Mujica and Hugo the Phoenix left the prison together and flew back to Caracas.

◆ ◆ ◆

A little boy, not quite three, put on his red shirt, and his mother took him to the march in the city. Like millions of Venezuelans, Luz Amelia was answering the call the president had made a few days before the coup against him. "The revolution is entering a more difficult phase, because we're taking it deeper—and the people must defend it!"

Her response was pure. She went out onto the streets because she believed fully in Hugo and his revolution. To defend him was to fight for her son's future, for the decent home she knew he was going to give her, for health, education, and a job. In the shelter where she still lived, she heard on the radio that her president hadn't resigned. Luz Amelia immediately found the Bolivarian Circle she was a member of and added her voice to the people's cry for the liberation of their leader and the dissolution of the *golpista* government.

Of course, many of these "collectives" were gangs funded by Prán's organization, fired up by agitation and propaganda organized by Mauricio. He was the first to learn what was happening in every city and, in particular, within every military garrison. Who supported whom? That was the question repeated throughout the military world, and the most reliable answer came from the Elite stores' customers. But that wasn't the only network Mauricio was running. He had other, more secret, ones, better armed and much better trained. Not for nothing had they practiced protocols to implement in the hypothetical event of the overthrow of the Venezuelan president.

Mauricio changed into worn workman's clothes, put on an expertly crafted wig that made his hair look longer, added glasses and a mustache that matched the wig, and headed out to get his own HUMINT. Passing for just another supporter, he assessed the atmosphere of the streets. He complied with the rule to not be in contact with agents from his networks or jeopardize his secret identity. And by daybreak, he had set in motion the plan rehearsed with the other Cuban agents, who were undercover as sports trainers, paramedics, and event organizers.

Luz Amelia and her son were just two little red fish in a river of people flowing down the city's main avenues. Some headed for the military base where the *golpista* generals were, thinking that that's where they were holding the true president. The more determined among them were intent on laying siege to this base, despite being unarmed and vulnerable to massacre. They wouldn't leave until Hugo was free and back at Miraflores. Other groups, organized by Mauricio's agents, marched to the TV and radio stations, which had just been showing footage of the new government, keeping suspiciously quiet about the person who had been president just a few hours before.

Pulled along by the current of fellow citizens, cries of protest mingling with revolutionary songs, Luz Amelia clutched her son with one hand while the other was a fist raised in a sign of struggle, which she periodically lowered to wipe away tears that came straight from her heart.

"Freedom! Freedom! Free Hugo now!" the boy chanted, an echo of the thousands of others, all dressed in red, marching with him and his mother.

Inside the palace, at the swearing-in, the nervous master of ceremonies made a stammering announcement: "We ask all those present to leave the palace. The event has been postponed."

Bottles of champagne were abandoned undrunk; there hadn't even been a chance to uncork them before the news of Chávez's return sent people running. Miraflores became a racetrack. The transitional president disappeared; no one knew where he'd gone. Men in tuxes and women in evening gowns ran like rabbits looking for a safe way out, while a squadron of over a hundred soldiers took the palace.

A retinue of ministers hurried down the corridors toward the main hall, followed by a cameraman. One announced that Hugo would be appearing at the palace in a few hours and sat in the presidential chair. "We have come to guard this chair for the president. We won't move until he's here."

Outside, Luz Amelia, her son, and the people still shouted: "Viva Chávez! Viva Chávez! Viva Chávez!"

From then on, the private TV channels showed nothing but cartoons. Very soon the revolution would once again be televised. Meanwhile, Eva was monitoring the street and media events through the elaborate CIA technology that was streaming street scenes and backroom conversations among the military and media to her underground office.

Hours later the president arrived, smiling, triumphant, surrounded by crowds who loved him, and in the palace he was received with hugs from the young soldiers of the presidential guard, ministers, and close friends. It was 4:40 a.m. at the end of Easter week, the Lord's Day. What a glorious way to start this resurrection day, hearing his people celebrate his return.

"He's back! He's back! He's back!"

Eva López woke her boss this time with a succinct text message: *Hugo is back!*

Less than an hour later, Eva was in the crowd gathered in a small square below the People's Balcony. She hadn't bothered to disguise herself; it wasn't as if it could be considered unusual to be interested in these historic events. Many people were there because they knew that at the end of the event they'd go home with a little gift: a bottle of rum, a chicken, or a bag of flour. But a large group always came to any official address because they adored their president. The People's Balcony was the perfect backdrop for TV cameras, now more than ever. That day, everyone was there.

Eva was on high alert. Though the coup was over, and there was nothing more she could do to salvage the situation, she knew the G2 lead agent must have been behind the popular uprising in support of Chávez. Like her, he would likely be on the streets witnessing the action. She scanned the crowd with her practiced gaze. A familiar face caught her attention, there, in an incongruous baseball cap . . . it looked like Mauricio, Mónica's boyfriend. She couldn't be sure, and as she tried to get a better look, he turned and slipped back into the thick of the crowd.

Just then, dressed in a tracksuit in the national colors, and holding hands with Eloísa, who'd decided to join him for this historic moment, the elated president appeared, and the crowd went wild with joy. He recounted his odyssey in detail. He spoke about the star that twinkled just for him and the words of Bolívar that had raised his spirits.

He continued with a violent tirade of accusations against Washington and the "unpatriotic" opposition, a word that would become fashionable. And he announced that from then on anybody in opposition would be considered an accomplice to the attempted coup in the service of the imperialist Yanks.

He shouted, bursting with pride: "My enemies will never return to power! They governed for thirty-six hours, and that's all the governing they're going to do in this century!"

The throng of supporters answered him with chants: "What do we say? Chávez must stay!"

Mauricio, lost among the crowd, smiled with satisfaction.

Chapter 10
Not as I Used to Be

The first shot is a warning, the second is to kill.

Eva López feared her days at the agency were numbered. She'd have to go back to being who she was: Cristina Garza. Nobody had said as much, but she knew that any day now they would "invite" her to Langley to report on what happened, and to take part in a process that her institution euphemistically called "lessons learned." What sounded like a mere formality was a detailed, exhaustive process in which mistakes were identified to ensure they'd never be made again. In practice it ended up being a trial of sorts in which the mistakes are identified not so much for learning as for dismissing those responsible.

Eva knew that the only thing that could save her from this bureaucratic defenestration would be the identification and elimination of the head of the Cuban spy network in Venezuela. The fact that she'd managed to infiltrate close circles of Hugo's friends, the fact that she'd recruited Juan Cash to influence Hugo via Prán, and her other successes would be of no use to her. Washington wanted a Cuban spy either dead or "turned." And it couldn't be just any Cuban spy. It had to be *that* one. The man responsible for Cuban intelligence's success in Venezuela and the defeat of the United States on this invisible but deadly battlefield.

They'd ask in Langley how this could have happened again. And how, even though she'd been living in the middle of the whirlwind that was Venezuela, their agent—the CIA's head of operations in the country—hadn't anticipated the coup against Chávez. How could Chávez insist it was planned by the CIA when the CIA didn't even know it was going to happen? How was it possible that they still had no idea who was behind it? Who organized it, financed it, and carried it out? Was there international support? And if so, from where? How was it possible that with their vast budget they were still no more than spectators in this whole business?

Eva knew her answers weren't going to satisfy her accusers. For some of them, it would be because she was Mexican, a woman, young, or tough, or because she hadn't put enough effort into cultivating friendships, loyalties, and support within the organization. Maybe it was a combination of all this and who knows how many other reasons. Some people would never accept her and that was that.

Those people mattered less to her than those in senior roles in the agency. They were the ones with influence, who'd cut their teeth during the Cold War as the Soviet Union and the United States secretly fought for control of the world, or through armed conflicts between allied countries who indirectly represented their respective interests on the battlefield. So even after the collapse of the Soviet Union, whenever there was a conflict, these CIA veterans' instinct was to find the country or organization behind the participants providing the dead bodies. For these old hawks, it was hard to imagine that something like what happened in Venezuela could be a combination of anarchy, Caribbean informality, and improvisation more than geopolitical calculations or covert operations.

Eva, Watson, and others within the CIA and the Pentagon ran up against this outdated vision daily. These bureaucratic opponents couldn't accept that all over the world power was fraying and that countries were confronting not just other nations but also, increasingly, organizations made up of terrorists, criminals, traffickers, insurgents, or fanatics who'd acquired vast power thanks to the new technologies accessible to everyone.

From her (always secret) conversations with Senator Brendan Hatch, Eva concluded that the old hawks' perspective was incorrect. Her electronic surveillance had led her to believe that despite the indisputable fact that Cuba was actively intervening in Venezuela—with a success that embittered her—it wasn't the leaders in Havana who were pulling the strings in Caracas. From the melee around the Cuban embassy, it was clear that this new coup also surprised the Cubans, as it had surprised her and the CIA, which she had heard repeatedly in a conference call the night before in which several of her superiors had taken part. Their surprise echoed the tone and content of the calls between Havana and Caracas that she'd listened in on through her taps. But how to convince her superiors in Langley?

It was Monday. The classes she taught at LUNA—the most expensive classes but also the most popular—had been canceled again because the instructor was "indisposed." As she had been for several days now, she was "unable to do yoga or come to work."

The receptionist was lying without knowing it. She was so busy with work she had no time to doubt her boss. The past weeks of political instability hadn't affected the flow of customers to the holistic beauty center. Many of them discovered that a few hours' refuge in Eva's spa was the best medicine for clearing their minds of the worrying—and often absurd—situations that were keeping the country on edge.

Eva knew just how to take advantage of the fact that LUNA had become a refuge for her clients. She had seen and heard conversations recorded by secret cameras and microphones. She asked questions about the future of the nation's politics with feigned and friendly concern. She delicately investigated Hugo's private life, the opposition's plans, the views of the business community, soldiers, and journalists. And it was all of some use to her, of course, though not enough to help foresee the coup that had her future hanging by a thread.

The reality of course was that Eva was not ill, but stationed night and day at her secret desk, where she followed events with dismay, measuring the significance of the coup to the United States and, on a personal level, to her career. She knew that the triumphal outcome for the president hadn't been due entirely to the passion of the people for their leader but also to the expert, appropriate, well-organized assistance of G2. Eva kept beating herself up over not yet having discovered the damn leader of this organization.

Another call from Watson only increased her anxiety. Her boss tried to sound casual, but she could sense he was nervous. He told her he was calling to share some of the comments his colleagues had made after the conference call they'd had the night before: "I can't lie to you, things don't look good. You know I understand where you're coming from and I share your view. But it seems like even with you in Caracas, the Cubans have more and more influence and we're further out of the game. I don't know what I can say to protect you. I just wanted you to know where we are and ask if you have any information I could use against your critics. Send me anything that could help."

Eva tried to stay calm, but her words rushed over one another, and her voice cracked. She barely managed to say: "Will do."

She hung up the phone and picked up another. She needed to call Hatch, her only friend.

◆ ◆ ◆

Hugo's return to power brought the first lady back to La Casona. After several months of separation as a result of Hugo's unexpected and fleeting fall, Eloísa decided to resume her role as the president's companion. She felt her husband needed unconditional support now more than ever. She could overcome the affairs with other women and conjugal quarrels by putting her love and faith in God. This time it would all be different.

Hugo had been shut up in his study for hours, drinking coffee and chain-smoking. His sullen silence troubled his associates, the first lady in particular. He'd given orders for another pot of coffee, for someone to get that buzzing fly under control, and for nothing to interrupt him or the total silence that reigned in his study.

"That's an order!" he said, slamming the door in the faces of his wife, bodyguards, and staff.

It worried her immensely. Hugo, smoking this much? Hugo, keeping this quiet? Hugo, on his own? From the outset, everything was different already.

Inside, deep in contemplation, the president picked up the train of thought he'd been on a few days before the coup: *I'm still a soldier. And if they drive me into an extreme position, if those privileged minorities at the top try to sabotage my revolution, I'm going to respond like the soldier I am and always will be. I've said it before: my hand won't waver because this struggle isn't for my benefit; it's for the country. This is a Bolivarian Revolution . . . It's about the poor, about the middle classes, and most of all, about those lower down, who for so many years were plundered and betrayed. I won't allow it! This is not going to collapse, you'll see! This revolution will not fail as long as I'm leading it and I have breath in my body.*

This very private speech addressed to the paintings of Bolívar and Jesus Christ that dominated the room moved him. Enveloped in nicotine, full of caffeine, and energized by the passion his people had shown him, Hugo had a revelation, a promise dressed up as an epiphany: *They aren't going to take power from me* ever again.

And so it was decided. He would do anything necessary to ensure he would remain in this palace; he would destroy anybody who stood in his way, anyone who contradicted his orders.

The first lady, alarmed by her husband's dark state of mind, dared to knock on the door.

"To hell with you!" Hugo's shout shattered the silence.

"It's me, my love, Eloísa." She tried to defuse the human bomb.

There was no reply.

"My love, I know you didn't want to be interrupted, but you've been shut away in here a long time," she said, coming into the study. Behind her, a fly slipped inside.

"Well?" he asked, his eyes glued to the nails in Christ.

"Aren't you pleased? I mean . . . having warded off a military coup, having seen your friends' loyalty proved, and the love and solidarity of the people?"

"I should be . . . ," he started to answer. But some words from José Martí enhanced his sudden unease: "Even a great man can be infuriated by a wretched little fly."

He *was* a great man, and this unbearable fly was getting on his nerves. He brushed it away from his face, moved the books on his desk, and got to his feet, waving a sheet of paper like a fan. His wife didn't understand, because he alone could see the fly. As if the fly were seeking him out alone, to infuriate him.

"You seem strange, Hugo," she said.

"I'm not as I used to be," he replied. "Please, leave me alone."

◆ ◆ ◆

Unlike Eva, Mauricio had praise raining down on him, enthusiastic recognition that, for obvious reasons, he couldn't share with his

171

beloved Mónica. He told her he had to go to Panama because of import problems.

"Seriously, you're going away again?" she asked.

"You know I've got to be on top of what happens there. My job is to cover the continent!" Mauricio answered.

"But we hardly see each other as it is! I'm lonely! Don't you miss me?"

Mauricio took her in his arms, kissed her for a long time, and repeated the promise he always made, that they would see each other again soon, very soon. He would try to recruit somebody, a new manager, and then he'd have more time for them. And he left feeling secure that she was satisfied. Almost.

He had been summoned to Havana to discuss a strategy to increase the island's control over its oil-producing ally. After making several stops en route and using every technique in his profession to make sure he was not followed, Mauricio arrived in Havana and hurried to G2 headquarters to meet Raimundo Gálvez.

"The president's charisma has gone as far as it can take him alone," Mauricio explained to Gálvez. "He's going to need other skills, and more effort, to stay in power. Most importantly, a broad base of well-organized political support."

Gálvez nodded.

"Of course, we'll need a counterintel op to identify threats and preemptively neutralize them. But that won't be enough. It wouldn't hurt . . . ," Mauricio said with a hint of irony, "if the government could actually start functioning. Nothing works, and Hugo doesn't care. Civil service is a disaster, and if it doesn't improve, public discontent will be overwhelming, and no amount of charisma will be able to save it. And there won't be much we can do either.

"Fidel has to explain to Hugo that he can't spend all his time bouncing from place to place. He's got to govern, for fuck's sake! And yeah, I know that's boring, but if he doesn't do it, they'll overthrow him again, and this time he won't get back into that presidential chair he likes so much."

Gálvez smiled. He understood what Mauricio was saying, and maybe he was right. He also knew it would never happen. Chávez would never be the kind of statesman who devoted his time to running the government. He was more about theater than overseeing the functions of the state. That's why Gálvez thought they needed to invest more Cuban military support for Hugo's regime.

"We need to prevent new coups," Gálvez said. "I think we should prioritize using our counterintel resources to identify Venezuelan officers who are potential *golpistas* and neutralize them. We need to increase the military budget and fill as many positions as possible with loyal soldiers," Gálvez mused. "But these loyal soldiers, just the same, do still need constant observation and monitoring. Perhaps the government ministries and other important public bodies, as well as the large state-owned industries and the private firms that are being expropriated, should all be under the leadership of military officers loyal to Hugo."

"That strategy is obsolete," Mauricio said boldly, to Gálvez's surprise. "It doesn't work nowadays, especially in a country like Venezuela, which is international and disorganized and has gotten used to democracy in the past forty years. Besides, you don't control countries through the armed forces anymore but through a civil society. Organized and controlled by us. Not with tanks on the streets, but with our own activists and intelligence agents embedded in the various barrios. Long-term, that's the only thing that works."

"Man, don't bring me that crap about military force being a thing of the past!" Gálvez snapped, annoyed.

"Of course, Comandante." Mauricio tried to sound conciliatory. "Right now, Hugo needs support from the military leadership, that much is obvious. But he needs a lot more of the kind of twenty-first-century help Cuba can offer him: intelligence, counterintelligence, propaganda, and technologies for social control and silencing opposition leaders."

"Technologies for social control . . ." Gálvez echoed him, interested and thoughtful.

"Yeah, technology," Mauricio continued. "It's more important that Hugo wins the next elections electronically than for us to arm his supporters! And only we can make that happen!" he concluded forcefully.

Gálvez smiled skeptically, his gaze trained on Mauricio. After a long pause, he brought the meeting to a close. "Let's leave it there for today. We'll think about it."

Mauricio was pleased. He knew, as everybody in G2 did, that "we'll think about it" meant it would be brought to Fidel.

◆ ◆ ◆

The president's radical transformation was obvious to everyone now. In the presence of his ministers and closest allies, he seemed like a boxer after a tough round, who, aching all over, was fired up and ready to kill in the round to come.

In the hall of the Council of Ministers, as he evaluated everything with his cabinet, his face darkened and his words turned threatening. Willy García noticed the president's resentment and mistrust, and he immediately informed Prán.

All the same, Hugo tried to resume his political agenda, his diplomatic tours, his *Hello, Mr. President*, and even his exercise routines.

It was a practice he'd always shared with Ángel, his truest friend of all, his one-time brother-in-arms, a kindly soul, with no ambitions of his own and a total disinterest in palace intrigue. One morning, after a jog and lifting weights together in the palace gym, Hugo dared to confide in his one loyal friend.

"Ángel, I can't trust anyone but you. Not anyone. Not those spineless ministers, and certainly not those two-faced generals. They just hid and waited to see who came out on top, me or the *golpistas*. How many of those celebrating my triumph today would have been celebrating just the same if the coup had succeeded? They'd have switched sides, no doubt," he said, disgusted and disappointed.

Ángel, who knew how to listen, looked him in the eye but didn't interrupt. He knew talking about what happened could calm his comrade, and Ángel had learned to moderate his old friend's agitation. Hugo's mood swings and sudden shunning of people in his closest circles were habits that Ángel knew well, and since long before his friend Hugo transformed into Chávez, the president.

Hugo confided that in his captivity he had realized that, for him, a life without power was not worth living.

"You really felt that?" Ángel asked him, respectfully.

"Power has to be *total*, Ángel, in order to be real power," Hugo answered. "Power is forever, or it's not really power."

"Mmm . . ." Ángel didn't know what to say. Deep down, he was scared to contradict him.

"After that attack I don't trust anybody, you hear? *Nobody*. I'm not going to risk losing the power the people have given me. I'm resolved— I'll do anything to keep it, and to increase it. Anything! You understand?" Hugo paused. "I'm not as I used to be," he said again.

"I understand. But I hope you still know you can count on me, right?"

"Thanks, Ángel," Hugo answered, and fell silent for a few seconds. Then he said, gravely: "No one but Fidel has told me the truth; I only trust him. And you . . ."

As they left the gymnasium, the two friends parted ways.

Totally lost in his thoughts, Hugo went to his bedroom, took a bath, and dressed in his old military uniform and red paratrooper's beret. Analyzing his defeat, he looked in the mirror and suddenly had an important revelation. He sat down and wrote:

*In this country, power depends on five things: money, informa-
tion, intimidation, centralization, and firepower.*

He drew a big box with five control levers sticking out of it:

1. money: control oil

2. information: control media

*3. intimidation: control population through selective, anony-
mous violence & judicial persecution*

*4. centralization: control state organizations that limit the
power of the president, especially the National Assembly &
the courts of the National Electoral Council*

5. firepower: absolute control of armed forces

The president looked over his diagram with care and determination, folded the paper in four, and put it in his pocket. He adjusted
the red beret, smiled at the hero he saw reflected in the mirror, and
left his bedroom, inspired, energized, and resolved to do what must
be done.

They're not going to fuck me over again, he said to himself over and
over.

His new mantra.

Neither the luminous April sky, nor the cherry trees in bloom, nor the
colors and scents of springtime, nor being home brought any happiness
to Cristina, who'd resumed her true identity for a few days.

Cristina feared she had been called back to Washington, DC, only to be fired. There was no poetry in that. She immediately called Brendan Hatch. His life as a senator, a political leader, a public figure, and a father and husband filled every moment of his day. But as soon as he heard from her, he postponed meetings and gave excuses in order to spend a few hours with her, the woman he adored.

Their relationship had changed considerably, of course. At first it was a secret affair complicated by Senator Hatch's visibility and political importance. And Cristina, despite being very attracted to the senator, and despite how good things were when they were together, had never managed to give herself over entirely. The guilt of being the *other woman* was something she couldn't overcome, even while she couldn't give him up. He, in turn, struggled to balance how wonderful their relationship was in terms of love and sex with the huge risk it posed to his political career and marriage. They both wanted to end the relationship, and they tried several times. But after a week or two, one of them would call, they'd meet up, and everything would start all over again. They couldn't be together, and they couldn't be apart.

To the relief of them both, the mission in Venezuela took Cristina away just as the relationship was entering a new crisis period. She had left for Caracas and become Eva years ago. And this distance and change seemed to suit them both.

They were perhaps each other's most genuine friend. Though they didn't see each other often, they talked regularly. Hatch was still married and devoted to his political career, but the distance from Cristina had done nothing to weaken the admiration and love he felt for the brilliant spy.

Brendan arrived at Cristina's apartment at 7:00 p.m. She opened the door looking more beautiful than ever in a knee-length emerald-green dress that set her off against the background of peonies filling her apartment with every shade of pink. They were her favorite flower, and the moment Brendan had learned of her return, he'd had a hundred delivered anonymously to her door. Despite the bags under her eyes, evidence of long insomniac nights and the devastating anxieties that haunted her, she looked radiant.

Cristina greeted him with a hug more friendly than passionate, but he held her tight and kissed her deeply. She pulled away reluctantly, sighing.

"This is your doing?" She gestured to the vases covering every surface, smiling knowingly.

"Guilty as charged." He laughed, closing the door behind him. She poured two glasses of Nikka Yoichi ten-year single malt, the expensive Japanese whisky she knew he loved.

"So, what happened in Venezuela?" he asked, once they were settled with their drinks on her couch. The fact that Brendan was also chair of the US Senate Intelligence Committee made the conversation easier. There was no one better than him to share her dismay, her distress, and her crushing feeling of failure.

"Hugo's return to power is a kind of victory for the Cubans, though it had more to do with the incompetence of the *golpistas* and the fragmentation and lack of leadership of the civilian opposition," she said. "But I can still complete my mission. Neutralize the Cuban influence. If I could just go back and continue my work, I'd prove it. Anyway, whoever they send now will take years to get the degree of infiltration I've managed in Venezuelan society."

Hatch nodded, already convinced. He was predisposed to do anything he could to help her. And besides, it suited him, too, that she was far from Washington. *It's been the best way*, he thought, *of keeping her close.* But for the moment, it was just the two of them. He slowly pulled her into his arms. His kiss was soft at first, but quickly deepened into something more passionate. He reveled in feeling her soft skin in his hands. Between them there were no politics or spy games. Right now, she was just his Cristina. Their clothes were shed so quickly neither could have said who undressed whom. In a flurry they were horizontal entwined flesh, finding new ways to get closer and closer. Nothing could have come between them.

A couple of hours later they said goodbye with the usual "See you soon," which always suggested a secret encounter. They would talk again when the agency had notified Cristina of her change of mission or her dismissal. Alone again, Cristina called her mother in Arizona, promising to come visit her sometime soon.

◆ ◆ ◆

Mauricio followed Gálvez into a secure conference room in one of the Cuban leader's secret residences. He was visibly awed, aware of the great opportunity he was receiving: to explain his proposed strategy for Venezuela in private to Comandante Fidel Castro himself. In Mauricio's eyes, he was about to play a game of chess with the greatest of revolutionaries, with his boss in the middle.

"Gálvez says you've got something interesting . . . ," Fidel began.

"Comandante," Mauricio started respectfully, "it is an honor for me to present my ideas on our patriotic engagement in Venezuela. I believe we can expand our efforts in two ways: social programs and technological surveillance. First, we could strengthen popular support for President Chávez by helping him with massive social assistance programs—especially medical care. Our doctors are the best in the world, and their help in hospitals and community clinics would be well received."

Fidel watched Mauricio with a penetrating gaze. Arm on the desk, fist under his chin, he didn't say a word.

"Equally important right now is surveillance," Mauricio continued, confidently. "My suggestion is to deploy experts from the Computer Sciences University. Clearly we need to keep the leaders under constant observation, especially those in the military who remained neutral during the coup, and all the opposition politicians. Also, the journalists and business leaders still in the country. And we've got to infiltrate the universities too, of course."

Fidel's eyes, trained on Mauricio, were two black stones, inexpressive and yet simultaneously inquiring. But Mauricio didn't allow himself to be intimidated.

He continued: "Venezuela's opposition is disjointed, and the United States has withdrawn after having supported the coup. They can't openly intervene in Latin America against a democratically elected, popular, and progressive government like Hugo's. Now is the time to proceed with intelligence and *secretly* ensure our total control over Hugo, his revolution, his oil, and his resources."

"We already know all that," Fidel said, impatiently.

"Cuba can offer Hugo things he doesn't have: first-rate counterintelligence services, selective suppression of the opposition leaders, and experience in controlling a society." Mauricio smiled, sure of himself. "The first thing we have to do is take electronic control of the organization that issues citizens their proof of identity, as well as registry offices, the public notaries, and of course the National Electoral Council. *Without them seeing us.*"

Mauricio felt his confidence surge with every word.

"What's crucial," he went on, "is that nobody in Venezuela die or be born, get married or divorced, sell or buy a house, a car, or a business, without the document certifying that transaction being controlled and stored by us. Venezuela has oil for us, but it also has information—data. And data is the oil of the twenty-first century."

Fidel seemed to like what he was hearing.

Mauricio registered this and moved forward: "No Venezuelan should be able to vote in elections without their vote being processed by our software. We must make the Venezuelans believe the government is watching them *all the time*, even if it's not true and they could never prove it."

Gálvez opened his mouth to say something, but the boldness of the strategy seemed to have left him mute.

"And that's how you conquer a country in the twenty-first century," Mauricio concluded, "not invading them with brute force, like the Americans did to Iraq. Just look what happened! Cuba needs Venezuela's oil resources; it's vital, a matter of life or death. With all due respect, Comandante, the twenty-first century will belong to civil society, not to the military. And for Cuba's benefit, we must learn to disguise ourselves as civil society!"

The king of this game, bearded, wise, with an impenetrable expression, took in the whole situation from the height of his throne. He understood the game of chess that Mauricio was proposing. Barely even processing the importance of the strategy, he heard the final words of this pawn who couldn't stop himself from asking the crucial question, which he did, with a bold change in protocol:

"So what do you say, Fidel?"

The uncertainty was nearly over for Cristina, who was still waiting for a decision that would either send her back to Venezuela or remove her from the agency altogether. Oliver Watson had not been keeping her in suspense intentionally. He, too, was unsure of what was going on in his superiors' heads.

Without much to do in her office, a deeply worried Cristina demanded that Watson tell her something. He—being cautious—didn't give her any false hope, nor did he discourage her. He merely justified the wait by the fact that the current "war on terror" had monopolized Washington's whole agenda.

"Now Al-Qaeda, bin Laden, Iraq, and Afghanistan are all more important," Watson said. "We're going to have to understand that.

There are very real threats there. Latin America is no longer a focus of our attention."

"And that leaves the field open to Chávez!" Cristina said. "If nobody's watching him, he'll be able to do whatever he wants. Imposing his political and economic model—that's a threat too, isn't it?"

"Neither Venezuela nor Latin America can compete in today's world," Watson answered. "Not even as a threat. They haven't got nuclear weapons, or suicide bombers, and they're not an economic power like China. Even their poor people aren't all that poor."

Cristina took a breath, nervous. She understood Watson's reasoning, but she believed the US and the global economy could be affected by the relationship between Hugo and his country's oil company. That same war in Iraq and Afghanistan was transforming Venezuela into the world's most secure source for the supply of oil to the United States. The government shouldn't underestimate that.

On that same day, without Watson or Cristina knowing, the CIA director received Senator Hatch in his office. Hatch made it understood—with the greatest courtesy—that objections had suddenly arisen in committee about the budget increase the agency had requested for its operations in AfPak—the acronym referring to Afghanistan and Pakistan.

"They're the two most dangerous countries in the world, Senator," the director said, agitated. "You know that, and your colleagues on the Intelligence Committee must know that too."

"Yes. Well, some people do think it would be best not to make changes to the way we're doing things, for example, in Venezuela, and allow the agents currently on the ground to act," the Senator responded, keeping a safe distance from any possibility of being accused of interference in decisions that are the domain of the CIA director alone.

The director nodded, understanding what was being asked of him. Before nightfall, Oliver Watson notified Cristina that, contrary to what they'd both expected, she would continue to be in charge of operations in Venezuela. The spy was flooded with relief. She would have one more chance.

Watson gave her some advice. She shouldn't waste her time on the business with Juan Cash, the fraudulent pastor.

"Leave that to the DEA or to the FBI. You have one priority: find and neutralize G2's top agent in Caracas. If we manage that, we'll stand a better chance of containing the progress of Cuban control over the Venezuelan government. They'll find it very hard in Havana to replace somebody who's as good as the guy they've got there now."

Cristina nodded. She suspected Hatch's hand in her superiors' decision, though she would never ask him directly and he would never tell. Their parting in her Washington, DC, apartment was long and smoldering. She loved meeting him in her own home, where he felt completely hers. She could forget about their outside lives, her nightmares, and his wife. As usual, she wished the moment could last forever. As she reluctantly started to get dressed, she felt him come up and stand behind her. His arms wrapped slowly around her waist, and he pulled her in close.

"I'll miss you," he said quietly. "I hate being away from you." He rained kisses across the back of her neck. Her clothing soon lay forgotten again in a pile on the floor. They drew out every earthly pleasure from each other that they could while they still had time together.

A couple of days later, Cristina left once again by private plane to a private airport in Mexico. From there she traveled by car to the suburbs of Mexico City, where a taxi under the agency's control took her to the main airport, and finally she boarded an Aeroméxico flight to Caracas.

In her economy-class seat, as the plane took off, she shut her eyes and tried to meditate, but she couldn't do it. There were too many things going around and around in her mind. She tried to identify them and put them in order, to calm herself down and fall into the trance that always helped. The exercise confirmed what she already knew. She wanted three things. And she wanted them all desperately.

She wanted a good night's sleep.

She wanted to go back to being Eva.

And she wanted to find the leader of the Cuban spies.

Chapter 11

LOVE IN THE TIME OF REVOLUTION

"Last week, President Chávez announced that, in the interests of the people's security, he'd created Bolivarian militias and had signed the new Venezuela-Cuba Plan," Mónica said grimly as she opened her program. "Today, we'll take a look at what this means for Venezuela in practice. As President Chávez put it in his statement . . ."

The journalist's face was replaced on-screen with that of the president. "We're expanding and deepening our previous agreement. We'll have a commercial exchange that's greater and better balanced, meaning what we export to Cuba will be of equivalent value to what we import from our island friends. We're going to set up primary-care modules and community clinics to house doctors in the most modest barrios in the cities and in small villages in rural districts," he said enthusiastically. "Get ready for two thousand doctors to arrive from Cuba—and our goal is to get that number up to forty-five thousand!"

Mónica reappeared. "The agreement includes low-cost surgical programs for seniors and grants for scientific, technical, athletic, and educational research. But the primary component is the Misión Barrio Adentro, the Mission into the Barrio, an ambitious family-medicine program to bring the famous Cuban health care to the Venezuelan poor, from doctors to diagnostic centers and schools of holistic medicine. Following this announcement, the Venezuelan Medical Association called an emergency meeting. I was invited to join the call, to share with you, our viewers, Venezuelan doctors' objections and concerns about this unprecedented development."

The dinner had finally been scheduled for 8:00 p.m. in the usual restaurant, the only one where Mónica felt she could get real privacy, free from fans, and above all, free from the critics always ready to ambush her. Being a critic of the government now meant she was subjected to insults and threats wherever she went.

But when she tried to leave the studio for this so-often-postponed gathering, which happened to coincide with her birthday, Mónica found herself stuck. They'd been preparing a special report for the following week: a close, in-depth look at the Misión Barrio Adentro. And one of the doctors taking part in the special had vanished.

Though she'd been looking forward to this dinner for weeks, Mónica couldn't abandon her reporter, a woman in charge of investigating the Caracas experiences of Dr. Avellaneda, who had now disappeared. So she called the restaurant and asked them to seat her guests and apologize that she was going to be half an hour later than planned.

Eva arrived five minutes early, true to a punctuality that was not just American, but military. The waiter led her to the terrace where she'd dined with Mónica on other occasions, and offered her the menu. "Miss Parker is going to be half an hour late. Please accept her apologies," he said. No sooner had he left than he was back again, this time with a handsome man to whom he'd already said the same thing, and who was carrying an enormous bunch of roses in one hand and a gift bag in the other. As he approached the table, he smiled with real excitement to see his girlfriend's best friend waiting.

"Nice to see you!" Mauricio Bosco said in a jovial Dominican tone.

"Yes, it's a pleasure," Eva answered, genuinely feeling that pleasure and exaggerating the Mexican lilt of her speech. Their greeting was friendly, but formal.

Mauricio put the flowers and the bag on the table and sat across from Eva. The conversation was awkward at first but gradually gained in intensity. Eva was wary, coming across as pleasant but reserved, trying to recycle information she'd gotten from Mónica.

"Mónica says you've been too busy to come to LUNA again. You can't work all the time!"

"I'm sorry, I truly am. The fashion business is like a running race—if I stop for a moment, I lose. It's a weakness, taking my work too seriously."

Mauricio's apology was so charming that Eva found it impossible to stop looking at him, curious and impressed. As he talked, she studied every feature, every gesture, trying to decipher this man who'd managed to unsettle her.

He looked at her too. He could tell he'd caught her interest and reflexively did everything in his power to convert interest into enchantment.

Finally Mónica arrived, agitated and anxious. Even as she came into the restaurant her mind was still on the new program, a special she was making about the Cubans in Caracas. When she reached the terrace, she saw Eva and Mauricio laughing and was delighted that things seemed to be going well, that they were no longer mere ghosts to each other.

"I'm so sorry, I'm so sorry," she said, interrupting their laughter. "Only the Cubans could make me late for my own birthday dinner."

Mauricio smiled and got up with delight. He kissed her and handed her the flowers. And then he looked at Eva. And Eva looked at him. Looked at them. And she finally understood what Mónica had told her so often: there was something special about Mauricio.

There really was. But what was it?

The dinner flew by. Three hours and three bottles of wine later, once dessert was finished and promises were exchanged to repeat this pleasant gathering, they headed for the parking lot. There they said goodbye and parted ways: Mónica and Mauricio to his house, where she always preferred to go because of her father. She knew that her father had a deep distrust, bordering on hatred, for Mauricio. He had warned her more than once that he could sense there was something off about the man. Was she certain about these work trips of his? Mónica defended Mauricio vigorously, though deep down she, too, sometimes had doubts.

Eva drove toward her apartment, alone. She felt infected by the flirtatiousness at the table, by a desire to be desired. It made her feel very much alone.

Impulsively, she called her lover in Washington.

As was becoming usual, after a number of rings, the call went to voice mail.

Eva had been obsessively looking for the spy leading G2 in Venezuela since the failed coup. In the past few months she'd managed to expand her networks, from which she was receiving increasingly reliable information. Her agents had also infiltrated Hugo's government. But they were always several steps behind the Cubans. She was frustrated by what her informants and sources confirmed: the Cubans had immense influence on the Chávez government. There were Cuban officials everywhere, and the government itself was giving them leadership roles. Still, the Cubans took great pains to ensure that their presence at the highest levels ended up being invisible.

She inevitably discussed some of these conclusions with Mónica, because Mónica couldn't stand what she called an "invasion" and often referred to it. It was an invisible, secret invasion, the impact of which was unprecedented. The hardest thing for Mónica to believe was that it had been done with consent, even support, from Venezuela's own government.

"It's impossible to hide how powerful the Cubans are in Venezuela," she said. "There's almost no part of the government that doesn't have an *adviser* at the very highest levels."

Eva didn't know what to do. This invasion was enormous, uncontainable, and essentially invisible. Her bosses in Langley had decided, correctly she believed, that they couldn't stop or reverse the Cuban invasion and that the only practical course they had left was to sabotage and mitigate its effects. They'd ordered Eva—yet again—to identify its leaders, to spy on them, to try to turn them, and if necessary, to neutralize them.

Eva was trying to carry out these orders as best she could, but every day she discovered new obstacles that limited what she was able to do. Privately she was convinced that it was an impossible mission. Hugo's willingness to let the Cubans furtively take over his government was as stealthy as it was bold. She sensed that this defeat would end her career, possibly even her life.

Why not quit and be done with it? Wasn't this whole thing just a whim, a battle led by her ego, by her eagerness to stand out amid the pack of bureaucratic hounds and veterans in DC? Who did it matter to, ultimately, if she gave up her post, her mission, her whole LUNA lie? What would happen between her and Hatch if she were to start over, on her own, someplace else?

It was in the midst of this that she had met Mauricio again. Why was she always so drawn to him? Was it a professional intuition, or an attraction?

She had looked into his background long ago, but found herself compelled to do it again. Mauricio Bosco, Dominican businessman, fashion entrepreneur. Her standard background check revealed a neat life: school in Santo Domingo, then an MBA in Puerto Rico. A large family, still in the Dominican Republic, except for a cousin who worked in the business here in Caracas. Nothing out of place, no arrests, no unusual travel, no hidden string of wives. Not even a speeding ticket. She accessed a picture of him from his passport and ran it through her CIA facial recognition program. Nothing. She sighed, annoyed she'd allowed herself to get distracted, and turned back to her mission.

She pulled out a box of unedited material from Mónica's program, which she'd gotten from one of her agents, a journalist on the show. Eva watched hours of video and listened to recordings from a clinic in Petare, one of Caracas's most infamous shantytowns. In order to understand Misión Barrio Adentro, one of Mónica's reporters had followed Cuban physician Dr. Avellaneda.

During the months in which she had been interviewing him, she and Mónica, and above all Eva, listened to the doctor complain about the violence in Venezuela, so unlike his life in Cuba. He talked about taking bullets out of the chests of teenagers, treating young girls who had been raped, and giving tranquilizers and sleeping pills to the victims' mothers. How he fought to keep patients from overdosing on the strangest, most potent drugs he hadn't even known existed, whose devastating effects left him baffled.

Misión Barrio Adentro had been the focus of much attention—it was the greatest work of the Bolivarian Revolution, unusually well financed from the increase in oil prices. It already involved nine hundred new clinics and five thousand new doctors. It was, to the eyes of the poorest people, a demonstration of the greatest love, compassion, and inclusiveness they'd ever received, proof of the commitment of Hugo, their beloved president.

For Dr. Avellaneda, meanwhile, that life was physically exhausting, emotionally numbing, and terrifying. He feared that a stray bullet might find its way into his own skull someday. So he fantasized about freedom: he daydreamed about hanging up his white coat and losing himself forever in the Andes. Or better still, the Alps. Far from all the death. All the inhumanity. And in that fantasy, between each interview, he became more and more connected to the reporter who came to see him.

Eva got instructions to the reporter that she should go as far as she needed to. So one night, in the midst of their first passionate encounter in the clinic, Dr. Avellaneda confessed an impassioned rejection of the "revolution" to which he'd been subordinated against his will. He admitted that he wanted to leave Venezuela and forget about the Cuban Revolution and everything it stood for. And he asked her to go with him. The reporter, a perfect actress, led him to believe that she would, and that same night she shared her recordings with both Mónica and Eva.

Eva had rejoiced! A prospective Cuban deserter through whom a direct path might perhaps open into the enemy lines.

The next day, Dr. Avellaneda was taken from the clinic and pushed roughly into a van. The women who lived next door to the clinic told this story to the reporter, who was detained by two armed men who threatened to kill her and Mónica Parker if she ever showed her face on those streets again. Mauricio Bosco's agents, charged with monitoring the thousands of volunteer medical workers, had been keeping tabs on the suspicious relationship between Dr. Avellaneda and the reporter. Their suspicions were confirmed when Mónica herself told Mauricio, idly, that one of her reporters was seeing a Cuban doctor and that the doctor seemed unconvinced by both the Cuban Revolution and the mission in Venezuela.

Mauricio had maneuvered his network with the usual skill, through two trustworthy lieutenants with whom he had very occasional secret meetings. These two agents in turn interacted only with one or two people they trusted, who repeated the pattern until a large network of total strangers was able to act in coordination, following Mauricio's orders. In practice this was an efficient and sometimes lethal tangle of cells that operated independently, without knowing who the others were or what they were doing. Gathering information, influencing decisions, neutralizing the enemy, and anticipating threats: these were their main tasks. The only person who knew for sure about Dr. Avellaneda's end was Mauricio, and it was an end he'd been very uneasy about. To him and to his bosses in Havana, the case was far from unusual. On the contrary, it was increasingly common. The number of Cuban doctors and other professionals sent to Venezuela who fled to a third country was growing at an alarming rate. The controls, the espionage, the threats of jail and retaliation against their families had all failed to stanch the flow of Cubans who used their mission to Venezuela as a springboard to another country, often the United States.

Eva went on listening to the audio and going over the footage in search of new details and clues. Anything that would give her the slightest hint about who the man behind Dr. Avellaneda's disappearance was, the man who had to be the lead G2 spy in Caracas.

Eloísa had decided to go public on Mónica Parker's news program. They knew one another in passing from LUNA, and people needed to know that *El Libertador*'s *Libertadora* wept over the anguish of being betrayed. That after such a great effort, she could no longer live with an unrecognizable man, a tropical Dr. Jekyll and Mr. Hyde. They needed to know that Eloísa had renounced her role as first lady of her own accord.

It was not just that he was different, but that the affairs had never stopped. She had finally learned that Manuelita Sáenz's words to Simón Bolívar didn't apply to her life: "You know well that no other woman you have met could delight you with the fervor and the passion that bind me to you." There were so many others who delighted him, so many others who would allow themselves to be delighted by him . . . It was enough, really enough. No one could say she hadn't tried, that she didn't love him, that she wasn't a match for him, that she didn't measure up, or that it was her fault the marriage had failed.

"What's the matter, Eloísa?"

Eloísa responded to Mónica's first question with trembling lips. "It's no secret that the president and I have been separated for some time," Eloísa answered. "But this situation, which I find so painful, has now developed from a personal matter to a legal one, and it's time for me to tell the country. I think everyone has been expecting it. It won't come as a surprise."

"What do you mean it's 'developed into a legal matter'?" Mónica asked.

"I mean I'm in the process of getting an annulment. It's just a matter of waiting for the president to formalize the documents and sign the divorce," she answered, mildly. "This will give him more time to govern, and it will give me a great deal more peace of mind."

"But what happened? You seemed so happy in the beginning."

"A lot of things changed," Eloísa said. "The president has changed significantly since we met. We've had our share of problems. I want to be clear: we're not divorcing because I'm his enemy, or an enemy of the revolution. This should not be used by the opposition to attack him. We're separating simply because, as a couple, we share nothing except our daughter. He has affairs, for example, and I can't tolerate that."

"And what about your commitment to the president's government?" Mónica asked. "You were involved in drafting the constitution, your social projects for kids, your policies for the advancement of women."

"For now, I'm going to devote most of my time to my family, though I'll still fulfill my commitments to the Children's Foundation, of course."

"It's a little strange hearing you talk like this, especially because you've been a vocal defender of your husband's government."

"Well, politics have had a huge influence over my life recently, and in my marriage. But I didn't marry the Bolivarian Revolution. I don't want to be a martyr to the revolution."

"I imagine everything has been more difficult since the failed coup?" Mónica asked.

"So difficult!" Eloísa sighed. "I was firmly by his side during those moments, as you know. But I no longer want to be the target of the attacks, slander, and malicious comments from the president's own people as well as his opponents. His opponents, for example, have tried to destroy him by attacking my moral integrity. It's a nightmare for my family, living constantly under scrutiny from the president's opponents, as well as his followers."

"And there's no possibility of reconciliation? This isn't just a passing crisis, Eloísa? You've been together five years."

"No, Mónica. I won't have a marriage of convenience. The president is not the Hugo I first met. I've never seen anyone as obsessed with power as he is. Power has changed him. On top of that, he's abusive, and a womanizer, and to be totally honest, the spark has gone out of our love life."

For the first time in her career, Mónica Parker didn't know what to say. For a few seconds, she was speechless, and to her and her audience it felt like an eternity.

Eloísa left the studio with her head held high, defiant, with the bearing of a woman who'd bravely defended her dignity. She certainly felt brave. She'd confronted the president of the Bolivarian Republic of Venezuela. Maybe she should have been afraid, but she wasn't. She felt she'd gone beyond petty political calculations, fame, and power.

But this wouldn't be the simple parting she had expected. A judicial tussle began over the president's visiting rights with his four-year-old daughter, whose custody remained with her mother. Eloísa insisted it had to be him, in person, who picked their daughter up and brought her back at the end of visits. She feared for her daughter's safety in that political climate. Journalists harassed her on her way in and out of the courtroom, though the president himself never made an appearance. In the end, he yielded, and Eloísa withdrew into private life and sank into a silence from which she would only emerge much later in an election campaign against her ex-husband.

Chapter 12

WAR GAMES

Juan Cash's sermons worked in Prán's mind like divine commands.

God wants you to be rich here on Earth.

Define your personal mission and you will triumph.

The true nirvana is success.

Prán wasn't quite sure what nirvana was, but he repeated the word effusively, and he even wrote that last line on the altar in his cell.

His main source of funds continued to be drug trafficking. Despite the Venezuelan president's problematic support for the FARC, his main rivals, Prán had managed to secure a number of senior military men's assistance. He needed their help to export drugs to Europe via "the African route." This involved sending cocaine by any means possible—cargo ships, sailboats, even fishing boats—to Guinea-Bissau, in Africa. From there, the drugs were transported by SUV to Morocco or Libya, reaching the insatiable and lucrative European market on fast boats that crossed the short distance between northern Africa and southern Europe. Prán's organization wasn't the only drug-trafficking network to use that route, but it was the best managed. And Prán wanted it to be bigger and more efficient. And Willy García—still finance minister—had recently recruited a well-respected army officer with great influence in the highest echelons: Colonel Gonzalo Girón.

"I met him at the presidential palace some time ago, and we've become friends," Willy told Prán, continuing with the conviction of someone who's done some serious investigation. "He's proved he has unlimited material ambitions, and that he's smart, well informed, and trustworthy. The colonel enjoys Hugo's esteem, and his promotion to the rank of general is being widely anticipated."

Prán's eyes glittered. He loved having such distinguished people on his payroll. "And," Willy added, to Prán's delight, "I have it on good authority that he doesn't have a communist bone in his body!"

"Extend an invitation to the colonel for our next meeting," Prán instructed his second-in-command. He poured them each a glass of rum, toasted their health, and felt his nirvana getting closer every day.

It was raining in Caracas. It had been for three hours, but inside the palace the rain couldn't be heard. The president was holding one of his marathon meetings, at which all the ministers were learning about new developments in military matters. The guest of honor at this meeting was Colonel Gonzalo Girón, the leader of the new Amazonian Defense Force. This project entailed, among other massive costs, building a system of early-detection radars for enemy aircraft or missiles, a sophisticated antimissile shield, modern regiments of surface-to-air antiaircraft defense, mobile missile launchers hidden under the Amazon jungle, and a series of apps that pulled everything together into an underground computerized nerve center.

Colonel Girón had carefully prepared his presentation, and it was obvious he had a gift for manipulating the president's delusions of grandeur and unyielding opposition to US imperialism. As he described the weapons system, Girón mentioned the great convenience to national security of acquiring everything from Russia. And he closed with an impressive 3D war game simulation projected onto a large screen, in which the US invaded Venezuela.

Everyone watched in silence, afraid to say anything that might get them expelled from the meeting. Ángel Montes had been invited as Hugo's personal adviser. Though he was impressed, and terrified at the expense it entailed, he just nodded and smiled when his boss leaned over and said, "Nice toys, huh?!"

Colonel Girón invited the president to command the simulation, and in that moment the training he had received during an extensive military career had transformed into the thrill of a little boy playing a video game. The special effects and realism of the simulation's leaders, who looked alarmingly like the real Presidents Chávez and Bush, made everyone's hair stand on end. What if the president really went to these lengths? And yet, nobody said a thing. They already knew that their only real duties were watching and approving of Hugo's eccentricities.

Gripping the command console, Hugo said, rapt: "And what if the gringos come over like they did in Iraq? They'd launch an air strike on me like they did to Saddam Hussein. Bombers coming from . . ."

"Norfolk, Virginia." Girón supplied the name of a US naval base.

"Exactly—Norfolk!" the president repeated, delighted, while Girón wrote the word in bright-green letters on the huge screen.

Outside the Council Chamber, it was still raining. The ministers' cell phones buzzed insistently. There were many things that needed doing, but nobody dared move.

Hugo, focused on the war game, continued: "Let's see what the Amazonian Defense Force can do against those F-16s and Skyhawk missiles . . ."

"From the USS *Abraham Lincoln*," Girón suggested, completing the president's phrase.

"How do I put aircraft carriers on this thing?" Hugo tapped clumsily at the keys of the console.

"May I, Mr. President?" Girón expertly input the data.

"Put in two—no, *three* destroyers with cruise missiles, Girón," he ordered. "The *Farragut*, the *Churchill*, and . . . the *Dunham*. Okay, okay, but now leave it to me, Girón." Hugo was anxious to start playing.

The stunned ministers watched the colossal war, which—thank God—was merely the fantasies of an anti-imperialist Latin American soldier. The president shrieked excitedly every time one of his missiles brought down an American F-16, and the ministers clapped as Venezuela won the first battle and a tricolor flag fluttered on the screen.

The president wiped the sweat from his brow. Ángel shifted, uncomfortable, trying to hide his disapproval. Willy García and the colonel exchanged a barely perceptible glance of complicity.

When the lights came back on, and the ministerial war gathering was finally over, everyone sighed to see that the only things pouring down from the sky were raindrops, and that the storm was coming to an end.

◆ ◆ ◆

The new general was preparing for a meeting of great significance, though his battle dress remained in the closet along with his medals, insignia, commendations, jewels, ribbons, bars, and crosses. One is still a soldier even dressed as a civilian, so the general nonetheless followed a detailed protocol for "excellent standing, magnificent impact, and an irreproachable display of obedience and discipline by all its members." He'd learned it by heart.

He'd dressed in a smart white long-sleeved shirt from Charvet in Paris, with white-gold Bvlgari cuff links, an Hermès belt with a discreet silver buckle, and a black calfskin attaché case: these three accessories alone had cost ten thousand euros. As he walked confidently through the labyrinth of tunnels to Prán's apartment in *La Cueva*, the recently promoted General Gonzalo Girón altered his bearing from officer to impeccable financial executive. Even the two armed hulks who guarded Prán's apartments were hypnotized by the subtle, deep scent of amber and pepper.

Inside, Yusnabi Valentín and Willy García invited him to sit down and poured him a glass of Dalmore Selene fifty-year scotch, eighteen thousand dollars a bottle. That morning, Hugo had personally notified Girón of his promotion to general and authorized the purchase of a complete antimissile system from a Russian supplier, conveniently represented by Prán, via a firm anonymously controlled by Willy. Prán and Willy toasted the news with the new general, and Willy handed the general a check for seven million dollars; his commission for the Amazon defense system.

"A pleasure working with you gentlemen," the general said, impressed.

"God's glory only comes in the form of gold coins into the hands of the bravest, most enterprising men," Prán said. "And we have an opportunity to invest in a business operation that's significantly more lucrative than selling Russian arms."

"Mexican cartels bring in about forty billion dollars a year." Willy took over, speaking directly, as he preferred to when discussing business. Girón's eyes lit up.

"I want some of that business," Prán interjected.

"We already have an operation like this," Willy said, "but I think it could be bigger."

"And for that, we need you, my dear general," Prán added.

Their glasses clinked again as the smell of roast pork filtered in, announcing dinner.

As soon as the servants left and they were alone again, Willy continued. "Bringing drugs into the US has become almost impossible. The Mexican cartels are powerful and violent, and at war with one another over territory."

"I confess, I'm not ready for that. I don't want that slaughter in my country," Prán admitted. "Call me a patriot . . . That's why we're leaning toward Europe. The Mexican cartels aren't there yet."

The general saw that Prán was thinking big. And he could relate.

"Cheers!" Girón remained stoic as his two new partners explained their need for a vast logistical operation and armed protection, no more nor less than an army.

"Your army, Gonzalo!" Prán said.

"Your army will give this business a great advantage," Willy added.

The momentary silence in the apartment was, simultaneously, a shared cry of joy in the hearts of this trio of partners.

"I want to take the product to Europe via Africa. I need a new cartel to rely on: *the Generals' Cartel*," Prán declared.

"That's more profitable, and much safer, than launching a coup against Chávez," the general said after a moment of silence.

Then they laughed, and poured another drink, and joined together in chorus: *"Salud!"*

◆ ◆ ◆

The cameras focused in closely on a pretty young woman in a red T-shirt and beret, smiling nervously at the vertigo of speaking in person, live, to the president. She couldn't believe the president was broadcasting from the victims' shelter.

"How are you, Luz Amelia, my dear?" the president asked with genuine sweetness.

"I'm so happy, Mr. President, to see you and talk to you. I'm a Bolivarian from the bottom of my heart, I swear."

"Beautiful, Luz Amelia. That's what this revolution needs: Venezuelan men and women committed to our movement, standing up for social change, and confronting the oppression of the oligarchy honorably."

Luz Amelia didn't fully understand the meaning of the word *oligarchy*, but she believed passionately in everything President Chávez said.

"Let's see what we can do for you, shall we, love?"

"I've got a five-year-old son, Mr. President," Luz Amelia began. "I'm on my own, a single mother. I live with my mom, my grandmother, and my son here in the shelter. We lost everything in the landslides . . . And, well, Mr. President, my biggest dream is having a little house, anywhere, wherever's easiest for you, somewhere to go with my son, my mom, and my grandma, who's very frail and can hardly walk . . ."

"Oh, I see you've got your patriotic beret on? So you're a real Bolivarian?"

"Of course, Mr. President! I swear it, I'm a Bolivarian head to toe. You can count on me for anything. You're the only man I trust, and I know you won't let me down."

"That's what I like to hear, people of Venezuela!" The president clapped. The viewers clapped. "You'll see, we're going to sort out a home for you, your family, and all the victims of the disaster we still grieve for. Keep faith in the revolution, my dear Bolivarian friend, and you'll see, you'll get your hands on some of that oil money that's been hoarded by the rich who believed the country's wealth belonged to them. Where's my coffee?!"

After hours, Hugo said goodbye to the inhabitants of the shelter. Luz Amelia received, for now, a hug! A kiss! Neither she nor her neighbors could sleep that night, elated by the hope of their dream coming true. They were sure that after years of waiting, their faith was at last going to be rewarded.

The next day she decided she was going to concentrate on "giving her life for the revolution." Her heart was full of pride, and hope, and a hint of anger at those who would dare to get in the way of her president's revolution. She wanted to fight for her president, for her country, for her son's future. It wasn't hard to find a group to join in her barrio, a

Bolivarian militia under the leadership of a fierce revolutionary named Lina Ron, who everyone called *Bala Loca*, Crazy Bullet.

In a matter of weeks, Luz Amelia had completed military training in a field on the outskirts of Caracas. She had learned to say she was fighting to defend her president, to give her life to the revolution, and to defeat the oligarchs, fascists, and Yankee imperialists who were trying to take the country by force. When her training was complete, she was issued an automatic pistol that she kept under her pillow while she slept beside her son.

Her boyfriend, a police corporal, followed Luz Amelia on her revolutionary path. They had met when he was doing community service in her victims' shelter. But now Miguel was a motorbike militiaman responsible for "taking care of" anyone in the barrio who was hostile toward the government or who organized counterrevolutionary activities. He was part of a group of rapid-deployment bikers based in police stations and local community centers. He, too, had been trained by Cuban agents, and he would shout, with great conviction: "Socialism, the *patria*, or death!"

Lina included him in one of the groups that occupied buildings, under the direction of Mauricio's agents. Their mission included forcibly breaking up anti-government demonstrations and intimidating and threatening the participants. They had a lot of work to do.

"With Chávez: we stand tall! Without him: we fall!" Lina had them shout again and again.

Though petite, Lina was commanding. Her hair was dyed a scandalous blonde, her brow was always furrowed, and her furious voice was sharp against her opponents and in favor of the disfavored. Her air of power had put her in the spotlight ever since she had begun, surrounded by men, to show the country what it meant to be a patriot. First, she violently took the palace of Caracas's archbishop. She showed up with her followers, evicted all the employees, and addressed the people. She ordered the Catholic leadership to stop criticizing the president, to take the revolution's side, and above all, to respect Hugo—"the only one in charge around here." Months later she tried the same at Mónica Parker's studio. For the first and last time in her life, she was imprisoned. Two months later, thanks to Mauricio's discreet intervention, she was released, and she became fiercer than ever.

Her "messiah," her "heart's true love," the "big boss," as Lina called the president, didn't dare disarm her, but following his Cuban adviser's suggestion, he sent a message asking her to tone down her acts and to focus on organizing local populations, introducing her to two of Mauricio's agents who would help her train new recruits and provide resources. He didn't bring up her actions against private property because it was good to intimidate the middle and upper classes. Which is why, though he denied it to the press, his associates also supplied the groups with weapons and money.

And Lina, no pawn to be controlled by others, submitting only to the words of Chávez, put on her red beret and continued on her way, somewhere between delinquency and armed propaganda.

"It's what my Chávez says: the struggle is between the classes—the poor against the rich," she pronounced on her radio show, an imitation of *Hello, Mr. President*.

The president again announced: "I repeat it a thousand times: this is a peaceful revolution, but an armed one. The people, in arms!"

As a fifth arm of the state—alongside the Army, the Air Force, the Navy, and the National Guard—he recognized the Bolivarian militias, and named a general trusted by the Cubans as its leader, who would answer to him, and to Havana.

Two hundred thousand volunteers, including Luz Amelia and her boyfriend, registered, enlisted, and put on their olive-green camo. A few of them received Russian AK-47 assault rifles. These are a people in arms, who love Jesus Christ, the world's first revolutionary. A people in arms, who read biographies of Fidel Castro, Che Guevara, Sandino, Túpac Amaru, Lenin, and Marx.

A people in arms, who organized a guerrilla movement and went into the mountains, not to fight the government but to defend it. A people in arms, who learned war rhetoric, pledged to destroy the opposition, lived in bastions of Chavismo, and paid tribute to the FARC. Who offered their blood, bodies, and souls to prevent Hugo from becoming a victim of the evil empire. Who believed that "after Bolívar, Chávez is the only good thing God has sent us."

Or who thought that the president was God himself, whose words were sacred when he said:

> The threat of a counterrevolution isn't gone. I know there are conspiracies to assassinate me. And if that happens, my brothers and sisters in the militias, stay calm. You all know what you must do: take power into your own hands—all of it! Expropriate the banks, the industries, the monopolies still in the hands of the bourgeoisie. The right are preparing another coup, but now the people are armed! Long live the national militia! Long live the people in arms! Long live the revolution! Socialism, the *patria*, or death!

Luz Amelia offered her rifle up to heaven: "Socialism, the *patria*, or death!" She continued to obey Lina. There was work now, at least, but she still waited for the promised miracle of a home and a peaceful life.

Eva, not having slept much, woke before sunrise to start her day. After meditating and her usual two cups of tea, she read over a brief that had come in during the few hours she'd been unconscious, struggling with her dreams.

A ship had docked safely at a coastal port in west Africa, carrying cargo that had been taken by military transport from the plains of Venezuela to the port in Guiria, overseen by no less a figure than Minister Willy García himself. At the port, men had separated the eight tons of cocaine into compact blocks, preparing to conquer the market in fifteen cities across the Old World. General Girón had received the good news on vacation with his wife and three teenage daughters on the Greek island of Santorini, while a report was immediately transcribed and sent to Eva in Caracas.

She knew that not long ago, the president and General Girón had received a FARC delegation in the presidential palace. In civilian clothes, the delegation had included Rodrigo Granda, the FARC's "foreign secretary," who managed their relations with the rest of the world. Her agent reported that they had spoken like family, and that the president had said, emphatically: "You can count on my support, in every way." The organization had started to receive refuge and resources from Venezuela for their "righteous struggle." And now Prán's organization was transporting the FARC's drugs to Europe. A business as roundly comprehensive as it was global.

Eva knew by then that Prán had significant influence with Chávez and that he had his own distinctly non-Cuban agenda. Though she knew firsthand the damage that allowing drug-smuggling operations to flourish could wreak on a country, she kept telling herself that with a little more maneuvering, she would be able to secure US interests in Venezuela, and then she could move to shut Prán down and be done with him. The whole thing made her feel nauseated, but she was too far committed to the mission to question the strategy now. Another thing for her nightmares. She stretched and made her way out of her private office into the foyer in time to greet the students coming in to the class.

She was hoping to see Mónica, whom she hadn't seen since the night of the birthday dinner. Mónica had gotten busier and busier, and Eva found that she genuinely missed their afternoon teas and chats over wine. But to her dismay, Mónica seemed to be missing class again. Eva took her place at the front of the room and rolled out her mat. She took a deep breath, and just as she began the first asana, the door opened. Mauricio slipped in, more graceful than sheepish, and set out a mat at the back of the room. Eva let out her breath in a sigh and reached her arms to the sky.

After class, Mauricio lingered until the last student had left the studio. Eva started rolling up her mat, feeling a little fluttery, maybe from the lack of sleep, and maybe from the intense yoga class she'd just led. But maybe it was because she had hoped when he walked in that he would approach her after class. Maybe he would even join her for some lunch? After all, Mónica was her best friend, and she really should get to know her boyfriend better.

"Great class, as always," Mauricio said, and leaned in to greet her with a familiar kiss on the cheek.

Eva flushed, grateful that it could have been as easily attributed to the workout as to anything else. Something about Mauricio always seemed to put her slightly off-balance. It was an unfamiliar feeling, and it made her uncomfortable.

"Thanks." She tried to smile casually. "It's nice that you're coming to class more, even if Mónica is too busy hunting for Cubans these days!" Eva laughed.

"Yeah, I'm surprised she can make time for me with how everything is going." Mauricio laughed in agreement.

"Well, tell Mónica for me that her best friend misses her post-yoga lunches," Eva tossed over her shoulder as she put the last of the mats away. "It gets boring around here without someone to gossip with."

Eva turned to find Mauricio standing behind her, close enough that she could feel the heat radiating from his body. He handed her his mat. She held her breath involuntarily.

"If you're free for lunch"—he paused, considering—"perhaps I could join you?"

"Oh. Well . . ." Eva avoided looking at him, searching for an excuse. She was usually so adept at lying—it was part of her job after all—but she felt the silence grow longer and couldn't come up with anything remotely convincing. "That sounds nice!" she finally finished, with a little too much enthusiasm.

"I'll just clean up and meet you on the terrace, then," Mauricio said, a dark glint in his eyes. Eva felt a little light-headed and nodded, smiling as he turned toward the men's showers.

Twenty minutes later Eva had also showered and thrown her hair up into a loose bun, long dark wisps framing her bare face. She rarely wore much makeup, especially at the spa, and her cheeks were still glowing from the class. She had thrown on a long, loose white maxi dress with brightly embroidered flowers around the scoop neck, and at the last minute added a touch of mascara and pale-pink lipstick. She walked barefoot out onto the terrace from the French doors of her office, and found Mauricio already at a table in the corner.

He rose to greet her, pulling out a chair for her. *A bit of a traditional gentleman,* she thought. Not that that was a bad thing. Immediately a waiter came over, and Eva ordered her usual grapefruit avocado salad with fennel and a glass of white wine.

"That sounds perfect. I'll have the same," Mauricio said. "That's a lovely dress," Mauricio said, once the waiter had disappeared. "Is it a Carolina Herrera?"

"I'm not sure!" Eva laughed. "I don't know the first thing about fashion," she admitted. "It was a gift from a client. Honestly, I don't even know where half my wardrobe comes from. I'm most comfortable in yoga pants."

"Well, we'll have to see if we can change that." Mauricio smiled, teasingly.

Eva's heart fluttered. "That's right, Mónica said you were in fashion." Eva pretended not to know anything about his business operations. "What do you do, exactly?"

"It's a lot of boring travel, business meetings, and socialite parties," Mauricio answered, with a dismissive wave. "Honestly, I thought fashion would be more exciting, but it's a business just like any other. I rarely get to see such beautiful women in beautiful dresses, unfortunately."

"Is that what brought you to Caracas?" Eva tried to ignore the compliment, though she felt a smile appear on her face despite herself.

"Yes, though it's not the only thing that keeps me here." Mauricio winked. "What about you? I'm sorry to say Mónica hasn't told me much about you."

"I'm from Mexico," Eva began, slipping naturally into her backstory. "I'd always wanted to open a place like this, and Caracas seemed like just the right city." She held back the details she'd developed about a Venezuelan boyfriend, thinking that it wouldn't feel appropriate to share such an intimate story on a first date. *Not a date.* She caught herself. *A friendly lunch.* Still, she didn't want to open up too much, even if it was just a story.

Their food and wine arrived, and Eva found herself relaxing as the conversation flowed naturally from their work to the things they'd found interesting about living in Venezuela. Two outsiders sharing their experiences of the city, of the people. She had worried that they wouldn't have much to talk about other than Mónica, but after the plates had been cleared and they were finishing a second glass of wine, Eva realized with a pang that they'd been talking for almost two hours and Mónica had hardly come up at all.

She made a show of looking at her watch. "I'm sorry, I let time get away from me. I have some work to do." She looked at Mauricio, genuinely sorry to end their afternoon together.

He rose and pulled her chair out for her. As she stood, he put one warm, large hand on her back, and brushed his lips softly against her cheek. Her skin tingled where he touched her.

"It's been a real pleasure," he said softly. "We must do this again."

"Definitely." She gathered herself, squeezed his hand in a friendly parting gesture, and turned to walk back toward her office. She felt his gaze on her back, until she shut the door behind her with a heavy sigh.

Sitting at her desk, she decided to look a little more into Mauricio, if only to assuage the tiny seed of guilt sitting in the pit of her stomach. He had some charm, that was for sure. She'd thought herself immune to the easy flirting of a playboy, and given Mónica's history with unfaithful men, the least she could do was to find out if Mauricio was deserving of her friend's trust. She didn't know what she'd tell Mónica if she found anything worrying, but she could cross that bridge when she came to it, she told herself.

Chapter 13

Black Gold

Mónica woke long before Mauricio did, though only in a manner of speaking, since she'd hardly managed to sleep. Ever since Lina had attacked her TV studio, the reporter had been constantly harassed. The threats made against her, her team, and even her father never stopped and had turned her life into a nightmare. Venezuela was magnetic. She was drawn to it, and it entrapped her.

The people were *her* people, and they were wonderful. The beaches, mountains, villages, and food—all the smells and tastes, lights and shadows, the sensations that turn a piece of land into a *patria* bound her to this place. It was her country. Still, the reality was, she was being pushed out. Every day, something new happened to repel, repulse, and threaten her. How long could she put up with the dangers and constraints, from shortages to the risks inherent in living in a country rife with kidnappers, armed robbers, and hit men?

And then there was her father: sicker every day, increasingly weak, almost constantly drunk. Maybe it would be better for them both to leave, to go back to Boston, the city where he was born. But though they still had relatives there, they no longer had real roots. They both felt that Caracas was the place they truly belonged.

Besides, Mónica felt an obligation to her team, and to her loyal viewers, who depended on her to know the truth about the government. Her journalistic and moral responsibility kept her here, with a front-row seat to her beloved, dangerous Venezuela.

And what about Mauricio? Of course, they could go to Panama, or somewhere in the Caribbean. But talking to him about the future was impossible. When the subject came up, he was evasive, listless, unreadable. "Do you think it's serious?" Eva had asked her a few times. But though they had been seriously dating for some time now, Mónica had no idea, because Mauricio would never talk about it. Not that things were going perfectly, anyway. He never shared details about his frequent trips. When he left, he didn't call, and sometimes he was gone for weeks. He never apologized, and he refused to even answer her questions. He just showed up as if nothing had happened. What was he doing? What was he hiding? She'd asked this many times, both to herself and to Eva.

Mónica turned her attention back to the coffee and read the front-page headline with interest: **Until He Goes!** The unions, merchants, businessmen, teachers, and students announced another strike, this time until the president resigned. The opposition was persistent, despite the failed coup. They even called for a constitutional referendum against the Chávez government.

Mauricio disrupted her reverie with a kiss, putting his arms around her from behind. He saw the headline and couldn't help but laugh.

"Impossible to know who's crazier in this country," he said, "the president or his opposition."

"Want a coffee?" She resisted saying anything more. She knew these conversations didn't go anywhere with Mauricio. *We should let this go now. This relationship hasn't gotten any deeper than it was when we first met,* she thought to herself, not for the first time.

"What's the matter, kid? Didn't sleep well?" Mauricio asked her.

"Not really," Mónica said, focusing on the paper. "I don't think living in Caracas is good for me. It doesn't feel good living where you know people want to kill you."

"I swear, I won't let anyone kill you," Mauricio said, meaning it, though he knew Mónica couldn't really understand the promise behind the platitude. He had come to realize that he loved her, in a way he'd never loved anyone before, never allowed himself to. But he was still the head of G2 operations in Venezuela, and his work always took priority. He knew this spelled trouble for their romance; he knew that Mónica wanted more than he could offer: to truly know him.

They fell into a contemplative silence, each on an island of their own thoughts. Their shared coffee was over quickly. Mauricio stood to leave, giving Mónica a passionate kiss that only momentarily distracted her from her worries. After he left, Mónica sat staring into her empty cup of coffee. Again, he had said goodbye and she didn't know when they would see each other again. Again, she was left alone, feeling empty. What's the point of having someone to love if you always feel empty?

That afternoon, Mónica was preparing her nightly bulletin in the office. Between phone calls and documents, she was trying to see into the future. Would the opposition manage to destabilize and remove the president this time? She tried to keep some distance and develop an analysis. The oil company's senior management, who previously had total autonomy, had clashed over and over with Hugo. He wanted absolute, direct personal control over the goose that lays the golden eggs. The coffers were full, and Hugo needed to get his hands on them.

Her on-the-ground team reported that worker tensions were palpable at the oil company. Factions shifted like shoals of piranhas: some were part of the shoal, but some had begun to devour their own. The tension between those defending PDVSA's autonomy and those ingratiating themselves with the government was rising. Soon, she thought, it would become a full-fledged battle. Her numbers showed that 80 percent of the oil sector would be joining the opposition protest and that 60 percent of those polled supported the strike. Of course, Chávez refused to believe the facts, as usual. He was preparing to confront the strike by riling up his populist support groups. Mónica was sure the Cubans were involved, somehow, but she still had no evidence.

The streets of Caracas had been deserted for a week. All the gas stations were closed. There was no fuel for anyone, not for the carriers of food and passengers, not for ambulances, fire trucks, or squad cars. No gas for people's homes, for businesses or factories, or crude to sell on the international market. For the first time in history, this oil-rich country had to import gas. It was hard to believe Venezuela had just bought a million barrels from the United States. The evil empire Hugo denounced regularly was not only his leading buyer of oil but also his supplier when necessary.

As soon as the national strike began, the president ordered the National Guard to prevent employees from entering oil facilities, bringing production to a complete stop. The board of directors had asked employees not affiliated with the union to continue working "normally" so as not to have to suspend production, refinement, processing, loading, or shipping. A total shortage of gas would hurt them too. But the president was playing a hard strategy: in order to win this battle he needed fuel shortages; he needed people to suffer.

Mónica spoke into the camera with the intensity her viewers respected. "Despite having no means of transport, millions of people have marched every day, continuing through the night, banging pots and pans to protest the persecution of political leaders, union leaders, oil executives, the press, and the protesters themselves. Once again they are demanding President Chávez's resignation. Today, in the middle of these protests, gunfire erupted. Though the president blamed the opposition for the shootings, no one can be sure.

"As part of the strike, a tanker loaded with two hundred eighty thousand barrels of crude oil is anchored in the middle of the channel of Lake Maracaibo, blocking the only shipping route to get Venezuelan oil to international markets. Many see this rebel captain as a symbol of the resolve with which the strikers are confronting a government they condemn. After twenty days without oil production, the supermarkets are empty and people are starving. How much longer will President Chávez continue to ignore the Venezuelan people's suffering?" Mónica put her papers down and looked into the camera, and the red light went out, indicating they were off the air.

Mauricio, now a trusted behind-the-scenes adviser himself, knew they had to break the strike. Like Chávez said, at any cost. Mauricio called Willy García.

"Willy, we have to get the oil out past that fucking tanker in Lake Maracaibo. What can you do for me?"

Willy García always had a connection. He called Augusto Clementi, a local subcontractor for the PDVSA fleet, and made a quick introduction to Chávez's inner circle. Clementi was assured that he would be very well compensated if he could get the oil out around the blockading tanker. Within hours, Clementi called Willy García.

"Okay, my friend, I did it. My fleet of small oil transport ships are filled and, as we speak, are getting around the tanker and out to the open seas. The oil is going to market now."

"Excellent!" Willy was delighted and contacted Mauricio to share his success and to make sure he got credit for future favors.

Mauricio knew that punishment of the tanker captain had to be swift. He marshaled his local and Cuban military contacts, and, within forty-eight hours, the rebel tanker had been boarded and the captain thrown in prison. The tanker was put into service for the glory of the Chávez regime.

"They thought they could topple the government with this oil coup," the president said after it was done, on his Sunday program, "but it backfired. Our Venezuelan oil firm, our dear—and vital—PDVSA is already starting to recover. And now we will have new managers and workers who are working for the people of this country and not the oligarchy. We'll bring criminal charges against the saboteurs and the traitors, and honor the soldiers and civilians who served the *patria* with distinction in this struggle. Like I told you, my Bolivarian brothers and sisters, this battle is ours. PDVSA belongs to the people!"

Mónica looked into the camera, a serious expression on her face. "Recent weeks have seen the reopening of oil wells, exploratory drilling, petrochemical plants, and refineries. Though everything may seem like it has returned to normal, there has been a sharp rise in accidents, fires, and barge sinkings due to pressure to work at faster-than-normal speeds. This reporter continues to wonder how far the president will go in ignoring the safety of his people, after weeks of near starvation and total social breakdown. This is Mónica Parker. Good night."

The red light on the camera blinked off, and her producer called, "Clear." Mónica stood with a grim look on her face, smoothed her skirt, and headed back to her office. She had immediately begun to wonder about this Señor Clementi. Where had this savior come from? She started to investigate with her usual intensity, and it didn't take long to discover that Clementi had already been rewarded for his work with high-value contracts. As if he were flaunting his sudden enormous wealth, Clementi had spent an absurd amount to buy two pistols that had belonged to Simón Bolívar as a gift for the president. The Bolívar pistols had starred in a long segment of the following *Hello,*

Mr. President, in which Hugo held them as he taught an improvised lesson in Bolivarian history.

Sitting at her desk, wondering whether to report on any of this, Mónica felt devastated to realize that the only winner to come out of the strike was the president: he finally had unilateral control over the torrent of money that flowed into the country as crude prices rose higher and higher.

Eva, turning off the TV at the end of Mónica's report, immediately wrote to Watson: "I'm warning you, the president's ambitions are no longer local or regional. He wants international influence. He already has the oil production in his hands, and he'll spend whatever is necessary to make the world pay attention. This black gold will finance his socialist expansion. Hugo's narcissism is global now!"

Over two months ago, during the strike, Mauricio had told Mónica he had urgent business in Panama, and he hadn't called since. He never answered his phone.

"Have you heard anything?" Eva asked over their third glass of wine that Friday evening. She was sorry to hear about Mauricio's sudden disappearance, but secretly relieved. He seemed to be out of the picture now, and she didn't need to spend any more time thinking about him, wondering why it was she felt so drawn to him, and at the same time so suspicious. Mónica had resumed coming to LUNA twice a week since the end of the strike, and Eva was happy about the restoration of normalcy to their friendship.

"Nothing. It's like, Mónica-the-journalist knows better than to pine over a relationship with no future. But Mónica-in-love misses him and all the joy we shared. I thought we were serious . . . I was ready to make sacrifices in order to make the relationship work. I feel so stupid." Mónica tossed the rest of the wine back, finishing her glass. Eva immediately refilled it.

"You're not stupid," Eva said firmly. "We all do things for love that don't make sense." She was thinking of her own now-defunct relationship with the senator.

"I mean, it's been two months. There's no way this is going to work. It's probably another woman. Mauricio met another woman and chose her," Mónica said, eyes glinting with anger. This was exactly what had happened with Willy García. She couldn't believe she'd let herself waste her time with another narcissistic playboy.

"Well, either way, you dodged a bullet here. Who would want to be with anyone who thinks it's okay to just disappear from a serious relationship without a single word? If there is another woman, she'll find out the hard way too," Eva said sympathetically.

"Let's talk about something else. How about you? Any news on the romance front?"

"Well, that guy I'd been seeing . . ." Eva had mentioned that she was sort of seeing someone secretly, but that she wasn't sure where it was going. "He's married."

"No!" Mónica was surprised.

"Well, I knew that when I started seeing him, but he said the relationship was over, it was just a marriage of convenience . . ." Eva trailed off.

"That he'd leave his wife, that he loved you," Mónica finished. "Oh, I know the script. I've been there, remember?"

"Well, we haven't even spoken in months. I've been so busy here, and I don't know, it just feels like he could never really be part of my life. Neither one of us officially ended things, but I think it's over." Eva sighed. "I think I even hope it is."

"I know exactly what you mean." Mónica nodded.

"To it being over!" Eva said suddenly, raising her glass in a toast. Mónica clinked her glass, smiled sadly, and they both drank deeply.

However intense his feelings for Mónica were, Mauricio was in the eye of a storm of emergencies that didn't leave him the time for anything beyond his mission. Cuba was achieving something previously unimaginable with Venezuela. Venezuela was rescuing the Cuban economy and restoring the revolution's lost strength. And he was at the center of this historic movement, one of the main characters.

It filled him with pride, and sometimes with doubt, though he didn't want to admit what worried him. Only in the early hours of the morning, woken by anxiety, was he frank with himself. Cuba was exporting its weakness to Venezuela. *These poor people, especially Mónica, don't deserve what's coming to them.* Whenever he found himself thinking this way, he would quickly banish the thought from his head and try to get back to sleep or, failing that, to work on one of the many problems he needed to attend to.

For example, despite defeat after defeat, and the lack of any clear leadership, the opposition wouldn't give up. In fact, they were collecting signatures for a recall referendum. On their advice, Chávez had added a clause into the current constitution under which a referendum could be called, and if the president failed to obtain a majority vote, his mandate would be revoked and he would have to resign the presidency.

The opposition didn't realize this was precisely the opportunity Chávez and the Cubans were waiting for. Hugo was going to win that referendum through precisely the tactics that had brought him results in the past: gifts, promises, charisma, and propaganda. And cyber traps.

But Mauricio needed time to prepare. First, the government claimed the opposition's request was untimely, that they could only ask for the president's resignation after the first half of his term. Then it claimed there was fraud and asked the Electoral Council for the register of signatories, so it could denounce what they called the "megafraud." But the opposition persisted and started collecting signatures all over again. Meanwhile, following his plan, Chávez flooded the country with money and initiatives to benefit the poor. He financed massive programs for jobs that didn't exist but which paid salaries to the lucky people who managed to get them, as well as subsidies, grants, gifts, and donations of all kinds. He funded the "missions," a whole range of social programs. Hugo knew he needed to deliver some incentive to the almost 50 percent of Venezuelans who lived in poverty if he wanted them to go on supporting him.

One morning, as Mauricio was about to go into a briefing session, he received another call from Mónica. Maybe it was his guilty thoughts that day, but something made him answer the call, ducking into a bathroom for privacy.

"Mónica?!" he said, feigning surprise.

"Mauricio, thank God! Are you okay? What happened to you?" Mónica asked, giving him the benefit of the doubt one last time.

"I'm so sorry. Something came up . . . I should have told you . . ." Mauricio was stalling. "I couldn't summon the courage to call you. Please forgive me. I've been in Europe. This opportunity came up . . ."

"It's fine, Mauricio," Mónica interrupted him angrily. "Don't bother. There are phones in Europe. You've made it clear to me now. Your work is your life, and I'm not part of it. Well, thanks for picking up. At least I know you're not dead. And good luck with the Elite chain in Europe."

"Look, Mónica, what happened—"

She hung up before he could finish, shaking with rage. Devastated and furious, she picked up the phone again and texted Eva: *Drinks tonight, the usual spot? Need to talk.* Moments later her phone buzzed with Eva's reply: *See you at 8!*

Mauricio turned his phone off and went into the meeting, more relieved than sad. He had no time for regret. This was how it had to be.

And larger things than himself were at stake. As soon as he walked in, Adalberto Santamaría, G2's second-in-command in Venezuela, began to explain what he called the mechanism. Elections in Venezuela would take place electronically from now on, thanks to a platform developed in Havana using voting machines that print receipts for the votes cast.

"On-screen, voters will see a ballot they tap on to vote. We store the votes locally on each machine," Santamaría continued. "At the end of voting, the votes are encrypted and sent through an isolated network, with multiple levels of security and authentication. No external computer can gain access to the electoral results. At the end of the day, the results will be printed. The decision will be known that same day, and *it will be transparent.*"

Mauricio was surprised by this final statement.

"How does the secrecy of the ballot work? Are we going to be able to know for certain how each Venezuelan voted? What can we do to maximize voter support for Hugo?"

"You'll soon see, Mauricio. Technology is on the side of the revolution," Santamaría answered with a smile. "Hugo will never lose an election," he added, looking Mauricio straight in the eye.

"Next we'll be talking to Señora Clorinda de la Rosa, who is seventy-one and struggling with arthritis. Señora, you just received bad news from the bank. Can you tell us what happened?" Mónica turned to her guest, who was sitting beside her on a living room couch in front of the cameras, producers, lighting technicians, makeup artists, and everyone else that helped make her segment the most popular in the country.

"I went in because my pension hadn't been deposited in my account. I've been retired for ten years, and this had never happened before. I didn't have enough money to get to the end of the month," Señora de la Rosa began, her trembling voice full of emotion.

"That must have been worrying," Mónica said encouragingly. "What happened at the bank?"

"The young man said my pension had been suspended *indefinitely*. That my name was on *the list*. I couldn't breathe. I almost fainted I was so upset." Her eyes filled with tears remembering the fear, the humiliation.

"Indefinitely?" Mónica turned to look at the camera. "Your pension was suspended indefinitely because you wanted to vote?" she asked, mostly rhetorically.

"That's what the man said. I asked him the same question, and he just said: 'That's how contracts work, lady. Next time look more closely before you sign something,' and walked away." Señora de la Rosa began to sob. "I don't know how I'm going to live."

Mónica put a comforting hand on her shoulder, and the camera cut back to Mónica sitting at her desk.

"The list that Señora de la Rosa's name appeared on, along with two million, four hundred thousand others, was a petition to hold a referendum about the legitimacy of President Chávez's government. Almost one in ten Venezuelans gave their signature, name, and address. Now, reports are coming in that the list is being used to fire public employees, suppliers, or contractors whose names appear on it. Citizens who apply for a job, a loan, or a passport, or who receive a pension, are being denied the services they have a right to if their names appear on this list. This is a serious allegation, and if true, a serious violation of civil liberties and human rights."

A few days later, engineer Jorge Sosa, a prosperous forty-two-year-old construction contractor, arrived at the Ministry of Housing project office. He had been there many times before; the head engineer was a friend of his. He greeted the receptionist with a smile and was about to walk in, when she gestured to him to stop.

"I'm afraid he's . . . in a meeting," she said.

"In a meeting?" asked Sosa, incredulous. "With who? Nobody *likes* him!" Cheerfully, without being announced, he walked straight into the office where the head engineer was indeed alone. Seeing Sosa, he went pale, looked embarrassed, and glanced down at his desk.

"What's this bullshit, Luis Arturo? You, in a meeting?" Sosa asked confidently.

"Just as well you came in . . . It's better this way," answered the head engineer. "I've got bad news for you, and I wanted to find a good time to tell you."

"There's never a good time for bad news. But go on."

"Your contract has fallen through," the head engineer said, looking uncomfortable, and then continued quietly. "I think it was because you signed against Chávez."

"What?! But the contract was approved by two committees and you signed it!" Sosa became upset. "The bank already advanced me the money to cover payroll. They can't do this to me. It's unconstitutional! They've got to pay me!" At the height of his anger he shouted, "The vote is secret, Luis Arturo. They can't do this to me. You're going to ruin me!"

"Shh!" the head engineer brought a finger to his lips. He was sorry, but there was nothing he could do.

One day, in the noisy dining room of a ministry, as the employees lined up at the buffet for lunch, a supervisor in a red T-shirt climbed onto a table and read a list of names: "Arnal, Carolina; Blanco, Alexis del Valle; Bracho, Sandra; Buenaño, Alejandro; Espinel, María de Lourdes . . ." The supervisor looked around for the people named.

At one of the tables, a woman was surprised: "What's all this?"

"You signed that referendum, didn't you? You signed to get Hugo out, yeah? You look the type," a colleague said, reprimanding her.

"What's it have to do with you?" she answered angrily. "How do you even know?"

"Well, I know—if you signed to get Hugo out of office, you're on the list! And that means you're outta here!"

Those who'd signed it dropped their forks, outraged, in disbelief.

Their coworkers started chanting a provocative refrain: "What do we say? Chávez must stay!"

Soon, thousands of employees in hundreds of public organizations were fired with no justification. The disk with the list became a best-seller on the streets of Caracas.

A peddler carrying a small case of burned CDs walked through rows of cars at a stoplight, saying: "Find yourselves, look for yourselves, see if you're on the list! Save yourself time and grief: find out now!"

"Life is hard now for anybody who opposes the president," Mónica's report concluded. "There is a lot to lose and not much to gain against a president who controls judicial power, the National Assembly, the military, the oil company, electoral registration, and of course, the private data of all Venezuelans. The petition to call for the upcoming recall referendum has cost many citizens dearly. And now, that very referendum is their one hope to recover their freedom. I'm Mónica Parker. Good night."

The Sunday of the referendum, a polarized Venezuela went to the polls. The thousands of employees sacked from PDVSA went out to vote "yes" to revoking Hugo Chávez's popular mandate. Mónica voted "yes" too, though she no longer thought it would matter. There was also a huge number of Venezuelans supporting the president. They went to their polling places early and voted "no." By evening the polls had closed.

To the bafflement of his opponents and the delight of his followers, the official winner was—for the *seventh* time—"the savior of the *patria*." Hugo emerged on the legendary People's Balcony, despised by his opponents and revered by his followers, seemingly imperturbable, totally calm, and utterly sure of himself.

"I thank God," he said, "for this clean and transparent conclusive victory for the Venezuelan people."

The opposition didn't see it that way. There were immediate accusations of vast, highly sophisticated electronic fraud. They knew the government must have manipulated the voting data, and they knew Cuba must have been behind it. They didn't, however, realize the true extent of the foreign power's influence.

Mónica presented an extensive debate between the two Venezuelas: those who believed Hugo and those who didn't. Finally, teams of international observers confirmed the results of their scrutiny. They said there had been some irregularities, but no fraud.

Chapter 14

FEET ON THE GROUND

"These are the facilities"—Mónica gestured sweepingly—"that, according to Chávez, belong to the people." The camera panned over barren, dilapidated warehouses before cutting to an arid piece of land. Mónica was producing a series on the effect of land expropriation. Someone had to do something about the millions of acres taken by force that turned the government into the biggest landowner in the country, while doing nothing to improve the quality of life of Venezuela's poorest.

"Land that gets expropriated is land that's made unproductive," said the grandson of one of the founders of Agrícola Canarias into the camera. "A firm that's expropriated is a firm that gets plundered and shut down."

In one of the most striking episodes she'd broadcast to date, she featured the fifty-year-old wholesale company, the main source of seeds, fertilizers, agricultural technology, and other essential components for the majority of Venezuela's producers.

The founder, grandfather of the current owners, was a rural peasant who had immigrated to Venezuela from the Canaries in the early seventies. Venezuela was a land of promise, and he was a man with a dream. One of his sons had been determined to grow his father's small family company, and through their hard work they had grown to have eight huge silos and sixty branches, and they were now selling their products to tens of thousands of small producers.

"We support the farmers that produce 70 percent of the country's food. Without them and without us, we'd have to import all our food, or people would go hungry," the founder's grandson told her.

But what could have been an example of successful industry was viewed by the president as a "nest of foreign exploiters." He appropriated and rechristened the company with a name that was as nationalist as his initiative: Agropatria.

Mónica had been monitoring the consequences of this expropriation for a few months, and now the reporter showed the before and after of the nationalized Agropatria. What was once a vast, well-stocked storehouse was now a desolate wasteland.

The report cut back to a small property in the countryside, a piece of arid, barren farmland. Its three acres of land belonged to Don Segundo, a modest farmer, who told the reporter: "I used to plant tomatoes here. When the president nationalized Agrícola Canarias, I was pleased because he said prices would go down for everything: the tools, fertilizers, and pesticides. He said he was going to give us seeds for free! It wasn't that I had anything against the owners, but I thought if the government bought the company, things would be better for me—but it wasn't like that!"

Don Segundo showed the camera rusted, broken tools that he hadn't been able to replace, flooded irrigation channels, weeds, dry earth—his land in ruins.

"The sad thing," the man continued, "is thinking about how it was actually better before. The owners of that company would give me seed, fertilizers, and pesticide on credit. If I broke a hoe or mower, they'd sell it to me on credit 'cause they knew I was good for the money. The tomatoes I got out of this place were enough for us to live on. It was tight but at least we could live on it, me and my wife. Now she's sick, and you know how expensive medicine is . . . if you can even get it at all!"

Mónica asked if Don Segundo had ever gotten anything from Agropatria.

"Yes, of course," he answered. "On the first day, they gave me everything free! Seed, fertilizer . . . Of course, to get it you had to sign up for the president's party, and go to these courses they teach on that guy Che Guevara and all that. I did it all. They offered me some credits and I put myself down on the list and filled out the forms. I don't know who did get that credit, but it wasn't me. So, yes, señorita, they did give me things one time . . . But I've got nothing at all now!"

"What do you think happened here, Don Segundo?" Mónica asked.

"I couldn't say, señorita." Don Segundo looked into the camera, his answer reluctant. "I don't know what could be going on. I think that Hugo, my president, who loves his people so much, doesn't know what's happening. That has to be it. Otherwise, how could you explain him leaving us like this?"

Mónica persisted, despite being in the government's sight line. The president called her out on his show; his spokespeople publicly told her to shut up, to stop making accusations against him and his revolution, and to show the good things Hugo has done in Venezuela over the past eight years.

The journalist had talked about all this endlessly with Eva. She went to yoga classes at LUNA whenever possible, trying to manage the tension that seemed to flood her life. She admitted to Eva that she was afraid, but while things were getting harder and harder, there were more and more reasons not to give up.

Just having Eva to talk to brought some relief. Over the years, their closeness had given each of them strength at difficult times. Mónica knew that Eva was a very private person, and her confession about being in a relationship with a married man had been a turning point in their friendship. The two women relied on each other for support, and it seemed to work better for both of them than counting on a man. Mónica had decided to devote herself entirely to her career since Mauricio had disappeared from her life. It had been seven months, and she still found it hard to believe he'd left her like that, with no explanation. That cup of coffee, that morning, had been their goodbye.

"You should stop, Mónica—you said it yourself: there are dark forces that want to silence you," Eva said.

"I will . . . I'll just finish this expropriations thing, then I'll stop. Just for a bit. I'd like to spend a few months in India," Mónica replied.

Mónica's next piece in the multipart report focused on the life of Franklin Brito, a forty-nine-year-old biologist who'd voted for the recall referendum and was consequently fired from his job as a teacher and had his land taken. He was not a substantial landowner—the Land Law also allowed the government to dispossess small-scale farmers.

Mónica had already traveled a few times to visit Iguaya, the property in the sub-Amazonian region. She knew that in the past fifteen years, Brito had invested in these lands and worked them productively. Thanks to his efforts, the farm had become a model of intensive cultivation of rice and coffee, as well as successful fishing. The farm also ran holiday camps for school-age kids and vocational workshops to teach farming skills.

Everything had been going well in his life until the day a group of rural peasants, accompanied by a squadron of soldiers, invaded the farm. Neither the bus drivers nor the escort from the National Guard heeded the warning: **ACCESS FORBIDDEN. PRIVATE PROPERTY**. His sign was a joke: this was no longer private property; it belonged to the state, and passage through it was free.

It was early in the morning. After crossing five acres of fallow, overgrown land, the caravan stopped. The three rusty old buses discharged their passengers: 180 peasants—men and women, young and old—along with dogs and cats. Each person was carrying something: a hammer, tools, pots, lumber, bits of plastic. They were going to build a makeshift camp before dark. They were going to win back the lands that had been usurped from them in some distant past. They chanted, in chorus: "We're not invaders, we're rescuers! Viva the Bolivarian Revolution!" By occupying this allegedly "private" property they were claiming their right to have a piece of land to cultivate. They had come to stay.

There was nothing improvised about what they were doing. They'd been planning this for months, ever since the president announced the expropriation of land. They organized themselves into a socialist cooperative, dressed in the red T-shirts that identified them as followers of Chávez, studied the constitution, learned about their ancestral rights, and began to make their revolution. The National Guard had accompanied them, because those estate owners meant business: they even had weapons, and they'd be ready to do anything to protect what they'd stolen. The rescuers had rifles and an order from their president: "If the landowners open fire, we can do the same."

Before putting up the improvised tents where they would spend the next several hundred nights, the newly arrived "rescuers" sat in a circle.

Their leader and his assistant spread a map out on the ground and explained: "These were the lands of our forefathers, our great-grandparents, our grandparents, and our parents. One day thieves arrived and started to take them, moving fences during the night, taking possession as if they were God. But today justice has come, compañeros, thanks to our President Chávez. Socialism, the *patria*, or death!"

His compañeros answered in unison. They had no water, no electricity, and they hadn't yet sown anything they could harvest, cook, or eat. But they had the land. Rural peasants knew what it meant to have land. One of them asked how they were going to cultivate it. But their leader insisted the revolution knew what it was doing. They just needed to have faith.

Brito was surprised, and at first he didn't challenge them, but as the days went by, he began a persistent, protracted passive resistance. He was transformed into a tireless pilgrim to courthouses and newsrooms. He said he had been promised payment for his expropriated lands, but he never received it. He accused the government of ruining him and his family.

In his bureaucratic race around Caracas, Brito managed to meet Mónica, and she promised to bring his situation to the attention of her viewers. The reporter accompanied him on the day he decided to go back home and face the hostile environment that the invaded farm had become. Many of the "rescuers" had been brought in from other remote villages, people he'd never seen before, and they treated him with particular cruelty.

The hardest part for Brito, however, was seeing years of hard work go to waste. Though he tried to take everything in stoically, he also tried to persuade them to keep the farm operational, but they weren't interested. They just wanted a place to live, and to get cash paid from the government. Mónica managed to get footage of the peasants killing dairy cows and holding barbecues with beer and music. Bit by bit, the whole herd of dairy cattle would be sacrificed, the land would end up filled with weeds, and the lakes, previously full of tilapia and trout, would become breeding grounds for mosquitoes.

Moved by what she saw, the journalist returned to Caracas and put out the first segment on the Brito case. Some months later, the biologist was back in the news. The injustice had turned him desperate, and he had returned to Caracas. He announced he was going on a hunger strike, then chained himself to the doors of the headquarters of the Organization of American States, the OAS. He demanded that the government pay him for the land they took. He denounced the harassment and violence he'd been subjected to. The president, in response, declared himself unmoved: "I'll get rid of large estate ownership or die in the attempt."

It broke Mónica's heart to watch Brito languishing during nine consecutive days on a hunger strike. In the final weeks of his life, Brito was taken by the political police, against his will, to a military hospital. He was unable to move or speak. He was suffering from respiratory failure, pneumonia, hypothermia, and liver and kidney damage. Ultimately, his protest had resulted in nothing more than his death.

A year later, divided up into teams of workers, the people who took his land had transformed the landscape. Working from early morning, with no machinery and with sheer manpower, they had built twenty precarious houses, dug seven wells, and opened up three paths to connect the separate pieces of land. They had learned how to use the seeds and the first and only supplies trucked in by the government: fertilizers, food, pesticide, tools. Plantains had started to grow, and cassava, peppers, and squash. Some tomatoes, onions, and maize. A chicken run, a pen for goats, another for pigs.

That's how you make a revolution!

And though neither the National Guard nor the government officials had come back since the day the land was taken, though the new landowners didn't have a TV set on which to watch *Hello, Mr. President* or even a phone to call in, they praised him as a kind, loving, generous father who cared for them as no other politician ever had before.

Life was hard there. But things were going well. It was a clear success for Hugo and his revolution.

Mónica was busier than ever. She found story after story to tell to her viewers, about the government's corruption, abuse, and lies. There were more people to talk to, more truths to reveal, and more faces to put to facts than ever before. Sometimes she felt dizzy with a sense of responsibility to show what was really happening in Venezuela. Her current story focused on Don Segundo, the farmer who had lost everything after the government nationalized Agrícola Canarias.

In an attempt to feed his sick wife, with no choice but to beg, Don Segundo had joined others who were down on their luck and started scavenging in the municipal dumps on the outskirts of Puerto Cabello in Carabobo near the country's main shipping port. One day the garbage diggers made a huge find: a row of half-buried shipping containers filled with poultry, meat, and powered milk, all in a state of decomposition. Don Segundo took a load of this home, hoping it was still okay to eat. Within a few days many neighbors, including Don Segundo's wife, were taken to emergency rooms in local hospitals, where several of them died of food poisoning.

These stories also reached Eva's ears, via her agents monitoring Prán's venture, Petro-foods, a public company Hugo had set up in accordance with his claim to be distributing subsidized food to those in greatest need. The new company imported food on a massive scale using the money from the national oil.

"No Venezuelan should ever go hungry!" Hugo shouted on his program, while the studio audience in their red T-shirts jumped to their feet and clapped enthusiastically. "The biggest weapon of mass destruction we have on this planet is hunger—and why do we have hunger in the world? Because of you, the capitalists, who exploit minorities. Because the powerful on this planet are against its people," Hugo said on his program.

Eva had traced the chain: Willy García's friend had become the senior manager of PDVSA, which carried out the purchases of food for the subsidiary company, Petro-foods. He took his instructions from

Willy, who, of course, took his instructions from Prán. The business was a huge illegal operation in which the government apportioned currency at well below the market rate. Those cheap dollars were meant for importing food on a massive scale to replace the fall in the country's own food production, to be sold at very low prices or, better still, to be given away to those who needed it the most.

The problem was that many of the subcontractors weren't actually importing food, and others were importing food that was already spoiled. And they got to keep the millions of cheap dollars the government had given them. The whole complex process involved Augusto Clementi's shipping network, which could rely on the complicit protection of the corrupt senior military, led by the talented, ambitious—and ever more important—General Gonzalo Girón.

Since "importers" weren't actually selling food to consumers, dozens of containers went straight from the port to the dumps, in order to temporarily hide their tracks. Temporarily, because of course the tons of rotting food began to stink, making these dumps public and notorious.

"While people go hungry, food imported by the government is left to rot," Mónica said, concluding her report standing in front of the landfill, gesturing to mountains of decomposing food.

And that was the report that sealed the fate of her TV station. Her father, sadly and a little bit drunkenly, warned her there would be reprisals. And he was right.

◆ ◆ ◆

"Wake up, Papá. Come on . . . let's get you to bed." Mónica's father was on the living room floor, passed out in a drunken stupor. "Come on, Papá. I know you can hear me. Please, try. I can't bear to see you like this . . ."

"Leave me alone!" the old man mumbled in his native English.

Mónica shook him, cooled his face with a damp cloth, then gave up, lay down beside him, and started to cry. He'd been like this for so long. So much suffering over the man she'd most admired in her life. She still didn't understand how he'd come to this, ruining his life, their lives, her life. She was constantly paying the price for protecting him, hiding his reality from the world.

Without realizing it, she'd fallen asleep. Mónica woke with a start in the morning. She was late; she had to be at the editorial meeting in an hour.

Her father was sitting at the kitchen table. He looked terrible. Without apologizing, Chuck Parker held out an envelope.

"This came for you," he said in English. Mónica raised her eyebrows.

KEEP QUIET, MÓNICA PARKER. SHUT YOUR MOUTH, OR WE'LL SHUT IT FOR YOU.

"Where did you get this?" she asked her father, but he couldn't remember how the piece of paper had ended up in his hands.

On her way to the station, Mónica asked the driver to turn off the radio. Her head hurt. She was shaking. Should she report that she'd been getting threats, day after day? No, better not. Who could help her, anyway? The threats had to be coming either from the president or his people.

She looked out the window at the walls covered with political graffiti, uninterested. Presidential elections, again. Hugo at the wheel, again. And another victory, no doubt about that. He'd been in power eight years; he'd easily get another six. The opposition couldn't organize themselves. None of the opposition leaders held a candle to Hugo in terms of charisma. They were few, scattered, and disorganized. They seemed to be living in a sleepy hopefulness: *We'll wake from this nightmare, one day . . . maybe . . .*

The president, on the recommendation of his advisory team, had softened his revolutionary message so that the middle class, which was largely against him, might be persuaded by his love for Venezuela. Mónica read a huge billboard as they waited at a stoplight. The president was smiling fondly.

I HAVE DONE EVERYTHING FOR LOVE, ALWAYS.
FOR LOVE OF TREES AND RIVERS, I BECAME A PAINTER.
FOR LOVE OF KNOWLEDGE, I LEFT MY VILLAGE TO GO STUDY.
FOR LOVE OF SPORT, I BECAME A BALLPLAYER.
FOR LOVE OF THE *PATRIA*, I BECAME A SOLDIER.
FOR LOVE OF MY PEOPLE, I BECAME PRESIDENT, YOU ALL MADE ME PRESIDENT.
I HAVE GOVERNED ALL THESE YEARS FOR LOVE. AND THERE IS STILL MUCH TO DO.
I NEED MORE TIME. I NEED YOUR VOTE.
YOUR VOTE FOR LOVE.

When Mónica arrived at work, her team noticed how distant and frail she seemed.

"I'm fine, just tired," she lied.

In the following weeks Mónica decided to tone down her reports a little. She wouldn't toe the government's line, but she did always present the official version, too, so she couldn't be accused of being biased or compromised and so they wouldn't kill her.

More and more, she censored herself.

Then a private company bought the station. Since when had it been for sale? Who was the new owner, and where had their capital come from? She was told that all she'd have to do was make a subtle change in her program's editorial approach. *Something's off,* Mónica thought, but it wasn't yet clear what it was. She felt trapped.

She covered the results of the election: having won a large majority of votes, the president would govern for another six years. And this time his power was supreme: the majority of deputies in the National Assembly wore the red shirt. Hundreds of mayors and governors enthusiastically supported Hugo's politics. And he controlled the goose that lays the golden eggs, the oil that was financing his revolution.

"I feel so small as I stand here before you," he said from the People's Balcony on the day of his victory. "You are the giant of the twenty-first century, the magnificent people of Venezuela."

The crowd shouted, wept, celebrated the revolution's success.

Eva, Mauricio, Fidel, Prán, and all of Venezuela watched the televised speech, each with quite different feelings about what they were seeing.

Mónica had never been more unhappy in her life. She told Eva over dinner one Friday, after her yoga class: "It's getting worse every day. They don't let me have an opinion. They censor all my reports. I can't do anything, but leaving doesn't seem like the answer either."

Eva again suggested she leave the country for a while, reminding her of her dream to travel in India.

"I can't leave my dad," Mónica told her, though she hadn't shared the full story behind Chuck Parker's illness.

The following day, Mónica went shopping with her dad. It was a miracle he wanted to leave the house at all, much less go with her to the market. Chuck decided to give the driver the afternoon off and do the driving himself. Mónica didn't argue; she was glad to see her father taking the initiative, and delighted he was sober and capable of driving.

Back home, about to unload their shopping, Mónica saw three men, tall, strong, and smartly dressed, approaching the car. She started shaking. She knew who they were, and she suddenly realized that in the back of her mind she had been expecting this moment for some time.

Chapter 15

FIDEL IS A GENIUS

Eva and Mauricio arrived at the church at the same time. There were dozens of luxury cars parked all along the streets.

Eva, dressed entirely in black, saw him first. He looked impeccable even in mourning clothes. She ignored him and, making no attempt to hide, sat down in the back pew, so she could get a full view of the social mobilization produced by murder.

The day before, Mónica had left her a message in a terrified voice, a cry of pain and a cry for help: "They've killed him! They've killed him!"

Mónica had seen them getting out of their car. Three men, dressed identically, walking at the same steady pace and with the same terrifying look in their eyes. Their movements gave them away: they were soldiers. Alarmed, she had told her father to stay in the car.

"Can we help you, Mónica?" one of them asked, reaching for the bags she was carrying. Mónica's mind started racing in time with her heart, which was beating so ferociously that she could feel each pulse. She should have been more cautious, more subtle. Maybe if she had . . .

"No, thank you, I don't need any help," Mónica said firmly. She was happy to hear that her voice did not betray her fear. One of the men moved around behind her and grabbed her by the waist.

"That mouth of yours is going to get you into trouble, you know that?"

"You aren't going to intimidate me, if that's what you've been sent for."

"Of course not," said the third. She was surrounded. "We just want to help you. Not to carry your shopping, you're too strong for that, aren't you? No, help you to leave Venezuela."

Mónica froze. She felt a gun against her back.

"You're like a snake, Mónica Parker Medina," said the first one, speaking politely and enunciating each word slowly. "If you bite your tongue, you could die from the poison."

At that moment, Chuck stepped out from the car and saw his daughter surrounded by three men.

"Leave her alone! *Stop that!*" he shouted, in a rage, and pulled a gun from the holster beneath his jacket. Mónica started to flail, kick, and bite, crying out for help. She thought her neighbors would hear them, but within seconds her face was on the asphalt. One man put his foot on her back, grabbed hold of her hair, and pulled her head up so she could see her father, while a second man fired a shot into her father's head and the third fired one into his heart.

And then . . . silence. She stayed on the ground and watched them leave. The blood. The terror.

When the neighbors arrived, Mónica pulled her phone out of her car. She didn't know who to call. Who were those men? Were they from the government? Maybe they were Cubans, or just bandits, or Chavista fundamentalists. Instead of the police, she called Eva, her friend, but she didn't answer. She managed to leave a message, then, choking with tears, she dropped down beside the body of her father. She cried and cried, choking on her grief, and let the neighbors deal with everything else.

The following day at the funeral service, she raised her head bravely. This time she was the main story. But she didn't make any statements or accusations. She kept quiet, breathed, waited.

Mónica walked at the head of the cortege, and she didn't shed a tear. As the casket was lifted into the hearse, Eva came to embrace her. Mauricio approached too, as if nothing had happened. In that moment, Mónica hated him with all her might. Eva felt her crumble and over Mónica's shoulder mouthed "not now" at Mauricio, who had the decency to turn and leave.

News of Chuck Parker's death reached Miraflores like an arrow. The president expressed his regret on TV. He had flowers sent to the cemetery and made sure the admirable Mónica Parker knew how sorry the government was about her loss. He regretted not being able to attend the funeral himself, but he was just about to leave on an official visit to Cuba.

"Here lie the remains of one who lives today in us, and with us, and who gave his life for the dignity of our people."

President Chávez was visiting the memorial to Che Guevara in Santa Clara during one of his trips to Cuba. He had wanted to pay tribute to the revolutionary on the fortieth anniversary of his death—or rather, his murder. The guerrilla leader's tomb was covered in flowers and Cuba was decked out for a party.

Hugo regretted that Fidel wasn't with him, but his mentor and friend wasn't well. He'd spent many months resting in his home, which had come to look more and more like a hospital. Fidel charged Raimundo Gálvez with hosting duties, and joining the Venezuelan leader on *Hello, Mr. President*, which was broadcast live from the square with a statue of Che in the background. Mauricio had been instructed to stay in Caracas—no need to take an unnecessary risk in revealing his identity when Gálvez could handle the operations in Cuba. He watched the program, broadcast live, and wished he were there himself.

Though Fidel couldn't be there in person, he did call in to the program. The president asked Fidel to share some stories about the guerrilla struggle and the life, work, and death of the "sower of the seeds of conscience who was Che." At one moment, visibly moved, Hugo said that he finally understood how the poverty, humiliation, and suffering of his childhood were a preparation for this struggle.

And staring straight into the camera and savoring each word, Hugo tossed out his latest big idea: "Our countries, Cuba and Venezuela, could very well form a confederation of republics sometime in the near future—two republics in one, two countries in one."

The listeners, drenched from the gentle drizzle, applauded and cheered. Gálvez and Mauricio simultaneously had the same thought: *Fidel is a genius. He's taken Venezuela without firing a shot.*

"*Hasta la victoria siempre!*" Chávez brought the program to an end five hours later with Che Guevara's famous line. *Ever onward to victory.*

After the Venezuelan delegation returned to Caracas, Gálvez went back to Havana, straight to a meeting with Fidel Castro and his brother Raúl. Mauricio joined by encrypted satellite phone. They had to analyze the options they now had for Chávez's next six-year term in power.

Fidel spoke emphatically about the development of the revolution: the time had come to consolidate control of Venezuela.

"We have to persuade Hugo to take charge of the whole economy. With the *golpistas* defeated and PDVSA in his hands, Hugo no longer has any substantial opponents . . . except one."

Mauricio knew he meant General Raúl Mujica, the current minister of defense. He was one of the few high-ranking soldiers not afraid of openly criticizing the revolution or Hugo. It wasn't out of bravery, since he didn't feel he was taking any risk. Hugo was his compadre, and he had rescued Hugo from prison. It was thanks to Mujica that Hugo was still president. Mauricio played them a recording of a phone call between Mujica and another officer who said he needed to be more careful about his criticisms.

Mujica had said: "Hugo can get angry with me, but only the way compadres get angry with each other. It lasts a little while, then it passes. Besides, he needs someone like me. Someone who doesn't revere him but who tells him the truth about what's happening on the streets of this country."

Then Mauricio played them a recording of Mujica having lunch with his colleague Willy García.

"Willy, what happens is, people recognize me and they talk to me. Only yesterday I was in the supermarket with my wife, and people gathered around me, talking about the trouble they're having getting food and medicine. There are a lot of shortages of basic goods, even with so much oil. The other day an old friend approached me at an event at my kids' school to tell me about the growing wave of criminal violence: robberies, kidnappings, homicides with no identified culprits. It can't go on like this, Willy. We should do something. Hugo has to correct the course."

"When the time comes, Mujica, haven't you thought about running as a candidate for the presidency?" García asked.

"Yes, of course I have. If Hugo doesn't change course, something's got to be done. He has no right to destroy our revolution," Mujica answered.

When the recording ended, those listening in Havana exchanged silent looks.

"We can't let this general continue controlling armed men and all that firepower," Fidel said after a moment. "He's dangerous. I'm going to talk to Hugo about it. He's got to neutralize him. If he doesn't, this guy's going to end up bringing him down."

◆ ◆ ◆

The president arrived dressed in his paratrooper's uniform. Ángel Montes had requested a private audience with him, and Hugo had surprised him with an early breakfast in his study. The sense of old camaraderie uniting them was palpable.

"Let's talk openly," said the host. "Like we always have, my dear Ángel. Go ahead—what's this about? What's on your mind?"

Ángel blinked nervously. He'd never been able to control the tic when he was nervous. And Hugo knew it. The two friends knew each other well, but Hugo pretended not to notice.

Ángel was nervous because he knew how delicate he'd have to be to raise concerns about the progress of a revolution for which both men had risked their lives and careers.

"Well, Hugo . . . ," he started. "You know I'm constantly observing the revolutionary process, and . . . I've been thinking . . . I've been thinking it's appropriate to analyze certain questions . . ."

"What questions, Ángel? For God's sake, say what you've come here to say!" Hugo was getting impatient. "Don't ramble, just say it, spit it out! Tell me, tell me!"

"We're experiencing an amazing oil-producing boom, right?" replied Ángel. "But the economy doesn't seem to be doing well . . . and nor does the honesty of many government employees . . ." Hugo's attention was divided between his friend's rapid blinking and the dish of arepas, eggs, and beans in front of him. He'd had three coffees already.

"Of course you've allocated a lot of money to social programs," Ángel continued, "and I think it's good to continue your direct subsidies, giving money to those most in need, but since the oil strike ended, and now with the exchange control, I sense, and I've suffered from this myself, a growing shortage of everyday basic products. Life is so expensive, Hugo! There's so much inflation. The analysts say it's because the economy's being poorly managed. And every day there are more products that can't be obtained for love nor money; they just don't exist."

"Ahaaa . . . ," Hugo said, raising his eyebrows.

"It's not something that can be explained completely," Ángel went on. "I'm not an economist, of course, but I'm a father, you know, and

I've got a big family . . . And it's something I see every day on the streets, in the markets: I *know* something's not working. I don't know why it is. There's a lot of money in people's pockets . . . but the shelves are empty."

Hugo listened silently. His expression hardened. He was upset at his friend's boldness more than at what he was saying. Better for them to stop here and consider the meeting over. But Ángel went on.

"The worst part is the corruption, Hugo," he said. "You said it yourself in your speech from the People's Balcony. The corruption of a lot of our guys . . . We fought to end it, but you must know there's more corruption today than before!"

Hugo dropped the cup of coffee he'd been holding in his left hand. His right struck the table with a dull thud. He got up without having finished his breakfast.

"Thank you, Ángel. I'm sure you mean well, but you are not an economist, or a politician, and you're badly informed. Now, if you'll excuse me, I'm going to make some important calls. We'll have to continue this some other day." He spoke coldly.

Ángel withdrew, dispirited. He sensed that he would pay for his daring. And indeed, Hugo had already decided to move him out of his inner circle of allies.

You don't owe anyone anything, Hugo! He kept repeating Fidel's words over and over in his head.

That evening, after a long day of appointments, still wearing his paratrooper's uniform, the president sat down for a few minutes in the solitude of his study. Among the many documents on his desk he found a sealed envelope he recognized as having come from Fidel. He opened it immediately. It was a report incriminating General Mujica in corruption cases.

Very good, very good, Hugo thought. He decided to keep the file under wraps until necessary. For now, he would just remove Mujica from his position as minister of defense. No reason to maintain a false friendship.

Mónica followed the news reluctantly. The president had announced he wouldn't be renewing the channel's broadcast license. For millions of viewers, it felt like a personal attack, shutting down the channel with telenovelas, game shows, music, and entertainment programs. For the opposition, it was another sign that the president was willing to violate fundamental democratic principles; it was an unacceptable abuse of power. For Mónica, it was almost a relief. She hadn't been on air since her father's murder.

Living in a place that no longer resembled her home country made her ill, and she felt almost ready to leave, at least for a while. In her remaining days, there was only one thing that mattered to her: finding out who killed her father and, even more importantly, identifying those who had given the order. Since that day she had dressed only in baggy pants, with her father's holster and revolver always at her waist. When she found the killers, if she wanted justice, she knew she'd have to dispense it with her own hands.

The decision to shut down the public television channel spurred thousands of students across the country to demonstrate in defense of free expression. It was a spontaneous movement, with no leader, no funding, and no clear organizational structure. The young people's capacity to mobilize, their creativity in communications, and their imaginative propaganda took Hugo and his advisers by surprise. An unexpected adversary had appeared, and they didn't quite understand it. But the security forces could disperse the young demonstrators with tear gas. And sticks, if necessary. And if that wasn't enough, then with bullets. Period.

This unexpected student uprising gave Eva some new ideas. She read public opinion polls, voting intentions, and reports about marches on Caracas's main avenues and rallies in the streets. There was another call for elections, and Eva knew that if he got his way in these elections, the president would take his socialist plans to a catastrophic and irreversible extreme. She wasn't in Caracas just to watch this happen. Eva needed a plan.

The call for elections had become as common as Christmas, coming up at least once a year, and there was nothing like an election to divide a society, or to make existing divisions deeper and more explicit, Eva thought. And there were no surprises: the people were always split between those who were in support of the president's proposals and those against him, but his supporters always seemed to win out no matter how much or how many people were suffering under his actions. So the elections were primarily an opportunity for Hugo, with his usual skill, to embolden his followers and demonize his opponents, whom he didn't characterize as political rivals but mortal enemies with no right to exist. Eva decided to finally move the Juan Cash piece in the game against Hugo Chávez, via the powerful Prán. If G2 was, as she suspected, using technology to guarantee that the president won every election, her strategy couldn't be any less aggressive. And if the Cubans thought technology was the future, Eva decided to put her hopes in the young people fighting for a better future for themselves. She had two big moves: gain control over Prán via Juan Cash, and help the students organize. Eva contacted Cash.

"We have to act now," she told him. "The network must connect, and maintain connections between, the anti-Chávez groups, especially the young people. We need to use the best in all media to keep the anti-Chávez movement alive. I expect to see more opposition voices online right away. Do you understand me?!"

Juan Cash knew he'd better get results or he'd make an enemy of the CIA, which was never a good move.

Despite the protests, Mauricio felt more confident than ever. He knew his team had prepared the electoral process expertly.

"We've got our software in computers and our hardware on the streets," he told his bosses in Havana. "On the streets we have our network of bikers, taxi drivers, bus drivers, activists, collectives, and agents taking voters to the polls and making sure they know we'll know what they vote. Victory is guaranteed."

Fidel had recommended that Hugo frame the vote as being not about the changes but about support for the president they love. And that he should say openly anyone who votes "no" will be treated as a traitor. Hugo couldn't agree more.

"To those who vote 'no,' I will also say, 'no!'" shouted Hugo at campaign rallies. "'No' to their jobs, 'no' to their homes, 'no' to the social programs they like so much!"

The students were protesting for a thousand different reasons. The closing of the TV station was one, but the brutal repression of defenseless young people brought thousands more defenseless young people out onto the burning streets. Eva knew that the student movement needed a leader, a sympathetic young person that the public could relate to, who could inspire them. And she had just the person in mind: Antonieta Girón.

Antonieta, along with her mother, had been a regular at LUNA ever since her father, General Girón, had become involved in Prán's operations. Eva had already started to befriend the young woman and was well positioned to begin subtly coaching her. She knew that Antonieta was involved with one of the student protest leaders, as she'd listened in on her talking about the relationship with her mother during their manicure appointments. Eva planned to maneuver her further into the spotlight. The wealthy daughter of a corrupt general, beautiful and innocent, she was the perfect person to be the public face of the student resistance. She could help reveal the levels of corruption within the Chávez government, just in time for the next election. And Eva had the resources to bring Antonieta's voice to a national level.

Fate seemed to be on Eva's side. Just as Eva was preparing to put her plan for Antonieta into motion, Arturo Solís, Antonieta's boyfriend, was wounded by riot police during a peaceful protest and dragged into a prison van by three men in civilian clothes. With exceptional courage and dignity, Antonieta led a throng of students to rescue the young man. It was all televised. The demonstrators, who had been almost completely dispersed by tear gas, pellets, and the "whale"—the high-pressure water cannon—rallied and regrouped upon seeing her bravery and followed her.

Eva watched the broadcast twice, three times: Antonieta, as she'd suspected, was a leader with dazzling oratorical skill. Eva could see the results of her clandestine coaching, as she had encouraged the young woman to speak up, and of her motivation of the CIA networks to get the message out that young people were standing up to the Chávez thugs. Eva made sure that Antonieta's personal call for opposition mobilization was heard loud and clear, arranging for one of the few remaining journalists to interview her.

"Where did this movement come from? Where have you all been?"

Antonieta smiled into the camera. "We were growing up. I was nine when Hugo Chávez came to power. Now I'm twenty, and he wants to govern for the rest of our lives."

A few days later, Eva saw Antonieta at LUNA and invited the young woman to have lunch with her after her appointment. They had started to become friends, but Antonieta was almost always with her mother, and Eva's finely honed instincts told her she needed to get some one-on-one time with the girl if she was to make any progress.

Antonieta emerged from the door leading out to the terrace fresh-faced and glowing and saw Eva sitting at her usual corner table with a book and a glass of wine. Eva glanced up as Antonieta sat down, put a bookmark in, and closed the book. Antonieta looked at the title: *No One Writes to the Colonel* by Gabriel García Márquez.

"I saw your interview at the protests," Eva said by way of an opening. "Very impressive!"

Antonieta smiled, keeping steady eye contact, not a hint of self-consciousness in her assured manner. "Thank you."

"Would you like a glass?" Eva gestured to the bottle of chardonnay and the second wineglass. She didn't wait for an answer before she poured. This girl was all manners; she needed her to open up a little.

Antonieta accepted the glass and raised it as Eva said, *"Salud!"* and took a small sip.

"So you're at the university? What do you study?" Eva asked, as if she didn't already know.

"I haven't declared a major yet," Antonieta said, "but I really love literature. I want to be a writer. Or maybe a journalist, like Mónica Parker."

"Oh, that's wonderful!" Eva smiled broadly. "You know Mónica is my best friend? I'm so impressed by her, sometimes I can't believe she'd want to be friends with someone like me. She's doing serious work, and I'm just teaching yoga!" Eva laughed self-deprecatingly.

"Really?" Antonieta's eyes lit up. "I admire her so much. She's fearless. She doesn't let anything stop her." She paused a moment, then added, "I really miss her program."

"Me too," Eva said sincerely.

"Do you like García Márquez?" Antonieta pointed to Eva's book. "I loved *One Hundred Years of Solitude* when we studied it in class."

"Oh, yes. I think this is my fifth time reading this book!" Eva laughed. "It's my favorite of his. He said once that he had to write *One Hundred Years of Solitude* so that people would read *No One Writes to the Colonel*, you know?"

"Really? I haven't read it," Antonieta said, turning to pull out a pen from her bag, to write down the title.

"Oh, here, borrow my copy. I've read it so many times, I practically know it by heart." Eva handed her the well-worn paperback.

The waiter brought over a plate of fruit, cheese, and bread for the women to snack on, and as the afternoon stretched out they found many more things to talk about. At some point, they started to feel like old friends, and Eva smiled, satisfied that she'd done her job well once again. After hours of conversation, they had formed a genuine bond, and Antonieta seemed at ease with her, sharing some of her hopes and fears about the future. As they finished the last of the wine, Eva leaned over and placed her hand on Antonieta's warmly.

"I'm so glad we got to do this. Let's have lunch again, next time you're here?"

"I'd love to. I'll be here on Tuesday."

Antonieta was delighted that she had finally found someone she could really talk to about what was going on in Venezuela. Her friends in school all shared her feelings, but none of them had any more perspective than she did. All the older people she knew were friends of her parents, part of the Venezuelan elite, not people who saw eye to eye with her on her political views. Eva was like a godsend: she was old enough to have experience and wisdom to share, but she was also clearly on the side of the students. As they chatted, Eva gave Antonieta tips on how to express her feelings and speak with authority. Antonieta felt immensely grateful to have someone to talk to about everything she was involved in, everything she cared about.

◆ ◆ ◆

Mauricio couldn't believe it. "No" received significantly more votes than "yes." The margin was so great that the software couldn't alter the trend without the manipulation being obvious.

The president shut himself in his study, ordered his hundredth coffee of the day, lit a cigarette, and turned out the lights. He read the report he'd requested when he realized that "no" might win, detailing steps that could be taken, in legal, political, and military terms, as well as in terms of propaganda and political repression, in the event that he decided to reject the referendum result.

Just then, there was a knock on the door, and a very meek Donato Gil, one of his most loyal aides-de-camp, came in.

"A thousand apologies for interrupting you, but there's a group of generals, and they're . . . *demanding* . . . to see you at once." Chávez didn't know whether to be annoyed or alarmed. He was quiet for a few long moments.

"Who's in charge of the group, Donato?" he asked.

"I don't know, Mr. President," he replied, "but General Raúl Mujica was the one who asked to see you."

"Mujica can come in—but just him. Nobody else comes in here," he ordered.

Chávez received him standing between the door and his huge desk.

"How can I help you, Raúl? What are you doing here? You know how busy I am," Hugo said with no attempt to conceal his impatience.

"As your comrade and compañero, Hugo, but most of all as a committed and loyal servant to the revolution, I've come to urge you to concede defeat in this referendum. We don't know what will happen if we fail to accept it and the people who voted 'no' come out onto the streets to protest. The generals who are here with me have come to tell you they can't guarantee that their troops would obey the order to quell the protests that will certainly happen all over the country if their vote is ignored."

"Nonsense, Raúl!" Hugo said, his voice loud and indignant. "I have never—listen to me, *never*—planned to disregard the will of the people. If they got more votes than us, then they've won and that's that. Nothing more. And now, please, let me work. I've got a lot to do. Good night."

A few hours later, the Electoral Council released the referendum result: "no" won by a slim margin, but enough. The opposition, and especially the students, celebrated Hugo Chávez's first electoral defeat. The celebratory kiss between Antonieta and her boyfriend, Arturo, was broadcast live.

Alone in the presidential palace, Hugo fell into an uncontrollable rage. He smashed several chairs and a glass table. Donato Gil listened and kept quiet. Finally, after a long silence in the president's study, Donato dared to bring him a pot of coffee. It was one in the morning. He opened the door shyly and found the study plunged into darkness. The only light was from the tip of the cigarette the president was smoking.

"Turn on the lights," Hugo ordered.

The room was in chaos. Chairs knocked over, an armchair upside down, sheets of paper on the floor, and dozens of cigarette butts everywhere. Donato was surprised not by the mess, but by the look on the president's face: a wild expression of exhaustion, rage, and frustration. He'd never seen him like this. On the desk in front of Hugo were the two old pistols that had belonged to Simón Bolívar and the automatic Glock that the president always carried.

Donato didn't know what to say, so he poured a cup of black coffee silently and turned to leave.

When he was at the door, Hugo spoke. "We didn't lose, Donato," he said with feigned calm. "We learned."

A few weeks later, the National Assembly began to approve a series of laws that contained many of the proposals rejected in the referendum.

Chapter 16

YES OR YES!

"Of course I believe in the Bolivarian Revolution," Antonieta said to Eva, almost in tears. She had come in not for spa services, but to see her friend, a woman she considered almost a mentor by now. "The ideals of greater justice, less poverty, more equality, and freedom. But I can't bear the authoritarian government, the oppression of anyone who thinks differently or dares to criticize them publicly. The rural poor are being armed, and I'm afraid of the increase in murders and kidnappings, the suffering and violence hidden behind this revolution. And the corruption. But I can't live like this anymore. I don't know what to do."

Her discontent had started a few months before, when Antonieta had given a pair of name-brand sneakers to the youngest son of her family's maid for his fifteenth birthday. Antonieta had known him since he was a baby.

That Sunday he put on his new blue shoes for the first time and went to see his girlfriend a few blocks away. In the neighborhood where he'd lived his whole life, two men attacked him for his precious shoes—they stabbed him, and he died. Antonieta was devastated; she went with the maid to collect her son's body from the morgue, where the weekend corpses were waiting: fifty-eight altogether. "About average," they were told.

"It was horrible," Antonieta had said to Eva in tears. "It was such a long line to collect the bodies. The woman behind us was sobbing. She was there for her son, the second one she'd lost to gunfire between narco gangs in her barrio. She said she didn't know what she was going to do with him: most undertakers won't take young men who've been shot, for fear of gang violence during the funeral. And she didn't even have the money for a funeral, a burial, for anything." Eva nodded silently; she knew when to let things take their own course. "I gave her all the money I had, but of course that won't solve anything. The system is broken." That night, her parents had thrown a party for their friends. Antonieta couldn't stop thinking about what she'd seen that day at the morgue, the poverty and suffering she'd become increasingly aware of every day since.

The cost of the drinks alone at one of her parents' parties would be enough to pay for all the funerals of the murdered sons. That night, Antonieta couldn't bring herself to join the party. She lay on her bed, crying, with the lights out. Her mother had been up twice to fetch her. Antonieta promised she'd come down soon, but she still hadn't. Finally, her father knocked on the door with a general's firmness. He said everyone was waiting, and they wouldn't serve dinner until she was there. She dragged herself out of bed to avoid an argument, hardly bothering to clean herself up.

When Antonieta arrived, the general stood and tapped his crystal glass delicately with a spoon. "There are many reasons to celebrate, but there's one of particular importance to me and my wife today: our daughter Antonieta has once again gotten the highest grades in her class. It's normal by now, but we've decided Antonieta deserves special recognition," he said in his military leader's voice, holding up a set of keys. "These keys symbolize the bright future she has ahead of her. But they also open the doors of the new blue BMW outside, which is her graduation present. Enjoy it, my dear!"

Antonieta flushed, tears springing to her eyes. She couldn't contain the mix of pain, rage, and indignation boiling in her heart. As her father handed her the keys, Antonieta managed to say "No!" It was a whisper at first, as if she were talking to herself, but she kept saying it like a mantra—"No! No! No!"—louder each time until she was shouting. Her mother looked lost; the general, for the first time, didn't know what to do, what to say.

"My father is corrupt," Antonieta said to Eva with a quiet rage. "There's no other explanation for the decadence, the luxury. I'd never wondered before how we had so much on a soldier's wages. But I finally understood."

A few hours later, Antonieta was having a tearful conversation with her mother. Money was a drug, ill-gotten money even more so. She suspected her family's wealth had shameful origins, and it couldn't be enjoyed without guilt. Their wealth was toxic.

Finally, Antonieta stopped crying and said, quietly:

"I'm leaving, Mamá. I can't live here anymore. I can't live like this. You know that . . . You could come too . . ."

She knew, deep down, that though her mother understood and even commiserated, she would never be able to leave.

She packed a small backpack with clothes and a few photographs and mementos of her childhood. She called Arturo and asked him to come get her. Then she called Eva. "I'll stay with Arturo at the dorms for now," she told her. "But can I see you tomorrow? I don't know what I'm going to do next . . ."

From one of the house's big picture windows, General Girón watched her leave. His daughter wasn't his daughter anymore, he thought. She was a victim. She'd been brainwashed by that boyfriend, who forced her to go to protests against the government, against his government—against him, even. He swore he would find out who this boy was and cut the problem off at the root.

Mónica went to LUNA for the last time. She hadn't been there for an appointment since her father's death, but she accepted Eva's invitation to meet her there for lunch.

"So . . . you're really leaving? Are you sure?" Eva asked her.

"I'm leaving. Sometimes I think it's just for a month, other days I think it's for good."

Eva could see that Mónica was changed, a different woman from the one she had met years before. Her eyes no longer shone, and she seemed to have no interest in searching for the truth, no desire to open the morning news bulletin with a bombshell revelation. Her eyes had become distant, her voice passive.

"Where are you going, and what will you do?" Eva asked.

"Boston for a while, where my father's siblings are. I need quiet—you know? Get out of this dark, violent place. I'm sure I'll recover the strength I need to . . . go on. I don't know. I'll decide. I've got a Venezuelan colleague who's always wanted me to work with him in the United States. But I'm not in any state to work. I need some distance from everything."

Eva restrained the tears she felt threatening. With Mónica leaving, she, too, would be even more alone.

"I'm sure I'll still be here when you decide to come back," Eva said as they hugged. "I'll always be here for you. Call me, write me. Don't forget about me."

Mónica accepted the massage Eva had arranged for her, but when she was done she didn't have the strength for another goodbye. Her driver picked her up, took her home, loaded the suitcases into the car, and brought her straight to the airport. Eva's hidden cameras captured her departure.

While Mónica was on her way out of Caracas, Eva was preparing for her last Ashtanga class of the day. As usual, the participants arrived gradually, rolling out their mats and chatting. Eva put on some background music and greeted each student as they arrived. It was a typical class, until Mauricio walked through the door, dressed in workout clothes and carrying a dark-blue rolled-up mat.

"What a surprise!" Eva greeted him, smiling awkwardly. "We're starting in two minutes. You can put your mat back there," she said, pointing at an empty space.

Mauricio greeted her with a friendly kiss but said nothing. He got ready and started along with all the others. Eva noticed that he was as familiar with the rhythm and positions of Ashtanga as everyone else, and his athleticism was very apparent in his poses.

After the hour-and-a-half class, Mauricio waited to talk to her.

"What a great class!" he said, with a charming smile. Eva returned the smile, noticing his lips, not for the first time.

"I'm sure you must think the worst of me . . . ," Mauricio started, acknowledging the tension in the room. "And I wouldn't blame you if you hated me."

Eva's heart twinged in an unfamiliar way. She didn't think it was hate, but she couldn't be sure. "The way you treated Mónica is unforgivable," Eva said coolly.

"I know. I feel awful. There's no excuse for the way I left things. And I'd do anything to make you believe that it wasn't my intention to hurt her, or to leave her. Things with work just got out of hand, and—"

Eva cut him off: "Why do you care what *I* think of you? It's Mónica you should apologize to."

"You're right. I tried to call her, to apologize, but the timing was never right. She didn't care anymore, I think, after what happened with her father." Mauricio's voice turned somber.

"Yes. She's been through hell." Eva remembered the look of anguish on her friend's face as she said she was leaving Caracas.

Mauricio interrupted her reverie. "Well, I just wanted to clear the air. I'd hate to not be able to come to your classes, but if that's what you'd prefer, I'll respect that."

"No, I don't mind if you come to class." Eva found herself answering without thinking. She immediately reproached herself: this was the man who'd broken her best friend's heart, who'd treated her terribly. She should banish him from the spa entirely, not just her classes. "Anyway, I've got a meeting in a few minutes," she said, cutting the conversation short. It was one of her strategies for social interactions: always be friendly but never a friend. Her conversations with customers were usually short. She didn't need long to tell what steps she'd have to take to shift a conversation to a source of information.

"I've got to go too, Eva," Mauricio said. "I'll see you another time."

"Of course."

They exchanged a kiss on the cheek and Mauricio left. She should banish him from her thoughts too, but somehow she didn't think she'd be able to do that.

◆ ◆ ◆

"Oh, Eva, it was terrible," Antonieta sobbed, nearly frantic. "There are bruises all over his body. Dried blood around his mouth and nose. He has broken ribs and fingers. They beat him and left him on the edge of a remote deserted highway with a warning: 'If we see you with Antonieta again, we'll kill you.'" The young woman wept inconsolably.

Eva put her arm around her shoulders, truly sorry for her pain. "Will he recover?"

"Yes, thank goodness. I was at his bedside the whole time until he regained consciousness. When he opened his eyes, I was holding his hand. When he saw me, he looked terrified."

Eva squeezed her shoulder comfortingly. Eva knew that before Arturo's hospitalization, Antonieta had been busy campaigning in the poor barrios, talking to the president's supporters and trying to make them understand that they were being manipulated and deceived. President Chávez had, yet again, called a referendum, this time to remove presidential term limits. Once again, Hugo was campaigning in the most aggressive, outrageous way possible. And successfully.

Antonieta had been finding it hard to persuade such desperate people. She came to confide in Eva more and more, and Eva was able to give her suggestions for approaches, for organizing her peers. But often the president's supporters drove them violently out of the barrio, throwing stones. Still, the young woman didn't give up. She had faith in her efforts. But seeing her boyfriend lying in bed, his body mutilated, had completely demoralized her.

"I'm sure it was my father," Antonieta went on, having gathered herself. "Arturo said we have to stop seeing each other. That our relationship is too dangerous. Of course, I agreed to respect his wishes. The love of my life, my partner and soul mate, is now out of my life. Because of my father." Antonieta's tears had dried up, and there was a glint of anger in her big brown eyes. "I don't think a person can cause others so much pain without consequences." Her voice took on a determined edge. "Life's balance ensures that my father's transgressions won't go unpunished. And if I can, I'll contribute to justice being done."

Eva marveled at the young woman's strength. Turning a tragedy like this into fuel for her cause was impressive. Eva hadn't really needed to do anything to support Antonieta's fight against President Chávez; all she had done was offer a friendly ear and some advice on organizing strategies.

And all on its own, thanks to the fire of people like Antonieta, the student movement continued to gain strength. Millions believed that their freedom was at stake, and they disapproved of the president's attempts to take the country toward the Cuban model. They organized into the National Command Unit for "No." The opponents emphasized that Venezuelans must consider the consequences of continuous, indefinite reelection: dictatorship disguised as democracy. They had rejected the proposal because it was unconstitutional, but they would try to defeat it again at the ballot box. The "no" campaign had an unexpected flurry of success when Eloísa, the former first lady, decided to emerge from her relative anonymity to appear in a persuasive commercial.

"Don't allow them to steal your freedom forever. Learn about the consequences. For a free Venezuela, vote 'no' to keep the status quo! 'No' to communism! 'No' to dictatorship!"

Taking advantage of her name being a draw for the press, she appeared on TV. She said it was her duty to warn her compatriots about concentrating power in one single person and about the gradual restriction of freedoms. She had herself taken part in drafting the current national constitution and rejected the planned amendments.

"I know the person in question. Don't believe anything he promises you. He's going to fail you the way he failed me."

She thought the very existence of the referendum was a mistake: "If the president has bypassed all legal grounds to call a referendum, he's going to keep cheating in the same way."

◆ ◆ ◆

From his mansion in Miami, and following orders from the CIA, Cash began his offensive against Hugo through Prán. Eva wanted him to urge his Venezuelan follower to confront the president and his revolution. Most of all she wanted to inform Prán about Hugo's ties with Cuba. Prán was no patriot, but he was sensitive to humiliation. There was a long list of people who'd humiliated Prán—sometimes inadvertently—and many of them had paid with their lives. Cash used his rhetorical skills and his influence on Prán to persuade him that the humiliation of the country was almost a personal affront against him.

"The president is an enemy of capitalism, and therefore opposes God's plan for our success." Prán listened in silence. "From here it's clear, my friend," Cash continued, "that Venezuela's economy is significantly affected by that man's antibusiness policies and by the ineptness of his comrades-in-arms at managing public administration. In a world like the one you and I dream of, and for which God wants us to fight, soldiers are in their barracks, not in the most important positions in the government. We can't support that. He has become an evil presence, and it is your duty to fight him."

The preacher's messages were divine wisdom for Prán. Already in the habit of lowering his defenses with Cash, Prán put aside his skepticism and his natural suspicion.

"Now I understand," he said. "How could I have been so stupid, to go along with Hugo? What can I do for you, for my God, and for my country?"

"My dear friend, you have great resources and a fighting spirit. You can bring these to bear to prevent the destruction of the country that the president is carrying out."

In a single stroke, Cash turned one of Hugo's first influential supporters against him. Prán began to secretly finance the "no" campaign. He ordered his men to vote against the amendment and to acquire votes, or buy them, at any cost. The president had become a harmful presence. He had to be moved out of the way.

Eva was sitting on the terrace at LUNA in the late afternoon. Antonieta, who had in some ways taken Mónica's place in Eva's weekly routine, had come to have lunch with her. Eva felt grateful for the infusion of youth in her life; despite being young, she sometimes felt so tired, so jaded. She supposed that was what this kind of life did to a person, after a while. Antonieta's passion, her innocence, her true belief in the possibility of change, they gave Eva hope.

They talked about politics, but also relationships, fashion, books, the everyday things that friends share with one another. That day they were immersed in a contemplation of the film adaptation of Gabriel García Márquez's *Love in the Time of Cholera*, which they'd seen together on its opening night. They shared a passion for García Márquez.

"I just wish it were less Hollywood," Antonieta said. "If only it had been a Latin American director—" She was interrupted by her phone, which rang loudly, repeating, "Why don't you shut up?" over and over again.

Eva laughed out loud as Antonieta smiled sheepishly and answered the call.

A week before, at a summit of heads of state in Chile, President Chávez had denounced the former prime minister of Spain, José María Aznar. Spain's current prime minister, who was accompanying the king of Spain, Juan Carlos de Borbón, asked Hugo to refrain. Hugo, in a rage, began to talk over the Spanish leader, when the king interrupted with a resonant "Why don't you shut up?" leaving the hall stunned and grateful. It was all caught on video, and it had gone viral. Bands had set the words to music, it had become a bit on comedy shows all over the world, and apparently there were even versions of it for cell phone ringtones.

Of course, Eva also knew that the Spanish firm that had secured substantial contracts to build ships for the Venezuelan government had just been officially notified that the offers were rescinded. There were always consequences when Chávez was offended.

"I'm sorry, I have to run!" Antonieta said, slipping her phone into the pocket of her light jacket. "But I'll see you Tuesday?"

Eva nodded and waved as Antonieta bounded out, guessing that there was an important opposition leadership meeting. Eva found herself entirely alone on the terrace, a half-full bottle of chardonnay in front of her. The late afternoon air was warm, with a hint of a cool breeze. Eva sipped her wine and let her mind wander over recent events.

"Yes" had won the referendum, and President Chávez could return to the political arena in the next presidential elections, and in the ones after that, and after that, for ever and ever, without end.

She had watched on TV as the president appeared on the People's Balcony, greeted by joyous shouts of *Gloria!* and fireworks.

"Viva Venezuela! Viva *la Revolución*! Viva socialism! Viva the people! Viva Bolívar!"

Immediately following the victory, that seed of doubt, the report implicating General Mujica in widespread corruption, finally bore fruit. Eva had seen the report, and suspected Cuban influence behind it, though she still had no solid intel on the head G2 agent in Caracas. Accused publicly by the president himself of corruption during his time at the Ministry of Defense, General Raúl Mujica was sent to military prison after a speedy court-martial. Eva learned that Hugo refused to even see the wife and children of his faithful friend. Their lifetime of comradery, his loyalty on the night he had been overthrown, it meant nothing.

"May I join you?" A soft, deep voice interrupted her reflections. She looked up and saw Mauricio, his tanned skin shimmering with a post-yoga glow in the fading afternoon light. God.

"Yes, of course. Lovely evening."

He pulled out the chair across the table and sat with one calm, fluid motion, like a dancer. Eva's defenses were down after the long day and the wine, but her natural wariness was still there. Mauricio caught all this in a glance. He leaned back and smiled.

"You look as if you are thinking deep thoughts. May I lighten your mood?"

She sighed. "You're welcome to try. Anything but politics."

Chapter 17

The True Bolívar

Donato Gil had been working close to the president for several years now, and their relationship had changed with time: he was no longer just a simple errand boy, he'd become a confidant. The relationship had deepened when Hugo discovered that Donato was a devout practitioner of Cuban Santería, which Hugo had taken an interest in after his first visit to Havana years earlier. Hugo's religious interest had been subtly encouraged by Mauricio over the years. Mauricio had been paying special attention to a group of Cuban *babalawos*, Santería priests who'd come to Venezuela to expand the Yoruba faith. Some had become very close to the president. But in this area Mauricio moved with great care, because although he didn't share their beliefs, he'd learned to respect the power that the santeros had over mere mortals like him.

One night, Adalberto Santamaría reported to Mauricio that Chávez and the orderly, Donato, had become close. Hugo had started to think of him as a close friend. "Hugo loosens up when he's talking to this kid. He's like his shrink. Donato says Hugo wants to have Bolívar's spirit always with him."

Mauricio's Caribbean creativity for mischief was spurred. "What he wants is a Shango ring!" he exclaimed, delighted. "Made with a bone from Simón Bolívar. And we can give him that, of course!"

Santamaría, surprised, brought his hands to his forehead. "Oh please, Mauricio—don't talk crap. Aren't you a socialist? You really believe in those things?"

"I don't believe them or not believe them. But it can't hurt. And if he wants Bolívar's spirit in his pocket, he might as well be indebted to us for it, right? And if he wants to stay around forever, well, then we'll help him do just that. We can use this to ramp up Hugo's tendency to think of himself as possessed by Bolívar's spirit. And flattery is a powerful tool. See if you can encourage Donato's proselytizing Santería to Hugo."

Donato's exhausted body was about to drop. For hours he'd been trying not to succumb to sleep. *How can Hugo work without rest till four in the morning?* the young soldier asked himself over and over. Meanwhile he, a disciplined, strong, well-trained soldier, couldn't make it through a whole night.

That night Donato tried to read a book he was interested in, that had been given to him by a friend, but he was defeated by his rebellious eyelids that closed against his will. He hummed songs, drank coffee, and paced back and forth outside the door of the presidential study. But sleep finally got the better of him at the very moment when Hugo came out to stretch his legs and clear his head with a walk through the corridors. He found his orderly in a corner snoring, book half-open in his hands.

"Wake up, soldier!" he barked, half laughing, and the orderly leaped from his chair, with an apology.

The book fell to his feet.

"What are you reading, Donato?" Hugo asked, interested. He was aware of the unusual hours he kept, and besides, he was fond of Donato and interested in his spiritual beliefs.

"I'm reading about Bolívar's murder, Mr. President," replied Donato, retrieving the book and holding it out. The president frowned as he read the back cover. Donato continued: "It's an amazing book. You learn the actual truth: *El Libertador* didn't die of tuberculosis—he was poisoned by his enemies. And that's not something we get taught at school, Mr. President."

"Mmm, interesting. What does it say?"

"The author is a serious historian," Donato went on. "He says he was killed by the oligarchs who had infiltrated his friends."

"I didn't know you read history," Hugo said, leafing through the book.

"It's not my favorite subject, but a friend recommended it highly. And you see, Mr. President, it's got me thinking."

The president asked his orderly for a coffee and to borrow the book. Then he shut the door, lit a cigarette, glanced at the portrait of his hero, Bolívar, and sighed before starting to read.

Well, Father, *seems it's time we found out what they did to you. Our enemies are never very far away!*

In December 1830, Simón José Antonio de la Santísima Trinidad Bolívar was in the throes of his death. A Spanish friend, one of the few he had left, took him into his house in Santa Marta, on Colombia's Caribbean coast. The dying man was forty-seven years old. He'd liberated five nations, fought in over four hundred battles, and written thousands of letters, declarations, manifestos, and speeches. He'd traveled the world, confronted Spanish rule in Latin America, survived assassination attempts, drafted constitutions, and been, in the slanderous opinion of

Karl Marx, a fickle traitor, a womanizer, a hypocrite, a power-obsessive, a petit bourgeois.

On his deathbed, he tossed between the painful coughing fits that characterized tuberculosis. Sweating and mournful, the "Genius of Liberty," to the confusion of the few people present, said in a weak voice: "Jesus Christ, Don Quixote, and I have been the greatest fools of this world."

Many already considered him a hero. And yet he called himself stupid and chastised himself for many things he'd said and done. Sickness and poverty had diminished him, and he no longer had the time or the strength to conclude his vital mission, his magnum opus: uniting South America into a single federal republic with himself becoming leader of the independent lands.

Some one hundred thirty years after his death, a cheerful high school student read his first speech in the square of a hot little town on the Venezuelan plains. As he read, the young man vividly imagined the rebel troops advancing against the Spanish soldiers, with himself as leader in the battles, defeating the enemy. He contemplated eternity sculpted in statues of bronze.

And that was how the spirit of *El Libertador* began to overtake Hugo. What did it matter that one had been a member of the aristocracy and the other the descendant of a modest family? Both were born to save their peoples, to fight against the Spanish Empire and, as Bolívar put it, against "the United States of North America, who seem destined by providence to plague America with miseries in the name of freedom."

One afternoon, in a televised speech on the anniversary of *El Libertador*'s death, the president announced that the father of the *patria* had not died of tuberculosis. Hugo decided to prove, with incontrovertible evidence, that Bolívar's political enemies had plotted with senior figures in the US government to murder him.

Donato was encouraged by Santamaría to talk to the president about the power of his belief in the supernatural. With the idea of helping Hugo find his relic, Mauricio also promoted talk of the cult that encouraged the ritual desecration of tombs and the use of the remains of people who were exceptionally gifted—whether in personal valor or intellect—for forging amulets to ensure that their owners possess the same virtues as the deceased.

The president was electrified. He loved this idea. A direct connection to his patron saint. Nothing in this world could be more urgent.

He ordered the exhumation of Bolívar's remains. He organized a visit to the old Caracas church and walked slowly toward *El Libertador*'s coffin, followed by the TV cameras and flanked by an honor guard of soldiers wearing the dress uniforms used at the time of the War of Independence. In front of the tomb, he stopped and fell silent for a long time.

Finally, the president spoke. "I have come here to swear that, just as we have sworn not to pause or rest until we've freed Venezuela from the imperialist, anti-Bolivarian threat, so I will not rest in my search for the truth of how our father, *Libertador* Simón Bolívar, died—where, how, why. Bolívar today is more alive than ever!" he declared, his voice faltering with genuine emotion.

Donato, unblinking, watched as a group of men in protective white uniforms, with masks and gloves that made them look like astronauts, approached the tomb, moving with the discipline of soldiers on parade, and carefully opened the coffin that had been sealed in 1830. The images looked like fragments from a 50s horror movie.

Bolívar's remains were to be subjected to anthropological, anatomo-pathological, radiological, odontological, medical-forensic, and genetic examinations, using the most advanced techniques and processes of the day to ascertain *the truth*.

The unusual exhumation took place in the early hours of the morning. Only a part of the investigation was filmed, and everyone wore outfits covering their faces. Very few people knew what happened before and after.

Donato was one of them, but he couldn't remember the experience because no sooner had the prayers begun than he went into a trance—it was the most powerful ritual he'd ever attended. He did remember some details of the ceremony: it took place on July 16 at three in the morning, the day of Oyá, the divinity who lives at the doors to cemeteries and who in Catholicism is syncretized with the Madonna of Mount Carmel.

Not all those present were forensic scientists. Most, presumably including the president, were practitioners of Santería. Between chants and prayers, the president received an amulet of Shango, the warrior divinity who would give him strength and courage, an amulet made with one of *El Libertador*'s bones.

"May your brother in Shango, Simón José Antonio de la Santísima Trinidad Bolívar, accompany you and protect you and never take from your heart the land of his brother, José Martí: Cuba," said the *babalawo*.

Hugo took a deep breath and sensed that deep inside him lay the essence of eternity. Now he really did feel guided by the immortal spirit of Bolívar.

I'm ready, he said to himself, very quietly.

A few days later, there was a press conference that all the media were obliged to cover. The historian appointed by Chávez announced the results of his investigation: "After exhaustive investigation, we have reached a conclusion that Simón Bolívar was poisoned in Santa Marta with high doses of Spanish fly powder and arsenic, which led him to suffer acute renal failure. Yes—he was poisoned. The exhumed remains correspond to a forty-seven-year-old male, five feet five, mixed race, slim and strong, with handsome white teeth, fine wavy hair, and remains in the area of the sacral bone by which they could determine he was a horse rider."

Eva woke that morning with uncharacteristic excitement. She was looking forward to that afternoon's class. It was the one Mauricio had been coming to without fail, and they had started having a regular after-class drink together, just as she and Mónica had always done. She couldn't really figure out why she was investing precious time and energy into this relationship; Mauricio's work in the fashion industry didn't seem to be anything she could leverage for her mission, and frankly she wasn't particularly interested in fashion either. Still, when they were together, she seemed to forget all about everything: her troubled nights, her endless, struggling mission, her loneliness. She felt a comradery between them that she chalked up to being foreigners living in Caracas, and their mutual care for Mónica.

It had been weeks since she and Mónica had really talked. At first they had exchanged lengthy phone calls, keeping each other up to date on all the daily happenings in their lives. But as Mónica settled in to her new life and developed new relationships, the calls started to be shorter and less frequent. Now they hardly talked on the phone at all, just sending occasional emails. Eva hadn't told Mónica that Mauricio had been coming to LUNA; she probably wouldn't care, or want to know, Eva had told herself.

Nonetheless, an uncomfortable sense of infidelity gnawed at her again, not unlike the guilt she'd had every time after seeing Brendan. She and the senator barely saw each other anymore, and they hardly spoke either. The distance had ended up burying what once upon a time had been the dream they'd shared of a life together.

The day had passed tediously, the hours dragging by in the morning as she did the office work that kept LUNA running and read briefs for her true work. She felt like she checked the clock every ten minutes, and only five had gone by. Finally, she gave up on working and went for a walk around the gardens to try to clear her head. She had been feeling more and more unsatisfied with her job lately, though she didn't quite understand why. It felt like no matter what she did, the universe had other plans. Her work was mostly unappreciated by her higher-ups, who were far more focused on the Middle East. She had been here for years now, and though she had successfully been involved in several opposition operations, she was no closer to finding out who the G2 lead agent was, much less counteracting Cuban influence in the government here. She felt like she'd been treading water, the student protest movement was sputtering, and she didn't quite know what to do next.

Finally, it was time for class. She went into the studio, late-afternoon sunlight streaming in through the massive windows, and started to prepare for class. As the students came in, she found herself holding her breath, looking expectantly for one face in particular. But the hour struck, and he still hadn't appeared. Scolding herself, she took a deep breath, exhaled, and began the class. Mauricio had never been reliable with Mónica, and he and Eva weren't even dating! Why was she so disappointed that he wasn't there?

After class, a young Argentine woman who was new to the class introduced herself to Eva. "Hi, I'm Camila," the woman said, smiling. "I've wanted to start a serious yoga practice for a while, but I've had to travel so much . . . My company just placed me in Caracas, and I'm going to be here for a while. I loved your class . . . Do you teach private classes too?"

"Nice to meet you, Camila," Eva replied pleasantly. "Honestly, I'm usually too busy for private classes. But I can recommend one of the other instructors."

Eva gave Camila her contact information and asked her receptionist to put Camila in touch with Maya, one of her best instructors/agents. Camila handed Eva her business card: *Camila Cerruti, Financial Adviser.*

"I hope I'll see you in class again, Camila."

"Definitely," she said. "It was a great class! Thank you."

Eva finished storing the mats in the quiet solitude of the studio and retreated to her office before taking a book out onto the terrace for a glass of wine. She had her rituals, even when she was alone. And being alone was peaceful, at least, she thought.

Yoga was the only thing that gave her the balance she yearned for. It was the antidote to the stress of her real job. She found herself wondering if it had been a bad decision to work for the CIA, to sacrifice her youth and emotional stability for something that, ultimately, would fall into the black hole of the past. But this afternoon her tumultuous thoughts were too much even for yoga to calm.

And just as she found herself wishing that Mónica, or Antonieta, or anyone were there for her to talk to, Mauricio walked through the terrace doors. Eva felt a smile light up her face, and he responded with a delighted grin.

"I hoped I'd find you here." He gestured at the empty seat. "May I?"

"Of course," Eva replied. He wasn't dressed for a workout, in a slim-cut slate-gray suit that highlighted his broad shoulders and a dusty-rose button-down shirt with gray pearl buttons. She suddenly felt underdressed, in her yoga pants and T-shirt, which she hadn't bothered changing out of.

"I was sorry to miss class today, but I had a last-minute meeting. Still, I didn't want the day to end without seeing you."

Eva felt a light flush appear along her collarbone. "Oh," she said, a bit unsure of how to respond. "Well, I'm always happy for the company. It can get a bit lonely here, sometimes."

"I can't imagine a woman like you ever wanting for company."

From anyone else it would sound like a pickup line, a bad one at that, Eva thought. But something about his tone, the way he made eye contact, made it feel straightforward and sincere. She laughed.

"How's business?" She shifted the conversation to more neutral ground.

"Terribly boring. Even if you were interested in fashion." Mauricio laughed. "Which I'm almost certain you are not."

"Guilty as charged," Eva admitted, not for the first time. "Well, let's discuss something else, then. Did you see the exhumation of Bolívar's tomb?"

"How could I miss it? It was all anyone talked about last week." Mauricio trod carefully, maintaining a studiously measured tone. He hadn't revealed anything to Eva about his political leanings, sympathies, or interests. Eva remembered Mónica complaining that he always seemed disinterested in the bulk of her work in political reporting, and only ever made the most passing comments.

She continued, hoping to coax something out of him. "I wonder if Chávez really believes all this, or if it's just part of a political strategy."

"Who could know?" Mauricio shrugged and raised his eyebrows questioningly. "With a man like Chávez, anything is possible. I heard that he kept a bone from Bolívar, as some kind of Santería amulet." He paused, and just as he opened his mouth to say something more, the waiter arrived with a second glass for him. He smiled graciously, relieved as Eva poured him a glass of wine. Something about Eva made him drop his guard and say more than he intended.

"To Bolívar!" He raised his glass, half joking.

"To Bolívar!" Eva said, sarcastically. They both laughed, and drank.

The sun was already beginning to set, and Eva shivered in the cooling breeze. Without missing a beat, Mauricio took off his suit jacket and draped it over Eva's bare shoulders. An intimate gesture, one of caring, of familiarity. His fingers brushed the back of her neck as he adjusted the jacket, and she shivered again.

"Thank you."

Mauricio and Eva exchanged a glance that lasted a long moment. A look that said more than either one of them could acknowledge just then. Mauricio looked down, breaking his gaze.

"What did I interrupt?" Mauricio said, after a long moment.

"What do you mean?" Eva asked, puzzled.

"Well, when I arrived, you looked lost in thought. Something serious, I'd guess."

"Oh. Well, I was just wondering if I'd made the right decision in life. Coming here, doing what I do." Eva skirted the truth of her presence in Caracas, but she had answered truthfully nonetheless.

"Why is that?" Mauricio was a good listener, Eva thought. She felt that he truly cared about what she said and what she thought.

"I honestly don't know. Maybe I'm restless? Lonely? Bored? Things are going fine here, but it still feels unsatisfying, you know? Like there's something missing." Eva felt comfortable being vulnerable just now. Maybe it was the glass of wine on an empty stomach, but she felt like she could share her feelings with this man, and that he would somehow understand them.

"I know the feeling. Like there has to be something more." Mauricio looked out over the garden, speaking softly.

"Exactly."

They fell into a comfortable silence, each lost in their own thoughts.

"Maybe it's the feeling of being a foreigner in a strange place." Mauricio gave a little laugh.

"I think I've always felt like that," Eva said, acknowledging a feeling she'd never truly been willing to confront before.

"I hope that you find a place that feels like home, someday, then," Mauricio said, meeting her eyes with his dark gaze. She felt as though he looked right through her. She shivered.

"It's getting late, I should get some dinner," she said, more to break the spell than because she was hungry.

"Could I take you to my favorite restaurant? It is Friday night, after all, and two young, beautiful people like us shouldn't be sitting alone at home," Mauricio said, with exaggerated flirtation.

Eva thought for a moment. She wanted to accept the invitation, but something was holding her back. She could never truly open up to anyone, not while doing what she did. And the feeling she had of being vulnerable to Mauricio was new, and startling.

"Thanks, maybe another time? I have some more work I have to do, and an early class tomorrow. The life of a yoga instructor is never dull!" she said, with forced enthusiasm.

"Of course." Mauricio stood, and Eva handed him his jacket back. He leaned down to kiss her on the cheek, but suddenly seemed to change his mind. His lips brushed hers softly, tentatively, slowly. It was a question, and an offer. She closed her eyes and leaned toward him, parting her lips slightly: an acceptance. Then they both pulled back, as if surprised by their own actions.

"Good night," Eva said, turning toward her office door without waiting for a response and almost running inside. Her heart was pounding, and she didn't know if it was excitement or fear.

Chapter 18

THE UNFORGETTABLE PARTY

The next day, when Mauricio walked into Eva's yoga class, a current ran through his body, throwing him off-balance for several long moments. He didn't usually come to LUNA for her morning class, but he couldn't stop thinking about their brief kiss the night before. He needed to know if she felt the same way. As her other students settled in, he approached her with his usual goofy flirtatiousness that, he hoped, made her melt.

"Could we talk after class?" he asked. Eva smiled and nodded, saying nothing.

Taking a yoga class had never been difficult for him before. He tried to avoid looking at his ex-girlfriend's best friend, but their eyes ended up meeting anyway. As class finished, he felt himself trembling. Must be the exertion. He couldn't be nervous about asking her out.

"Have you got a moment?" he asked when the last student had filed out of the room.

"Sure."

"Well," Mauricio said. "I've been invited to a party that could be really fun. It's tonight. I don't suppose you'd like to come with me?"

An answer rushed out before she had time to think. "Sure, why not? I have to work till seven, but you can pick me up here."

Mauricio grinned with devastating mischief. "Wonderful. I have to run, but I'll see you later!"

He seemed almost boyish with delight, as he turned and sauntered out.

Eva kicked herself—she'd forgotten to even ask what kind of party it was.

◆ ◆ ◆

Gunther Müller rolled around Caracas in a dazzling black Mercedes, as elegant as its owner. Handsome, slim, blond, with gold-frame glasses, an unvarying black HUGO BOSS suit, an Hermès tie, an incredibly white shirt, Italian shoes, and a very thin white-gold Piaget watch on his wrist, Müller was the epitome of a high-flying financier. He was cool but friendly and spoke several languages fluently, in a voice that was quiet but commanding.

He was often seen in the most elegant restaurants with Camila Cerruti and Ángela Paz, who were personal account managers for high-value clients on Müller's team of professionals. The Swiss bank they worked for was neither large nor famous, but in the right circles its reputation was impeccable. It specialized in providing financial services to the world's richest people, especially those who lived in emerging markets with limited or nonexistent democracies, with a large number of nontransparent businesses.

The banker had come to Caracas, attracted by the rise of a new class of rich people. These huge, very recent fortunes were the fruits of the Bolivarian Revolution—which was why the class was called the Bolivarian bourgeoisie, or *bolibourgeoisie*.

Müller settled in a luxurious but discreet suite of offices, from where he operated with a very small team: Camila and Ángela, both investment experts, and Frank Stanley, a South African who was a genius with computers and technology. On the bulletproof glass door a sign read simply **GM, Financial Advisers**. There were closed-circuit cameras everywhere and not a single sheet of paper on the desks.

In order to inspire confidence in potential *bolibourgeois* clients whose fortunes he would like to manage, Müller shared letters of recommendation from Russian billionaire oligarchs, vastly wealthy Arab oil sheikhs, and Chinese tycoons. These affluent clients could bank anywhere in the world, but they chose him because he offered very high returns, investment security, and most importantly, total discretion. "Our technology guarantees that nobody will ever be able to hear our phone conversations or read our emails," he told his clients, his voice always quiet.

They loved this last point. Or rather, they loved all of it. Soon dozens of *bolibourgeois*, including a number of generals and senior government officials and their relatives, were depositing their money with Müller. The intensive public relations carried out by the banker and his highly expert, beautiful managers quickly started to produce lucrative gains.

Six men and one woman gathered around a circular table in a totally secure room. Three of the men were over sixty, white-haired, overweight, with the look of people who'd seen everything and believed in nothing. Two were about forty—thin, athletic, intense—one dark haired, the other blond. The sixth was a young man covered in tattoos and piercings. He was the only one with a computer in front of him, and he didn't take his eyes off the screen. The woman, about fifty, was tall and slender, with dark Mediterranean skin and quick green eyes that darted about, missing nothing. It was clear she was in charge, and she ran the meeting with few words, precise questions, and sharp looks. Everyone was drinking very black coffee in little cups.

The meeting was in a building that easily went unnoticed, in Ramat HaSharon, a city just north of Tel Aviv. It was the headquarters of Mossad, Israel's national intelligence agency. The woman asked the tattooed young man to summarize the developments that had led them to call the meeting. They had been monitoring the Venezuelan president's aggressive, unusual behavior toward Israel for some time. Venezuela had never posed a threat to their country before, but its foreign policy positions were being increasingly influenced by Cuba. And Cuba had long had a friendly relationship with the government of Iran.

"An anti-imperialist fighter can't be a friend of Israel," Fidel had once said.

The Venezuelan president had voiced his own thoughts on the matter on *Hello, Mr. President*, when he referred to Israel as "a terrorist, murderous state!"

The tattooed young man gave his colleagues a presentation that strongly suggested that, with the support of Venezuela's government and military, Iran was establishing a center of operations for Hezbollah in that country. He showed a video in which a number of Hezbollah activists known to the Israelis were coming and going from elegant apartments in Caracas. Another video showed Hezbollah leaders at the immigration checkpoints in Europe using Venezuelan diplomatic passports. Another analyst began to give more evidence, but the director stopped him.

"That's fine, that's fine," she said. "I get the message. We need to devote more resources to Venezuela. Let's talk about what we're going to do. David? What does the psychological report say?"

The director turned to Dr. David Katz, who summarized the Venezuelan president's career, from the first failed military coup against then president Pérez up to the present. "Hugo Chávez's psychological profile indicates an extreme case of narcissistic personality disorder. His hypersensitivity to criticism makes him react with explosive destructiveness against those closest to him, and even against himself.

Characteristic of this personality disorder is a need to feel superior to other people, which then would give him the right, in his mind, to be a transgressor. A person with this disorder wouldn't feel any obligation to respect laws, rules, customs, or commitments."

The director took the floor again. Hezbollah's presence in Venezuela, Chávez's relations with Israel's enemies, his clear anti-Israeli position, Venezuela's solidarity with the Palestinian militant organization Hamas, and Palestinians claiming to be medical students going to Venezuela to be trained by Cuban soldiers all justified setting up a permanent Mossad operation in Caracas. The agreement was unanimous.

And the agent tasked with carrying it out in the field, she decided, would be Uri Abarbanel, one of the organization's most respected agents. Abarbanel would take the identity of Gunther Müller, a Swiss banker, and lead a team of financial advisers in Caracas, also, of course, experienced Mossad agents. His real mission would be infiltrating and combating the expansion of Hezbollah and other Iranian organizations in Latin America. Meanwhile, they had to learn as much as possible about Iran's allies in the Venezuelan government and their associates.

A few weeks later, Camila Cerruti and Ángela Paz started to recruit new clients for Müller among Venezuela's *bolibourgeoisie*. The intelligent and charming women touted Müller's expertise, and with the profits he promised and his excellent references, new contacts came rolling in.

One of his first clients was a middle-aged man who claimed to be a Venezuelan of Persian origin, whose business was in trade between Iran and Venezuela. Müller opened an account for him and discovered that his new client was not Venezuelan, that he worked for the Iranian government, and that the funds he deposited were the product of the coarsest corruption.

This man secured multimillion-dollar contracts with Venezuelan state firms to whom he sold "machinery and equipment" imported from Iran. In reality, the "machinery" was secondhand and in some cases practically useless. But the Venezuelans paid for it as if it were all new. And the money from the sales didn't entirely go to Tehran; more than half was diverted to the very secret personal account of Gunther Müller's new client.

Müller was able to learn this and much more thanks to his most powerful secret weapon: Frank Stanley. If G2 thought they had the very best hackers as part of their team, they would have been devastated to encounter the genius of Frank Stanley, an expert in IT and data encryption. Stanley had worked with Mossad for years, and his role in this operation was vital. The security of their information was one of the most attractive pieces of bait to the *bolibourgeois*, who urgently needed to hide their illicit gains, the identities of their partners, and their financial assets.

Frank was actually in charge of high-tech information gathering, tracking and identifying targets, and long-distance facial recognition. He used the most sophisticated methods of digital anthropometry and the most advanced databases. His genius consisted in being able to learn everything about a person extremely quickly, sometimes in a matter of minutes. All he needed to do was take a photo of his subject and submit it to his database, which immediately returned all the public information, and supposedly confidential data, of the person photographed.

A few months later Uri Abarbanel shared some of his Venezuelan discoveries with his bosses. Everybody was astonished. The presence of Iran went far beyond what they'd suspected, and the collaboration between the governments in Tehran and Caracas was significant.

"We've got to put an end to this . . . quickly, whatever it takes," muttered one of Abarbanel's bosses to the spy.

"Do whatever you have to do. Ask us for whatever you need."

◆　◆　◆

Eva could not shake her guilt. It felt like she was betraying Mónica, even though she'd been gone for months, and had been over Mauricio long before she left. Eva had received a few brief emails in which her friend told her that she was starting to feel better, that she was considering returning to the journalistic arena, and that she had been offered a producer position for CNN in Atlanta. Eva also felt as though she was betraying Hatch. But that was totally absurd. Betraying a man who had been betraying his wife with her?

She was inexplicably drawn to Mauricio. But she knew there was no point dreaming that her feelings might someday lead to love. She'd already accepted that love didn't exist, just as she, Eva, didn't exist. She, her backstory, her reality, and her future were all provisional fictions. Lies. So Eva decided to keep Mauricio to herself. Investigating him further, or reporting their relationship per protocol, meant sharing him with her colleagues, the spies in Langley.

When had she become attracted to him? When they met and talked in that restaurant while waiting for Mónica? Even before then? Maybe it was all just a fantasy, an intense, intimate need to have some private space in which a relationship was possible, a space where she could experience her feelings without suspicion, material interests, or secret ulterior motives. All Eva really wanted was to love somebody freely. Something as simple, essential, and impossible as that.

So despite having doubts, after reconsidering again and again, she decided to go with him to the party. She daydreamed about sleeping with her arms around him. Serene. Without the nightmares.

Around two in the afternoon, a courier showed up with a delivery for Eva. The receptionist called her up to the front; she was under strict orders never to allow anyone into Eva's office. Eva signed for the delivery and was handed two black boxes wrapped with emerald ribbon, with a single rose-colored peony tucked under the knot. There was no card, but she knew they were from Mauricio.

Eva had spent extra time on her usually minimal makeup and had set-tled on wearing her hair swept up in a loose bun, strands of hair framing her face and held strategically in place with a filigreed silver barrette. She had gratefully dressed in the beautiful gown Mauricio had sent: a long raw-silk silver dress in a mermaid silhouette that draped perfectly over her body. He'd sent matching heels and a purse with a delicate silver strap, all designer, though the names meant little to her. The slightly V-shaped neckline showed her collarbone and silky cinnamon-colored skin. She smoothed the dress over her hips one more time, fighting the anxious butterflies in her stomach, and checked her makeup, and there he was, precisely on time, in an elegant suit, with that devastating smile.

"You didn't even say who the party is for," Eva said, as he offered her his arm and they went down the front stairs of the spa.

"The daughter of Augusto Clementi, one of our investors," Mauricio answered, not mentioning that he was also a friend.

Eva rummaged through her mind and found the name. He was the subcontractor who'd helped Hugo break the oil strike and who was now one of the richest men in the country.

"Oh! A friend of mine, Jessica, planned it. I've heard all about it." Jessica was a smart, vivacious woman, a devoted student of Pilates, and their friendship was, as usual, a result of Eva's strategic manipulation. The *bolibourgeois* had an insatiable appetite for showing off their wealth, and Jessica had capitalized on it. Parties all ended up being the same no matter how much money they spent on them, she told anyone who would listen.

Eva went on. "What matters is differentiating the product, the mes-sage, Jessica always says. You've got to give the party a *brand*. The only way to make people remember a party is to give it a theme that makes it unforgettable. Jessica has made themed parties all the rage. She's done caveman parties, Victorian-era parties, *Lord of the Rings* parties, rocker parties, French royalty parties set in halls decorated like those in the

Palace of Versailles. They usually cost over a million dollars, can you believe it?"

Mauricio smiled, saying nothing, and took her hand in his, helping her into the car. Once seated in the back beside Mauricio, Eva couldn't stop herself from babbling on about Jessica's parties. Anything to ease her nerves. His leg pressed against hers.

"And since this woman is marrying a descendant of an aristocratic Spanish family, Jessica suggested the theme be the court of Isabella the Catholic and the discovery of America. She said the food was imported from Spain and they built a small-scale replica of the *Santa María*. They also hired Spanish actors to play the king and queen, Columbus, and others. The servers' costumes are in the style of the Spanish court in 1500. Oh, and the guests were encouraged to do the same!" Eva looked at her dress, dismayed.

"You look perfect to me," said Mauricio, bathing her in a look of such admiration that Eva fell silent.

Thanks to her relationship with Jessica, Eva had managed to get valuable information about a number of government employees who spent millions of dollars on parties to impress other people just as corrupt as they were. But until now, Eva had only experienced these parties via reports and video footage. The opportunity to attend in person proved to be quite a stroke of luck. If she could just concentrate on her mission.

Mauricio and Eva arrived at a mansion in Caracas's most exclusive neighborhood. Though neither had accepted the invitation to dress in the style of the Spanish court, they made a couple impossible to ignore.

Eva immediately recognized a number of faces whose files she had studied, among them Augusto Clementi, Willy García, and General Girón. She noticed how senior revolutionaries mingled socially with the new millionaires as they made their way through the crowd with glasses of the most expensive champagne in the world. Eva knew how to blend in. She took Mauricio's arm and for a few minutes acted as his—what, girlfriend? The unease of the first few minutes was relieved by seeing somebody she knew: Jessica.

"What a surprise seeing you here, Eva!" she said. Eva smiled, happy to see a familiar face and have small talk without ulterior motives.

"I'm glad you've finally deigned to come to one of my parties!" she said with a wink. "Let me give you a special tour of the *Santa María* and introduce you to Admiral Christopher Columbus!"

Eva laughed and playfully asked about the guests and gossip of the party. How many charter planes from Spain? And from Cuba? Who's the Middle Eastern–looking gentleman? And that sheikh over there?

While Eva added to her visual inventory, Mauricio turned to greet another guest. Just as he was about to return to Eva, he found himself face-to-face with someone whose presence chilled his blood.

"Iván Rincón—in Caracas!" exclaimed a delighted red-headed woman. Mauricio panicked at his real name. It was Chloe, the Dutch activist from Havana.

Chloe was in Venezuela to get a good look at Hugo Chávez's "revolutionary experiment" and offer it support. She never thought it would be where she'd bump into Iván again, the man who had disappeared from her life so suddenly.

Iván felt lost. For a long moment he didn't know what to do, how to react. He worried that Eva had heard Chloe, but she was still in an animated conversation with Jessica several feet from the unexpected encounter and the music was playing loudly.

After the initial surprise, Iván turned on all his charm. "Chloe! What a wonderful surprise!" He bent to kiss her cheek. "What on earth are you doing in Caracas?" Before she had a chance to answer, he continued. "We must catch up. Where are you staying? I'll come tomorrow for a drink, around eight?"

Chloe, caught off guard, just answered: "The Tamanaco."

Iván said goodbye with a wink and a complicit smile. No one noticed a thing.

Then Iván returned to being Mauricio and, calmly, wandered toward the garden where Columbus's ship was and where Eva and Jessica were headed. But his knees were still trembling and his heart was beating wildly. The chance encounter with Chloe could have cost him his life. And it still might. He knew what he had to do, and as soon as possible. He reached Eva, who introduced him to Jessica and the others, and Mauricio chatted with them briefly. Then he took Eva's hand and asked her to walk with him around the large garden. They found a secluded spot to sit, champagne in hand, and for a few minutes they talked about the party's excesses.

"Don't you think, Eva, that something's happening here."

"What kind of something?"

"Hard to say. What's happening between us isn't something you analyze or describe. It's something you feel."

"And what do you feel?"

"The desire to kiss you."

"How odd, I feel the same," Eva said. And she smiled, standing, and started walking toward the music.

He followed her, confused, but hopeful too.

Frank Stanley had managed to be hired as part of the event photographer's team of videographers. Later in his studio he reviewed the pictures of all the guests. There were many people the Israeli agents had already identified as "persons of interest": Clementi himself, General Girón, and the senior government ministers, including Willy García. He checked each of the images against the vast Mossad database. His attention was drawn to a handsome man who seemed to know many of the guests, accompanied by the woman who spoke to Jessica, the party planner.

Once the images were processed, he discovered that the unknown man was in fact one of the top G2 spies. His real name wasn't known to Mossad, but he had appeared in pictures from various operations carried out by the Cuban agency around the world: Argentina, Angola, Paraguay, Central America, Spain, Colombia, Canada, the UK, Germany, and elsewhere. Frank immediately reported the information to Gunther Müller. The man went by the name of Mauricio Bosco and he was operating in Venezuela as a wholesaler of luxury clothing and accessories. Gunther Müller decided to follow him, to learn as much as possible. But who was the stunning woman with him? The database Frank consulted didn't recognize her; this beautiful woman didn't exist.

Mossad's Caracas team quickly discovered that Eva was Mexican and owned LUNA, the upscale holistic beauty center. But going deeper, they found a backstory that was so normal and boring that they immediately knew they needed to learn more about her. It was a long-held philosophy of the profession that if you find nothing surprising in a person's past, it was probably because they were hiding something.

"There's no way the girlfriend of one of the top G2 agents is just some Mexican woman," Gunther said to Frank, frustrated.

"Why don't we ask our Langley friends for help?" the techie replied.

"Yeah, you're right. I'll call my contact in Washington, see what he can tell me. He owes me a favor anyway."

In his office, Oliver Watson couldn't believe what just popped up on his screen. His old friend from Mossad, Uri Abarbanel, was asking for any information about a woman in Caracas who was of great interest to him. She had attended a function together with a known G2 operative, and Uri wanted to know if she was an undercover operative as well. If so, she had stayed under the radar thus far. Did the US have any intel on her? When he opened the encrypted file, Watson's heart skipped a beat. He was looking at a photo of his protégé, Cristina Garza, at a party of Caracas's ruling elite.

There was nothing unusual about that in itself. That was her job, after all. What made Watson panic was seeing her holding hands with a Mossad-identified G2 agent he didn't know was in Venezuela. He didn't know because Cristina hadn't told him. He looked at more photos and the short video Abarbanel sent him. The looks they exchanged showed obvious attraction, maybe even genuine intimacy.

If she was dating this man for work, she would have reported it. If she was in a genuine romantic relationship with him, she should have reported it—she knew well that the rules of her profession required that any romantic contact be reported, justified, and approved. Cristina was an absolute stickler for the rules. She followed them to the letter. And so either way, the fact that Cristina had kept this relationship unknown to Langley was very suspicious. A horrifying possibility had to be seriously considered: that Cristina had become a double agent.

In a tangle of rage, panic, and grief, Watson told Uri that the CIA didn't recognize her either. He lied to the Israelis, but he couldn't do the same within his office—he had no choice but to inform his superiors. They immediately concluded that the head of the CIA ops in Venezuela had been turned by Cuba's G2 and had been acting—and who knew for how long!—as a double agent. It would explain why she'd had so many failures and not managed to accomplish her mission.

They took the necessary precautions. From this moment on, they would consider all Cristina's reports compromised, untrustworthy. The agency's handbooks recommended that they should use the double agent to get false information to the enemy. The manuals didn't say so explicitly, but eliminating the double agent once they'd been used was also good practice.

Cristina's bosses were careful to ensure that she detected no change in her position or her relationships with her colleagues and superiors. Containing the damage Cristina might have done by revealing the CIA's secret technologies, methods, and sources to the Cubans was top priority. Watson knew his career was over and that Cristina Garza's days were numbered.

Meanwhile, in Caracas, the only thing that changed from Eva's point of view was her acknowledgement to both herself and Mauricio that there was something powerful between them, a spark of something that led her to fantasize about a different kind of life—one in which she could share her future with him.

Chloe was trying on dresses in one of Caracas's best boutiques.

"I want to look like a Venezuelan beauty queen. Nobody dresses as seductively as you do. I want the sexiest outfit you've got."

The assistant smiled at the flattery and expertly pulled from a rack a number of dresses. The Dutch woman settled on a long, slinky black one with a devastatingly low back. She looked stunning.

Tonight she would see Iván again. Chloe was determined to show him that she was not someone to be trifled with. She would demand an explanation for his sudden disappearance without a word. She would look irresistible, but she would not succumb to his advances. Not under any circumstances.

Chloe got herself ready, physically and mentally, and at 8:00 p.m. on the dot, the telephone in her room rang: reception said there was somebody waiting for her. Chloe put the finishing touches on her makeup, looked at herself in the mirror, and felt beautiful.

It's true, she said to herself. *There's really nothing like dressing* a la venezolana.

Arriving in the lobby, she saw a man waiting for her, elegantly dressed and smiling, who introduced himself as Luis Barrera. He said he was a friend of Iván's, who'd asked him to come get her. Chloe was disappointed to find that there were other guests, but Luis's pleasant warmth put her immediately at ease. They got in the back of a large navy-blue car with a stocky driver in a black suit and tie.

The car took a highway, left the city, and sped up. *Iván's house is further away than I'd realized,* thought Chloe after a period in which Luis had kept her entertained with questions and stories. In fact, the signs indicated they were headed toward the airport.

Chloe began to worry. Suddenly, the car took an exit and made its way along streets that looked increasingly dark and uninhabited. Luis's friendliness turned to silence and Chloe started to cry silently, trying not to make a sound.

They left the deserted paved road for an even darker dirt track, with no light nor signs of life. Chloe began to panic and started to shout and hit Luis, who restrained her forcefully. The driver stopped, got out, and yanked Chloe onto the ground. Luis shone a small, powerful flashlight into her eyes. He spoke quietly.

"I know you're scared, Chloe. And you're right to be. You don't know what's happening or why. And it's best that way. You should know that we could kill you and no one would ever know. But we're not going to. And we aren't going to hurt you either, so long as you follow my instructions to the letter."

"What do you want from me? Who are you people? Where's Iván?" she asked.

"Now listen, Chloe. Iván doesn't exist, he never existed, and never will. Your life depends on you understanding that completely. You're never to think of him again; you're never going to look for him. And if you ever happen to meet him by chance you won't acknowledge him, let alone speak to him. We would have killed you in order to ensure this, but Iván himself has asked us not to. So it's thanks to him you have the chance to keep living your life."

The color had drained from Chloe's face. Her whole body was shaking.

Luis went on: "If you talk to anybody about Iván or anything related to him or to tonight, you can be sure of two things: the first is that, sooner or later, we'll find out. The second is that you'll soon be dead. We know where you'll be, who your family is, and how to find you. On the other hand, if you erase Iván and all this from your mind and never mention it to anyone, nothing will happen to you. Understand?"

Chloe stopped crying. She said she understood and asked them to take her back to the hotel.

"Actually, we'll be taking you to the airport. We've got clothes for you to change into. You have a seat on the flight leaving in three hours for Madrid, and from there you connect to Amsterdam. Oh, and one other thing. You will never return to Venezuela, or Cuba, for that matter. Got it?"

Chapter 19

Life Surprises

Colonel Ángel Montes was the first person to notice the limp afflicting his friend Hugo.

"My knee's hurting, that's all," Hugo said when Ángel asked him. "Not a big deal, just my knee."

But those who had been close to him all along, like Ángel, knew there was more to it. On several occasions, he'd seen Hugo unexpectedly doubling up in pain, or needing support to stop himself from falling. Sometimes important engagements had to be canceled because the president was unable to stand. Hugo had, from time to time, gone into what those around him called "the black hole," entire days when he wouldn't see anyone or do anything. He would spend hours alone, chain-smoking in the dark. With the help of Cuban doctors he would always get out of it and quickly recover his energy. But lately both the pain and the "black holes" had been becoming more frequent. And more persistent.

One day, Hugo felt the need to visit Sabaneta, the village on the plains where he'd spent his early years. The trip was discreet, and he was accompanied only by his security personnel, his Cuban doctor, and his friend Ángel. Sitting with Ángel in the shade of a tree, surrounded by the infinite Venezuelan plains, he talked at length. The silences that punctuated the conversation seemed as important as the words spoken.

"I've got a lot still to do, my dear Ángel, a lot . . . ," Hugo said, talking more to himself than to his companion.

Ángel was quiet for a couple of minutes, then said: "But I don't think you can do it till you've seen a good doctor and found out what the hell is going on."

"I feel fine," he answered. "Never better. There's nothing wrong. Let's go back to Caracas, now. I've got a lot to do . . ."

A few weeks later, during a trip to Cuba, Ángel insisted that his obstinate friend undergo a thorough medical examination. Fidel received the medical report even before the patient himself had seen it, and the Cuban patriarch called an urgent meeting of his senior advisers, including his brother Raúl and Raimundo Gálvez.

Fidel told the group he had assembled, "We must ensure the continuity of the special relationship between Cuba and Venezuela in the event of losing Hugo in the near future. We can't afford a government in Caracas that's not friendly to us."

"I'm not going to stop thinking about the future of our revolution," Hugo said to Ángel one evening, eyes fixed on the sea from his Havana balcony. He was lost in a daydream of his ideal country: public services that are efficient and free, old age protected, childhood cared for, abundance and happiness, everything red, from the clothes to the murals showing a thirty-foot president surrounded by children of all races who adore him. Hugo was pulled out of the communist reverie by Fidel Castro himself; the patriarch had arrived to break the news to him personally.

"You've got an exceptionally aggressive cancer."

As Fidel advised him to undergo an urgent intervention, Hugo collapsed and wept.

"I made a fundamental mistake. I was so busy with our project that I forgot to take care of my health. It's my fault."

Ángel watched, stunned into silence by the news.

"What will happen to my revolution?" Hugo asked, between sobs of rage, devastation, and helplessness. Bit by bit he gathered himself again and said to Fidel: "I'm ready to die. But to die *while killing my enemies.*"

Since news of the illness could unleash premature struggles over succession, or an attack by the opposition, they considered carefully what steps should be taken. They decided that nobody could know what kind of cancer Hugo had, which surgical procedures would take place, and what their results would be. Fidel offered advice of a philosophical bent: worry about living one day at a time.

But soon the illness became impossible to hide, and a public announcement could no longer be avoided. Hugo returned to Caracas and told the country, on television, about his illness, without revealing how serious the prognosis was. He appeared optimistic, even energetic.

"I will soon be returning to Cuba to undergo an operation. I am going hand in hand with Christ," he said, his voice strong.

As Fidel predicted, the announcement sent the government—civilian and military—into a frenzy to prepare for a "post-Chávez" scenario. The weakened opposition came together too; the president's announcement was a ray of hope for them.

The Latin American countries that were Chávez's allies reacted with concerned solidarity. The presidents of Nicaragua, Bolivia, and Argentina offered an official expression of their regret and sent good wishes and support for the Venezuelan revolution. Brazil's president, Lula da Silva, offered care in a modern hospital in São Paulo. Hugo thanked him for his generosity but wanted to be treated in Havana. In private, suffering from unbearable pain that had moved to his groin, and filled with dread, Hugo felt himself falling into the blackest hole of all.

The day before his return trip to Havana to continue with his treatment, Hugo called Ángel to Miraflores Palace. Ángel, the person who knew him best, only needed to look at him to see the extent of his illness.

It was clear Hugo would die soon, though neither of them said it.

There was something distracting Hugo, irritating him.

"You see those flies, Ángel? They've been after me for ages! You'd think they could smell the death on me!" Hugo said, batting at something Ángel couldn't see. "And I, who dreamed about overseeing the transformation of this country, watching it brought to completion, I'm going to have to leave the stage . . . so young. With so many things still outstanding."

"That doesn't matter, Hugo." Ángel finally spoke, delicately. "Forget about the future of the revolution. You're leaving an impressive legacy, and the revolution will take care of itself. Concentrate on your health. That's what's important!"

"I'm going to keep fighting, Ángel. This will be the toughest battle of any I've fought. Don't leave me on my own, brother. I need you now more than ever. Help me with this final stretch."

They held their goodbye hug for a long moment.

As Ángel left the study, grief-stricken memories of a lifetime shared flooded him, along with tears. Hugo and Ángel throwing baseballs in Barinas, trying for the Caracas minor leagues, then as cadets carrying out their first military maneuvers. Hugo and Ángel marching, chanting: "Oligarchs quake with fear! Freedom is here!" Discussing political ideas with other colonels around a bonfire, surrounded by young NCOs and soldiers, the country's future liberators. Hugo and Ángel planning the coup, and on the day of Operation Zamora, taking the first step in their Bolivarian Revolution.

In the solitude of his study, Hugo crumbled, defeated, into an armchair. Hugo Chávez felt betrayed by life. Death had been allowed to gain the advantage.

◆　◆　◆

They were in a hotel on the outskirts of the capital, lying on an elegant king-size bed, covered in sweat, their legs entwined. There was a large picture window with a panoramic view of the mountains around the Caracas valley, but the lovers were totally entranced. Not by each other, or by the beauty of the mountains. They were watching TV.

"I will soon be returning to Cuba to undergo an operation. I am going hand in hand with Christ," a serene, serious President Chávez told his people.

Mauricio was surprised. Even he hadn't heard the news about Hugo's health. Eva couldn't disguise her surprise either.

"Do you think it's serious?" she asked her—what, boyfriend? Lover?

"Not at all. The guy's a rock," he replied.

Eva tried to focus, but she couldn't. She'd learned that trying to ignore her attraction to Mauricio was a losing battle. She'd already decided to let herself get carried away by the current of love, forget about Hugo and the rest, and embrace this man as best she could. The bouquets of roses he'd been sending to her yoga studio contributed to her fantasy of a genuine, pure romance, which could lead them to a happy ending. Eva knew this dream couldn't possibly materialize, but she nonetheless dove in and was enjoying it deeply. In order to do this, she had to disable the alerts her profession required her to keep constantly switched on. Mauricio was a vacation Eva needed and deserved.

There was a kind of simplicity and freedom to this man that Eva found extremely attractive. She wanted a relationship with no problems and no suspicions. Mauricio was all this, and a lover more comfortable and skilled than any she'd had before.

Sometimes, however, she got worried. Especially when Mauricio's eyes hardened in a way that scared her. She didn't know how to read it. What, Eva wondered, could he be thinking in those moments? It didn't happen often, and he usually noticed her response immediately and wiped it away, coming closer to kiss her. Neither Mauricio nor Eva wanted their relationship to become complicated. Both took refuge in the oasis of sincerity and transparency into which they felt the other had invited them.

After the announcement of the president's illness, Mauricio was summoned urgently to Havana, but he told Eva he had to go to Panama. To his relief, she believed him.

Eva's task was clear. She had to maneuver her agents in the government more boldly now. Whatever it took, she needed to get the medical information and the plans being prepared in the event of the president becoming incapacitated. Eva knew she couldn't risk allowing Hugo's successor to be named without her knowledge. And more than this, she had to do everything possible to influence that decision. This might be her last opportunity to restore her professional prestige and jump-start her career in Washington.

With all this in mind, Eva took her leave of Mauricio with a long kiss, smiles masking their true thoughts.

G2 and the CIA weren't the only organizations preparing for the end of Hugo.

In Gonzalo Girón's mansion, five army generals, two from the Air Force, two admirals, plus three generals from the National Guard met discreetly. In civilian clothes and without bodyguards, the soldiers had their intense, chaotic conversation interrupted by their host's cell phone.

"He's here."

Prán walked in, accompanied by an impeccably dressed Willy García. Everyone stood to greet Prán, but he just looked over his team and sat in the best chair in the room, which had previously been occupied by Girón. Willy sat to his right and Girón went to get more chairs like a hasty porter.

Prán remained worryingly silent for several seconds, long enough for the soldiers to feel uncomfortable, unnerved, and unsafe. Time and silences were tools Prán had mastered. It was another way of showing who was in charge.

"Friends," he started at last. "Thank you all for coming, and especially to General Girón for his hospitality. It's time to talk about why we're all here."

The other men in the room relaxed a bit.

"Soon we will be gambling for the country's future. And our own," he said, his voice quiet but clear. His tone left no room for doubt; his voice was the indisputable authority. He gave Willy García the floor.

"The time has come to prepare for the imminent disappearance of the president. Fortunately, we're well placed to take full advantage of the vacancies his death will certainly produce. We'll emerge even stronger from the changes. We'll be relying on the impressive network of friends and associates we've built within the national armed forces. A network of which you are the absolute summit."

"Yes. But that's not all," Prán said, interrupting him. "The most important message for today is this: I recently learned that G2 has dossiers on each of you, and your closest associates both within the armed forces and outside them, within the country and outside it. Their goal is to extort or eliminate any of you who don't obey orders or who interfere in Cuba's actions in Venezuela. G2 has even considered sending information about you to the US DEA. There are hard, dangerous, uncertain times ahead, which will affect all of us in this room today."

The officers were overwhelmed by fear, just as Prán had expected.

"I gathered you here to tell you this, and something even more important. I'm a bigger danger to you than Cuba," said the mollusk, making piercing eye contact with each man present, one at a time. "We're entering a period in which betrayals, cheating, and denunciations will happen every day. You'll find yourselves under immense pressure to betray me. And anybody who does, dies. The only people who will survive will be those who keep the loyalty of their people. And I know how to ensure that, and how to repay it. I also know how to detect disloyalty, informants, and traitors."

Another minute of unbearable silence began, and the officers shifted uncomfortably in their seats, fidgeted, and clenched their teeth.

"Be aware that what a man like me does to those who are disloyal is not just done to them but to their families, and anyone they love," Prán warned them, speaking slowly, with a deliberate coldness in his voice. "But I also know how to reward loyalty generously. That's how I've survived. The Cubans can keep control in Cuba. I'm the one who controls things here. Never forget that." Everyone in the room held their breath. The warning hung heavy in the room: loyalty to Prán, or death.

Chapter 20

Cancer in Havana

The freeway was a red artery pulsing with revolutionary slogans. Thousands of Chavistas in red berets, with flags and placards, came to show their love for the president as he left to attend to his health in Havana. Many wept at the sight of their leader. They knew that it could be the last time they would see him. From a jeep, the president greeted his people, pounding his left fist into his right palm to signify a fight, against everyone, against everything. And, of course, against his illness. Nobody knew for sure, but rumors were that it was cancer.

He boarded the plane accompanied by his older daughters, who since the diagnosis had never left his side, and a small group of ministers closest to him. Hugo watched the Venezuelan coast recede into the distance, and his eyes filled with tears. He sensed that he wouldn't emerge victorious from this battle. The wide presidential seat suddenly felt like a straitjacket, and he had neither the spirit nor the strength to free himself from these bonds. He held still, a prisoner, looking out the airplane window. Everything was black. Not a single star to be seen.

The meeting with Fidel was brief and emotional.

"You couldn't be in better hands anywhere in the world."

Hugo nodded.

While Hugo headed to the hospital, Fidel invited Nicolás Maduro to a "very private" meeting. Maduro was one of the ministers closest to the Venezuelan president, and Fidel already knew him well. Mauricio had been building a file on Maduro for years, and Fidel was extremely well informed. Maduro wasn't particularly intelligent, but he was loyal, one of his men—the essential qualities for the man he needed in Venezuela once Hugo was gone.

Maduro was struck by the situation and the caudillo's serious tone. The living icon of the Cuban Revolution looked troubled. And Maduro, in turn, looked awed.

"We're approaching the moment you've been preparing for all these years," Fidel told him. "You've come a long way since your days as a student activist in Caracas. Congratulations, brother. But never forget *it was long before the rise of Hugo*, and it was here in Cuba, in our cadre schools, where *we* made you a true international revolutionary."

Nicolás, afraid of saying something stupid, stayed silent. The caudillo went on.

"The moment is approaching for you to serve the revolution. When Hugo dies, it's *essential for Cuba* that you, comrade Nicolás Maduro, be the man to replace him."

The future president of Venezuela, as anointed by Fidel, smiled yet said nothing; both men knew he had nothing to say. And there was no need. Fidel stood, took his leave with a hug—which he'd never done before—and Nicolás left the room with the idea of power planted in him.

A few weeks later, Hugo made a TV appearance from "this dear, heroic Havana," in which he told his country that the doctors had found a growth in his pelvis that required emergency surgery. After the successful surgery they had begun an intensive treatment, but detailed examinations confirmed a malignant tumor, requiring another surgery.

"I'm making great progress," Hugo said with contagious enthusiasm. "I'm undergoing treatment to fight those cells and to continue on the path to a full recovery. In the meantime, I have been—and continue to be—in control of all my government's actions."

Before saying goodbye to his Venezuelan brothers and sisters, the president expressed his gratitude for the many demonstrations of solidarity he'd received from his Venezuelan people and from Cuba, especially "from Fidel, Raúl, and the whole medical legion who put themselves on the front line of this battle in a way that has been truly glorious."

◆ ◆ ◆

"Eva! So good to hear your voice. Did you see my last email?"

Eva froze. She clutched the telephone nervously and with both genuine and feigned delight.

"Mónica! Yes! Sorry I haven't had a chance to answer. You're coming to Caracas? When? Will I get to see you?"

"I'm actually on my way to the airport now—that's why I called so early. Hope I didn't wake you!"

"No, no, just sitting with my morning tea." Eva clutched the warm cup in her hand.

"I'll be in Caracas for three days, on work, but I really want to see you. How about tonight? The usual restaurant."

Eva wanted to invent some prior commitment, but she just couldn't do it. "Wonderful! See you there!" she said instead.

For the rest of the day, she struggled to focus on her work. Should she tell her about Mauricio, or not? Was Mónica planning to see him? Could Eva hide it even if she wanted to?

Eva poured herself a glass of water and sat back down at her desk. She had a more urgent matter to worry about. The only thing occupying her life these days: Hugo, his illness, and what would happen when he was gone.

Although her instincts told her there was something happening at CIA headquarters, she hadn't made any changes to her intelligence operations or stopped sending her bosses reports. She didn't know that Watson and a team of specialists analyzed everything she reported as "disinformation," trying to detect the purpose behind each message—an old spy trick to try to get information about the enemy by extracting it from the disinformation they're spreading.

No sooner had the president made the news of his illness public than Eva focused on compiling a detailed report on Nicolás Maduro, who, she assumed, would be his successor. The report also considered the options that would open up for Fidel Castro and Cuba with Hugo Chávez's death. In the silence of her secret office, Eva wrote:

> Nicolás Maduro isn't a soldier, nor did he complete his studies. He's famous for his limited ability to speak in public. His blunders in speaking have earned him the nickname *Bobolongo*.
>
> Despite this, Maduro has come far since his work as an ultraleftist activist in the eighties, during which time he lived in Cuba. His relationship with the island long predates Chávez's appearance. He took political education courses there and probably also received training in urban guerrilla fighting and explosives. He became close to Chávez thanks to his wife, Cilia, who was among the lawyers defending the soldiers imprisoned after the failed coup.

She attached several photos to the report. One, a photo of a group of young people who'd completed the course at the Che Guevara School of Revolutionary Cadres thirty years ago, showed him posing with Fidel Castro. Eva added an arrow pointing to Nicolás Maduro. There was also a photo of him with a Molotov cocktail in a square near Central University in Caracas, and others, from years later, in which he was taking part in family celebrations, in the company of Cilia. In one of the pictures he could be seen participating in a strange, rather macabre ceremony from the Indian religious sect to which they still belonged.

> Our information suggests that Maduro was recruited by the Cuban spy services a long time ago. In the twelve years of the Chávez government, Nicolás Maduro has been rising rapidly through government positions in the team closest to Chávez, thanks to his loyalty and, more importantly, thanks to the influence of the Cubans.

What Eva didn't know was that the most important pictures would be not those of his past, but those of his present. Her colleagues in Langley had been going over a series of high-resolution photographs taken by one of their spy satellites. They showed Fidel Castro himself talking to Nicolás Maduro in a secluded corner of his garden. In the last photo, the two men were hugging.

That night, after her class, Eva went to meet Mónica. It was as if no time had passed.

"Technically I'm here to do a report on the paramilitary groups for CNN. But between us, I'm still investigating if they killed my father." Mónica changed subjects quickly. "And how are things for you? Your health? The job? Affairs of the heart?" Mónica asked.

"Everything's more or less the same . . . ," Eva replied. "Except I met someone."

"That's wonderful! Who is he?" Mónica asked, genuinely pleased.

"Well, let's see where it goes. I'll tell you more when things have settled a bit." Eva blushed, more from guilt than embarrassment.

"Fair enough. But at some point, I want details!" Mónica winked, conspiratorially. She was used to Eva's reluctance to talk about her intimate life. "Well then, I'll go first. I love Atlanta. The Southern vibe and great food. I do want to hit the road and see a few fabulous places before I knuckle down to my studies at Emory."

"How exciting, Mónica! I'm glad you're so motivated. Seems like I just putter along."

"Well, Eva, you may be getting into something more exciting. We'll see!"

They clinked glasses.

"Here's to excitement," she toasted, "and may our next encounter be soon."

Adalberto Santamaría was supposed to kill his boss. That was the order he'd received during a brief visit to Havana. Adalberto was the second most senior G2 man in Venezuela, reporting directly to Mauricio. But now he was supposed to get rid of him.

"Mauricio must be eliminated. Do it. No questions. I trust you," Raimundo Gálvez, his boss's boss, had ordered.

During the years they'd spent together in Venezuela, Adalberto's resentment of Mauricio had been building. He envied Mauricio's privilege as a member of Cuba's governing elite. The dislike was mutual. Mauricio thought Adalberto was incompetent, and possibly disloyal. Both men did what they could to disguise their antipathy toward each other. Yet Adalberto didn't want to kill his boss and couldn't fathom why he had been ordered to. And not knowing was tormenting him.

Gálvez had been specific: act alone, and do it immediately. So Adalberto arranged an urgent meeting at their most secure safe house—one that only the two men knew of.

"I have some important information about what the army is planning when Hugo dies. We need to act," he told Mauricio.

Nervous, Santamaría arrived several hours early. Once there, he opened a bottle of vodka, trying to gather the courage to kill him. By the time Mauricio arrived, Adalberto was drunk. He was sitting in a chair, and when Mauricio walked in he launched into an incoherent diatribe against "the traitors to the revolution that gave us everything." Then he lunged clumsily at Mauricio.

Mauricio immediately deflected the attack, and in doing so he saw the knife clutched in Adalberto's hand. He grabbed the cord of a nearby phone, wound it around Adalberto's neck, and held it there until he'd almost passed out. Then he loosened it and demanded to know what was going on. Adalberto begged for his life, and Mauricio tightened the cord again. Finally, Adalberto confessed that he had been ordered by Gálvez to kill him. The admission seemed to inspire him to try to complete his mission. "You dirty traitor" he spat out and, with a renewed energy, raised his hand to try to plunge the knife into Mauricio's neck.

Mauricio tightened the cable one final time, and waited. Leaving Santamaría's body lying on the floor, he fled the house, no longer Cuba's top spy but a fugitive from G2's long arm of execution.

Why did they want him dead? He'd carried out his mission in Caracas scrupulously, with great success, and he hadn't violated any rules. What did G2 know, or think it knew, that he didn't?

Back in his house Mauricio stripped off his Italian suit and changed into blue jeans and a black T-shirt, with a light jacket hiding the handgun tucked into his waistband. He switched his luxury car for a motorcycle and, blending in with all the other motorcyclists, he raced through the clogged Caracas streets. He decided to turn to the only person he trusted: Eva.

Lost in the vertiginous feeling of his death sentence, Mauricio parked near LUNA. He assessed his surroundings, half expecting that G2's agents were already waiting for him there. Sure enough, he spotted three separate men, all hidden, and all watching the yoga studio. But they weren't G2 at all. He recognized one as a G2-identified CIA agent. Mauricio's alarm turned into confusion. What interest could the CIA have in LUNA? Were they after him too?

He had to act at once, and without attracting attention. Leaving the motorcycle on the street, he went into the restaurant next door to LUNA and headed straight for the bathroom. He broke a window and climbed out onto the roof. From there he jumped onto LUNA's back balcony and slipped into the hallway. Within moments he'd found her.

"What the hell, Mauricio? Why are you dressed like that? What's happening?"

"Eva, you're in terrible danger, right now. Please, trust me. Let's go!" Eva grabbed his hand, and they raced up to the balcony in the back, climbed to the roof, and then jumped to the restaurant roof next door. They dropped down into the restaurant's garden and raced out onto the street where Mauricio had left his bike. Eva didn't know why she trusted him, but she did.

"Quick, this way!" Mauricio pulled her toward the motorbike.

Eva looked down the street and was shocked to see two CIA colleagues she had not known were in Caracas, who were part of the unit used to kill enemy agents when that became necessary. Why were they there? Was she the target? And if so, how had Mauricio known?

Mauricio pushed her toward the waiting bike. They had a little lead on their attackers, but not much.

Even as they ran, they had the same questions ringing in their heads:

Why do people want to kill me?

Who is this person I'm in love with?
Why are they also running away with me?

◆ ◆ ◆

Mauricio took them to Luz Amelia's house in the barrio. Long ago, Mauricio had chosen this place as a refuge in case of another coup against the Chávez government. Luz Amelia owed her modest home to him, and he knew she would always offer him protection.

Some years ago, impressed by Luz Amelia's commitment and moved by her tragedy, Mauricio had used his influence to get her one of the homes built by the government for the victims of the disaster. It wasn't the house of her dreams. The barrio quickly became a kind of hell, plagued by drugs, rapes, thefts, hit men, and gunfights between gangs. It was the center of operation for gangs of kidnappers, and one of the main gathering places for paramilitary groups armed and financed by the government, the subject Mónica Parker had come to investigate.

If there was any kind of order here, it was imposed by Prán's organization; he was the barrio's real master. In that impregnable territory, he held absolute power, enforced the unwritten laws, and was the all-seeing ruler of this underworld. And like any good manager, he didn't deal with it directly. Others did it for him.

In this case, Lina, *Bala Loca*. Small and extremely dangerous, she was known for having young lovers who disappeared suddenly after a few months. She controlled the drug trafficking and received a percentage of each ransom paid for kidnappings coordinated from within this barrio. She had a long, striking mane of hair, dyed red. She only obeyed orders from Prán, and did so unquestioningly and unconditionally.

Some years back, rumor had it, Lina had tried to betray Prán. No one knew exactly what had happened, but one day she disappeared. Months later she returned, converted into a disciplined, loyal, efficient executive for the criminal network headquartered in *La Cueva*. And though she never spoke of it, it was clear Lina lived in terror of Prán's disfavor. Once, in a liquor-soaked conversation, Lina said: "Death is better than being one of Prán's enemies." Maybe that's why Prán had no known—or living—enemies.

As Eva and Mauricio, drained and nervous, ate the cheese arepas Luz Amelia had made for them, Lina showed up. Nothing happened in the barrio without her knowing. She knew Mauricio, at least superficially. She thought he was a Dominican businessman who was supportive of the revolution and who'd made generous contributions to her barrio's collectives: money, motorbikes, guns. Lina watched them with curiosity and mistrust.

"Well. I'll let you stay in my barrio, for now. And I'll offer you some . . . protection. It's dangerous here, so I'll have a couple of compañeros keep an eye on you. Just so nothing happens to you. I'll come another time and we'll have a drink and you'll tell me why you're here. You're on the run, and I'm sure it's not nuns who're after you. But we'll talk about that later, okay?"

Mauricio agreed with a forced smile. Lina stood, gave him a kiss on the cheek, and left, ignoring Eva.

Luz Amelia gave them her bedroom, saying she would sleep in her son's room. The three of them sat in the kitchen in silence, the TV blaring. Luz Amelia switched channels every few seconds, not letting any program capture her attention, but suddenly she stopped on CNN. Mauricio and Eva jerked to attention when they heard a familiar voice. Broadcasting live from that very barrio was none other than Mónica Parker. She was calling it a refuge for paramilitary collectives created and financed by the government, while the camera panned across the steep hillsides.

"Stupid bitch!" Luz Amelia shouted at the TV, and stormed out of the house, leaving Mauricio and Eva there, stunned, watching the report. Minutes later, Luz Amelia's wild face appeared on screen.

"Now you're in for it, you whore, traitor, *escuálida*! Shut up, shut up! You'll get what's coming to you!"

Horrified, Eva and Mauricio watched as Mónica dropped her microphone and pulled out her father's revolver. The women stared at each other for a long moment, deadly defiant. Both were shaking. Luz Amelia, trained for confrontations, lunged for Mónica's gun, and they struggled before the terrified audience.

Then a gunshot echoed, and the women fell on top of each other. Luz Amelia pulled herself up and raced away, plunging into the labyrinth of her barrio.

The last thing Eva and Mauricio saw before the camera cut away was Mónica on the ground in a pool of her own blood. Dead.

Eva screamed and jumped out of her chair. Mauricio continued staring at the blank screen, as if in shock. Alone in the house of Mónica's murderer, they held each other silently for a long time. They were both utterly devastated. Neither one of them wanted to talk about Mónica. Or anything else. They were afraid of beginning the conversation about who they were and what they were running from. Mauricio thought about Mónica, whom he'd loved and whom he'd abandoned for the revolution. He was overwhelmed with the sense that he could not allow another person to be hurt by him in the name of his cause.

To hell with the revolution, he said to himself. *Keeping Eva safe is all that matters now.*

He knew he had put her in the line of fire just by being close to her. And he knew that, in order to survive, he had to disappear, erase himself from the map. His former colleagues would do everything possible to carry out the death sentence issued by Havana. Who knows, it might even be Lina who would fire that final bullet.

But why did they want to kill him? The more he tried to answer that question, the more confused he became. Mauricio couldn't make sense of it. There was some missing piece of information. The only thing he knew for sure was that the attack on Eva was his fault. The CIA must have identified him, followed him, and discovered his relationship with her. They were going to kidnap her to use her as bait. Maybe Adalberto Santamaría had been turned by the CIA and was lying about the order to kill him coming from G2. But then why would they kidnap Eva? No, it still didn't make sense.

Mauricio's thoughts jumped around frantically between the past—why he was sent to Caracas all those years ago—and the present—why G2 wanted to kill him. And amid it all, there was the miracle of having discovered that he was capable of having feelings first for Mónica, and now, even more intensely, for Eva. In the course of his mission, Mauricio's feelings had evolved in other ways too. He knew he was a man who had benefited from the Cuban Revolution, and he had spent his career in defense of that revolution. But the more he saw the effects of Cuba's intervention in Venezuela, the more ambivalent he'd become. And now the revolution had condemned him. At this point, all he really wanted was freedom and peace, and a life alongside Eva. But how could that ever be possible?

After the long silence, Mauricio stood up and began pacing.

"I'm going to make arrangements for you to be taken somewhere safe," he said.

Eva flatly refused.

"No, I'm not leaving, Mauricio. I want to be with you, and I don't care what happens."

Eva, accustomed to being suspicious, had gone into a kind of tailspin of her own since the escape. All she knew was that her lover, a Dominican fashion wholesaler, had rescued her from a CIA ambush. It wasn't exactly typical for a businessman. And his familiarity with one of the most dangerous barrios in the city suggested he was much more than a salesman. But what? She recalled her earlier look at his file. His slightly too-perfect record. She began to have a terrible suspicion. One that could change everything, threaten everything she'd been working for, everything she could hope to accomplish in the future.

Mauricio took Eva's words as the pledge of a woman in love. Overwhelmed, suddenly, by the rush of love he felt for her, he took her face in his hands and kissed her. "I love you, Eva. You mean the world to me."

She closed her eyes, unable to answer.

Some time later, Eva was stretched out on the bed pretending to sleep while Mauricio watched her. He imagined a normal life beside her. Was it really so out of reach? Everything was so complex, so dark. What if he just pulled back the curtain? The spy decided that the only option he had left was to be honest. He had to put all his cards on the table and let Eva decide what to do with them.

As day broke, he prepared himself; for the first time he was going to tell *the truth*.

"Eva, Eva . . ."

No answer.

"Eva, wake up."

Still no answer.

"Eva, my name isn't Mauricio Bosco. I'm Iván Rincón . . ."

Nothing.

"And I'm not Dominican, I'm Cuban. I work for my government . . ."

The woman beside him sat up in a daze and shivered. She looked at him. Was she dreaming?

Mauricio—that is, Iván—tried to touch her. She recoiled as instinctively as a mimosa, that sensitive plant that closes to defend itself against predators. But she felt a confused kind of nervous relief. This started to explain things.

"I'm so sorry I couldn't tell you. I wanted to, believe me. And I shouldn't be telling you now. I'm sorry I got you into this mess. I've been leading Cuban operations in Caracas for years, but something changed. I don't know what. They ordered my elimination, and I managed to escape, but I didn't know where to go, or who to trust. You were all I could think of." He waited for Eva to emerge from the shell in which she had shut herself. "I love you, Eva. That's why I'm here. I love you and I couldn't lie to you anymore."

Eva asked just one question. "You're the head of Cuban espionage in Venezuela?"

"Yes."

She stared at him. Nobody had ever looked at him like that before. It wasn't just a look, it was a laser shooting from her eyes. She said nothing. Her mind was racing. Iván might already know who she really was. Maybe he was preparing to act. What if he tried to kill her? What if she had to kill him? But for the moment, time had stopped. They fell into two separate silences, heavy with questions, confessions, and fears.

Eva was tempted to level with her nemesis, but caution hadn't left her entirely. She said nothing. Iván, meanwhile, had nothing left to lose.

"I'm at a dead end, Eva. I'm guessing there's some plot against me . . . I'm no saint, and I know I've got enemies in G2, but it looks like my time has come. They ordered me killed!"

Eva hid her panic. She remembered everything she'd read about him over the years in the detailed archives she'd compiled on the skillful, elusive Cuban spy. The CIA had spent years trying to identify him and eliminate him. And he'd always eluded them. She remembered her own mixture of hatred and admiration. She always came to the same conclusion: "He's an exceptional agent. We have to get rid of him."

Now he was right there, in front of her. Eva could probably kill him here and now if she wanted to. She could break the glass of water he'd gotten for her and plunge it into his neck. It would take a matter of seconds. But . . . he seemed sincere. Was he? Or was this a trap? Did he truly love her, or was he manipulating her? And if he was, what were the Cubans after? If they wanted information, why not just kidnap her and attain it through violence and intimidation? Were they going to try to turn her? And did Langley somehow already know that he was the lead G2 agent in Venezuela? That would explain why the CIA was after her now. She hadn't reported their relationship; if they knew about the relationship, maybe they thought she was working with him.

She didn't know what to do. In a moment, her entire life had been turned upside down. Her career was over, and her life was likely under threat. The only thing she knew for sure was that she did love this man. Not the Cuban spy, the man she was under orders to kill, but Mauricio. There must be a lot of one in the other. She was confused, and without thinking about it, she hugged him with a tenderness she'd never felt for a man before.

She still didn't know whether to believe him. All she knew was that she desperately needed to embrace him. That moment was all there was. With no more certainty than the heat of their bodies, they surrendered themselves to each other.

Chapter 21

To Die Killing

According to the confidential report prepared for Fidel by an international team of surgeons, the first surgeries in Havana had been a failure. Fidel had already begun planning his next steps. He knew what was at stake was not only his friend Hugo's life but his own historical legacy.

To the relief of the expectant public, a minister appeared on television to announce that the surgery had been a success. The president was in good physical condition and recovering rapidly. He said that the tumor was only a recurrence of the cancer, not new growth, and that Chávez would start a second round of chemotherapy. Even so, he would continue devoting all his energy to the future of Venezuela and the well-being of the poor.

One morning, his head shaved and his body swollen from the treatment, a hopeful president appeared on every TV screen. Full of joy and energy, Hugo announced that his body was cancer-free.

In the next broadcast he wore an indigenous headdress, listening with eyes closed to the prayers of a Yanomami shaman in the Venezuelan Amazon. The shaman, crouching, blew healing incense over the president. Other indigenous people watched respectfully, surrounded by soldiers, reporters, and the usual presidential delegation: a few of the president's relatives and his closest allies, including, of course, minister Nicolás Maduro and his wife, Cilia.

A number of signs appeared in the background: **COMMANDER PRESIDENT, GIVE YOUR ORDERS!** At the end of this sacred ceremony, amid the trilling of birds and crickets, Hugo announced that he had won his battle against cancer and was ready to win another battle for the presidency. Hugo was selected as his party's candidate for the presidential elections scheduled for the end of the year.

"Chávez is going to be around for a while!" he shouted. And millions of his followers were ecstatic.

◆ ◆ ◆

Sitting in a car decked out for the electoral tour, Hugo couldn't stop his body from convulsing. The pain made him writhe. Nicolás Maduro, Cilia, and Ángel Montes tried to persuade him to cancel the event.

"The people will understand," Ángel said.

"Don't worry, Mr. President, Nicolás could give the speech for you," Cilia added, receiving a withering glare from Hugo in response.

Barely audible, he commanded the Cuban doctor who was always with him to administer a powerful painkiller.

"That's an order!" he shouted with the little breath he had left.

Throngs of supporters wearing red T-shirts and holding placards crowded the square in the center of San Fernando de Apure, where their beloved leader was about to speak to them. The music was loud, people were dancing, and free rum and beer were flowing. For all the world, it looked like a party. Hugo, enlivened by the medication, climbed to the podium on his campaign float, which was specially designed to make it look as if he were standing, though it supported the weight of his body for him. He set off toward the rally. The float moved slowly through the streets, and there was nothing to suggest that he had one foot in the grave.

Seeing him, his followers understood the words he'd said a few months before: "I'm not the horse I used to be; I'm like a buffalo now."

But his very presence was a miracle, and his followers believed him when he accused the opposition of practicing witchcraft to prevent him from campaigning. He had to limit himself to appearing on radio and TV, and at a few huge gatherings in the main cities, while his young rival went to every corner of the country: walking, running, on a bicycle, on a motorcycle, on a tractor. A race between a buffalo and a hare. But it wasn't always the fastest runner who got to the finish line first.

And of course, he used his illness as a campaign tool. Why not? It was another resource his rival didn't have! At a Mass held for his health, standing with an open Bible and looking at Jesus of Nazareth hanging over the altar, Hugo had a genuine emotional moment of faintness.

With beads of sweat on his brow, his eyes filling with tears, and his voice cracking, he begged before Christ, and the TV cameras: "Give me your crown, Christ. Give it to me so I may bleed, give me your cross, a hundred crosses, and I will carry them, but give me life! Even if it's fiery, a life of pain, I don't mind. Don't take me yet, oh Lord, give me your thorns for I'm ready to carry them, but with life, Christ, oh Lord! Amen."

The video went viral, not just in the country but across the Americas. Millions of people were rocked by this moving scene. The other candidate couldn't compete.

The national and international press followed the political contest closely, especially as it accelerated in the final hundred days of the campaign.

Iván and Eva also followed along, sitting intertwined on a small couch in front of the TV in the new safe house that Lina had secured for them. Murdering Mónica live on television had been considered reckless and stupid by the group, and Luz Amelia's fanaticism had been rewarded by her comrades handing her over to the police. The spies had now spent almost two months alone in a shabby one-room house in the barrio, never setting foot outdoors and relying on Lina to leave basic groceries on their doorstep every week. Under normal circumstances the living conditions would have been hard to bear, but after all that had occurred, they found they almost relished the forced confinement, and they were astonished by the ease and comfort with which they settled into living together. Iván discovered a joy and relief in sharing his true thoughts with the woman he loved, and Eva was surprised to discover that his beliefs were closer to her own than she would ever have imagined possible. They both firmly agreed that it was irresponsible for Hugo to run, because however his illness progressed, he was unlikely to be able to complete his constitutional term. They worried together for the future of the Venezuelan people and wished for an end to the corruption and for peace. Mónica's death had shaken them both to their cores. For both of them, it had been the final straw.

"I don't know what to believe anymore," Iván said, turning the TV off. "I've known for as long as I can remember that the revolution was the best—the only—way to help the people. I knew that power and resources shouldn't be concentrated among the ruling capitalist class. I thought that's what we were working toward, not just in Cuba, but here." He returned to the couch and gathered Eva in his arms.

Eva said nothing, putting her hand on his shoulder gently.

"But now . . . it seems like everything we've done has hurt people." He paused. Eva knew he was thinking about Mónica. She had been, too, and wondered how much her government's actions were responsible for the death of her friend, and for the circumstances surrounding them in the barrio.

319

"You were doing what you thought was right," she said comfortingly, finding that she actually believed that to be true. They both had been.

After a long, heavy silence, Eva kissed his cheek brightly, hopped up, and said, "How about some coffee?"

That night, Iván and Eva's refuge came to an end. In an instant, the house was surrounded, and the spies were pulled from their bed, cuffed, and shoved into an armored car with tinted windows.

Speeding through the dark streets, escorted by armed bikers, Eva tried to calm herself. *At least we'll die together,* she thought to herself, holding back her tears. Their imminent death made her feel even closer to him.

When the car stopped, hoods were roughly placed over their heads, and they were forced to walk for several minutes before entering a building. They heard loud music, shouting, metal doors opening and closing. There were strong, unpleasant smells. When they were made to stop, they heard a big electric door opening. Once they had stepped through, the door closed again. The noises and smells were suddenly gone. The murmur of air-conditioning and soft music made the atmosphere feel positively serene in comparison. They were pushed down into chairs, and the hoods were taken off. They were facing Prán.

They'd never seen him before, but they both knew exactly who he was, and what he was capable of doing.

He sat in a comfortable armchair, drinking a glass of rum. His presence gave them a feeling they struggled to identify. Was it hopefulness? It was like being greeted by Satan at the gates of hell. He could be giving them one final chance to save themselves, to play a final hand, which, if they won, would spare them from their fate.

Prán was intrigued by their inexplicable presence in the barrio. His instinct told him these two could give him valuable information. Lina had some fragmentary, confused bits of information about the Dominican clothing wholesaler. But Eva was an enigma to everybody.

"Who are you?" Prán demanded. Eva didn't answer; she was trying to assemble a credible story, to buy time while writing a script that might possibly save them.

There were seconds between life and death.

"Who are you?" Prán asked again.

"Eva López. I own LUNA," she said, deciding to stick with her cover. She saw immediately that he wasn't convinced.

"Who are you running from?" Prán asked.

"I don't know." Eva played dumb.

Iván said nothing.

"Why are you in Venezuela?" Prán demanded.

"Well, my boyfriend was Venezuelan . . . ," Eva began. "We'd always talked about moving here together. After he died, I felt like I needed a new start."

Prán stared at her in angry disbelief.

He asked question after question, and she gave evasive answers that he interpreted as disrespect. In Prán's world, disrespect carried the death penalty.

Finally Prán lost patience. Standing, he gave the quiet order to take them "out for a walk."

They all knew what those words meant. Eva and Iván looked at one another, their only way of saying goodbye. The look in Iván's eyes was one of indescribable sorrow. Eva imagined their bodies in a garbage dump somewhere. Just as Prán was about to leave, Eva mustered all her strategic brilliance.

"Wait, Yusnabi. Listen to me. Your name is Yusnabi Valentín, and I know all about you. And before you kill us, I'll tell you who we are. It'll be worth your time to listen; you've got nothing to lose."

Iván looked at her in shock.

Eva didn't wait for Prán to respond. "My name is Cristina Garza, and I'm a former US Marine. I've been in charge of CIA operations in Venezuela for many years."

The mollusk's eyes widened, giving him an immediate panoramic view. He watched for any sign of deceit, but mostly he was savoring the delicious, spicy dish that destiny seemed to have just served up to him. He sat back down to listen with an incredulous, devilish smile. Surely it was nonsense, but once he'd had a bit of fun he could send them off for their walk.

Iván felt paralyzed and cold. Was it possible that his Eva—the woman he wanted to be his partner in a new and different life—didn't really exist at all? She wasn't Mexican but an American? She wasn't a yoga instructor but a CIA agent? The woman he loved and who said she loved him was evaporating in front of his eyes in this hellhole.

He struggled to process the story she was revealing and make sense of it all. A Cuban agent must have found out that Eva was the head of the CIA mission in Venezuela and convinced the CIA that Eva had been turned and that they needed to neutralize her urgently. This way, the Cuban spy in the Pentagon spared G2 the risky—and so far impossible—task of killing the lead CIA agent in Venezuela. Instead, they got the CIA to attack itself. *A brilliant move,* Iván thought to himself with admiration.

Furthermore, his Cuban colleagues must have discovered his relationship with Eva and thought he had been turned. They would have to get rid of him. Iván was starting to put the puzzle together, but he was still missing some key pieces. And it felt like the pieces kept changing shape.

Nobody moved.

"Alright, Ms. Spy," Prán said doubtfully. "Why should I believe you?"

"I can prove it," Cristina said. "We know that you orchestrated Chávez's first political campaign. We know that you arranged for Willy García to become finance minister, and that he is also the second-in-command in your 'business' operations. We also know that you've recruited high-level military officers to expand your market to Europe. And that you're funding both the Bolivarian militias and the opposition."

She was careful not to reveal any sensitive aspects of her operation. She'd been honest with Prán, but if it came to it, she would die before she put members of her network at risk.

"None of that proves that you're with the CIA." He was looking at her with curiosity, but he didn't believe her. The story wasn't particularly believable. With the bored flippancy that comes from absolute power, the mollusk praised her imagination and, with a weary gesture, waved his men over.

She had one move left, though.

"I wouldn't do that if I were you, Yusnabi," Cristina warned him, her voice strong and sibylline. "Juan Cash wouldn't approve. Ask him yourself if you want. He's in Miami. I'll give you his private number. Tell him you're planning to kill Cristina Garza, and see what he says."

The man who took orders from nobody froze, right there, thin and stiff as a rod. Prán couldn't comprehend how this woman could know so much about him. And about Juan Cash. The uncommon sensation of being shocked knocked him off-balance.

After several long moments, Prán pulled a phone from the back pocket of his Armani pants and put in the number Cristina gave him. Cash took the call at his mansion in Miami. His heart skipped a beat when he heard Prán's voice. Prán didn't have his phone number, let alone this private one. Prán, surprised that the number worked, explained the reason for the call.

Cash listened carefully, then, with a firm, forceful voice, gave an order: "Don't even try it, Prán. If that really is her with you, don't touch a hair on her head. It could be a costly mistake. Don't do it, for God's sake! I'll come to Caracas, and I'll explain everything. But don't do anything to her. Wait for me!"

With heroic effort, Hugo Chávez won the presidential election: he would be in power for another seven years. Beneath the balcony a torrent of people applauded, shouted, and wept.

Miraculously, Cristina's stunt in *La Cueva* had worked. Juan Cash had immediately boarded his private jet to Caracas to come to Cristina's rescue, unaware of course that she had fallen out of favor at the CIA. He persuaded Prán to form an alliance with them.

"These two are a gift from heaven. Use them!" Cash insisted.

Prán gave Willy García a call. "Hello, my friend. Seems we have a couple of spies in hand. What do you think? Is this a good opportunity or a problem?"

"Listen. I think this is golden! Let's get everything we can from them and use it as a battering ram to attack Hugo's fortress."

Cristina and Iván spent long hours telling Prán and García everything they could about the Chávez government: strategies, chains of command, vulnerabilities of the Chavistas and their rivals, strengths and weaknesses of the most important players, their finances, relatives, and lovers. Who was on whose payroll. Who was sleeping with whom. And a whole lot more.

But they all knew that Cristina and Iván needed to get out of the country fast. Prán pulled together the logistics. Their first stop was to be a remote port in the east, where they would board a cargo ship bound for Guinea-Bissau. Both of them understood immediately; they knew about the African route, and they knew that this ship was one of its carriers. Of course, this being Prán's network, the ship wouldn't be taking just them to Africa but also twenty tons of cocaine. From there, the drugs would travel to Europe, where they would be bought and consumed in palaces, nightclubs, business offices, universities, on the streets, and in the most elegant living rooms of the Old World, yielding hundreds of millions of euros.

Weeks later, Cristina and Iván disembarked in a strange Colombian-Venezuelan enclave in a beautiful, deserted cove in Guinea-Bissau. Scores of Prán's Colombian and Venezuelan employees had set up base there to handle his fast-growing business. The time aboard the ship had been another strange interlude in their gradual opening up to each other. Rather than discuss their present-day lives, in which they were supposed to be enemies, they talked about their pasts, revealing the first truths about themselves slowly. Cristina told Iván about crossing the border, about her childhood as an undocumented immigrant. Iván told Cristina about his mother leaving. They found solace in their shared abandonments, their shared vulnerabilities. For those blissful, treacherous weeks, they could pretend that they had fully escaped their previous lives and that the future was theirs.

Over arepas, listening to vallenato and merengue, in a simple but charming house beside a river, Cristina and Iván continued talking until there was nothing more to reveal. Each made the decision to believe the other. They no longer cared about their careers or fighting for their countries. They no longer wanted to give their lives for their governments or sacrifice everything for national defense. They loved each other and wanted a quiet life together. It was as simple, and unlikely, as that.

Chávez appeared before the TV cameras to share his final plans before he returned to Havana to face another battle against his greatest enemy: cancer.

> If by chance it should happen to incapacitate me in some way, my firm opinion, irrevocable and absolute, is that in a scenario in which the constitution requires you to call another presidential election, I ask you to elect Nicolás Maduro as president of the Bolivarian Republic of Venezuela. I ask you this from the bottom of my heart. God knows what He is doing! If I cannot

continue, I will leave you with a young leader with the greatest ability to proceed with a firm hand, with that look in his eyes, the heart of a man of the people, his intelligence, his gift with people, the international recognition he has won for himself, his leadership, at the head of the presidency of the republic, leading— alongside the people, always, and subordinate to the interests of the people—the destiny of this *patria*.

I've always lived from one miracle to the next. And since I have held fast to Christ for so long, with God's favor we will, as on previous occasions, keep going. I have absolute faith.

The president's speech lasted exactly thirty-seven minutes; those live broadcasts lasting many hours were a thing of the past.

Even as they tried to live in the present, Cristina and Iván had watched the broadcast together, and they both knew that the death of this person whose life had driven theirs for so many years was imminent.

"I can't believe this is all falling apart. We had such a great opportunity to add Venezuela, a big rich country, to our Cuban world."

"My love, I have a feeling that this Cuba-in-Venezuela story is not over yet. Your clever compatriots have wrapped their fingers around that idiot Maduro."

"I guess all our favorite players—the Yankees, Russians, Cubans, the oil barons, the drug cartels, and everyone else—will be stuck in this world-class telenovela for a while. Let's go take a walk."

It was the first time either of them had broached the subject, and in some ways it was the end of their suspension of reality.

As they walked along the beautiful river, Cristina turned toward Iván and started the long "what next?" talk. Their governments wouldn't stop chasing them; they were too valuable as assets, knew too much, to be left alone. What could they do to keep their enemies at bay? Where would they live, and what would they do to shore up their protections? The air filled with questions. They stopped for a lingering, deep kiss.

"Hugo . . . Hugo is leaving us," Fidel said to Raúl and Gálvez. "Fortunately, he's leaving a vast, positive legacy for his country and for ours. For all the Americas. But we can't take risks with Venezuela. Hugo's death must be handled so there's only Nicolás and ourselves. We must control this transition carefully. Which means we control when it begins. That's what we'll decide here."

He tried to stand up, laboriously. His butler appeared from nowhere to help him to his feet.

"Since we already have Nicolás in place, I've decided Hugo shouldn't die in Cuba." With a strange look on his face, he concluded, "He is only going to *start* dying here . . ."

Nicolás Maduro, the vice president and designated successor, continued to report on Hugo's health status to Caracas.

"Our president has returned to Venezuela to continue his treatment here!"

From day to day, the unfavorable developments continued to be announced: "He's in recovery in the military hospital . . ." "He's in a huge battle for his life . . ." "He has another very severe infection . . ." "His respiratory function has worsened . . ." "His condition remains very delicate . . ." "He is in a long-term coma."

Fidel sat beside the bed where Hugo was lying in the half-dark room. The only sound was the song of the many monitors, their rhythms slowing. Finally, a long, last whistle of extinction and it was over.

Fidel shut his eyes and took a deep breath.

◆ ◆ ◆

A phone call woke Oliver Watson in the middle of the night. It was Cristina Garza, speaking to her former mentor from across the Atlantic Ocean on one of Prán's encrypted satellite phones.

The CIA had lost her trail, and Watson had assumed she was dead. Though he knew she had betrayed him, the organization, and the country, he was still filled with grief about what had become of her. Hearing her voice in the middle of the night was a shock. On the one hand, he was glad she was still alive, but on the other, he could not forgive her for having become an enemy agent. Cristina kept the conversation short. She said she was calling to inform him that she had escaped the country with an "asset" who could be very valuable to the CIA.

"I have the head of G2's operations in Venezuela. He's prepared to share decades of information on Cuban intelligence in exchange for political asylum, American citizenship, and protection by the US government. All accusations against me must be dropped. The CIA has to assure me I can return safely. You have twenty-four hours to decide. Then I'll make the same offer to other governments."

Watson called an immediate meeting with his bosses at the CIA, the Pentagon, and the State Department. Meanwhile, Cristina made the same call to Senator Hatch. She asked him to take the information to the CIA director and to the president.

In Washington, Watson and Senator Hatch managed to convince the heads of the CIA and other US intelligence agencies not to take both spies and their valuable information out of circulation for good. Once they accepted her offer, Cristina hired a well-known Washington, DC, lawyer to negotiate the terms of the handover to guarantee their safety, as well as Iván's political asylum. A few weeks later, two small private jets landed at a secret airport outside the village in Guinea-Bissau.

The pilots and the four accompanying agents told them that for security reasons they would be traveling separately. The pilots insisted that they had to take off right away before an impending storm, so with confidence in the agreements they had negotiated, they agreed to board the planes. Rushed, Cristina and Iván managed a quick goodbye, a hug, and only a fleeting kiss. But they would be together again very soon. And forever.

Cristina's plane took off first. The captain said they were flying back to Andrews Air Force Base, and the flight time would be eight hours and forty-three minutes.

Cristina's flight took precisely that long, and they landed at the familiar military airport. Cristina saw that they were being met by eight armored vans carrying a large number of heavily armed men. She disembarked and realized she didn't recognize anyone. Nobody said a word. They gestured for her to get in the back of a van, and once she had, the convoy pulled away at high speed.

She asked her escorts about Iván and about Watson. "I don't have that information, ma'am," the one who seemed to be in charge replied coldly. None of them said another word for the rest of the drive.

Cristina was tired, hungry, and uncomfortable from travel and fear. After a lifetime of planning every step, here she was with no idea what would happen next and no control of her life or the lives of her loved ones. She hated this.

After traveling for two hours along back roads, the convoy turned into a large field planted with corn. They drove several miles along a dirt track, past three checkpoints, until they arrived at a wooded hill with a large house as noble as it was austere. Cristina saw two boxlike buildings behind the main house, which had no windows. The roof of one of those box-buildings was dotted with antennae. There were armed guards everywhere.

She was met by a pleasant but curt older woman who introduced herself as Rita Ferguson and welcomed her to what she called "the Mansion." She showed her to her room and told her that she would be expected in the dining room for dinner in an hour.

"You'll want to go to bed early and try to get a good night's sleep, since the conversations start tomorrow and it's important you're well rested," Rita concluded. Cristina knew exactly what the conversations consisted of. She'd taken part in several of them, always from the other side of the table. They were intense, detailed, repetitive questionings.

Cristina answered that she had no intention of taking part in any conversations until she was allowed to make some telephone calls, and until she was told where Iván Rincón was.

"As you wish, Cristina," Rita said, with a cold smile. "You're a professional so you know the rules. You can refuse to cooperate, but the longer you refuse, the longer you'll be here. It could be easy: tell us everything you know, and you'll be done. But you know you can't have any contact with anyone until your conversations are over."

"My lawyer is waiting for a call from me," Cristina said, livid. "And if he doesn't get it, it will trigger a series of public revelations that compromise the entire operation. I made an agreement with Oliver Watson and Senator Hatch, with concrete commitments."

Rita Ferguson stared at her for several seconds.

"Our commitments to you haven't changed," Rita said quietly and calmly, "and we'll keep our side of the agreement. After you keep yours and tell us everything. As for your lawyer, we've been in touch with him, and he knows you're with us. He won't do anything until after your conversations are concluded."

Cristina was annoyed but knew Rita was telling the truth. She said she wouldn't be having dinner.

"First I have one question I need you to answer, please," she said with anxiety she couldn't hide. "Where's Iván Rincón?"

Rita thought for a few moments. "All I can tell you is that he arrived safely and that he'll also start his conversations with us tomorrow."

"But where? Where are you keeping him?"

"Guantánamo," Rita answered, then turned and walked away.

Cristina couldn't sleep. Her new, very real nightmares were combined with those that had never left her, making sleep totally impossible.

The next morning she was exhausted but determined to dive straight into the questioning and get through it as quickly as possible. *You have nothing to hide, and you don't want to hide anything,* she told herself over and over. She persuaded herself that her freedom depended on the government knowing everything she'd done, learned, discovered, and experienced in Venezuela. She arrived ready to tell them everything. Her challenge, of course, was getting them to believe her. But she assumed that when her interrogators saw she wasn't hiding anything, everything would get easier. She hoped this would last only a couple of weeks at most. Then she would be reunited with Iván. At first, this hope did help her to handle the long days of questioning. But Cristina, the experienced spy, was wrong. Two months later, they were still questioning her. And she continued to have no news of Iván. Or anybody else.

She spent every day with her interrogators in a freezing room with mirrors, recorders, TV monitors, files, photos, and the omnipresent lie detector, recalling and reconstructing her life in Venezuela. Her interrogators worked in several teams, taking turns. They arrived fresh and rested, while she was more exhausted every day. She'd lost weight, and anxiety had become a permanent part of her physiognomy. She was also overwhelmed by boredom: they made her go over the same things again and again, always looking for some contradiction, some mistake, an answer just the tiniest bit different from an answer she had given on one of the hundred previous occasions.

Reconstructing her Venezuelan life in these interrogations also meant reconstructing her relationship with Iván. Or rather, with Mauricio. Or with . . . who? Which of them had she fallen in love with? And similarly, which version of her had Iván fallen in love with? Telling the story over and over became for Cristina a process of dissecting her love. And of dissecting the love Iván said he felt for her too. How could they both have lied so much, so well, and for so long? Of course, it was their job. But what if lies and lying were addictive? Would they ever be able to trust each other? She felt she knew Mauricio well, but Iván less so, though she forced herself to remember that Mauricio and Iván were the same. Or were they?

Thousands of miles away, Iván thought the American spy he'd fallen in love with had laid a trap for him. No sooner had he boarded the other plane than Iván had asked the captain where they were going. The captain apologized; he wasn't authorized to divulge their destination, but said not to worry. Iván should relax and enjoy the flight.

His plane landed at the US naval base in Guantánamo, in southeastern Cuba, and from that moment his interrogators had done nothing but abuse him. They threatened to push him over the other side of the fence, turning him over to the Cuban government. Iván knew that would mean certain death.

His interrogations were similar to Cristina's. All day, every day, questions and more questions. Often the same ones. And like Cristina, Iván had decided to tell them everything, but it wasn't enough to satisfy them. When they asked him about Cuban secrets he genuinely knew nothing about, the interrogations turned violent. On three occasions, he was subjected to waterboarding.

At first, Iván asked about the agreement he and Cristina had reached with the US government and the promises that had been made as to his legal protection and his physical safety. His questioners laughed and told him mockingly that was a different department.

"Our department is Questions and Encouragements," one of the cruelest interrogators said, his words dripping with sarcasm. "I don't know anybody in Commitments and Promises. We're a big machine, after all. And not a well-oiled one. We don't know what our colleagues have decided to do. What we do know is what we're gonna do to you if you don't tell us everything we want to know."

Iván didn't know whether to believe them. Maybe there never was any agreement, and Cristina had just handed him over to the CIA. Sometimes Cristina's betrayal felt obvious. At other times, he had doubts. Her love did seem real. And he knew that he truly loved her. Or did he? Who did Iván love—Cristina or Eva? And which man did Cristina love—Iván or Mauricio? How could he ever know what was real?

Several months later, the interrogations finally ended. The CIA kept its promises to Cristina, and they allowed her to resign without a trial. She returned to her family in Yuma, Arizona, where she eventually opened a spa.

Iván, too, was freed, and the American government got him a Spanish passport under a different name, documents allowing him to construct a new identity, and a small sum of money. Iván settled in a small town in Galicia, where he rented a simple house on the seafront.

Neither knew about the other's fate. Neither tried to find out.

Cristina occasionally remembered their musings as they'd strolled along the beach, Iván's hand in hers: Maybe we should live in California where all dreams come true? Or Canada—we could escape to the north, although it would be too cold. Hmm. Australia, no one would find us there and we could have a little garden and start a family of Aussies and teach the kids Spanish.

Iván couldn't get her out of his mind. Her smooth skin. The weight of her breasts in his hands. The scent of her body after making love. He wanted to find her, grab her, and carry her away to another world. They could eat and sleep and make love all day long in a lavish home with curtains flowing in a tropical breeze. Oh Cristina, Eva, Cristina.

Both felt betrayed. They didn't know if they could trust somebody who lied so skillfully. But they could dream. And they did.

A year or so later, Cristina was sitting at the front desk of her spa when she got an unexpected surprise. That afternoon, which had started out like any other, Oliver Watson walked into the spa. Cristina's heart leaped. She was overcome by an avalanche of memories. She didn't know whether to hug him or punch him. To invite him for coffee or ask him to leave.

They looked at each other, face-to-face, for a long time.

Finally, Watson broke the silence: "I've got something I've been wanting to give you for a while now." He handed her a folded piece of paper. Then he turned and walked away. When she could no longer hear his footsteps echo in the hall, Cristina opened the note. It contained two words and a phone number.

Iván Rincón: +34 555 378 200

ACKNOWLEDGMENTS

I have written several books, but none has been through as many versions as this one.

One of the reasons I changed it so much is that I was fortunate enough to have friends, colleagues, and family members who wouldn't let me be satisfied with a previous version. Their criticisms pushed me to constantly edit, add, cut, and redraft.

I have thus accumulated a huge debt of gratitude to those who so generously commented on this book in its various drafts. The list is long, and they are all mentioned in the Spanish edition of this novel. Once again, gracias.

Here I want to recognize the extraordinary support I received from my longtime publishers at Penguin Random House. Pilar Reyes and Miguel Aguilar helped me in countless ways. Their then boss, Claudio López de Lamadrid, who is no longer with us, was not only a dear friend, but surely one of the best editors of books in the Spanish language. I miss him.

My children, Adriana, Claudia, and Andrés, and my wife, Susana, also read various drafts carefully, and as usual, made me happy in myriad ways.

Liza Darnton, my editor at Amazon Crossing "discovered" this novel in Spanish and decided to make it available to English readers. She enlisted for this journey legendary translator Daniel Hahn and exceptional editor Erica Mena. It was a privilege to work with this world-class team. I am immensely grateful to them.

This novel is set in a wonderful country that has been plundered. I am sure the country's wonders are permanent, while the devastation it is suffering these days is transitory. The country will recover and be able to welcome new generations who will give it the love it has been so sadly lacking. I hope Emma, Lily, Sami, and Ari, my grandchildren, will be a part of the generation that will rebuild Venezuela.

And so, this novel is dedicated to them.

Moisés Naím

ABOUT THE AUTHOR

Photo © Susana Naím

Moisés Naím is a Venezuelan author and prize-winning journalist whose writing on international affairs is read worldwide, appearing in such publications as the *New York Times*, the *Washington Post*, *Newsweek*, *Time*, *El País*, and many others. He is the author of twelve nonfiction books, including *Illicit* and the *New York Times* bestseller *The End of Power*. A former contributing editor to *The Atlantic*, Naím was also the editor in chief of *Foreign Policy* magazine for fourteen years. *Two Spies in Caracas*, his first work of fiction, is based on his experience as a former member of Venezuela's economic cabinet. He lives in Washington, DC, with his family. For more information visit www.moisesnaim.com.

ABOUT THE TRANSLATOR

Photo © John Lawrence

Daniel Hahn is a writer, editor, and translator with nearly seventy books to his name. He chaired the Translators Association for two years and served four years as a director of the British Centre for Literary Translation and four years as editor of the journal *In Other Words*. Recent translations include Juan Pablo Villalobos's *I Don't Expect Anyone to Believe Me*, Julián Fuks's *Resistance*, and Carola Saavedra's *Blue Flowers*. For more information visit www.danielhahn.co.uk.